Praise for Susan

The Night Drifter

"Carroll writes sparkling dialogue and exquisite prose."
—TERESA MEDEIROS,
author of *Yours Until Dawn*

"Carroll has topped herself and proved her genius by creating a romantic situation without equal."
—*Rendezvous*

"Carroll has a gift more powerful than the St. Legers': the ability to bring a sense of joy and true peace to her readers. Her magical romances give life to remarkable characters and superb stories, but also to the idea that hope and faith prevail."
—*Romantic Times*

"Susan Carroll definitely has star quality."
—IRIS JOHANSEN,
author of *Blind Alley*

The Bride Finder

"An intriguing tale that proves the wounds of the heart can be healed by the magic of true love."

—NORA ROBERTS

"An absolutely beautiful love story, a spellbinding combination of magic, passion, and destiny."

—KRISTIN HANNAH

"A beautiful, tender, funny, unique story that captures the essence of romance . . . One of those magical books that touches all the right buttons, bringing you joy and a deep sigh of pure pleasure."

—*Romantic Times*
(Gold Medal review)

"Paranormal reaches a new high through the unique talents of Susan Carroll. Her dark sensual hero inflames the reader's passion as much as the heroine's. Time ceased to matter as I turned the pages."

—*Rendezvous*

"Spellbinding from its first page to the last . . . Sensational sorceress Susan Carroll scores a big-time success with this magical story."

—*Affaire de Coeur*

Midnight Bride

"Fascinating . . . Once again, Carroll, who sets the standard for paranormal romance with her beautifully crafted tales of the gifted St. Legers and the women who love them, enchants readers by subtly enhancing her alluring love story with lush historical details."
—*Booklist*

"[A] compelling, mesmerizing tale . . . This [novel] is beautifully crafted, laced with occasional humor, and rife with Gothic atmosphere."

—*Library Journal*

"Bewitching nineteenth-century historical romance . . . Carroll's swift-moving tale won't disappoint."
—*Publishers Weekly*

"The power of Ms. Carroll's writing is truly amazing, and *Midnight Bride* teems with emotional intensity . . . There is also magic and wonder and such an intense pace that when you turn the last page, you will want to start reading all over again. This is a special book; a rare, eloquent tribute to the love of man for mankind. Brava Ms. Carroll."

—*Romantic Times*

The Courtesan

Also by Susan Carroll

WINTERBOURNE
THE PAINTED VEIL
THE BRIDE FINDER
THE NIGHT DRIFTER
MIDNIGHT BRIDE
THE DARK QUEEN

The
Courtesan

A NOVEL

SUSAN CARROLL

BALLANTINE BOOKS · NEW YORK

The Courtesan is a work of historical fiction. Apart from the well-known actual people, events, and locales that figure in the narrative, all names, characters, places, and incidents are the products of the author's imagination or are used fictitiously. Any resemblance to current events or locales, or to living persons, is entirely coincidental.

A Ballantine Books Trade Paperback Original

Copyright © 2005 by Susan Coppula
Excerpt from *The Silver Rose* copyright © 2005 by Susan Coppula

All rights reserved.

Published in the United States by Ballantine Books,
an imprint of The Random House Publishing Group,
a division of Random House, Inc., New York.

Ballantine and colophon are registered trademarks of
Random House, Inc.

This book contains an excerpt from *The Silver Rose* by Susan Carroll.
This excerpt has been set for this edition only and may not reflect
the final content of the forthcoming edition.

Library of Congress Cataloging-in-Publication Data
Carroll, Susan.
The courtesan/Susan Carroll.
p. cm.
"A Ballantine Books trade paperback original"—T.p. verso.
ISBN 0-345-43797-7 (pbk.)
1. France—History—Henry II, 1547–1559—Fiction. 2. Catherine de Mâdicis,
Queen, consort of Henry II, King of France, 1519–1589—Fiction. I. Title.

PS3553.A7654C68 2005
813'.54—dc22   2004062269

Printed in the United States of America

www.ballantinebooks.com

2 4 6 8 9 7 5 3 1

First Edition

This one is for my real-life heroes:
My big brother, Tony, and my outlaws, Jerry, Tom, and Pete.
Love you guys, always.

The Courtesan

Prologue

Mist rose off the Seine, the ghostly vapor drifting over the banks of Paris, obscuring streets that were already a labyrinth in the fading light. But the woman stealing through the haze appeared oblivious to both the perils of becoming lost and the damp chill of the autumn evening.

Shrouded in a hooded gray cloak that fell to her ankles, her face was hidden behind a black velvet mask, the kind court beauties used to shield their complexions. It completely shielded her identity as well, only the sparkle of her eyes visible and a few blond wisps of hair. Wooden pattens protected her brocade shoes from the dirt of the streets as she marched forward with a sure step, unaware of the man who followed her.

Captain Nicolas Remy hung back as far as he dared without losing sight of the lady in the misty evening. He was clad in a dark jerkin and black venetians that blended with the oncoming night. His worn garments and his dusty boots appeared to have seen better days, as had the captain himself. Tangled dark blond hair spilled across his brown eyes, his lean features obscured by a heavy beard that had been allowed to run wild. With both sword and dagger affixed to his belt, he was a dangerous-looking man, even by the standards of Paris.

Passersby gave him a wide berth, making it difficult for him to lose himself in the crowd as he dogged the footsteps of the lady in gray. The streets were swiftly emptying of all other company. Artisans and street vendors scurried for home. Shutters of shop fronts slammed shut, all of respectable Paris retreating behind locked doors.

Captain Remy would soon stand out like a lone soldier left surviving on a battlefield, but he could not risk putting any more distance between himself and the woman. She had a distinct advantage. She *knew* where she was going.

Any knowledge he had ever had of this cursed city, he had done his best to forget. Remy was not only unfamiliar with the streets, he was not even certain he was following the right woman. He angled a glance at his companion, a rangy youth of about eighteen years who went by the sobriquet Martin le Loup.

A fitting name, Remy thought. The lad bore much of the aspect of a wolf with his mane of sable-colored hair, sharp features, and green eyes. Although the Wolf styled himself as an "adventurer, a gentleman of fortune," he looked regrettably more like what he was, a scoundrel and a cutpurse. But Remy would have trusted the boy with his life. He already had on many occasions.

However, this time he wondered if his clever Wolf had made a grave mistake. As the woman led him deeper into narrower streets, Remy tensed with the apprehension that he was being led into the sort of trap laid for many an unwary traveler in Paris, lured on by a beautiful woman only to be set upon and robbed.

Remy's hand shifted to the hilt of his sword and he muttered to his youthful guide, "Are you certain that this is the lady I sent you to find? Because if you've made some sort of mistake—"

"No mistake, Captain!" Wolf protested, looking wounded

that Remy should doubt him. "I swear on the grave of my father . . . or at least I would if I knew who he was. That is indeed the lady you asked me to seek, your Mistress Gabrielle Cheney."

Remy allowed himself a moment of regret. No, she had never been his Gabrielle, nor was she ever likely to be.

"She is said to be the most dazzling woman in all of Paris," Wolf said, kissing his fingertips. "Do you recognize nothing about her?"

Remy's eyes narrowed, studying the distant form of the cloaked woman. He tried to discern some familiar gesture or movement of the young enchantress he had once known. But it had been over three years since he had last seen Gabrielle, not since that long-ago summer in that mysterious place known as the Faire Isle.

He had heard that Gabrielle had changed, the warm, passionate girl transformed into a woman, seductive and dangerous. They said that she was consumed with cold ambition. They said that she had grown more adept at intrigue than the Dark Queen, Catherine de Medici herself. They said . . .

Remy's mouth set in a terse line. He simply did not want to believe all the things that were being said of Gabrielle. It was far too painful. But he could hardly escape the fact that people who ventured abroad at this hour were either remarkably careless of their lives or else bent upon some purpose that would not bear the light of day.

So which was true of Gabrielle? All he had to do was overtake her and ask her. But he was reluctant to do so. After so long an absence, he didn't want their reunion to take place here in the street. She believed him to be dead and perhaps it would be better if he remained that way.

"Just let her go," something inside him urged. *"Don't entangle her in this desperate quest that your life has become."*

The voice was a faint echo of the man he'd once been,

honorable and chivalrous. But any nobility inside him had been killed that hot August here in Paris, three years ago, a night of blood, betrayal, and madness. The mere thought of St. Bartholomew's Eve was enough to make his stomach clench, his brow go cold with sweat.

Remy thrust the nightmarish memories aside and continued doggedly after Gabrielle. Despite the risks, he needed Gabrielle Cheney's help with the dangerous enterprise that had brought him back to the city. But first, he needed to be sure of her.

As Gabrielle stalked onward, the houses towering around them grew more decrepit, the street more filthy. Little as Remy knew of Paris, it was obvious even to him they were plunging into one of the less savory quarters of the city.

Beside him, Wolf growled in a low voice, "The rue de Morte? Have a care, monsieur. Even the worst of rogues dread to come here by night. Your lady must be quite mad to venture here alone, without even the company of her maid. Has she always been this reckless?"

"Always," Remy murmured with a grim smile. At least that much about Gabrielle had not changed. "She once stole my sword and prepared to fight an entire cadre of—"

"A cadre of what?" Wolf asked with great interest.

Remy already regretted his impulsive words. The doings on Faire Isle that summer had been strange enough to him. If he were to recount some of those tales, even the insouciant Wolf would become alarmed.

Remy was spared the necessity of answering when they lost sight of Gabrielle in the mists. Both he and Wolf came to an abrupt halt, listening. The street was clear of the daytime clatter from the traffic of carts, horses, and mules. Remy could hear the hollow echo of Gabrielle's shoes in the distance.

"There!" Wolf pointed across the street.

The rising moon pierced the clouds enough for Remy to make out Gabrielle's shadow. She approached the iron gates of what had once been a great manor done in the Gothic style, set

behind high stone walls, the gatehouse flanked by pepperpot turrets. The rambling stone house bore a ghostly aspect in the
moonlight and mist, many of the windows boarded over, the garden wall crumbled and broken in places.

Nearby lots were vacant despite the current rage for construction that had seized hold of Paris. The house stood isolated
as though the rest of the city shrank from drawing too near.

"Nom de Dieu!" Remy heard Wolf gasp.

"What is it?" Remy asked.

"The—the Maison d'Esprit." Wolf whispered, pointing a
trembling finger in the direction of the imposing house.

"What! You know this place?"

Wolf gave a jerky nod, his eyes full moons in the sharp oval
of his face. "The place . . . it—it has a dreadful reputation, monsieur. The house once belonged to a powerful bishop who fell
under the spell of a witch. She enchanted him, caused him to fall
desperately in love with her, forget all his holy vows. He made
her his mistress, kept her hidden away in this house for many
years. She even bore him children, daughters like herself, evil
witches."

Wolf shuddered. "Finally one of the bishop's servants summoned the courage to inform the authorities. Witch-hunters
raided the place, seized the sorceress and her daughters, dragged
them away to be executed. Everyone thought that would break
the spell for the bishop, but the poor man hanged himself in the
garret, driven mad by the witch."

Wolf rolled his eyes heavenward and crossed himself. The
boy had a penchant for high drama and enjoyed terrifying himself with any legends he chanced to hear, the more gruesome the
better.

If Gabrielle was familiar with the story, it hadn't daunted
her. Remy made out her cloaked figure heading straight up to the
gates. After a moment's hesitation, Remy risked getting closer.
Moving stealthily across the street, he positioned himself behind
an ancient oak in one of the vacant lots.

Wolf scrambled after him, not so quietly. Remy shot the boy a quelling frown. The dark house waited in the distance, a silent shadow, not a sign of life stirring. What could Gabrielle possibly want in this wretched place?

"Who lives there now?" Remy demanded in a low aside to his companion.

"No one," Wolf whispered hoarsely. "The place is haunted and cursed besides. Before she died, the witch declared that anyone who ever enters these grounds would go as mad as her lover did."

Remy didn't believe in curses, but there was something disquieting about the abandoned manor that caused the back of his neck to prickle. He felt an odd sense of relief when Gabrielle passed by the iron gates.

But Remy should have known locked gates would not be enough to stop Gabrielle Cheney. She moved along the stone wall until she found a large break. With a furtive glance over her shoulder, she gathered up her skirts and climbed through. As she vanished from sight, Remy stepped out to follow.

Wolf frantically seized hold of his arm. "No, Captain! You must not go in there after her. The place is cursed, I tell you."

"Don't be absurd, boy." Remy attempted to shake him off, fearing that he might lose Gabrielle, not to any curse, but to the mist and darkness.

"Ah, please, Captain! Don't you see that it is too late? Your lady must already be seized with madness or else why would she go into that terrible place?"

Why indeed? Remy had no idea what would draw Gabrielle to this neglected wreck of a house, but he intended to find out. However, it was clear he would have to go on alone. Wolf was not indulging his usual flair for melodrama. The boy's terror was genuine, his face pale, his fingers trembling. Wolf might not flinch from tangling with the fiercest brigand, but he had a deathly fear of anything hinting at the supernatural.

As Remy pried the boy's fingers loose and commanded Wolf

to wait behind, his conscience pricked him because he knew he had been less than honest with the lad. When he had first sent Wolf to find Gabrielle Cheney, there was one significant fact Remy had neglected to tell him.

The lady was something of a witch herself.

Chapter One

GABRIELLE CHENEY PEERED THROUGH THE SLITS OF HER MASK, picking her way carefully along the path overgrown with weeds. The courtyard of the Maison d'Esprit was silent as a cemetery and twice as eerie. The moon cast a pale light over moss-blackened fountains and broken statuary. Some headless saint presided over the withered remains of a rose garden. The flowers were long gone, but the thorns were not, one branch catching at the hem of Gabrielle's cloak.

As she bent to free herself, she was beset by the troubling sensation that had afflicted her all evening. The feeling that she was being followed. Straightening, she curled her fingers over the hilt of the sword hidden beneath her cloak and whirled around. The iron gate and stone wall were nothing more than vague outlines in the fog-bound night. But as she stared, another figure took shape, that of a tall proud warrior.

Her hand fell away from the sword and she uttered a soft choked cry. Not of fear, but more of despair because she had seen the silhouette of this man far too many times in her dreams. She took a step forward only to check the motion, knowing it would do her no good. There would be no smile to greet her, no strong arms to welcome her because he didn't exist, this phantom man. All she would find was empty space and silence.

Ghosts left no footfalls and memories cast no shadows, except perhaps on the human heart. She watched the figure of the man evaporate into the mist as he always did. Gabrielle had never once seen his face, but she knew beyond certainty who he was.

Nicolas Remy, the captain from Navarre. Whether it was his ghost she kept seeing or only a figment of her own tormented imagination, the effect was always the same. Gabrielle's heart constricted with sorrow and guilt.

"Oh, Remy," she murmured. "I've asked your forgiveness a thousand times. What more do you want from me? Why can't you leave me in peace?"

She knew she would never gain any answer to that question, at least not in this damp, misty courtyard. With one last glance behind her, Gabrielle turned and hastened toward the house.

The stone manor loomed ahead of her, splintered wood and a great hole where the front door should be, gaping like the jagged mouth of some fierce beast ready to devour her. But Gabrielle feared the ghosts of her own memories far more than she did the sinister aspect of the house. Besides, she knew the truth behind the legends of the Maison d'Esprit far better than the superstitious Parisians who blessed themselves every time they had to pass those rusting gates.

Easing past the shattered remains of the door, she entered the house, the darkness swallowing her. The boarded-up windows blocked out what pale moonlight there was to be had. Gabrielle stripped off her mask and reached beneath her cloak for the large pouch fastened to her belt. She groped until she found the candle set in its small brass holder, along with the tinderbox she had brought. After much fumbling between flint and wick, she managed to coax the taper to light.

The tiny flame spluttered to life, casting a small circle of illumination. Gabrielle moved deeper into the room that yawned before her, the grit crunching beneath her feet. Holding up the candle, she surveyed the wreckage of the once-magnificent great hall. The bishop had done very handsomely by his mistress until the witch-hunters had come.

A beautiful high table of carved oak had been pulled from the dais and overturned, the broken remains of chairs and stools littered nearby. Tapestries had been dragged from the walls and sliced to ribbons, the musty scent of rotting wool heavy in the air. Even the iron candelabrum had been wrenched from the ceiling and left with its chain snaking around it. Everything was coated with thick cobwebs as though time had sought to weave a shroud for this house.

The witch-hunters had done their work well. Gabrielle shivered with a mingling of horror and pity, remembering the night those fiends had invaded her own home on Faire Isle. She and her sisters, Ariane and Miri, had only been saved by the intervention of the Comte de Renard, the man who eventually became Ariane's husband.

But no such rescue had come to poor Giselle Lascelles and her daughters. How terrified those women must have been, dragged from their home, crying and shrieking to meet the worst sort of torture and death that could befall any daughter of the earth. All of them lost, save one . . .

The appearance of the great hall was calculated to make any chance intruder believe that the Maison d'Esprit was uninhabited by anyone but ghosts. Gabrielle was one of the few who knew better. Lifting her skirts, she moved to the stairs stretching upward. The small glow of her candle could not reach far enough to penetrate the upper regions of the landing, to detect whoever or whatever might be lurking there.

"Hello?" she called tentatively.

Her voice echoed, swallowed up by the vast silence of the house. "Cassandra Lascelles?" Gabrielle called more loudly.

She was met with more unnerving silence, then she thought she heard a floorboard creak. Gabrielle moistened her lips and tried again. "Cass? Are you there? It is me . . . Gabrielle Cheney. I need to talk to—"

She checked abruptly at a low rumbling sound. Staring up at the landing, she caught the shadow of movement. Her heart leapt into her throat as two baleful yellow eyes glared back at her, the rumbling escalating into a fearsome growl. The creature sprang forward, a large brownish-black mastiff with a heavy muscular body.

"Merde!" Gabrielle cried.

As it bounded down the stairs, Gabrielle scrambled back, nearly dropping her candle. Hot wax splashed over the brass holder, searing her hand. She winced with pain, but managed to keep a grip on the taper.

Retreating across the room, she stumbled up against an aumbry, the wooden shelves gouging against her spine. Her pursuer skidded to a halt a few feet away, cornering her against the cupboard. Baring cruel-looking incisors, it snarled.

"C-Cerberus. Good d-dog," Gabrielle quavered. "Don't you remember me?"

Apparently he did not. The mastiff issued a series of savage barks. Her younger sister could have crooned a few words to the dog, soothing him at once. But Gabrielle had never possessed Miri's strange affinity with all four-legged creatures.

Fortunately, Gabrielle had long ago learned the weakness of this particular beast. One wary eye on the dog, she inched aside enough to set her candle down on the aumbry shelf. She groped for the pouch hidden beneath her cloak. The cursed drawstrings refused to budge or perhaps her fingers were too clumsy with nervousness. Somehow she got the purse open, and drew forth a cluster of slightly squashed red grapes.

Swallowing her fear, she croaked, "Nice Cerberus. S-sweet beastie. Look what I have for you."

She carefully extended her arm, the handful of red grapes glistening against her palm. The dog gave a sharp bark. Gabrielle jumped and tossed the grapes wildly. The cluster hit the floor with a dull thud, causing the dog to shy back.

Cerberus crept forward again, snuffling her offering. The dog emitted a delighted whine and began greedily gulping down the fruit. Gabrielle ventured a few steps away from the wall. Cerberus would make no objection to her movement, at least until the grapes ran out.

"What have you done to my dog?" An imperious voice rang out.

Gabrielle twisted toward the sound and breathed a sigh of relief as the mastiff's owner finally put in an appearance. Cassandra Lascelles stood poised at the top of the stairs, a tall, thin silhouette. How long she had been there, Gabrielle had no idea. She seemed to have materialized out of nowhere.

"I haven't done anything to your precious Cerberus," Gabrielle retorted. "Merely bribed him with a few grapes to keep him from devouring me instead."

"Gabrielle? Is that you?" Cass asked sharply.

"Yes."

Clutching the banister, Cass began to descend the stairs with elaborate care. She had been blind almost from the moment of her birth. A young woman, she was not much older than Gabrielle's own twenty-one years, although there was a hard, brittle quality about Cass that often made her seem much older.

A tattered red gown half-hung off her thin frame, baring one shoulder. The weight of her mass of gypsy-dark hair appeared too heavy for her slender neck. She had an exotic face with high slanting cheekbones and an ice-white complexion that seldom saw the light of the sun. Her sightless dark eyes were fixed and without expression, all emotion centered in her mouth, which at the moment was slashed thin with displeasure.

For one deprived of her vision, she moved with a remarkable amount of grace and stealth. It was only when she cleared the last step and let go of the banister that she faltered, stretching out one hand cautiously into the vast empty space of the room.

"Cerberus! Come," she commanded.

The dog's ears pricked up, but he hesitated, still searching for more grapes.

"Cerberus! Come here!"

The formidable beast whined and lowered his head, slinking guiltily over to his mistress. Cassandra groped until she seized hold of the dog's leather collar.

"Bad dog. Heel!"

Cerberus sank even lower. As the chastened dog positioned itself beside her, Cass grumbled, "Blasted fool. Just like any other male. Ruled by your stomach."

She softened her scolding by scratching him behind the ears. The ferocious-looking beast transformed, his eyes going limpid, his tail wagging, his massive body quivering with adoration.

It was the mistress who now seemed the more formidable of the two. One hand resting protectively on her dog's head, Cass straightened and scowled.

"Damnation, Gabrielle Cheney. I have warned you before not to come here without first sending word through my servant. I do not like to be taken unawares. Bribe or no bribe, you are lucky Cerberus did not tear out your throat."

"I am sorry," Gabrielle said, taking a cautious step closer. "But I was desperate to see you and I didn't have time to contact you through Finette. I have been here enough times before that I thought Cerberus might recognize me."

"He is trained not to *recognize* anyone. Otherwise he would not be much of a protector."

"But surely you do not need such protection from another daughter of the earth."

"Not all daughters of the earth are to be trusted. You above anyone should know that." Cass gave a scornful sniff. "And I hate such mincing terms as 'wise women' and daughters of the earth. Let us just say witches and be done with it."

"Yes, but let us not say it too loudly." Gabrielle replied wryly.

Cass's rigid features melted into a reluctant smile. She bent and muttered some low command to her dog. With her hand still poised on Cerberus's collar, she walked forward with a sure step that Gabrielle always found astonishing.

Gabrielle had seen her sister Miri accomplish some astounding feats with animals, but the degree of rapport between Cassandra and her dog, the way she had taught Cerberus to be her eyes, was nothing short of magic.

Cerberus led Cass straight over to Gabrielle. Another low command and the dog took up position, sitting beside her, eyes trained on Cass as though waiting her next order. Cass reached out boldly until she made contact with Gabrielle. Drawing her forward, she enveloped Gabrielle in a brisk hug.

"I did not mean to make you feel unwelcome, my friend," she murmured. "But *next* time, let me know when you are coming."

"I will," Gabrielle promised. As she hugged her in turn, Gabrielle was uncomfortably aware of the thinness of Cass's frame beneath her worn gown. She wished that she could persuade Cass to give over living like a recluse in this depressing abandoned house. Or at least allow Gabrielle to provide her with a few comforts like better food and clothing. But Gabrielle was all too familiar with Cass's fierce pride and sense of independence.

Cass released her and stepped back, her lips quirking upward in a faintly teasing smile. "Well, to what do I owe the honor of this unexpected visit? Surely you cannot have already used up that last bottle of perfume I brewed for you. I gave you enough to bring every man at court to his knees."

Cassandra Lascelles could concoct some of the most powerfully seductive perfumes and skin ointments Gabrielle had ever discovered. Gabrielle started to shake her head and then checked herself. It was often difficult to remember that Cass was blind.

"No, I need no more perfume."

"Cream for your complexion then. Or another lotion perhaps?"

"N-no . . ." Gabrielle said, glad that the other woman could not see her face. She liked to feel cool and in control, but it had been sheer desperation that had blazed her path to Cass's door.

Now that she was here, she discovered it was more difficult to blurt out what she wanted than she had imagined it would be. Gabrielle found it hard to display her vulnerabilities to anyone, but if she did not manage to overcome her pride, there was no point in having taken the risk to come here.

As though she sensed Gabrielle's reluctance, Cass said in a softer tone, "Out with it, my friend. What do you want from me?"

Clearing her throat, Gabrielle confessed haltingly, "I need your help, Cass. To—to find someone who is lost to me."

Remy, her heart whispered with the familiar dull ache.

Cass's fine brows arched upward in surprise. "I would be delighted to assist you in any way I can, my dear," she said dryly. "But as you may have observed, my eyesight is not all that keen. Hadn't you better hire yourself a tracker or some mercenary who is good at that sort of thing?"

"I—I can't. The person I seek is . . . no longer in this world. I have heard—that is—Finette told me that you possess remarkable skills in the art of necromancy."

Cassandra's face darkened with annoyance. "Rot Finette! That scrawny little witch talks far too much."

"So is it true then?"

Cass didn't answer her, something in her face shutting down. There was an ancient magic learned by most wise women during their childhood, the art of reading the eyes, those mirrors of the soul. Those who became adept at it could divine the very thoughts of their subject, but unfortunately Gabrielle had never mastered the skill.

Such an art would not have served her with Cass in any case. Her eyes were like twin lanterns with the lights burned out, giving none of her thoughts away.

"Necromancy," she repeated slowly. "The raising of the dead. Perhaps I do possess some ability in that arena. But you are a witch the same as me. Why don't you conjure for yourself? I am only the bastard child of a wild gypsy woman and a foolish holy man who forgot his vows. Your lineage is certainly more impressive than mine, Gabrielle Cheney. Your father was a renowned knight and your mother, the incomparable Evangeline, such a queen among sorceresses, she was known as the Lady of Faire Isle. The noble descendant of a long line of strong and clever witches."

"Regrettably, I don't seem to have inherited my share of the family gifts." Gabrielle tried to speak lightly, but she felt her throat tighten. "Whatever magic I did possess, I lost it a long time ago."

"Then go to your sister Ariane for help," Cassandra said. "She is the present Lady of Faire Isle, reputed to be as wise and clever as your late mother."

"You know full well I cannot do that. Ariane and I have not had any contact for the past two years." Gabrielle experienced the familiar rush of pain and regret at the thought of her older sister. "She didn't approve of my decision to come to Paris."

"Because you became a courtesan? Very few respectable women would approve of that."

"Yes, well, it is all very fine for Ariane to pass judgment on me," Gabrielle said. "She is quite happily married to her Comte Renard. For her, everything is simple and perfect and that makes it impossible for her to understand that other women might find life a bit more . . . complicated."

Gabrielle tried to sound indifferent, as though Ariane's disapproval was of no consequence. But the loss of her sister's love and respect weighed heavily on her.

"It doesn't matter," she went on briskly. "Ariane wouldn't have helped me in any case. She confines all her skills to healing the sick. She would never dabble in the darker arts."

"How wise of her and how unfortunate for you," Cass said. "Because I don't dabble in them lightly either. I don't share my peculiar talent for necromancy with anyone. Not even you, my friend. Now why don't you just forget all this nonsense and come have a cup of wine with me?"

She gave Cerberus a light tap and the dog sprang to its feet. Both woman and dog turned as one and headed back toward the stairs.

Gabrielle stood a moment, dismayed by Cassandra's refusal. But Gabrielle never easily surrendered anything she had set her heart upon and few things had ever meant more to her than this. The hope of seeing Nicolas Remy, speaking to him one last time.

She hurried after Cassandra, seizing her by the elbow.

"Cass, wait, please—"

Cerberus bristled and issued a warning growl. Gabrielle hastily drew her hand away.

"Cass, you must help me or—or I don't know what I shall do. There is someone who has passed to the other side who I am desperate to contact. It is more important to me than you can possibly imagine. I—I will pay you any amount you require."

"Money doesn't interest me. If it did, I have ways of getting it myself."

"What about jewels then? Gowns from the finest dress-maker in Paris."

Cass flushed and shoved the drooping sleeve of her tattered frock farther up her shoulder, the gesture a trifle self-conscious. Her jaw jutted to a stubborn angle. "I don't care about such fripperies either."

"Then name your price," Gabrielle pleaded. "I'll give you anything, do anything you ask."

Cass gave a bark of laughter. "*Anything?* You are very rash, Gabrielle Cheney. Didn't your Maman ever tell you of the old fairy tales about what dire things happen to ladies who make such promises?"

"Well, what could you possibly demand? My firstborn child?"

"No, I abhor children," Cass drawled. "I doubt they'd even taste good in a stew." She fell silent for a moment, then said slyly. "There is only one way I might consider your request. Let me read your hand."

Gabrielle tensed. This was not the first time Cass had made such a request of her, but Gabrielle had always been wary of granting it.

She whipped her hands nervously behind her back. "Why? Why do you need to do that?"

"Because I am the only one left in a family of women who were tortured and burned for practicing witchcraft. I have learned to be damned careful about whom I trust. If I am to consider granting your request, I need to probe the depths of your innermost heart. Other wise women are adept at reading the eyes. Obviously that skill is barred to me. I am, however, good at reading hands. Let me examine yours."

Cassandra held out her own hand in a demanding gesture. Gabrielle still hesitated. Probe the depths of her innermost heart? That was something Gabrielle had never allowed anyone to do, not even her own sisters, and she had only known Cass for three months. She was disquieted by the notion that Cass might somehow be able to draw out the secrets of her soul through the touch of her palm. Was such a thing even possible? Gabrielle didn't like the idea of it, but if she wanted Cass's help, she had no choice but to cooperate.

"A-all right." Gabrielle started to extend her own hand. Cerberus, suspicious of the gesture, let out a fierce bark.

"Down!" Cassandra ordered. As the dog subsided at her feet, Gabrielle uneasily rested her hand in Cassandra's grasp.

The woman turned Gabrielle's hand palm up and began to trace her finger across the surface. Gabrielle shivered, finding Cass's touch disturbing and cold. It was rather like being probed by a needle of ice.

"This is a well-formed hand," she murmured. "Elegant, the skin smooth as silk. But it was not always so. Once there were calluses here—" Cass touched the pads of Gabrielle's palm. "And here." She touched Gabrielle's fingertips.

"Calluses from . . . from working with chisel and marble? And these well-manicured nails were chipped and flecked with paint."

Gabrielle started a little at this observation, and then said dismissively. "I used to dabble a bit with sculpting and the like. A girl has to amuse herself somehow. I found it more entertaining than needlework."

"It was more than mere entertainment. This hand could once perform a great magic. Breathing life into stone. Taking a blank canvas, filling it with light and color, conjuring images that mesmerized the eye and moved the heart. The hand of an extraordinary artist."

"Perhaps I did have some such ability, but I *told* you," Gabrielle replied with some asperity. "Any magic I ever had, I lost a long time ago."

"And exactly how does a wise woman go about losing her magic?" Cass asked softly.

"How should I know?" Gabrielle snapped, but she knew all too well how and when she'd lost her magic. She simply didn't care to discuss it.

"It doesn't matter," Gabrielle said. "No woman can ever find fame and fortune as an artist. That was an old dream and a foolish one."

"You never used to worry so much about fame and fortune. At least not then."

Gabrielle flinched and tried to close up her hand, but Cass forced her fingers back open.

"Yes, a very lovely hand, but an empty one," Cass murmured.

"I told you that I could easily fill it up with jewels and coin for you."

"I am not talking about that kind of emptiness, but the sort that would not be apparent to most. You are a beautiful woman, much sought after and desired. But your life is empty all the same. You abandoned all that you ever knew when you came to Paris, your two sisters, your home and friends on Faire Isle, and now you are quite alone."

"Nonsense. I have a house full of servants and I am frequently at court. I attend the banquets, the masques, the balls. People surround me all the time, seeking my favor."

"Women you don't trust and men you despise. Fools who see nothing but the glittering façade you present and never come close to touching the real Gabrielle. This hand speaks to me of darkness, isolation, a vast loneliness."

Then her hand was telling Cassandra a great deal too much, Gabrielle thought. "Is there a point to all this?" she asked, trying to draw her hand away. "I didn't come here to have my palm read."

Cass only tightened her grip, her long, thin fingers continuing their inspection. "Ah!"

"Ah, what?" Gabrielle asked anxiously.

Cass traced the creases on Gabrielle's palm. "Here I feel a pulsing vein that marks great ambition . . . a strong desire for power, fame . . . invulnerability. But right next to it runs the line of the heart, the hunger for passion, romance, a fervent wish to love and be loved."

"That line must be very short," Gabrielle said, pulling a wry face.

"No, the lines are equal in length and converging upon each other, reaching a point where a choice will have to be made. Love or ambition."

"I have already made it."

Cass smiled and shook her head. "No, you haven't. But your choice will be a difficult one. There is an old scar getting in the way."

Gabrielle straightened haughtily. "I have no scar. My hand is flawless."

"The scar is on your heart, Gabrielle Cheney. An old wound that never properly healed, left upon you by an unworthy man."

"I think I have heard quite enough—"

"You gave your entire heart to this man and he betrayed you," Cass continued softly, but inexorably. "With the most unspeakable injury a man can inflict upon a woman. One bright summer afternoon in the hayloft of a barn—"

"My God. You are a blasted witch!" Gabrielle cried and wrenched her hand away. She staggered back and clutched her palm, feeling as though Cass had sliced her open and left her bleeding, old and bitter memories spilling out of her. Of that June with Etienne Danton, the brutal afternoon she had tried her best to forget.

No, she *had* forgotten it.

Gabrielle released a tremulous breath, groping for her mask. "This—this is all the most arrant nonsense. I have no time for any more of this folly. If you don't want to help me, then fine. I clearly made a mistake in coming here. I bid you good evening."

Cerberus emitted a short bark as Gabrielle stalked away, but she had not even reached the door when Cassandra called after her, "Gabrielle, wait."

Gabrielle halted, glancing back at the other woman. Cass stood motionless, frozen in the pool of light from the candle Gabrielle had forgotten in her haste.

After a pause, Cassandra said, "I will do what you ask, but I warn you. There is a reason why the conjuring of the dead is considered black magic and forbidden. A séance is a dangerous proceeding, one that can easily go awry. Sometimes the soul one wishes to contact does not care to be disturbed, whereas there are others, more evil, who might welcome a portal back into our world."

Gabrielle frowned, wondering if Cassandra was merely seeking to frighten her. "Are you telling me that if you conjured wrong, you could—could what? Let loose some sort of ghost or demon?"

"Anything is possible when you tempt fate by playing with the darker arts."

"If it is so dangerous, then why do *you* do it?" Gabrielle demanded.

"Because my days are spent in darkness," Cass replied softly. "But when I conjure the dead, I can actually *see.* This is the only way I have of looking upon another face and so to me that makes it worth any risk. The question is, is it worth it to you?"

Was it? Gabrielle had to admit that Cassandra's words had daunted her. But then she thought of Remy, the way she had parted from him the day he had ridden out to meet his death, so much left unsaid between them.

"Yes," Gabrielle said, steeling her spine. "The risk is worth it."

"Then I will help you."

Gabrielle warily returned to Cass's side, her elation tempered with suspicion of this sudden capitulation. "You will? What made you change your mind?"

Cass shrugged. "Perhaps I might one day find it useful to have you in my debt. I will give you one séance, one conjuring of the dead in return for some future favor."

"And what would that be?"

"How can I possibly decide right now?" Cassandra protested. "But you will agree to perform some service for me, no questions asked, no refusal. Is it a bargain?"

"Do you require an oath in blood?" Gabrielle asked dryly.

"No, a simple handshake and your pledge will do." Cassandra extended her hand toward Gabrielle.

Gabrielle hesitated. She had not survived this long in Paris without learning some caution, and surely there could be nothing more rash than undertaking a commitment without knowing what it was.

"Come now, Gabrielle," Cass said. "I am not one of those backstabbing intriguers you associate with at court. I admit our acquaintance has been of short duration, but you may trust me in this. I would never ask more of you than you can give."

Somewhat reassured, Gabrielle shook Cass's hand. "All right. I—I agree. Do this for me and I am in your debt. You have the word of Gabrielle Cheney."

An odd smile tugged at the corner of Cassandra's mouth as they sealed their bargain, sending a chill through Gabrielle. But the disturbing expression was gone so swiftly, Gabrielle thought she must only have imagined it.

Cass turned toward the cupboard, groping along the lower shelf. Her hand collided with the candle Gabrielle had left burning there. Cass swore as she nearly knocked it over, hot wax splashing her hand.

"Move this candle out of my way," she said, "and then stand back."

Although mystified by the abrupt command, Gabrielle did as she was told. She stepped away from the cupboard, holding her candle aloft. With an intent look of concentration upon her face, Cass continued to feel her way along the shelf.

Gabrielle could not see what Cass did, but suddenly the entire aumbry shuddered and creaked. Cass scrambled back and Gabrielle gasped in astonishment as the cupboard swung outward, revealing a yawning hole in the floor. She crept closer, the light from her candle flickering over carved stone steps that spiraled downward, leading to a darkness that was cold and uninviting.

A hidden cellar. So that explained how Cass must have escaped the witch-hunters all those years ago. Gabrielle wondered why the other Lascelles women could not have been saved as well, but Cass was loath to discuss the tragic loss of her family. As one who fiercely guarded her own wounds, Gabrielle understood and respected Cass's reticence.

"You allowed me to read your palm, now I am trusting you with the secret of my innermost sanctum. Welcome to my real home," Cassandra said with a mocking flourish of her hand. When Cerberus attempted to brush past her and lead the way down, Cassandra collared him.

"No!" She bent down and muttered some command that sounded to Gabrielle like, "Go. Guard."

Head erect, the dog trotted away, looking like a soldier ordered to do sentry duty. Cassandra inched forward carefully and started to descend the stairs, pausing to call back to Gabrielle. "Clutch your candle tightly and follow me closely.

"The way down is always a very dark and treacherous one," she added with one of her strange ironic smiles, leaving Gabrielle with the uneasy feeling that Cass was talking about much more than the stairs.

Gabrielle swallowed hard, but she had already come too far to turn back now. Gripping her candle, she plunged after Cass into the darkness.

Chapter Two

GABRIELLE WISHED SHE COULD HAVE CONDUCTED HER VISIT with Cass where she usually did, in the small stillroom at the back of the house. But apparently, the conjuring of the dead required a more secretive and darker setting than the distilling of perfume.

Gabrielle had never liked underground chambers, abhorring the cold, the damp, the prospect of rats or, even worse to her mind, spiders. They had had a dungeon like this room at her home, Belle Haven. The concealed workshop was replete with the potions, herbal brews, and ancient texts of forbidden knowledge the wise women of Faire Isle had kept prudently hidden for generations. Gabrielle had usually fetched whatever she needed from the storeroom and made haste to return to the sunlight.

The underground room at the Maison d'Esprit appeared less of a workshop and more of living quarters. Someone, the serving girl, Finette, most likely, had taken great pains to make it as comfortable as possible for Cassandra.

A cot with many feather pillows took up one side of the narrow room, the thick mattress heaped with wool blankets. A braided rug covered the rough stones of the floor. A bright red shawl and several other dresses of faded finery similar to the one Cassandra wore hung from pegs, lending a touch of color to the gray stone walls.

The only other furnishings were a smaller version of the cupboard upstairs, a humble table, and two chairs arranged before a hearth that must have been connected to one of the chimneys above. It was obvious the fireplace was seldom used. Wisps of smoke wafting from the rooftops of the Maison d'Esprit could well give lie to the belief that only ghosts inhabited the manor.

Cass gave Gabrielle permission to ignite a few of the torches mounted upon the walls and for that she was grateful. But despite the additional light, she found the small room with its low ceiling far too bleak and confining. The prospect of the séance was daunting enough without conducting it in a room that had all the cheer of a blasted tomb. Gabrielle was eager to conclude her business and get out of there.

"Some refreshment?" Cass offered, picking her way over to the cupboard.

"No, thank you," Gabrielle replied and it was all she could do not to add, *"And I wish you would refrain as well."*

She had not been acquainted with Cass long before she realized that Cass suffered from a weakness for strong drink. But even hinting to Cass that she would be wiser to be more temperate was enough to rouse the woman's ire.

All Gabrielle could do was watch unhappily as Cass filled a goblet with liquid from an amber-colored bottle. Her fingers curled round the rim of her glass as a way of measuring, preventing the vessel from overflowing.

Gabrielle caught the reek of very strong spirits, some form of cheap brandy most likely. She fretted her lower lip as Cass drained the large glass as though it was nothing more potent than a goblet of water.

"Ah," Cass breathed. "I needed that." Wiping her lips with the back of her hand, she said, "All right. Suppose we begin by you telling me all about this man that you want raised from the dead."

Gabrielle started. "Man? How do you know it is a man? I never said so."

Cass gave a throaty laugh. Carrying her bottle and glass, she found her way over to the table and eased down into the nearest chair. "You are a beautiful, intelligent woman who has been pushed to the brink of desperation. Of course there must be a man involved. So who was he? Some long-lost lover?"

"No!" Gabrielle winced, fearing that her denial sounded too quick. But there had never been any question of anything like *that* between her and Remy. At least not on her part. She had never granted the man as much as a kiss.

She paced the confines of the small chamber, hard-pressed to sort through her own tangled emotions about Remy and define exactly what their relationship had been.

"He was a friend," Gabrielle said at last. "Only a friend."

Cass's eyebrows arched upward in skeptical fashion, but she made no comment as she refilled her glass. "And what was the name of this *friend?*"

Gabrielle had to moisten her lips before she was able to speak the name she had scarce allowed herself to utter these past three years.

"Remy. Captain Nicolas Remy."

Cass paused in the act of settling the brandy bottle back on the table. "Nicolas Remy. The great Huguenot hero? The one they called the Scourge?"

"Yes, but how do you know of him?"

"I am not a complete recluse. I have Finette to bring me tidings of the world." Cass took a swallow of her brandy, taking a little more time to savor her second drink.

"You intrigue me," she said to Gabrielle. "Your father, the Chevalier Cheney, was also acclaimed a great hero. What does the daughter of a celebrated Catholic knight want with a Protestant soldier?"

"On Faire Isle, we tended to ignore the religious wars. One summer, Remy came to the island, a fugitive and badly wounded. Ariane brought him to our home and nursed him back to health. We kept him safe, hidden from the—"

The Dark Queen.

Gabrielle paused, reluctant to speak of how and why Nicolas Remy had made himself such a powerful enemy, Catherine de Medici, the Dowager Queen of France, but far better known by other names. The Italian Woman, the Sorceress, the Dark Queen. A daughter of the earth herself, Catherine was the most skillful practitioner of black magic in all of France, perhaps the world.

Most wise women shrank from challenging Catherine's power and shied away from any witch foolish enough to do so. Gabrielle didn't want to frighten Cass off by revealing the enmity that existed between the Cheney women and the Dark Queen, a grim history that had begun long before they had snatched Remy from Catherine's clutches.

Gabrielle hesitated so long that Cassandra demanded impatiently. "You hid Remy from whom?"

Gabrielle stripped off her cloak, hanging it on a peg near the empty hearth, the action giving her time to think. "From—from the Catholic soldiers who were persecuting him."

Cass was silent for so long Gabrielle did not know if she had been fooled by Gabrielle's evasive answer. To her relief, Cass did not press her for more details of Remy's desperate flight to the Faire Isle.

Cass took another gulp of her drink and murmured, "So this Remy arrived on your doorstep, a wounded and tormented hero. I can conceive of nothing more romantic. And yet you deny that he won your heart?"

"Yes, I do," Gabrielle snapped. Why did Cass persist in believing that Gabrielle must have been in love with the man?

"If I had a heart, which I don't," Gabrielle went on. "I would never have given it to Nicolas Remy. The captain was far too solemn and earnest for my taste, one of those noble fools, all honor and duty. Every inch the soldier, no courtly manners whatsoever and—and very little experience of ladies."

"Then he must have been entirely bewitched by you."

"Perhaps he was a trifle smitten. I didn't want him to be." Gabrielle's throat constricted as she recalled, "I was not even particularly kind to him."

Not particularly kind. A glaring understatement. Gabrielle's heart ached at the memory of the way she had returned Remy's sword to him, the one she had stolen to fight off the witch-hunters.

"The morning he left Belle Haven, I—I didn't even say good-bye," Gabrielle faltered. "I never saw him again. He was here in Paris that St. Bartholomew's Eve in the summer of 1572."

Cass lowered her glass, her thin face going solemn at Gabrielle's words. "The night the Catholics went on a rampage, murdering Protestants? Not the best place for a Huguenot soldier to be."

"No, it wasn't," Gabrielle agreed, her eyes welling in spite of herself. She rubbed her knuckles fiercely across her eyelids. "Remy was killed during the massacre, but by the time I—that is we—my sisters and I learned of his death, we could not give him a decent burial. He'd already been tossed into one of the mass graves."

Her grief and anger over that was still so sharp, Gabrielle stalked back across the room, hugging herself tightly. Remy had been a valiant soldier, the most honorable man she'd ever known. He had deserved a far more fitting end, to be laid out like a knight of yore in gleaming armor, his sword clutched in his hands. Not dumped like refuse in a pit, no gentle hands to clean the blood from his face, no one to whisper a prayer.

Damn the Dark Queen for so callously bringing about his

destruction. Damn the jackals who had cut Remy down and then so dishonored his body. Damn them all to hell.

And most of all, Gabrielle thought wretchedly, damn herself for never being able to love Remy as he had deserved.

She turned back to Cass, disturbed to see the woman pouring yet another drink. She had lost track of the amount of brandy Cass had consumed in such a short period of time, certainly enough to put any ordinary woman under the table.

Cass's hand still appeared remarkably steady, but her nose and cheeks were getting flushed. She lolled against the back of her chair, saying, "What happened to the gallant captain is very sad to be sure, but the massacre was over three years ago. You say you didn't love Remy. Why not simply forget the man and let him rest in peace?"

"Because he is giving me none! It is perfectly absurd." Gabrielle tried to laugh, but the sound came out strained and hollow. "I can't get Remy out of my head, can't stop remembering. I even dream about him. He is haunting me and it is growing worse of late."

She dragged her hand back through her hair. "The other day I fancied I saw him in a crowd and made a fool of myself chasing after a stranger. Then earlier tonight I imagined I saw him out in the courtyard, by your gate."

"And so you would conjure his spirit to do what?" Cass demanded. "Ask him to leave you alone?"

"I don't know," Gabrielle said miserably. "To tell him I did try to find him and give him a proper burial. And to beg his forgiveness. I could have saved him, Cass. I knew how—how much he cared for me. I could have seduced him into staying on Faire Isle, safe in my arms.

"But I didn't," she added in a broken whisper. "I just let him . . . go."

Cass shook her head. "It never works, Gabrielle."

"What?"

"Seeking forgiveness from the dead." Cass sounded so bleak, Gabrielle wondered if the woman spoke from bitter experience. "Ghosts are not that easily laid to rest."

"But I need to try. I have to make my peace with Remy. Somehow I don't think I can get on with the rest of my life until I do."

"Very well, but it is difficult for me to conjure up the spirit of a person I have never met. You will have to describe Nicolas Remy for me so that I can fix some image of him in my mind."

The request, simple as it was, daunted Gabrielle. She had once been so good at capturing the essence of any person, place, or thing with the magic of her hands. Her skillful fingers wielding a brush could transfer all that she saw upon the blank expanse of canvas or paper. She had never been as adept at painting with words.

"Remy is . . . he *was*," Gabrielle paused to correct herself painfully. "Was a man of—of average height, but he had a very powerful body with a broad chest. His flesh was hard muscled, especially his sword arm, and—and he had a scar where he had been pierced with a shaft from a crossbow. As for his thighs, they were like iron."

"What an excellent description," Cass said in a tone laced with sarcasm. "But tell me. Did you ever happen to notice his face?"

"Of course I did. He—he—" Gabrielle floundered, perhaps because it was easier to focus on Remy's body and somehow far less painful than dwelling on his face.

Her memory of his face was distressingly vague. The impressions she retained were of a visage carved of infinite patience and kindness, of an unfailing gentleness, but those all seemed odd terms to apply to a man who had been a much-decorated warrior.

She said haltingly, "He—he had dark blond hair and a beard that he kept closely trimmed."

"You could be describing any of a million men. What of his eyes?"

"They were dark brown."

"I'm not talking about their color," Cass said impatiently. "What of their expression, their reflection of his thoughts?"

"I—I don't know." Gabrielle laced her fingers together in a helpless gesture. "I was never good at reading eyes. But my little sister Miri said that Remy's were far too ancient for his face."

"The eyes of a wearied knight, doing battle with the evils of the world," Cass murmured into her brandy glass. "Even when the cause is hopeless, never surrendering, never laying down his sword until the bitter end."

Cass's voice was somewhat mocking, but Gabrielle could not help thinking that Cass had hit upon an apt description of Remy.

Cass emptied her glass again. "That is still not enough. You don't by any chance happen to have something of his, do you?"

"Yes."

Gabrielle reached for the sword buckled to her side and slowly unsheathed it. It was a soldier's weapon, the hilt plain and unadorned, the blade fashioned of fine tempered steel. As simple, strong, and true as the man who had once owned it.

Gabrielle carried the weapon over to the table and guided Cass's hand until the other woman's long, thin fingers closed over the hilt.

Cass's lips parted in surprise as she felt the handle and discerned what it was. "Captain Remy's sword? How on earth did you come by this?"

"It is a long story." Gabrielle sighed. "My brother-in-law, Renard, was with Remy in Paris the night he was killed. Renard barely escaped from the mob with his own life, but he managed to bring Remy's sword away with him. R-remy wanted me to have it."

Cass gave a sly smile. "And you've cherished it all this time."

"Why not?" Gabrielle bridled. "I told you! Remy was my friend, the only friend I ever had outside of my sisters."

Cass fingered the hilt, stroking the pommel and finger guard, carefully testing the sharpness of the blade. She sucked in her breath with a sharp hiss. "This weapon speaks to me of—of a darker side to your gentle knight. A man who could be a ruthless enemy when possessed by the killing fury. Fierce, violent, even savage."

"You are obviously better at reading palms than swords," Gabrielle said, resenting such words applied to Remy. "Remy was nothing like that."

"They called him the Scourge, Gabrielle. I doubt that a man acquires such a title because of his kind and sweet nature."

"Remy hated that nickname!" Gabrielle blazed. "He was a soldier. He did his duty, nothing more."

"All right. All right." Cass flung up one hand in a peace-making gesture. Some unreadable expression softened her gaunt features. She continued to caress the sword in a slow, lingering fashion that stirred in Gabrielle a jealous impulse to snatch the weapon away from her.

She felt curiously relieved when Cass finally shoved the sword back toward her. "Here. Put it away."

Gabrielle seized the weapon, her fingers curling possessively about the hilt as she restored the weapon to its sheath. She was dismayed to see Cass turn immediately back to her bottle, fearing that Cass was going to drink herself insensible.

When Cass started to refill her glass, Gabrielle shot out her hand to stop her.

"Don't you think you've had enough?" she asked softly.

Cass scowled, attempting to thrust Gabrielle's hand away, but Gabrielle tightened her grip on the bottle.

"Please, Cass. You yourself said how dangerous conjuring the dead can be. Would it not be better to proceed with your senses fully alert?"

"I could conjure up the devil himself, drunk or sober."

"That is exactly what worries me."

Cass's lips tightened with a mutinous expression. She and Gabrielle tussled for control of the bottle until Cass grudgingly let go.

"I s'pose you are right," she grumbled. "Take the damned stuff and put it away. For now."

Gabrielle was relieved, even though it was a somewhat hollow victory. She realized the bottle was nearly emptied. She returned both the brandy bottle and the half-filled goblet to the cupboard shelf, all the while anxiously keeping an eye on Cass.

The woman rubbed her hands across her face as though trying to clear her senses. Gabrielle wondered in dismay if Cass was sober enough to proceed any further. Cass struggled to straighten up, shaking back her mass of unruly black hair. Her voice sounded astonishingly steady as she began rapping out commands.

"Go back to the cupboard and find a large copper basin and a black candle. Fill the basin with water. Light the candle and then place both of them on the table. Put out the torches and take up your seat opposite me."

Gabrielle hastened to obey, carrying out all of Cass's orders, her veins thrumming with a nervous excitement. Soon all of the torches were extinguished, the objects Cass had requested positioned in front of her. The black wax candle stood poised in the center of the table, burning with an almost unnatural intensity. The small but brilliant flame shimmered over the water in the copper basin and cast a strange white glow over the pale features of Cassandra Lascelles.

Gabrielle perched on the edge of her chair, aware of the tomblike silence that had fallen over the room. She heard nothing but her own quickened breathing and the thud of her heart. It was hard to remember that there was a vast city teeming just beyond the walls of this house. Paris, with all its noise and bustle, seemed very far away as Gabrielle braced herself to follow Cass into another world, a land of shadows.

"Give me your hand," Cass commanded.

After how easily Cass had been able to pry out her innermost secrets, Gabrielle was reluctant. But when Cass extended her hand with a gesture of impatience, Gabrielle gingerly took hold of her. She couldn't help shivering a little. Cass's fingers were so cold and dry for such a young woman.

"Now what?" Gabrielle whispered.

"Nothing. Sit still and be quiet. And whatever happens, don't break the contact of our hands during the conjuring."

Gabrielle glanced dubiously at the copper bowl of water and burning candle. They seemed simple objects to accomplish such a mighty feat as raising the dead. Even if the candle was black.

"Is nothing else required beside that bowl and candle?" she asked. "Don't we need a potion or—or something?"

"Potion." Cass's lip curled in a sneer. "Other witches might need such pitiful aids, but I possess a natural affinity for the world of the dead."

What a chilling way of putting it, Gabrielle thought. She was beset by an unwelcome memory, one of the more disturbing rumors she had heard about Cassandra Lascelles. That when Cass was a little girl, her gypsy mother had struck a hellish bargain, trading Cass's eyesight to the devil so that her daughter might be granted great supernatural powers.

A patently ridiculous tale, Gabrielle assured herself. More likely Cass had become blind through scarlet fever or some other bout of childhood illness. There was nothing sinister or all-powerful about the woman seated opposite her, looking almost childlike in her overlarge dress, her hand so thin it felt as though one hard squeeze might crush Cass's bones to powder.

And yet a voice inside Gabrielle warned, *"Do not be deceived by appearances. Maman always told us to stay clear of anyone who practices dark magic. You can still stop, Gabrielle. Now. Before it is too late."*

The voice sounded remarkably like her older sister, Ariane, whose hands were always too ready to reach out to protect even when one had no wish to be protected, to soothe and comfort even when one was too raw to be touched.

An image of her sister forced its way into Gabrielle's mind,

Ariane's clear gray eyes, her soft brown hair, her solemn smile so like their late mother's. It had been such a long time since Gabrielle had seen Ariane. Far too long, she thought with a pang.

But she resolutely thrust her sister from her mind and focused on Remy. If this dark magic of Cass's actually worked, in a few moments it would be his face Gabrielle would see.

As Cass flung back her head and closed her eyes, Gabrielle held her breath, waiting for Cass to murmur an incantation, the magic words that would bring Remy back to her.

But interminable long moments passed and the woman simply sat there, not moving, not making a sound. Patience had never been one of Gabrielle's virtues. She watched the wax drip down the sides of the black candle with mounting restiveness.

"Damnation!"

Gabrielle was startled when Cass swore, her grip tightening over Gabrielle's fingers. The woman's eyes fluttered open, her lips thinned with annoyance. "Will you please stop fidgeting. I am getting nowhere."

"Sorry." Gabrielle tried to sit still, but Cass continued to complain. "This isn't working. You have got to give me something more to work with."

"But I don't have anything else of Remy's."

"Then give me a memory."

"How am I supposed to do that?" Gabrielle protested. "I don't know what you mean."

"Close your eyes and concentrate," Cass said fiercely. "Think back to a time when you were with Remy. Not a time of any great danger or excitement. Just one quiet moment."

Gabrielle nearly burst into hysterical laughter. A quiet moment in a summer that had seemed filled with nothing but threats of death and disaster, Remy on the run from the Dark Queen. She had sent her soldiers to tear Faire Isle apart in their search for him. When that effort had failed, Catherine had resorted to far worse tactics, setting the witch-hunters upon them, led by that dread, half-mad fanatic, Vachel Le Vis.

The bastard Le Vis had arrested Gabrielle's little sister Miri, threatening to torture the child if Remy was not handed over to him. This threat had only been averted by the Comte de Renard, driving the witch-hunters back to the mainland. But all too soon Le Vis and his minions had returned under cover of darkness, this time attacking Belle Haven itself, nearly burning the house over all their heads.

Gabrielle opened her mouth to inform Cassandra that she had never known one quiet moment with Nicolas Remy hidden on Faire Isle. But she faltered, obliged to admit that that wasn't true as other memories flooded back to her.

Gabrielle had been so restless and bored that summer, still coming to terms with the pain of her past, not yet able to chart the mysteries of a future beyond Faire Isle, the present seeming locked in endless quarrels with her sister, Ariane. But in looking after Remy, aiding in his recovery, Gabrielle had found a measure of peace. She recalled days in which she had forgotten herself entirely in her efforts to keep Remy's mind off the pain of his wound. Doing anything to entertain him, even unpacking the remnants of girlhood she had put behind her, her books of poems and romances.

Remy's hands, so large and callused, had been better suited to wield a sword. He'd looked uncomfortable and awkward turning the leaves of her books, far preferring to have her read to him. But Gabrielle wondered how much sense he'd ever made of the words. She'd glance up from the page to find him staring at her with such a look of steadfast adoration. It had almost been enough to make her feel young and innocent again, untouched. *Almost.*

Gabrielle stiffened in her chair, shying away from the recollection. But she became aware of Cassandra gently stroking her hand and urging, "Go on, Gabrielle. Remember."

Against her will, Gabrielle's mind drifted to one particular afternoon when Remy had finally been well enough to rise from his bed and Gabrielle had persuaded him to steal away from the safety of the house, into the woods behind Belle Haven.

The grass had felt cool and crisp beneath Gabrielle's bare feet, the sun warm upon her face, but not as warm as Remy's hand clasped in hers. Gabrielle's breath snagged in her throat, her head filling with a clearer image of Remy than she'd had for a long time. Soul-weary eyes of a melting brown were shielded beneath thick dark lashes as he smiled down at her, his sensitive mouth so at odds with the rugged lines that time and hardship had carved into his face.

Remy had had an unusually sweet smile for a man, a little solemn, a little shy, made all the more endearing by the fact that he—

No. Gabrielle's eyes flew open, her throat clogging with the familiar grief.

"I can't do this," she said hoarsely.

"Yes, you can," Cassandra soothed, continuing her rhythmic caress of Gabrielle's hand. "You must if you ever want to see Remy again. Just listen to me and I'll carry you safely past the hurt."

Gabrielle sighed, unwilling to return to that August day, the last one she had ever shared with Remy before he'd ridden away from Faire Isle to meet his death. But as she fell under the spell of Cassandra's hypnotic voice, Gabrielle closed her eyes and fought hard to remember that afternoon by the riverbank.

She had been teasing Remy again despite the fact that Ariane had frequently scolded her for doing so. Tormenting the man, as her older sister had called it. But Nicolas Remy had needed to be teased out of his seriousness if ever a man did. He needed someone to ease that grave look from his eyes, to make him laugh, to forget for a time whatever heavy burdens he carried.

Gabrielle had coaxed him into setting aside his solemn dignity and joining her in a favorite flight of fancy from her childhood, playing at knights and dragons.

If she concentrated hard enough, she could still hear the rough timbre of his voice.

"So does this game include a part where the fair damsel rewards her bold knight with a kiss?" Remy tried to make the question sound like a jest, but his deep brown eyes were far too serious for Gabrielle's comfort.

Gabrielle moved away from him, sweeping her skirts in a grand manner. "A kiss? Fie upon you. It is clear you understand nothing of damsels. We are a cold and cruel lot, requiring our champions to worship us from a distance. The most we ever allow is our knight to kneel at our feet and swear eternal devotion and service."

She spoke with forced playfulness, never expecting Remy to comply with her request. But to her consternation, he stepped in front of her and began to slowly lower himself.

"Oh, Remy, I was only jesting—" she began, but Remy went down on one knee, the effort obviously costing him some pain from his recently healed wound. He flinched.

"Remy, stop," she said. "The game is over. Do get up."

But he remained where he was, even though he had paled a little. "Nay, milady. You suggested this. Now we will see it through."

"Don't be an idiot. Stand up before you hurt yourself." She tugged at his sleeve, trying to force him back up. But he captured her hand, imprisoning her fingers in the warm strength of his own.

Gabrielle attempted to tug free, but when Remy tilted his head to look up at her, she stopped, held spellbound. The sun spilled over him, turning his hair to burnished gold, accenting every line worn by pain and hardship on his beard-roughened features. But his eyes seemed to shine with a light of their own, strong, steady, and honest.

"Milady, my sword is ever at your service," he said, gathering her hand close to the region of his heart. *"I vow by my life's blood to serve and protect you forever."*

It was as though the embodiment of every maiden's dream

had sprung to life at her feet. The battered knight, after much toil and care, fighting his way to his lady's side, to sweep her off on his charger and into the shelter of his arms.

A man of complete honor, integrity, and courage, traits that she had once mistakenly supposed belonged to the Chevalier Etienne Danton. But Danton had only borne the title. He'd been no more a knight than Gabrielle was any longer a maiden.

Only Nicolas Remy was real and true. Unfortunately he'd arrived on her island much too late.

"Remy . . ." A husky voice breathed the name with a sorrow that might have come from Gabrielle's own heart. But the sound had emanated from Cass. Gabrielle opened her eyes and stared uneasily at the other woman.

"Remy," Cass murmured again. Her head was flung back, a succession of strong emotions chasing across her pale features. One moment her lips were parted with a dreamy sensuality, the next they tightened with despair.

It was almost as if . . . as if Cass was stealing Gabrielle's memories of Remy, draining them from her through her fingertips. Gabrielle instinctively fought to pull her hand free, but Cass's fingers tightened around Gabrielle's wrist like an icy manacle. Cass's head snapped forward and Gabrielle ceased her struggles, too paralyzed to move as Cass transformed before her very eyes.

Gone was any trace of the inebriated woman or the pale recluse. Cass threw back her shoulders and arched her neck, appearing to grow in stature until she resembled some legendary sorceress of old, a Circe or Morgan le Fay.

Glowing in the intense white light of the candle, her skin was translucent, a strong contrast with the bloodred of her gown, the ebony tangle of her hair. The candle's flame reflected points of light in her dark eyes, sharp and cold as some distant star.

"Nicolas Remy," Cass rasped. "I summon you back from the realms of the dead. Follow the sound of my voice and come to us. Gabrielle is waiting."

She groped for the bowl with her free hand, sweeping her fingers across the top of it. The water in the basin began to roil, vapor rising from the surface until it became a vessel of mist. Cass leaned forward eagerly, her lips parted. The more the water clouded, the clearer her eyes became, the sharper their focus. As Cassandra stared down into the water, Gabrielle realized with a jolt, the blind woman could *see.*

"Nicolas Remy," Cass called again. "Gabrielle has traveled a long way to find you. She is wearied and sore of heart. Do not disappoint her. Part the veil of the dead and let her look upon your face, hear your voice one last time."

At Cass's words, the mist began to swirl and a shape began to slowly emerge, a barely discernible silhouette, like the face of a man lost in fog.

"Show yourself, Captain," Cass demanded. "Do not keep us waiting."

The vapor shifted and Gabrielle's breath hitched in her throat as she caught the barest hint of a bearded countenance only to have it fade back into the mist. She bent over the bowl, her heart thudding with a painful mingling of fear and hope.

Cass intoned more fierce invocations, but the man remained a phantom, lost in the water and mist.

"He won't come for me," Cass muttered to Gabrielle. "You call him."

Gabrielle peered down at the ghostly shape in the water, her pulse thundering in her ears. "R-remy?" she faltered.

"Call to him as if you mean it. Put your heart into it, girl."

Gabrielle moistened her dry lips and tried again. "Remy, please. Come back to me—just one more time. I—I need you."

The mist whirled and parted and the image hidden beneath the surface gradually became clearer. Gabrielle's breath escaped in a half-sob as the water shimmered, assuming the contours of a man's lean face hidden beneath a rugged growth of beard.

But it wasn't Nicolas Remy.

Chapter Three

GABRIELLE RECOILED IN ALARM FROM THE APPARITION. THE OLD man's beard was long and thick, his cheeks sunken, forming deep hollows beneath eyes filled with a grave dignity. They focused accusingly on Gabrielle.

"Foolish witch! Why have you disturbed my peace?" The spirit's voice was deep, like the rumble of distant thunder.

"I—I didn't." Gabrielle shrank back in her chair. She tugged frantically to break the contact of their hands. "Cass, we've got to end this now."

But Cass refused to let her go. "No, don't be afraid. It is all right, Gabrielle."

To Gabrielle's astonishment, Cass leaned closer over the copper basin, her voice lowering to a tone of hushed reverence. "Good evening, master."

The water in the basin rippled, the steam rising higher with a soft hiss. Gabrielle's heart clenched with fear. And yet the old man hovering in the mist did not seem threatening so much as sorrowful, bowed down by a hundred lifetimes of regret. As his aged eyes fixed on Cass, Gabrielle thought she actually saw him shudder.

"Cassandra Lascelles. You perform this accursed black magic no matter how many times I have begged you to desist. Why did you summon me again?"

"I did not summon you this time, master," Cass replied. "You came on your own."

"Because I could not help myself. The mere sound of your voice invading the realms of the dead is a torment to me. And then there was that name . . . Gabrielle."

Hearing her name pronounced in that sepulchral voice caused Gabrielle to tense with fresh alarm.

But Cass persisted. "You know something about Gabrielle? Her name means something to you, master?"

"Cass, please," Gabrielle interrupted. "What is happening? Who is this strange man?"

"Nostradamus," Cass hissed back at her.

"Nostradamus?" Gabrielle's jaw dropped in pure astonishment.

"Yes, the famous doctor from Provence and former court astrologer. A man noted for being able to read the future. Surely you have heard of him?"

"Yes, what wise woman has not?" Gabrielle whispered. "But what I don't understand is what he is doing here when we were seeking Remy."

"Maybe if you'd be quiet, I'd have a chance to find out," Cass muttered. In a louder, more respectful tone, she addressed the ancient face drifting before them. "Master, you said something about Gabrielle. Have you seen her in one of your visions? Do you know her future? Tell us."

"I didn't come here to have my future told," Gabrielle said in another terse aside.

Cass ignored her. Rising taller in her chair, she was at her most imperious as she demanded, "Tell us now, master, and I will end the séance and let you depart in peace."

"No, you won't," Gabrielle protested. "What about Remy?"

Cass gave Gabrielle's hand a hard squeeze to silence her. The old man closed his eyes, as though trying to will himself back into the mists of his own world. He apparently realized the futility of the struggle because his mouth drooped with defeat.

Nostradamus opened his eyes and began to intone in accents of wearied resignation. *"The Lady Gabrielle has a mighty destiny before her. She will become a woman of great influence, wealth, and power beyond her greatest imaginings."*

"I don't want to hear this," Gabrielle said. "Tell me about Nicolas Remy."

"Gabrielle will hold sway over the heart of a king."

"King? What king?" Cass asked eagerly.

"The king of France. Gabrielle will rule the country through Henry. First she will become his mistress—"

"Henry Valois?" Gabrielle echoed with revulsion. "The son of Catherine de Medici? That perfumed fop? He is the cruelest and most perverted man I've ever known."

"I speak not of Henry Valois," Nostradamus replied. *"But of Henry, the present king of Navarre. It is his adoration you will gain and he will one day inherit the throne of all France."*

"That's impossible," Gabrielle said impatiently. "Valois is a young man and he has an even younger brother. Their mother, Catherine de Medici, would fiercely guard their right to the throne. Now about Nicolas Remy. He was a Huguenot soldier. It is him I want to—"

"The House of Valois will fall, the power of the Italian woman come to an end."

"Stop!" To Gabrielle's astonishment, Cass reared back, her voice sharp with alarm. "You will speak no more of the Dark Queen."

Nostradamus paid no more heed to Cass's attempt to interrupt than he had to Gabrielle.

"Beware the Dark Queen. She will fight to keep what is hers and destroy all who threaten her power. But she will perish along with both of her remaining sons. Her line will end. The king of Navarre shall become king of France, and Gabrielle will—"

"No more of this," Cass cried. "Be silent."

Cass's hand fought to break contact with hers and this time it was Gabrielle who clutched at her to prevent that from happening.

"Gabrielle will what?" Gabrielle asked the old man, intrigued in spite of herself.

"The Dark Queen's reign will end and Gabrielle's will—"

"No!" Cass shoved to her feet, wrenching free of Gabrielle. Before Gabrielle could stop her, Cass lashed out with her free arm, striking the copper basin and black candle from the table. Both hit the stone floor with a terrible clatter.

Gabrielle leapt up from the table, hoping to be able to do something, but it was too late. The water was spilled, the candle extinguished. The mist, the ghostly countenance, the predictions of Nostradamus, all gone. Even worse, so was her hope of seeing Nicolas Remy again.

A heavy silence fell over the chamber. Gabrielle stumbled through the darkness, fumbling with flint and tinder until she managed to relight one of the torches. The basin lay overturned on the floor, a dark spill of water pooling around it and the black candle. The wick was charred to black ash. The candle, which had blazed with such power only moments ago, looked absurdly harmless.

"Why, Cass?" Gabrielle asked, turning angrily on the other woman, her voice thick with a mingling of frustration and dismay. "Why did you do that?"

"Why?" Cass repeated shrilly. "Bloody hell, Gabrielle."

She hugged her arms tightly around herself. "Nostradamus was bandying about the name of the Dark Queen, foretelling her death and the downfall of her line. Do you know what she would do to us if she found out we were conjuring up such predictions?"

"Oh, don't be a fool, Cassandra," Gabrielle snapped. "We are hiding in an abandoned house, holding a séance down here in a room like a blasted tomb. How the devil would Catherine ever find out?"

"Because she *is* a devil. She possesses more evil powers than you could ever imagine. If the Dark Queen even suspected that you hoped to supplant her and her brats with Navarre, she'd destroy you and him, too. And then she'd come after me for conjuring up her dead court astrologer to fill your head with such ambitions."

"I didn't need Nostradamus to supply me with the ambition to end the Dark Queen's power. I have burned with the desire to see Catherine brought low ever since—" But Gabrielle checked her anger as she realized how genuinely distressed Cass was.

She had turned deathly pale, even for Cass, and she swayed a little as though she might be about to faint. Her ire dissolving, Gabrielle hastened to Cass's side.

"Are you all right? You look terrible." Gabrielle wrapped her arm bracingly around Cass's thin shoulders. "Come on. I think you need to lie down."

"What I need is a drink," Cass mumbled, but she allowed Gabrielle to lead her over to the narrow cot. Cass refused to lie down, but she did sink down on the edge, bowing her head between her knees until some of the color returned to her cheeks.

She sat up with a blurry sigh, seeking to shove back the straggling ends of her hair. Cassandra Lascelles dwindled right in front of Gabrielle's eyes, all trace of the formidable sorceress vanished along with the mist. The most marked change was in her eyes, the light in them snuffed out like the wick of the candle. Cass was lost, back in her darkness.

She moistened her lips, passing a trembling hand across her brow. "Lord, it—it is always hard on me when I end one of my conjuring sessions so abruptly. I—I am sorry I did so, Gabrielle. I know you think me a great fool. But when the master started going on and on about the Dark Queen—"

She shuddered. "I am not frightened of many things in this world. But I am wary of crossing her. At least now while she is still the strongest witch in France."

Gabrielle knelt down in front of Cass, gently chafing her wrists. "You need not be so afraid. Far too many of our kind ascribe to Catherine all the dark magic of hell. But I've had dealings with the woman and I promise you—she is just another daughter of the earth, flawed with weakness like the rest of us."

"But—but she is so powerful."

"So are you," Gabrielle said, trying to rub some warmth into Cass's hands. "I have never known any other witch as gifted at conjuring the dead as you."

Cass managed a wan smile. "Not that good, apparently. I didn't give you what you wanted, your Captain Remy."

"Well, that's no great matter," Gabrielle lied, swallowing her disappointment. "It was interesting meeting the great Nostradamus. My father used to bring us the almanacs of his predictions from Paris, although Maman never approved. She had little faith in the art of astrology. She always said that Nostradamus's predictions were but foolish poetry, irritatingly vague."

"Some of his predictions were, others were astonishingly accurate. I can tell you this much, Gabrielle Cheney," Cass said earnestly. "I have conjured Nostradamus many times since he passed over to consult him about the future. His skills have been greatly honed by death."

"Then you think all those things he said about me were true?"

"Oh, yes. You undoubtedly have a great future before you. I only regret I didn't have the courage to continue so he could have told you more."

"Never mind." Gabrielle sighed. Actually there was only one

more thing she wanted to know about the séance. She hesitated, fearing she might not like the answer.

"Cass . . . why did Nostradamus come to me tonight instead of Remy?"

Cass shrugged. "The master and I are linked together forever in a way, whether he wishes it or not. You see, when I was a little girl, my father, the bishop, took me to Dr. Nostradamus in the hopes he could cure my blindness—"

"That's not what I meant," Gabrielle interrupted her. "I understand how you were able to summon Nostradamus. What I don't understand is why Remy didn't come when I called for him."

Cass took a long time about answering, her head ducked beneath her curtain of hair. "I am not sure," she said at last. "Most likely because the captain didn't want to. I tried to warn you the dead can be very unforgiving."

"So you think because I rejected him in life, now he rejects me in . . . death?"

"It would seem so." Cass lifted her head, her face shadowed with sympathy. "I am sorry, Gabrielle."

"That's all right. I rather suspected as much myself," Gabrielle said. Then why did it hurt so much to hear Cass confirm it?

"I suppose if you wanted I could try again sometime when I am feeling better."

"No, what would be the point?" Gabrielle answered bleakly. "I daresay the outcome would be just the same. It was ridiculous of me to attempt it in the first place."

Cass gave her hands a comforting squeeze. "You should forget about Remy. He was only a soldier who passed briefly through your life, nothing to do with your destiny. If Nostradamus is right, you're going to have a king in thrall, be mistress of all of France."

"Yes, France," Gabrielle murmured, wondering why she did

not feel more elated. But at this moment she would have traded away the entire kingdom, all her ambitions and dazzling prospects, for just one more of Nicolas Remy's smiles.

A foolish thought, she chided herself. She was tired, that was all. It had been an eventful and exhausting evening. Releasing Cass's hands, she straightened up slowly.

"It is getting late. I should be going. And you should get some rest."

Cass reached up one hand to smother a mighty yawn. "I am feeling extremely weary. These sessions are always very draining for me."

Gabrielle strode across the room to fetch her cloak. By the time she had fastened it around her shoulders and glanced back, Cass had already stretched out on the cot and crawled beneath the blankets.

There was something curiously childlike about the way she hugged the pillow beneath her head. Watching her, Gabrielle was beset by a sharp pang. It seemed so callous to simply walk away and leave Cass in these melancholy circumstances, alone in this mausoleum of a house, which had to be filled with such terrible memories for her.

"Cass, I—I hate leaving you alone like this. I wish you would let me—"

But Cass cut her off as she always did.

"Don't worry about me, Gabrielle," she said with a drowsy smile. "I have looked after myself for a long time. You just remember your promise to grant my favor whenever I ask for it."

"Of course," Gabrielle murmured.

There seemed no more to be said as Cass nestled down under the covers and closed her eyes. Finding the taper she had brought with her, Gabrielle lit it to help find her way back up the stairs. As soon as she opened the door to the hidden chamber, she all but tripped over Cerberus, who was stretched out across the threshold. The dog had been mournfully resting his head on his paws. He perked up at once and without wasting a glance on Gabrielle, he darted down into the hidden chamber in quest of his mistress.

Looking back, Gabrielle's last glimpse of the blind recluse of the Maison d'Esprit was Cass cuddling her dog beside her.

✳✳✳

CASS HUDDLED BENEATH THE BLANKETS, LISTENING INTENTLY, HER sense of hearing almost as keen as her dog's. As soon as she detected the last of Gabrielle's footsteps on the floor above her, the distant thud of a door closing, Cass whipped back the covers and went in search of her bottle.

She heard Cerberus's claws skitter on the stone floor as the mastiff paced anxiously after her. Cass ignored him, groping her way along the cupboard shelves. Gabrielle had been the last one to put the brandy away and it was not in its usual spot. Cursing softly, Cass fought to choke back her impatience and feel carefully, terrified lest she tip the bottle over and spill out those few remaining precious drops. Her tension mounted until her fingers closed around the welcome shape of the bottle.

Clutching the brandy to her like a miser guarding her last coin, she made her way back to the table and sagged down in her chair. Uncorking the bottle, she did not even bother with the refinement of a glass this time, tipping the brandy straight to her lips.

The fiery liquid flowed over her tongue and down her throat. Only when the brandy pulsed its warmth through her veins did her dark need begin to ease.

Cass lowered the bottle to the table with a long sigh, feeling ashamed of her frantic haste. Cerberus came to thrust his head in her lap, his cold nose nudging her hand as he emitted a low whine.

The poor beast had seen her at the bottle too many times,

Cass reflected ruefully. Witnessed the loss of control, the rages, the unleashing of unbridled impulses that could make her a danger to others, even more so to herself.

She petted the dog, scratching him behind the ears. "Don't fret, old friend," she murmured. "There is not enough left in the bottle to get me drunk tonight. I'll have no more until that idiot girl Finette turns up here again."

Her fingers tightening around the bottle, Cass reflected that she would have a few sharp words to say to the girl about betraying the secret of Cass's ability to practice necromancy to Gabrielle Cheney.

Cass almost trusted Gabrielle as a friend, as much as Cass ever trusted anyone. But all the same, Finette needed to be taught a lesson. Cass lifted her bottle and took another long swallow although she despised herself for it.

The drink was a weakness, she knew, and one she could ill afford. But sometimes it seemed the only magic that could keep her ghosts at bay. Her sisters had risen unbidden from her copper bowl upon more than one occasion to stare at Cass with hard accusing eyes.

The dead did not forgive. That at least was one true thing Cass had told Gabrielle. Too often Cass had lain wakeful, tormented with memories of the witch-hunters tearing apart the house, her sisters' terrified shrieks as they had been dragged to torture and death.

But not tonight, Cass mused, as the brandy's warm haze enveloped her. Tonight she would entertain far more agreeable memories. Stolen ones of a war-weary soldier with hair of ashen gold and melting dark eyes. A lean, battle-hardened body and strong hands. Long fingers as capable of tenderly unlacing a woman's bodice as they were of killing without mercy, driving his sword up to the hilt through an enemy's heart. That sword of Remy's had pulsed with such dark ruthless power, the memory of it still sent a warm shiver through Cass.

Cass held a grudging admiration for Gabrielle. Her new

friend was clever and worldly wise. But in other ways she was a bit of a fool, because there was so much Gabrielle did not know about Nicolas Remy, including the most astonishing fact of all.

The great Scourge was still alive.

Cass laughed softly to herself even as she drained the last of her bottle.

"I have never known any other witch as gifted at conjuring the dead as you." Gabrielle had told her.

Gifted? Indeed she was, Cass thought. So much so that no spirit had ever failed to answer her call, willingly or otherwise. There could be only one reason why Remy had refused her summons from the underworld. The valiant captain from Navarre wasn't there. He still walked the realms of the living, this man who might prove invaluable to Cass.

He could possibly be the *one,* although Cass was not yet certain of that. Or how she would go about finding Remy. But Cass knew that she would, once she had made up her mind that the Scourge truly was the man she sought. She licked the last drop of brandy from her lips and smiled.

Her dear friend Gabrielle would be amazed to discover that poor blind Cass Lascelles had a few dreams and ambitions of her own.

Chapter Four

T HE MIST THAT HAD SOFTENED THE SHARP EDGES OF THE CITY
had faded, leaving only dark streets that seemed colder, harder,
and more dangerous than when Gabrielle had traversed them
earlier. As she approached the gates leading to her own courtyard, she fought a strong impulse to flee for the safety of her
house. A feeling far different from the determined spirit that had
inspired her to march through Paris on her secret errand to Cassandra Lascelles.

Now Gabrielle could only marvel at her folly in venturing
out unescorted. She knew the city well enough to realize how
perilous it could be for a lone woman traveling by day, let alone
at night. What had made her think herself so invulnerable?

Unfortunately she knew the answer to that. Her hand
groped toward the hilt of the weapon strapped to her side.
Remy's sword. Wearing it had always made her feel safe, un-
touchable, as though the blade were a sort of magic talisman infused with the strength and courage of its former owner.

Now when she curled her fingers around the hilt, all it felt like was cold, comfortless steel. It was as though any magic had fled that moment when the séance had failed, when she had been forced to accept the fact that Nicolas Remy truly was dead to her. She would never be able to speak with him, beg his forgiveness, or see his smile one last time. He was never coming back to her, not in any sort of conjuring, perhaps no longer even in her dreams.

She should have felt relieved to be released from her memories at last. Instead all she felt was strangely frightened, alone, and at a time when she most needed protection.

She was being followed.

Gabrielle had been aware of that ever since leaving the Maison d'Esprit. She was being stalked and this time not by any phantom of her imagination. The dark sinister man who dogged her footsteps was no ghost. Each time she chanced to look back she caught the menacing stranger ducking into alleyways, melting behind a drunken crowd that had spilled out of some tavern, fading into doorways, but not quite quickly enough. There was no longer any fog to disguise his relentless pursuit of her.

Gabrielle sensed him lurking behind her in the darkened street, watching her and waiting. But waiting for what? If he were a common thug or footpad, he could have attacked her already. He'd had dozens of opportunities, as careless as she'd been tonight. What if he wasn't stalking her at all, but spying? She had forgotten to don her mask upon leaving Cass's. Gabrielle experienced an urge to do so now, as if that would somehow shield her.

If he was a spy, the threat to her person was not so immediate. And yet the danger remained, peril of a far more subtle and insidious kind, but one that made her more angry than afraid. Gabrielle lingered near the gate, pretending to bend down to release a pebble from her shoe, all the while thinking furiously.

Who did she know who would dare set a spy loose upon her? She had enemies enough in the French Court, not the least of whom was the Dark Queen. Catherine tended to keep a close eye on Gabrielle when she visited the Louvre. Had the Dark Queen started mounting watch on Gabrielle outside the walls of the palace as well?

Gabrielle had mocked poor Cass for being so nervous about the Dark Queen, but perhaps Cass had been right. Gabrielle frowned as she thought back to the man she had seen earlier in the mist, the one she had dismissed as a figment of her imagination. What if the same man who tracked her now had followed her to the Maison d'Esprit?

No, surely Cerberus would have driven off any intruder who came too close. There was no way anyone could have known what she and Cass had been doing down in the hidden cellar. But report of Gabrielle's visit to the abandoned house might be enough to rouse Catherine's curiosity, impel her to investigate the Maison d'Esprit further. Gabrielle could have drawn the very peril Cass dreaded straight to her door.

Or Gabrielle could be merely letting her imagination run wild. There was only one way to know for certain. Slowly straightening, she resisted the urge to glance behind her again. Lifting the latch, she swung the gate open. It had been left unlocked according to her instructions. Gabrielle had wanted no curious eyes registering her coming and going this evening, not even any of her own servants. Now she was doubly glad she had left no guard posted, for it would enable her to set a trap.

She entered the courtyard with seeming casualness. Only when she was sure she must be out of view of the street did her demeanor change. She darted into the shadows, flattening herself against the stone wall that surrounded her property, positioning herself only yards away from the gate. Gabrielle inched Remy's sword free of the scabbard and winced, the rasp of the blade sounding as loud as cannon fire to her ears. Her pulse thudded as she waited for what seemed an interminable length of time.

Perhaps her pursuer would not be rash enough to follow her

onto her own grounds. Or having seen her return home, he would conclude there was nothing more to be learned of her movements tonight and simply vanish.

She almost came out of her hiding place when she heard it. The chink of the latch and the creak of the gate as it was being slowly opened. She quickly crouched back again. Gabrielle held her breath as the lean silhouette of a man stole through the open gate.

Moonlight washed over his features and Gabrielle could see that he was indeed an ill-favored varlet with long, tangled hair and a thick beard, his black jerkin and venetians worn and tattered. He paused, glancing from the abandoned walkway to the distant outline of the house and Gabrielle imagined that he must be puzzling over her sudden disappearance. She had best make her move before he had time to figure it out. Her heart banged hard against her ribs, but it was more from excitement than fear, a righteous anger at this interloper.

Gabrielle slipped from her crouching place beside the wall and circled behind him. Her footsteps whispered across the grass as she raised the sword and brought the point to bear directly in the center of his back.

"Don't move a muscle," she growled. "Or I'll run you through where you stand."

Gabrielle saw him tense, flexing his shoulders. She experienced a fraction of alarm as she realized he was taller and more muscular than she had first assumed. She also noticed too late that he had a weapon strapped to his side.

She had some skill with a blade, but no idea how she'd fare against some strange cutthroat in the dark. It occurred to her that perhaps she'd been a trifle rash to attempt to capture this spy alone. But she had him now. She had to do something with him.

"Raise your hands," she said fiercely. "Unbuckle your sword and drop it."

"I can hardly do both, Gabrielle," he murmured. There was

something familiar about the voice that caused her heart to miss a beat. He chose to obey her first command, raising his hands in the air.

Gabrielle recovered from her shock at hearing him use her name so intimately. She infused her voice with hauteur. "So you know who I am, do you, sirrah? I should like to know who the devil you are and why you've had the impertinence to spy upon me. Turn around, but do it carefully. One move toward your sword and I vow I'll slice your hand clean off."

"I verily believe you would, mademoiselle." She heard his voice more clearly this time, deep, a little hoarse like a voice that had permanently roughened from roaring out commands over the smoke of a battlefield . . . Nicolas Remy's voice.

Gabrielle's heart skittered and then seemed to stop entirely as her captive swung about to face her. Moonlight etched a gaunt visage all but lost in a wild tangle of hair and beard. The only things soft in that hard face were his eyes of rich, melting brown. Remy's eyes shining down at her. What madness was this? As he lowered his hands, Gabrielle felt far too stunned to try and prevent him.

"If you were bent on capturing an intruder, why didn't you go summon your servants? Do you have any idea how easily I could have disarmed you? Only you would be this rash, Gabrielle Cheney." He was scolding her, but his teeth flashed in a smile of rare and unexpected sweetness. Remy's smile.

Dear God, she was losing her mind. She had to be. Gabrielle's hand trembled. Her sword wavered and he attempted to come closer. She sprang back with a terrified cry, bracing her weapon again.

He froze in his tracks. When his voice came again, it was soothing, gentle. "Please, Gabrielle. Don't be afraid. Don't you recognize me? It is me, Remy."

"N-no," she choked. "Y-you lie. You can't be Nicolas Remy. He—he's . . ."

"Dead? I swear to you I am not. Please don't look at me as if I were a ghost."

Gabrielle backed away, trembling. A ghost was exactly what she was looking at. A phantom with Remy's voice, Remy's eyes, Remy's smile. But he could not be Remy, this rough-looking man with his wild, unkempt hair and haggard face. Not unless he'd marched to her across the plains of hell or back from the depths of the underworld. The mad thought seized hold of her that Cass's séance had worked after all, dragging Remy's tormented spirit from the recesses of his grave.

Gabrielle shook so badly she could no longer hold the sword. The weapon slipped from her fingers, tumbling to the ground with a dull thud. The stranger with Remy's eyes took a hesitant step toward her.

"I am sorry that I have alarmed you. I never meant to reveal myself to you this way, but you rather forced my hand. I had hoped to choose a better time."

"A better time?" Gabrielle stared up at Remy, still unable to credit the evidence of her own senses. "Is that why you did not come when I called for you earlier?"

"You called for me? I never heard you."

Gabrielle bit down hard on her lip to still its quivering. "I cried out to you in the mist, but you wouldn't come. I thought you had rejected me and turned back to the land of the dead."

Remy looked rather confused, but he cast her a gentle smile. "Gabrielle, I would never turn away from you, even if I was no more than a ghost, but I promise you I am not. If I were, your sword would have gone straight through me. Please let me get close enough for you to touch me and you'll know I am real."

Gabrielle wanted to beg him to stay away, but she could not seem to find her voice. She didn't want to touch him. She had an irrational terror that if she did, he'd evaporate like Nostradamus, vanish in a hiss of steam.

Remy kept coming closer. When his fingers curled around

her wrist, Gabrielle couldn't summon the will to resist him. He raised her hand and pressed her palm against his chest, over the region of his heart. He was not a man made of mist, but solid rock. The plane of his chest was all hard muscle and beneath his worn jerkin, she could feel the steady thud of his heart.

The hand that held hers was strong, callused, and warm. So was the other one that Remy used to caress her cheek. Gabrielle reached up and caught that hand, trapping it against her face.

She closed her eyes, savoring the rough texture of Remy's palm against her skin. She could almost feel the blood pulsing through his veins. The truth struck Gabrielle with all the force of the earth heaving beneath her feet.

Nicolas Remy was alive.

Her eyes fluttered open. Remy was gazing down at her.

"There. You see?"

Gabrielle nodded, her breath escaping her in a strangled half-sob. Still hardly daring to believe, she ran her hands wildly over him, his chest, his sinewy arms, his broad shoulders. Her fingers roved upward, feverishly caressing his hair and beard, his brow and his cheeks.

She heard Remy's breath quicken and she reveled in every rise and fall of his chest. When she traced her trembling fingers over the outline of his mouth, felt the warm rush of his breath, Gabrielle gave a broken laugh that bordered on hysteria.

"You are really not dead," she whispered.

"No," he replied huskily. Catching her hand, he pressed his lips fervently against her palm. "And for the first time in three years, I am actually glad about that."

She lifted her face, gazing straight into Remy's intense dark eyes. Her own misted with tears. By some miracle, she knew not how, the fates had brought Remy back to her. Not as a ghost, but wondrously, gloriously alive.

With a glad cry, Gabrielle flung her arms about his neck and she did something she realized she should have done years ago.

She buried her fingers in Remy's hair and crushed her mouth eagerly to his.

She felt Remy stiffen in astonishment, but only for a moment. Then he was kissing her back, ravaging her lips with a hunger and passion that left her dizzy. Gabrielle clung to his shoulders, returning his kiss just as greedily, seeking his mouth again and again, unable to get enough of him.

"Remy . . . my dearest Remy," she breathed. Her lips parted before his, giving him deeper access. Gabrielle moaned low in her throat as she felt the heat of his tongue against hers, tasted the vitality flowing through him. Her pulse seemed to thunder the wondrous tidings in her ears. *Remy is alive . . . alive.*

Gabrielle's heart swelled with such joy, it was painful. When their lips parted, she was panting hard and so was Remy. He gave her the uncertain smile of a man who could scarce believe his good fortune.

Gabrielle attempted to return his smile, but the full shock of Remy's return from the dead overcame her at last. Remy's features blurred before her eyes and she felt her knees tremble and begin to give.

Then Gabrielle Cheney did something she had never done before in the entire course of her life. Her head falling back limply, she swooned in a man's arms, sinking into a dead faint.

※※※

NICOLAS REMY HAD WALKED THE PATHS OF NIGHTMARE EVER SINCE the massacre of St. Bartholomew's Eve, but tonight he felt as though he had strayed into a dream. His thick boots sank into the luxurious Turkish carpet of a bedchamber fit for a princess, with a high vaulted ceiling, tall latticed windows, and magnificent paintings adorning the walls.

A stately bed carved of mahogany and hung with pale cream-colored silk curtains embroidered with roses dominated the room. Gabrielle seemed all but lost in the middle of that vast bed, her blond hair fanned across a large feather tick pillow. Gold-tipped eyelashes rested against her cheeks, her face so white and still that Remy's heart wrenched with a fear he'd never known on a battlefield.

"God in heaven, I—I've killed her," he muttered hoarsely.

"No such thing," the brisk voice of Gabrielle's maid replied. Bette was a buxom young woman with a competent air about her, her face completely calm beneath her lace-trimmed cap. She elbowed Remy aside, bending down to chafe Gabrielle's wrists.

He should have thought of that himself, Remy reflected, but both his mind and his limbs seemed to have gone numb. The quick reflexes that had enabled him to leap to the aid of many a fallen comrade seemed to have utterly deserted him. He felt completely helpless before the pale slip of a woman stretched out on the bed.

Remy was only galvanized into motion when Bette ordered him to fetch some water. He carried an ewer over from the washstand, sloshing half the contents onto the carpet in his haste.

Bette dampened a cloth, which she applied to Gabrielle's brow. As she started to loosen Gabrielle's bodice, she said, "You'll have to leave now, Captain Remy. Wait out in the hall."

"No!" Remy protested. "I can't just—"

"You can and will," Bette said. "When mistress comes round, she'd hardly thank me for displaying her teats to you."

Remy flushed at the maid's blunt words. "By God, madam, I would never look—"

"Out!" Bette splayed her hands against Remy's chest and propelled him firmly back toward the door. He allowed her to do so, but only because it was Bette's goodwill that had permitted him to remain with Gabrielle in the first place.

He had alarmed Gabrielle's entire household with his sudden arrival on the doorstep and Remy could scarce blame them for that. Such a desperate vagabond as he must have appeared, bellowing for help, bearing their unconscious mistress in his arms.

It was a miracle he had not been overpowered, Gabrielle wrested away from him while he was arrested and hauled off to face the nearest authorities. He had Bette to thank for the fact that he was not even at this moment clapped in irons.

She had been one of the serving girls at Belle Haven. Bette had grown up and filled out considerably, changed into the very semblance of an elegant lady's maid, so much so that Remy had scarce known the woman. He was fortunate that Bette's memory of him was far clearer and that she had not been as overwhelmed by his return from the dead as Gabrielle.

Remy craned his neck for one last glimpse of Gabrielle before Bette shut the bedchamber door in his face. Gabrielle still had not stirred and Remy tried to not let his mind leap to such dire things as heart failure and apoplexy. Gabrielle was young and healthy. Despite her resemblance to the fair and helpless damsel of folklore, Remy had long ago detected a strength and resilience in Gabrielle.

She would be all right. All he had to do was wait, not the easiest thing for a man accustomed to action. He forced himself to lean back against the wall, crossing his arms over his chest when what he really wanted to do was march restlessly up and down the hall. But he thought it less than wise to draw any more attention to himself. He was aware that he was being watched from the landing below by Gabrielle's footmen, the servants regarding him as warily as if he'd come to steal the silver plate. Their supercilious stares made Remy all the more conscious of his disheveled state.

He supposed that under normal conditions a vagabond such as himself would not even have been permitted inside the kitchen door of a grand establishment such as this. At this hour, most of the building was left in shadow, but when he'd carried Gabrielle up to her bedchamber, Remy had glimpsed enough of the place to discern this was a town house of opulent proportions.

He wondered how Gabrielle came to be living here on her own in Paris, so far from her sisters and the Faire Isle. When her father, the Chevalier Louis Cheney, had been lost at sea, it was said that the knight had sunk most of the family fortune with him. So how then could Gabrielle afford to maintain this costly mansion?

Remy knew what he had heard murmured in the streets about her, lies that even now caused him to grit his teeth and long to cut out someone's filthy tongue. *The most dazzling courtesan to descend upon Paris in many a day,* the old woman in the wine shop had cackled about Gabrielle.

Courtesan . . . a fancy name for a whore. If that hag had been a man, Remy would have run her through. By damn, he'd always hated Paris and this was but one of his many reasons. It was a viperous den of gossip from the palace to the backstreets, all scandalmongering and deceit. Small wonder that a woman as lovely as Gabrielle would become the target of such cynical and envious small minds.

If they had but known Gabrielle as he had that summer, none would dare to slur her honor. A woman-child, striving so hard for sophistication and yet so touchingly innocent in the ways of the world. Warm and cold, kind and cruel by turns, her moods came and went like the wind. Her blue eyes could sparkle with laughter or be haunted with melancholy, but only when she thought no one was looking. He'd often glimpsed a sadness shadowing her face, an expression that had gone straight to Remy's heart, the more so because he had never been able to discover the root of her sorrow.

He only hoped Gabrielle was happy now. She had always dreamed of traveling to vast cities, living in a fine house, and enjoying grand parties and balls. The one thing Remy was certain she had never dreamed of was him.

When he'd made the unfortunate mistake of hinting at the

nature of his feelings for Gabrielle that summer on Faire Isle, she'd made it clear she wanted none of him and the sooner he departed, the better. Never in his wildest dreams had he imagined that Gabrielle would greet his return with such welcome arms, such fire on her lips. Her embrace had stirred desires in him, fantasies of her that he'd always been too wise to ever indulge. But he couldn't stop his mind from running riot now.

Could any woman kiss a man the way Gabrielle had done and feel nothing? Could she swoon with happiness at his return if she was as indifferent to him as she'd once claimed? Was it possible that she cared for him after all, maybe even loved him?

And what if she did? a grim voice inside him demanded. You have no more to offer her now than you did three years ago, even less. The thought brought an abrupt halt to the mad hope flaring inside him, as effectively as if he'd been doused with cold water.

"Captain Remy?"

Remy had been so absorbed in his own reflections, he had failed to hear the click of the bedchamber door as Bette emerged. He straightened away from the wall at once, regarding the maid-servant anxiously.

"Gabrielle? How is she? Is she awake? I mean—has she—"

"The mistress is fine." Bette interrupted his harried string of questions in a soothing tone. "In fact, she is asking for you."

"Thank God." Remy breathed in relief, his shoulders sagging as some of the tension melted out of them. He pressed Bette's hand. "And thank you as well, mademoiselle."

"It is both my duty and my privilege to look after Mistress Gabrielle, monsieur," Bette replied with a dignified sniff.

"I know that. I meant thank you for intervening on my behalf earlier, not letting me be arrested."

"It is the footmen who should be thanking me. You looked quite wild at the prospect of being parted from my mistress and I remember your skill with a sword from the night the witch-hunters attacked Belle Haven. And you were then still recovering from your wound."

Bette's face dimpled in a coy smile as her gaze swept apprais-ingly over him. "May I tell you, Captain, despite the fact you need a haircut and a shave, you look remarkably fit for a dead man."

Remy's own mouth curved wryly. "You don't seem all that surprised to see me still alive, mademoiselle."

She shrugged. "When one has been in service to a family of wise women as long as I have been, very little surprises one. Now you had best go in. Mistress Gabrielle is waiting."

Remy turned to the bedchamber door and opened it. He ex-pected to have Bette hard at his heels, maintaining fierce chaper-one over her mistress. He was surprised when the maid slipped away, leaving him to enter the room alone. Remy took a hesitant step inside, closing the door behind him quietly.

The candlestick had been moved so that all light centered on the bed. The bed curtains were drawn, affording him a glimpse of the figure tucked beneath the costly brocade coverlet. Remy crept forward, his heart beginning to pound. He felt as uncertain as some raw peasant lad invading the bower of a princess.

"Gabrielle?" he called softly. He reached for the bed curtain and drew it back.

Gabrielle was propped up against the pillows and his breath stilled at the sight of her. Her hair spilled down over her shoul-ders in a halo of gold, framing a face that was pale except for a high flush of color spreading across her cheekbones. Remy had always been enchanted by Gabrielle's beauty, the more so because it seemed to emanate from some intense light that burned within her, finding expression in the glow of her jewel-blue eyes.

She was undressed, stripped down to little more than her shift and she peered up at him, clutching the coverlets high over her breasts in a way that was both demure and childlike, the ges-ture leaving Remy curiously moved. He experienced a strange urge to sink to his knees before her as he'd done that day on Faire Isle and renew his pledge.

"I vow by my life's blood to serve and protect you forever."

Instead he simply stood and stared at her until Gabrielle reached one hand up to him. Her soft, slender fingers curled around his, drawing him down to sit beside her. He sank on the edge of the bed. "You—you are well? You are recovered from your shock?"

"Recovered? I hardly know." She gave an odd choked laugh and continued to devour him with her eyes. "So I did not dream you. You really are here?"

If anyone was dreaming, Remy thought it was him.

"Yes, my lo—," he replied, the word almost escaping him before he could prevent it, a word he'd never dared utter before, even to himself.

Gabrielle did not seem to have heard. She tipped her head to one side, a tiny furrow appearing in her brow as she pursued her own line of thought.

"And you have been alive all this time."

"If you want to call it that." Remy cradled her hand, but Gabrielle slipped her fingers away from him, sitting up straighter.

"I thought that you were dead."

"Er, ah, yes—" Remy began.

But Gabrielle interrupted, her voice becoming sharp. *"You let us all believe you were dead."*

She screwed up her face like a little girl trying hard not to cry. Ducking her head, she disappeared behind her shimmering curtain of hair. Remy regarded her in complete consternation. He had never known the proud Gabrielle to weep, not even when the witch-hunters had abducted her sister and she'd been terrified for Miri's life.

"I am sorry, Gabrielle. Please . . . please don't cry," he murmured, seeking to brush her hair back.

Gabrielle's head whipped back. Her eyes blazed, not with tears, but with a fury hot enough to reduce a man to ashes on the spot.

"I am not going to cry. I'm going to kill you!"

Gabrielle doubled up her fist and cracked it into Remy's jaw. The blow caught him completely off guard and sent him flying backward off the bed. He fell to the floor, sprawling on his backside, blinking as much from sheer astonishment as the force of the blow. Gabrielle fought furiously with the bedcovers, flinging them off. She leaped to her feet and stood towering over him like a wrathful goddess.

"Bastard. You bloody bastard!" she cried. She stormed past him in a flurry of flapping night shift and bare feet.

Remy ran his tongue over his bottom teeth, tasting a trickle of blood from his split lip, feeling stunned. As he struggled to his feet, Gabrielle paced up and down, rubbing her bruised knuckles and swearing, using invectives Remy was shocked to discover she even knew.

All modesty was forgotten in her fury and she didn't seem to realize that the candlelight rendered her fine lawn shift all but transparent, revealing the soft swell of her breasts to him, every womanly curve of her body. She might as well have been naked.

The sight was a more formidable blow to Remy's senses than the punch she had given him. Looking frantically for something, anything to throw over her, he seized upon the coverlet and yanked it free of the sheets.

He came up behind her and wrapped the coverlet around her shoulders. "Gabrielle, calm yourself and let me see how badly you've hurt your hand. Give me a chance to explain."

Gabrielle flung the coverlet to the floor and smacked his fingers away from her. "What is there to explain? You've been playing dead for three years. Three God-cursed years."

She heaved with such indignation, her breasts looked in danger of entirely spilling out of her low-cut shift. Remy tried gallantly to avert his eyes, a struggle he was in danger of losing.

"Where the devil have you been?" she shouted. "What have you been doing all this time?"

Remy would have found it difficult to answer that question even without Gabrielle half-naked in front of him, looking as

though she wanted to rip out his throat. Ever since St. Bartholomew's Eve, his life had been a struggle to survive, to contain the
horrors in his head, above all else to let himself hope for nothing,
feel nothing. Within mere minutes, Gabrielle Cheney had managed to strip his heart raw again.

"I—I have been out of the country," he said at last. "Ireland,
then England mostly."

"Oh? And they are having a parchment and ink shortage
over there, are they?"

"I was a fugitive again, Gabrielle, still alive only because my
enemies thought me dead. It hardly seemed prudent to be sending letters."

"And there was no messenger you could trust to bring me
word?" she asked with cold fury. "Or were you struck dumb as
well? Something happened to your tongue, perhaps? From the
way you were thrusting it into my mouth earlier, it seemed to be
working well enough."

"Gabrielle!" Remy rebuked her, finding it almost profane for
her to speak so crudely of the kiss they had shared. "I am sorry if
you were distressed by the report of my death, but allow me to
point out one thing, milady. From the way we last parted, you
gave me very little reason to believe you would care."

Although she flinched at his words, she went on fiercely, "All
right. I suppose that I didn't. But what of my sisters? You must
have known that Ariane had grown very fond of you. And—and
Miri. She regarded you as the brother we'd never had. Do you
know how many nights I comforted her while she grieved and
wept for you? How many nights I—"

Gabrielle broke off abruptly and flounced away from him.
Even though she retreated into the shadows by the windows, he
could see what she fought so hard to hide, that her anger was no
more than a mask for the hurt she had endured. She *had*
mourned for him all this time. She *did* care. But any elation
Remy felt was swept aside by the realization of how much suffering he had inflicted upon her.

Tears trickled down her cheeks. She was crying in a way that Remy doubted the proud, stubborn Gabrielle had ever let anyone see her weep before. And those tears were a worse reproof than any hard words she could have hurled at him. He approached her as carefully as he would have done some injured woodland creature likely to lash out or take flight.

"Gabrielle. I am sorry if I caused your sisters or you any pain. I would cut off my right arm before I ever—"

She whipped away from him, presenting him with the rigid line of her back. That treacherous shift slipped, baring one smooth white shoulder. Remy eased the fabric back up, his fingers brushing against her soft warm skin. He struggled manfully to ignore the effect that the feel of her had on his body.

"There is one thing you must understand about me, my dear," he said, placing his hands on her upper arms. She stiffened as he forced her gently around to face him. "I have lived a rough life, not accustomed to any of the softer influences."

Gabrielle kept her dampened lashes lowered, refusing to look up at him.

"I never had a mother or sisters to worry and weep for me. Even my father is long gone and I have no other living relatives. Any friends I've ever had have been soldiers like myself who well understood the realities of our profession, that death always marches just a step behind. I am sorry for my thoughtlessness, but quite frankly, I am simply not used to thinking my life of any consequence to anyone."

"That—that's because you are a very stupid man." Gabrielle sniffed, but she relented enough to rest her forehead against his chest.

Remy brushed a light kiss against the golden crown of her hair. "Forgive me?"

She didn't answer, but she melted against him in a way that was far more eloquent than any words, nestling her face against his shoulder. Remy's arms wrapped about her, straining her close, holding Gabrielle in a way he'd always dreamed of doing.

He felt as though he could have been content to hold her thus forever, but Gabrielle squirmed free, dashing aside the last of her tears with the back of her hand. She no longer appeared angry, but her tone was still aggrieved, as she demanded, "So exactly when were you planning to announce your presence? Why have you been skulking after me all evening?"

"I wasn't skulking," Remy started to protest, then grimaced. "Very well. Perhaps I was. I have been waiting for an opportune moment to approach you and when I saw you set out tonight on some reckless errand, I felt I had no choice but to follow."

"To see what I was up to?" Gabrielle scowled.

"Yes," Remy replied, refusing to be daunted by her frown. "It was very imprudent of you, Gabrielle, to be out wandering in this cursed city alone at night, to visit some decrepit, abandoned house. What on earth were you doing there?"

A mutinous expression settled over Gabrielle's face and he thought she would refuse to answer him. Then she shrugged. "If you must know, Nicolas Remy. I was trying to bring you back from the dead."

"What?"

"There is a witch who hides in that old house who is especially skilled in the arts of necromancy. We were holding a séance to contact your dearly departed spirit."

Remy gaped at her. For most of his life, he had been a plain and practical man, skeptical of anything that smacked of magic or superstition. But his experiences with the Dark Queen and the Cheney sisters had altered his simple views of the world forever. In particular, he had seen and learned enough from Ariane that summer on Faire Isle to make him react to Gabrielle's calm pronouncement with horror.

"Necromancy!" he exclaimed sharply. "That is black magic of the worst kind. What were you thinking?"

"I was desperate. I had to see you one last time, to speak to you." Her lip quivered and she bit down to still it. "To beg your forgiveness."

"Gabrielle, what have you ever done that I would need to forgive you for?"

"I thought that I had gotten you killed."

"Gotten me killed?" Remy echoed in astonishment. "The massacre on St. Bartholomew's Eve was none of your doing. Even if I had died, how could that have been your fault?"

"Because I gave you back your sword, sent you away to Paris to—to die."

"You did not send me. I had to go. My king was in danger."

Gabrielle shook her head. "I should still have stopped you from leaving. I knew how attracted you were to me. I should have been kinder to you. I should have kept you safe on Faire Isle even if it meant holding you my captive. Even if—if I had to seduce you in order to do it."

"My God, Gabrielle!" Remy cupped her face between his hands and chided her. "Do you ever think that I would have allowed you to do that? That I am the sort of man who would have so lightly set aside my honor and what is worse, have taken such advantage of your virtue? No, my dear, and what is more, you could never have behaved in such a fashion either. Your own sense of honor would never have permitted it."

"My honor," Gabrielle echoed softly.

"Yes, you were but an innocent slip of a girl, although the most beautiful one I'd ever seen." Remy stroked her cheeks with the pads of his thumbs. "I admit that I was fairly bewitched by you. But my duty to Navarre had to come first. No matter how much I cared for you, nothing could have been any different."

Gabrielle had gone very still beneath his touch. Curling her fingers about his wrists, she slowly pushed his hands away from her. "Yes, you are right," she said dully. "Nothing could ever have been any different. Thank you for reminding me of that."

She drew abruptly away from him, leaving Remy with the dismayed feeling he'd just said something terribly wrong. He always had been a clumsy dolt when it came to any dealings with women and most especially Gabrielle. Instead of prating on about his duty, perhaps he should have told her how much he adored her, that leaving Faire Isle, believing he would never see her again, had been the hardest thing he'd ever done.

But the expression that had settled over Gabrielle's face was far from encouraging. Something had shut down in her eyes as she stalked over to her wardrobe and dug through her gowns and petticoats. He should have been relieved to see her seeking to cover herself up, but it was like watching her armoring herself against him. She selected a dressing gown of gold brocade that looked more costly than anything he could have earned by soldiering in a year.

"So after all this time, what finally brings you back to see me?" she demanded.

"I need your help with something," he admitted reluctantly.

"Oh?"

"And—and I did want to see you again," he was quick to add. That was putting it mildly. She had never been far from his thoughts or out of his heart these past years, but it seemed futile to try telling her that now. Not when the smile that she offered him was as cold and glittering as some distant star.

"Very well. Why don't you have a seat while I make myself a bit more presentable? Then you can regale me with your adventures these past three years and tell me how I may be of use to you, Captain Remy."

Captain Remy? What the devil? Remy frowned, wondering what he could have said or done to produce this change in a woman who had been all but melting in his arms only moments ago. But before he could question her, Gabrielle had disappeared behind a wooden dressing screen at the far end of the room. He had no right to hope that anything could come from his feelings for Gabrielle. He never had. But he felt as though he'd had a touch of heaven this night and had somehow let it slip through his fingers.

Chapter Five

GABRIELLE THRUST HER ARMS INTO THE SLEEVES, EASING THE dressing gown over her shoulders. The intricately carved wooden screen shielded her from Remy's gaze, but she had not retreated behind it out of any sense of modesty.

It was far too late for that after the way she had stormed around in her flimsy shift. But she had done far worse than bare the secrets of her body. She had exposed her heart to him as well, all the feelings she had long refused to acknowledge even to herself.

She *did* care for Nicolas Remy, far more than she had ever wanted to. Of course she was not in love with the man. She was incapable of that, but when she thought of how she had grieved for him all these years, she wanted to pound her fists against his chest and rage at him.

Why? Why the devil could you not have let me know you were still alive? If I hadn't thought you were dead, I would have . . . have . . .

Have done what? a voice inside her mocked. Not pursued a career as a courtesan? Saved herself for him? There had never been any question of that. Thanks to Etienne Danton, it had already been too late even when she had first met Remy. Her joy at finding Remy alive had made her momentarily forget herself, who she was, what she was destined to become, and it wasn't any man's blushing bride.

As she struggled with the ivory buttons on her robe, Remy's voice echoed sadly through her mind. *Nothing could have been any different.* His words had jolted her back to reality with a painful thud, but she was grateful to Remy for reminding her of that. Before she made any more of a fool of herself over him than she already had. Kissing him, swooning in his arms, almost forgetting all the ambitions that had enabled her to survive these past years.

Gabrielle looked up, her gaze drawn to the mirror mounted upon the wall, reflecting back the golden crown of hair, the creamy complexion and delicate features so many ladies envied her. All she saw was a woman haunted by the knowledge that her beauty was only a surface one, a thin disguise for all the dark stains on her soul. It was one thing to bewitch a man out of his senses, to keep him in thrall. She was certainly capable of that. But to inspire a love that was real and true, that was a magic she did not possess.

Remy thought her so beautiful. Very likely, he even believed that he loved her. But how could he love her when he didn't even know her? If he did, he would never connect her with such terms as *honor* and *innocence*.

But what the devil did it matter how Remy felt about her? She had long ago realized it was better to be a wealthy lord's mistress than a poor soldier's wife. Seduction . . . that was where a woman's real power lay. And power meant the ability to protect her family and herself from the machinations of the Dark Queen. To be strong, invulnerable to the kind of hurt that could be inflicted upon one by predatory men like Danton. Or even unintentionally by a gallant man like Remy.

According to Nostradamus, her future was set. She was destined to become the most powerful woman in all France, mistress of Remy's own king, Henry of Navarre. She wondered how Remy would react to that. Would he be stunned? Hurt? Angry? Would he turn away from her in disgust or do his best to persuade her to abandon her plans, leave Paris?

She would never do that. Paris was where she belonged. If anyone should go, it was Remy. This city was just as dangerous for him now as it had been three years ago. Gabrielle smiled bitterly at the irony of it. She had hoped, prayed, even risked breaching the realms of the dead to see Remy one last time. And now that she had him back, she was going to have to do her damnedest to drive him away again.

She closed her eyes in momentary despair, then forced herself to rally. She finished buttoning up her dressing gown to the very top where the high standing collar framed her slender neck like a ruff. Moving with the swiftness of long practice, she swept up her hair, confining it to a net caul studded with tiny pearls. The mirror reflected back a proud and distant woman.

With one last glance at her icy image, she emerged from behind the screen. She had taken so long she expected to find Remy pacing the room with impatience. But he waited by the chamber's imposing fireplace, looking as uncomfortable as any man possibly could, left to his own devices in such a thoroughly feminine room.

The hearth had been swept clean for the summer, the brass andirons polished and gleaming. The marble surround was whimsically carved with dolphins and mermaids, costly silver branches of candles situated at either end of the mantel. The expanse in between was cluttered with some of Gabrielle's fans, a leather bound book of poems, an hourglass, and some discarded hair ribbons.

One object in particular had caught Remy's eye. Some of the tension in his face relaxed as he lifted a miniature down from the mantel. It was a portrait of her little sister, Miri, one of the few things that Gabrielle had brought from home with her.

As Remy studied the portrait, the taut set of his mouth softened into a smile. His distraction enabled Gabrielle to do what she had been unable to before—take a good long look at him, and she was daunted by what she saw.

Remy had changed and in ways that went far beyond his unkempt appearance. He seemed leaner and harder than she remembered, looking like a man who gave little thought to food or sleep beyond what he needed for survival.

Gabrielle longed to urge him to rest while she ordered him up a decent meal and a hot bath to soak his wearied bones. Get him out of those travel-stained clothes, trim his beard, comb his hair, scold him and fuss over him, tease him into laughing as she used to do. Tuck him up in her bed and caress the lines of care from his brow while he sank into some obviously much needed sleep. And then—

Gabrielle hitched in her breath, checking her wayward imaginings. These were stupid thoughts to be having about a man she had just resolved she must be rid of. Especially the thought that involved bringing Remy anywhere near her bed.

With great difficulty, Gabrielle struggled to maintain her distant demeanor as she glided toward him. Remy glanced up at the rustle of her skirts. But the smile he had bestowed on her little sister's portrait faded at the sight of Gabrielle. His mouth turned down with a mixture of disappointment and confusion, clearly perceiving the changes in her and not liking what he saw.

Gabrielle steeled herself behind a glittering smile. "I am sorry I took so long about tidying myself. What must you think of my manners, Captain Remy? I trust I have not kept you waiting?"

"No," he muttered. He shifted his eyes back to the miniature in his hand. "I was admiring this portrait of Miri. It is a remarkable likeness, just as I remember her."

"Oh? Do you think so?" Gabrielle's cool manner faltered a little as she plucked the picture from Remy's hand. He was right. The likeness of Miri was very true to life. Gabrielle remembered the long-ago spring day in the garden when she had painted it, the sweet smell of Ariane's herbs filling the air, the drone of the bees amongst the flowers, a day when Gabrielle's magic had been at its strongest.

Bending over that small oval of ivory, working with her finest brush and softest colors, she had succeeded in capturing her little sister perfectly, no easy task with Miri, fairy child that she was. There was an ethereal quality about the girl in that portrait, as elusive as a beam of moonlight. Miri leaned forward, her long white-blond hair spilling over one shoulder, her quicksilver eyes dancing with impatience as though she might vanish at any moment to go romping with elves in the woods or hunting for unicorns.

There was no telling how much Miri resembled that portrait anymore. It had been over two years since Gabrielle had seen Miri and heaven only knew when she would do so again, if ever. That thought filled Gabrielle with a rush of sadness for the little sister who was as lost to her as her long-ago magic.

Gabrielle became aware of Remy watching her far too intently for comfort.

"Is that one of your paintings, Gabrielle?" he asked.

"Yes, I painted it back when I had time for such nonsense." She handed the miniature back to him with a show of indifference. "Of course Miri has grown up a great deal since then. I doubt you'd even recognize her anymore."

"I daresay I would not," Remy agreed with a sad smile.

Neither would I, Gabrielle thought, suppressing a pang.

"And what about Ariane? How fares the Lady of Faire Isle?" Remy asked as he replaced the miniature where he had found it. He scanned the mantel as though he expected to spy a portrait of Ariane as well and was puzzled when he didn't find one.

Because Gabrielle could no longer bear to look upon the image of the sister who now despised her. Because the portrait was too painful a reminder of the bitter way she and Ariane had parted.

Gabrielle managed to reply airily, "Oh, Ariane married Renard and she is now living happily ever after with her great ogre at his château."

Although Remy smiled, he chided her gently, "Why must you always speak so disparagingly of Renard? He is a good man and he saved all of our lives the night the witch-hunters came."

"I know that and I am fond enough of my great hulk of a brother-in-law. But the comte and I have always taken a peculiar delight in vexing one another. We used to drive poor Ariane to distraction. Once she even threatened to lock us both in our rooms until we behaved better." Gabrielle smiled ruefully at the memory. "Our quarrels were never serious until—"

"Until?" Remy prompted when she fell silent.

Gabrielle fretted her lower lip, vexed with herself for even broaching the matter. She continued reluctantly, "Until Renard got this damn fool notion in his head that he should find me a husband. That I could never be happy or content until I was wed."

"Is that such a foolish notion, Gabrielle?" Remy asked quietly.

For her, it was. Renard playing matchmaker for her might have been laughable if it also hadn't been unbearable, the idea that some nobleman, greedy for the dowry Renard offered, might be willing to overlook the fact he was getting damaged goods. Or worse still be enchanted with her beauty and fancy himself in love with her, a love she'd never be able to return. And when this prospective bridegroom had discovered the truth about her? What then?

Gabrielle knew there were ways a clever woman could deceive her husband into thinking he had acquired a virgin bride. But the thought of such deception sickened her. No, better at once to let a man know exactly what she was and be warned.

Then why was she still avoiding revealing the truth to Remy? Feeling the weight of his grave dark eyes upon her, Gabrielle finally answered him. "It was foolish for Renard to seek a husband for me for many reasons, but chiefly because I had no interest in being wed to some provincial oaf, being buried in the country all my life."

Seeking to change the subject, Gabrielle rustled over to the bedside stand, where a flagon of wine and a crystal glass were kept to slake her thirst should she awaken in the middle of the night.

"Can I offer you some Rhenish wine, Captain Remy?" she called over her shoulder. "I could also roust out my cook to serve you a late supper down in the hall."

"You mean on that great table that I glimpsed below stairs, the one that's the length of a battlefield?" Remy grimaced. "No, I am afraid I hardly appear grand enough for such a setting."

"Because you clearly have not been taking proper care of yourself. Just like most men when they are left to their own devices." Gabrielle poured out the wine and marched over to him. "You look as pale as the ghost I mistook you to be. Perhaps some wine will at least put a little color back in your face."

She forced the glass into his hand, saying sternly, "Here. Drink this."

"Yes, milady," Remy replied, his meekness belied by the glimmer of a smile in his eyes. When he took his first sip, he winced, and for the first time Gabrielle noticed the split in his lip where she had struck him.

She forgot her cool demeanor in the wake of her remorse. "Oh, lord, Remy. Did I do that to you?" She feathered her fingertips across his lower lip, dismayed to detect a slight swelling as well. "Oh, I—I am so sorry."

Although he winced again at her touch and caught her hand, he said, "It is no great matter, my dear. I've been dealt far worse blows, but probably none I ever deserved as much. After all you and your sisters did for me, I *should* have found a way to let you know I was alive."

He pressed a light kiss to her fingers. "It was natural that you should be angry with me."

Gabrielle's skin tingled from even so soft a pressure of his lips. She made haste to pull away from him.

"Natural, perhaps," she conceded, "but hardly civil, Captain."

"Is that what we are doing now, Gabrielle? Being civil to each other?" Remy asked quizzically.

She thrust up her chin with a determined smile. "Of course. Why should we not be cordial to each other? It has been a long time but we are still friends, are we not?"

"Yes, *friends*," Remy agreed, but the intense look in his eyes belied the word.

He reached up to tuck a stray wisp of hair back inside her net, his fingers lingering against her cheek. Gabrielle always had marveled how Remy's hands, so hard and callused, could still be so gentle. His touch was almost a seduction in itself.

She felt a quiver of warmth rush through her. It was all the fault of that heated embrace they had shared earlier. She had always known it would be a mistake to kiss Nicolas Remy. That one moment of folly had cracked a wall of reserve she had built around her heart for years.

Gabrielle shied back from his touch, saying nervously, "Unfortunately I—I no longer have the time to spare for old acquaintances that I might wish. My life in Paris is very different from what it was on Faire Isle."

"So I have heard," Remy said. The tender light vanished from his eyes. He took a long swallow of his wine, his brows drawing together in a heavy frown. "What are you doing here in Paris, Gabrielle? So far from your family and your home?"

It was the question she had been dreading. Her heart missed a beat as she wondered exactly what Remy *had* heard about her.

She had been told that they were taking bets in some of the taverns regarding who her next lover would be.

But whatever gossip he had gleaned, Gabrielle could tell that Remy didn't want to believe it. His gaze sought hers as though trying to reassure himself that despite all evidence to the contrary, she was still the innocent girl he always imagined her to be.

So why not make the truth plain to him and be done with it? Gabrielle's lips parted but no sound came. She just couldn't bring herself to do it, speak the words that would disillusion Remy, end any feelings he had for her forever. Damning herself for a coward, Gabrielle evaded his probing gaze. She rustled toward an ornate rectangular table positioned along the wall opposite her bed. The glossy surface was laden with an array of bottles of lotion, jars of cream, and those seductive vials of perfume Cass had brewed for her. She removed the gilded lid from one of the jars and scooped out a dab of cream for keeping her hands as smooth and white as possible.

"You always knew I longed to get away from Faire Isle, Captain Remy," she replied at last, working the cream into her skin. "To travel, to experience all the excitement and diversion of some great city."

Leaning his broad shoulders up against the wall, Remy positioned himself alongside the table where she could not avoid his eyes. "Yes, but how did you acquire this vast house? Forgive me, but I thought your family's fortunes were lost when your father did not return from his voyage of exploration."

"So they were." Gabrielle smoothed cream over her fingertips, hoping their slight tremor did not betray her tension. "This house belongs to or . . . I should say belonged to a woman named Marguerite de Maitland.

"My father's mistress," she added in a flat emotionless tone.

"His *mistress*?"

"Many men have them, Captain Remy," Gabrielle said tersely.

"I am aware of that. But I had heard . . . I had always thought—" Remy hesitated, taking another sip of wine.

"You heard all the stories about the great romance between the gallant Chevalier Louis Cheney and Evangeline, the beautiful lady of Faire Isle." Gabrielle believed herself long over the hurt of discovering her father's betrayal. But the old bitterness crept back into her voice. "Unfortunately, that is all they were—just pretty stories. Even while professing devotion to my Maman, my father was keeping this other woman here in Paris, lavishing Madame de Maitland with gowns, jewels, and this house."

Remy digested her revelation in thoughtful silence, frowning into his glass. "I still don't understand what *you* are doing here, living in the home of such a—a—"

Remy didn't finish, but he didn't have to. From his censorious tone, Gabrielle could easily guess what he meant. Such a *whore, a trollop, a slut.* Although she kept her expression neutral, some part of her flinched, wondering what Remy would call her when he realized she was little different from Marguerite.

Gabrielle picked up a small stiff brush and doggedly buffed her nails. "After my father was declared dead, Mademoiselle de Maitland experienced some fit of repentance. She determined to retire to a convent. Before she did so, she offered this house and her jewels to my sisters and me."

"And you accepted, Gabrielle?" Remy asked gravely. "But did that not seem to you like a betrayal of your mother's memory?"

Gabrielle flushed. "You sound just like Ariane, sentimental and impractical. It was my father's coin that paid for all of this. Why shouldn't I accept the offer?"

"I can see the justice of that," Remy conceded. "But—" Gabrielle could tell there was more he wanted to ask her, but he hesitated, probably because he feared the answers.

Gabrielle tossed the brush back on the table and flounced

away, saying, "Enough about me. I would far rather hear about what *you* have been doing these past three years."

Swirling the wine in his glass, he said, "You would not find it a very interesting tale, Gabrielle."

"Nonetheless, I insist upon hearing it." Sweeping over to the window seat, Gabrielle sank down upon the embroidered cushion. In the old days, she would have patted the cushion beside her, inviting him to join her in friendly fashion. Now she indicated a high-backed chair a safe distance away.

"Do sit down, Captain, and tell me everything."

Remy's gaze flicked toward the chair, but he made no move to sit. He positioned himself by the fireplace, cupping his glass in his hand. Something had closed off in his eyes with her inquiry into his past.

"Tell you everything? I'd hardly know where to begin."

"Why don't you start with what happened to you on St. Bartholomew's Eve?"

"That would make an even less entertaining bedtime story." Remy's fingers tightened around the stem of the glass so hard, Gabrielle was astonished it did not snap. No doubt Remy found it hard to remember or speak of that terrible night and she was loath to inflict any more pain upon him.

But Gabrielle had found it painful too, imagining the horrors of the way she'd thought that Remy had been brutally slaughtered. She desperately needed to know what had really happened.

"Please, Remy," she said in a gentler tone. "At least tell me how you survived that night. Renard said you had been cut down, mortally wounded. He thought you were finished or he would never have left you behind."

"I know that. The comte is an honorable and courageous man. I am glad he was able to escape with his life."

"Yes, but how did you?"

Remy took a long swallow of his wine, nearly draining his glass in one gulp. "I was saved by a wolf."

"What!" Gabrielle cried. If Remy had not looked so grim, if

it had been anyone else but him, she would have imagined she was being teased.

"A wolf? Here in Paris?" she asked incredulously.

Some of the tension melted from Remy's shoulders. His lips twitched as though at some memory that amused him in spite of himself. "Martin Le Loup, a young pickpocket and thief. He spied my body sprawled in the street and took a fancy to my boots. The lad sought to—er, relieve me of them."

Gabrielle was horrified, picturing too clearly the scene, Remy, wounded, helpless, while some street rat attempted to rob him before he even went cold. She didn't know how Remy could smile at such a callous action. She clenched her fists in her lap. "Why—why that scurrilous little bastard. He should have been hung, drawn, and quartered."

Remy shrugged. "If I had been dead, the boots would have been no use to me. But I let out such a groan when Martin touched me, I nearly gave the lad an apoplexy. He could have finished pulling off my boots and fled. I could never have stopped him.

"Instead he managed to drag me to a place of safety, kept me hidden from the rampaging mobs while he found someone to tend my wounds. An elderly priest highly skilled in the arts of healing."

Remy gave a bemused frown. "I never even knew his name or why he chose to help me. It was a dangerous thing to do. St. Bartholomew's Eve was not the best time for any Catholic to be caught trying to save a Protestant soldier.

"As for Martin, I've never understood him either. He is generally a very practical lad, good at looking out for his own hide. To this day, I don't know why he risked his life to help me."

Remy might not know, but Gabrielle did. There was something about a selfless man like Nicolas Remy, honest, valiant, honorable to his very core, that brought out the best in other people, made them eager to serve him even against their own interest and better judgment.

When Remy fell silent again, she prompted, "So you were saved by this Wolf person and an old priest. What happened then?"

"Martin is a lad of great resource. When I was well enough, he smuggled me out of Paris. Then we went abroad."

"Where?"

"To Ireland first, then England."

"And did what?"

"Worked. Traveled. Existed."

Gabrielle's gaze traveled up Remy's tall frame to shoot him a look of pure frustration. Remy had never been a great talker, but she was beginning to feel like it would be easier to extract the man's teeth than any information.

"So you just spent three years wandering the English countryside and then what? One morning you woke up and decided it was time to come back?" she demanded.

"Something like that." Remy fidgeted with the finely cut stem of the wineglass. He was not merely being his usual quiet self. The man was being deliberately evasive.

"Why?" Gabrielle persisted. "Why have you returned?"

"I am beginning to feel that I should not have."

"What? Not have come back to Paris?"

"No, I should never have come back to you."

Remy's words cut Gabrielle deep and she could not conceal it. When she flinched, Remy went on hastily, "I didn't mean that I did not want to see you again. I did. Far too much. I only meant that my life has taken a rather desperate turn and I have had second thoughts about involving you."

"I was involved in your life once before," Gabrielle reminded him.

"Not by my choice. I was a bloody fool that summer I descended upon Faire Isle, so obsessed with my quest for justice, I didn't stop to think what danger I brought in my wake." Remy finished his wine and set the empty glass down on top of the mantel. "You never fully understood the nature of the evil that I had uncovered, the reason why I became a fugitive."

"Oh, for the love of heaven!" Gabrielle rolled her eyes. It still annoyed her the way Remy had confided all his more dangerous secrets to Ariane, but had persisted in treating Gabrielle as though she were some innocent child no older than Miri.

She took great satisfaction in informing him, "I knew all about how Catherine de Medici assassinated your queen, Jeanne of Navarre."

"You . . . you did?"

"Of course I did! You suspected your queen had been poisoned, and you stumbled upon the only evidence, a pair of beautiful white gloves. When you fled Paris, you stole the gloves and brought them to Ariane, hoping that she could help you to prove the gloves had been tampered with. Have I got that all right so far?"

"Yes," Remy agreed, still frowning in surprise. "So Ariane finally chose to tell you everything?"

"No, I figured most of it out for myself. When I found the gloves she'd hidden down in our workshop, I tried them on."

"*You what?*" Remy looked appalled, then confused. "Then I was wrong? The gloves had not been poisoned after all."

"Oh, they were poisoned all right," Gabrielle said wryly. "I damn near died."

"Gabrielle!" Remy blanched with such horror Gabrielle regretted telling him. He strode toward her and sank down beside her, gathering her hands in his strong grip.

The concern that suffused his face was tender enough to thaw any woman's heart and Gabrielle had difficulty resisting it. Her fingers involuntarily interlaced with his, returning their pressure.

"My God! I am so sorry," he said hoarsely. "I should have told you the truth about Catherine and the gloves. If anything had happened to you, I would never have—have been able to—"

He broke off, so stricken with guilt it was all she could do not to wrap her arms about him. The only way she could resist the impulse was to pull free of his grasp and retreat from the window seat.

"Oh, don't make such a fuss." Her voice was not as steady as she would have liked it to be. "Obviously I am not dead. Renard came to the rescue. He was able to brew up an antidote. As it happens, the comte knows a bit more about the practice of dark magic than any man should. If we had realized that sooner, you could have taken the gloves straight to him. Unfortunately we don't even have them anymore. After we all thought you were dead, we were obliged to make peace with the Dark Queen as best we could."

Gabrielle's lips thinned, remembering how much it had galled her, had eaten away at her very soul to declare a truce with the woman who had threatened her family, the vile witch she had blamed so bitterly for Remy's death. One day she would make Catherine pay dearly, Gabrielle had vowed.

But it was a vow she had been unable to keep and gazing at Remy, Gabrielle was beset by the feeling that she had failed him.

"I—I am so sorry, Remy," she said. "We didn't feel we had any other choice. The Dark Queen had captured Renard. We had to trade the gloves back to Catherine in order to save his life."

"Oh, damn those gloves. As if I ever had any hope of bringing that evil woman to justice. It was a fool's quest. All I accomplished was nearly getting you killed." Remy slumped forward, his hands dangling between his knees, his attitude one of bitter defeat.

Gabrielle's fingers twitched with the urge to smooth away those lines of worry, to rid him of those shadows that haunted him. She had to bury her hands in the folds of her gown to still the impulse.

"Don't be so foolish. If I had been killed, it would have owed more to my own curiosity and impulsiveness than any fault of yours. You may have noticed," she added with an impish smile. "I can be a trifle reckless at times."

Her words did not provoke the answering smile from Remy that she had hoped for. His mouth remained set in a taut line of self-reproach.

"You would never have been in any danger if I hadn't brought it to your door. And here I am back again to—" Remy expelled a harsh breath, rife with self-disgust. "I should never have come. Forgive me."

He shoved to his feet. As though he did not trust himself to look at her again, Remy marched toward the bedchamber door. For a moment, Gabrielle was too stunned to react. But when she realized what he was about to do, she tore after him. Remy already had the door ajar, but Gabrielle shoved past him. She gripped the jamb to prevent him opening the door any farther.

"What do you think you are doing?"

"Leaving."

"Just like that? Without another word?"

Remy made no reply, but the answer was writ clear in his eyes. He was going to steal back into the night, vanish from her life as though he'd never returned. And this time she truly never would see him again.

She should wish for just that. Remy's return into her life had only served to confuse her, to stir up vulnerabilities and tender emotions she could not afford to feel. But the thought of losing him all over again filled her with something akin to panic.

"How dare you!" Gabrielle cried. "You let me think you are dead for three years and then you saunter back into my life one night. You scare the wits out of me, nearly shock me to death. You hint at some mysterious reason for your return, some favor you require of me. And now you've changed your mind and just plan to disappear again?"

"It will be far better for you if I do."

"Damn you, Nicolas Remy." Gabrielle tried to shove him away from the door. But it was like trying to budge a stone wall.

She glared up at him. "Stop treating me like I am some innocent damsel that needs protecting. I am more than capable of looking out for my own interests. Just tell me what you want and I will decide if the price is too high."

Remy shook his head, his jaw set in an inflexible line. In another heartbeat, he would shift her to one side and walk out that door. Fighting to conceal her mounting desperation, she prodded, "Tell me what you need. A place to hide? Money?"

A dark flush stained his cheekbones. "By thunder, Gabrielle! Do you truly think me the sort of man who would come to beg coin from you?"

He drew himself up to his full height, a rare spark of anger flashing in his eyes. His umbrage caused him to step away from the door. Gabrielle made haste to close it.

She caught hold of Remy's hand and tugged him farther into the room. "Oh, stop being such a stubborn ass and tell me why you came back to Paris. You know me well enough to realize I won't give you any peace until you do."

"Aye, how well do I know that." He resisted a moment longer, then relented with a wearied sigh. "Very well. I came back because of my king. The Dark Queen has been holding him prisoner since St. Bartholomew's Eve and it is my duty to rescue him."

"Oh." Gabrielle dropped Remy's hand as though she had been scorched. She managed to school her features to hide the fact that her mouth had gone dry with dismay. She stalked back over to the bedside table to fortify herself with a glass of wine.

So Remy had returned to Paris to mount a desperate bid to free his king. The same cause he had risked his neck for three years ago. Gabrielle reflected bitterly that she might have guessed as much. The fool. The insufferably noble, reckless fool.

"My information is correct, is it not?" Remy called uncertainly after her. "The Dark Queen does still hold him captive?"

"Navarre is not languishing in the Bastille, if that is what you mean. He is Catherine's son-in-law, after all. He has his own apartments at the Louvre, although he is kept under close guard. *Very* close guard."

"Nonetheless, it is my duty to get him out of there."

Gabrielle swore softly under her breath. Damn Nicolas Remy and his infernal sense of duty. She raised the wine to her lips only to set it back down untasted. Whipping about, she glared at him. "I see. You didn't manage to get yourself slaughtered on St. Bartholomew's Eve, so now you are determined to have another go at it."

"I trust it won't come to that . . . with your help."

"What do you think I can do?"

"I have heard that you are received at court and I wondered if you might contrive to get a message to the king, let him know I am still alive, that I have returned to free him. But I need information regarding the location of his rooms, the number of his guards . . ." Remy trailed off, raking his hand back through the uneven lengths of his hair. It was clear that he had not wanted to ask her. But it was equally clear that he was desperate for her help and that part of him hoped she would agree.

"So you want me to act as the go-between in this escape plot?" Gabrielle asked bluntly.

"Yes," Remy said, his eyes intent upon her face. Gabrielle was obliged to turn away so he could not see the full depth of her consternation.

She retreated to one of the tall windows near the bed. Oh, why couldn't the blasted man have wanted something as simple as money or a place to stay? Outside of her sisters, Nicolas Remy was one of the few people in the world she would have been willing to do anything for. Well, almost anything, Gabrielle corrected herself.

Others had tried before to spirit the captive Navarre out of Paris. The conspirators had been caught and condemned to death. Not only was Gabrielle unwilling to help Remy to hazard his life in such a dangerous enterprise, there was another problem with what Remy wanted her to do.

Navarre might be Remy's king, but he was also the man that Gabrielle was fated to ensnare as her lover, the man who was destined to make her the most powerful woman in all of France. Gabrielle didn't see how that could happen if Remy succeeded in turning Navarre into a fugitive, fleeing back to his inconsequential kingdom on the border of Spain.

Remy hovered behind her. She could see his reflection in the night-darkened windowpanes, like some ghost from her past. The specter of a brave soldier who had once pretended to be her knight and she, his lady fair. Unfortunately, that was all it had ever been, a pretense, and she was far too worldly-wise to be beguiled by make-believe.

Her heart felt leaden as she came about to face Remy. "I am sorry, Captain Remy. But I cannot do what you ask."

His eyes darkened with disappointment, but there was a certain amount of relief there as well. "No, Gabrielle. I am the one who should be sorry. I never should have asked you. The risk is far too great. You have reason to be afraid. If you were caught smuggling messages—"

"I am not afraid of that. I am very good at intrigue."

A deep furrow appeared between Remy's brows. "Then I don't understand. If you don't think there would be any risk, why won't you do it?"

Gabrielle compressed her lips together, wishing that she had let Remy leave when he had wanted to. Then she wouldn't have to face this moment, wouldn't have to tell him the truth. But she feared that even without her help, Remy would proceed with his dangerous plan. There was only one thing that might discourage him. If she told him about the prophecy, about Navarre's destiny . . . and hers.

She had to swallow hard before she could find the courage to speak. She began haltingly, "I—I won't help you because Navarre needs to remain with the French court. This is no time for him to disappear back into the wilds of Navarre, so far away from me. Because . . . because I desire him for myself."

Remy stared at her for a long moment, then his jaw hardened. "What the devil do you mean, Gabrielle? Are you trying to tell me that you have fallen in love with—with a king?"

"Kings are much the same as any other man, but in this case love has nothing to do with it. I admire and respect Henry." Gabrielle hesitated, then added, "He is my destiny."

"What sort of destiny do you imagine you could have with Navarre?" Remy asked impatiently. "He is already married."

"Perhaps you should ask the witch I consulted tonight. Among other things she conjured up the future for me. Navarre is going to be the king of France one day and I—" Gabrielle found it hard to meet Remy's eyes, but she forced herself to do so as she continued. "I am going to be his mistress."

Remy looked stunned for a moment, then he paced off several agitated steps, swearing. "Damnation, Gabrielle, you shouldn't be fooling about with that dark magic. You know better than that. It's all bloody nonsense anyway. You could never be anyone's mistress. You are a noble lady. Gently and properly reared—"

"Perhaps I was at one time—"

"No, you still are!" Remy paused in his pacing to glower at her. Beneath his rising anger, he had the look of a cornered man, fighting hard to hold on to his illusions of her, no doubt as hard as he had ever fought against impossible odds on any battlefield. Remy was not a stupid man by any means. But he was proving more willfully blind than Gabrielle would ever have believed possible. He stalked toward her and crushed her hands between his. When he spoke it was clear that it was costing him great effort to keep his voice level.

"Gabrielle, you have obviously been confused and hurt by your father's behavior. But you must not let it make you cynical or bitter. You have no idea what it would be like to sell your virtue." Remy added fiercely, "You couldn't."

"I think you already know the answer to that," Gabrielle said.

"No! I won't accept it. Not until I hear the truth from you. You tell me."

Gabrielle had to close her eyes briefly to shut out the tormented face of this man who wanted so badly to believe in her in a way no one else had ever done. No, not her, Gabrielle was forced to remind herself. Just some dream of her, a Gabrielle who had never existed.

Remy gripped her hands hard, offering her no quarter. So he insisted upon hearing all the painful details? Very well, then. She would give them to him. Gabrielle wrenched free of Remy's grip and stalked away, fortifying herself with a deep breath. She positioned herself behind the chair and faced him, assuming her iciest façade, the one that had stood her in good stead during all the most painful moments of her life.

"Of course I know how to barter with a man." She curled her fingers around the back of the chair for support. "How do you think I ever managed to get here to Paris to claim this house? With Ariane opposed to me, Renard was practically holding me prisoner. I had no choice but to run away. I finally managed to escape with the help of a wine merchant who was visiting the château."

Gabrielle dropped her gaze, staring rigidly at the gilt trim that adorned the chair. "Monsieur Duclous was a very kind, good-humored sort of man. He was more than willing to take me to Paris in exchange for—for my favors."

Gabrielle heard the sharp intake of Remy's breath, but she did not risk looking at him. "Once I arrived in Paris, Monsieur Duclous could not be of help to me in gaining what I really wanted. Access at court and the higher circles of society. I needed the duc de Penthieve for that."

"I don't want to hear any more of this," Remy growled. He stalked over to the windows and turned his back as though he could shut out the sound of her voice.

"No, damn you. You asked for this and you are going to hear it all," Gabrielle cried. She bit down hard upon her lip to still its trembling and then went on ruthlessly, "Monsieur le Duc was very urbane, witty and charming. I learned a great deal from him. Regrettably the duc suffered financial losses and felt obliged to retire to his country estate. I had no wish to leave Paris, so then I—"

"Stop it, Gabrielle," Remy grated. He braced one arm against the window frame, the line of his back looking rigid enough to snap.

"Then I found the Marquis de Lanfort. A nice boy, but with a tendency to write dreadful poetry. I probably still have one of his—"

"I said, *stop.*" Remy roared so loud that Gabrielle flinched and faltered to silence. Remy clenched the wooden frame so hard, his entire arm shook with the force of it.

As he whipped around, Gabrielle's breath hitched in her throat, fearing that she had gone too far. She had never seen such a look on Remy's face before, his mouth pinched white, his nostrils flared, his breath coming quick and hard as he advanced toward her. Gabrielle stumbled back, retreating to the other side of her dressing table, her heart thudding.

Remy dashed his hand across the table with a violent oath. Bottles and jars hurtled to the floor, shattering. Gabrielle shrank back, flinging up her hands to avoid the shards of flying glass. She emitted a cry that was part protest, part alarm.

Before she could even draw another breath, Remy was upon her. He grabbed her roughly by the shoulders and hauled her toward him. Remy's breath was hot on her face, his lips pulled back in a taut furious line. She was reminded suddenly of what Cass had said when she had touched Remy's sword.

"This weapon speaks to me of a darker side to your gallant knight. They called him the Scourge, Gabrielle. I doubt that a man acquires such a title because of his kind and gentle nature."

"What happened to you, Gabrielle?" Remy rasped, his eyes dark with anguish and rage. "How could you have changed so much?"

Though her pulse raced, Gabrielle lifted her chin, meeting his black anger with defiance. "I haven't changed. I have always been a very ambitious woman."

"No, you weren't!" Remy snarled. "You were never this cold and calculating, willing to do anything for money and power. You were restless and passionate, yes, but always honorable and innocent—"

"No, I wasn't. I had already had my first lover before I ever met you." Gabrielle flung the bitter words in Remy's face. It nigh sickened her to describe Danton in such a way, but she would have died rather than admit the shame of what had happened that hot summer afternoon.

Remy uttered a savage oath. His grip tightened so painfully, she gasped, certain he meant to shake her until she dropped in a heap. But he released her abruptly, all but flinging her away from him. As Gabrielle staggered to regain her balance, Remy retreated to the far end of the room.

A terrible silence ensued, broken only by Gabrielle's tremulous breaths as she struggled to compose herself. She trembled, rubbing her bruised shoulders, and stared at the shattered remains of all those lotions and perfumes Cass had so carefully brewed.

"So—so you see," Gabrielle concluded in a low voice. "You never really knew me at all."

"Evidently not."

Her confession about Danton seemed to have dealt Remy the final blow. His rage faded as swiftly as it had come. He dragged his hand wearily across his face and Gabrielle thought she could see every dream he had ever had of her dying in his eyes.

Remy placed his hands on his hips and stared up at the ceiling with a bitter laugh. "Lord! I have to be about the biggest fool of all time," he muttered.

No, Gabrielle thought sadly. Only an honorable man who expected the rest of the world to be the same.

She picked her way past the debris of broken glass and lotion that smeared the carpet and approached Remy tentatively. "I am sorry if I have hurt you," she said. "Truly that was the last thing I ever wanted to do."

Gabrielle reached out to touch his sleeve, but he shook her off with such a look of contempt that she recoiled. His rejection hurt so much, she wanted to wrap her arms around herself as though fending off a blow. But if there was one thing she had always been good at, it was taking her wounds and burying them deep where no one could see.

She kept her arms pinned to her sides and faced him regally instead. "At least now you understand why I will not help you with any of your schemes. You would do better to forget about Navarre. Escapes for the king have been tried before and failed. You will only end up getting yourself killed."

"Your concern for my welfare is touching, madame," Remy sneered.

His words stung. She *was* concerned for him, if only she could make the stiff-necked fool see that. Gabrielle made one last desperate attempt to reason with him. "I fully intend to make sure Navarre gains his rightful place of power in France. You will do far better by your king to just leave him to me."

"I would as soon leave him in hell."

Gabrielle tensed when Remy stepped closer and took hold of her chin. His grip was not rough this time, but inexorable all the same, forcing her head up so she had to look directly into his eyes. They were like points of steel, cold and hard, and that was somehow worse than his anger had been.

"I mean to have my king far away from the Dark Queen's clutches and yours as well. So be warned, Gabrielle, and stay out of my way. You never really knew me either. I can be damned ruthless to my enemies."

She had already seen proof of that, Gabrielle thought. A shiver of fear worked through her, but she refused to be intimidated by Nicolas Remy or any other man. She thrust his hand away, saying just as coldly, "It is you who should take care. You seem to have forgotten that after all, I am a witch."

"How could I have possibly overlooked that fact?" Remy strode to her bedchamber door, wrenching it open. He did not even glance back as he left, slamming the door behind him.

Gabrielle remained just as she was for a long time. As the events of this tumultuous evening overwhelmed her, she began to shake uncontrollably and was obliged to sink down onto the chair. She hugged herself tightly in an effort to still her trembling. Remy clearly despised her now.

What did you expect, you little fool, she chided herself. That Remy was somehow going to be able to understand, to forgive her for being who she was? Not even Remy could be that noble. Like most men, his views on women were appallingly simplistic. The fair sex only came in two forms, madonnas or whores. And there was little doubt how Remy now regarded her.

Well, what did it matter, Gabrielle asked herself, fiercely refusing to cry. It was not as though she and Remy had ever had any kind of future together. She should be feeling relieved. After all of this time, she had laid his ghost to rest. She was finally free to carry on with the rest of her life. Gabrielle closed her eyes against the sting of tears, denying their release.

Nicolas Remy would haunt her no more.

Chapter Six

A SINGLE CANDLE RESTED ON THE ROUGH-HEWN TABLE, CASTING its light over the only other furnishings in the small room, a narrow wooden bedstead and a washstand with a cracked pitcher. The lodging that Nicolas Remy shared with his young companion was cheap, affording few comforts. But the bleakness of the chamber appeared to suit the captain's mood tonight. Grim and silent, he readied for bed, removing his cloak and divesting himself of the dagger he kept tucked in his belt.

As Martin Le Loup unrolled his pallet on the floor nearby, his usual swagger was absent. He stole worried glances at the captain and felt more ashamed of himself than he had ever been in his life. He had failed his captain this evening. Wolf fetched a deep sigh. He might as well fling himself into the murky waters of the Seine. That would be the only fitting punishment for a miscreant such as himself.

Martin had ever prided himself on being as bold and fierce as the creature whose title he had adopted to give himself a surname. But tonight he had proved to be more like a jackal than a wolf. When the captain had ordered him to leave at the gates of the Maison d'Esprit, Wolf should have refused. He should have followed Remy straight into that devil's den. Instead he had allowed his great fear of witches and curses to get the better of him. Wolf had slunk away with his tail between his legs like a whipped cur, abandoning the man who had become all things to him.

Despite all of his hardship these past years, Remy had found the time to instruct Wolf in the arts of fighting. Not with clubs and knives like some mangy street thief, but with rapier and dagger like a true gentleman. But Remy had given Wolf a far greater gift than that. The captain had taught him how to read and to write his name.

And how had Wolf chosen to repay the magnificence of such a man? He had forsaken his captain when he had needed his Wolf the most and now something terrible had happened to Remy. The captain who had set out after his beautiful lady was not the same man who had returned to their lodgings. Remy always carried himself with an upright, military bearing. But there was an aura of defeat about him as he unbuckled his sword and dropped it carelessly to the floor in a way that was most unlike him. A good soldier always took painstaking care of his weapon and the captain was a *great* soldier.

At least he had been until he had followed the lovely Gabrielle to that devil's manor, the Maison d'Esprit. Wolf shuddered with the fear that the Captain had fallen prey to the witch's curse, no matter what Remy had told him to the contrary.

As Remy stripped off his shirt, Wolf stared at Remy's broad back, anxiously looking for witch's marks. He craned his neck, trying to see around to the other side of Remy. Straining forward, he lost his balance and tumbled into the little table. The candle nearly went flying and he grabbed for it, hot wax splashing on his hands.

"*Merde,*" Wolf muttered, wincing at the pain.

The commotion roused the captain from the black haze that enveloped him. "What the devil do you think you are doing?" he growled, stealing an irritated look over his shoulder.

"Nothing, m'sieur." Wolf hastily righted the candle. He rubbed the wax from his hand and then licked the spot where he had been burned. Remy was generally the most patient of men, but his temper seemed on a short fuse ever since his return.

Another bad sign that the captain was no longer himself. Wolf knew that Remy had already had a belly full of what the captain termed Wolf's "superstitious nonsense." But Wolf was far too worried to keep his fears to himself.

"Er-ah—Captain. I—I don't like to keep harping on this," Wolf ventured. "But old Tante Pauline, the closest thing I ever had to a mother, always told me that when a man is attacked by a succubus or cursed by a witch, he often acquires an extra teat. And I was just afraid that—"

"Oh, for the love of—" Remy muttered a fierce oath and spun around. The smooth, hard-muscled surface of the captain's chest was streaked with scars from more wounds than any mortal should ever have endured and survived. But the captain still only had two nipples like any normal man. Wolf heaved a sigh of deep relief.

"There, are you satisfied?" Remy demanded, flinging his arms wide. "No extra teat. I haven't been suckled by the devil or cursed by a witch. I never even went into the Maison d'Esprit. I merely waited in the courtyard until Mistress Cheney emerged. Now stop being such a bloody fool and go to bed."

Wolf drew himself up with wounded dignity. "Is it being a fool to fear for one's friend? Then plague take me for the dolt that I am, but I would rather perish a hundred times, have a thousand hot spikes rammed up my arse than—"

"Ah, Martin, please," Remy said tersely. "None of your theatrics tonight. I am too damned weary for them. I have told you I am well. Be content with that."

"Yes, m'sieur," Wolf grumbled. But as he stripped off his

own jerkin, his lips thinned into a stubborn line. He was far from content. A witch may not have suckled the captain, but there was something very wrong with him.

As Remy sank down on the edge of the bed to tug off his boots, his eyes looked as black as they did on those nights when he sprang awake from one of his nightmares. Wolf spread out his wool blanket on top of the pallet, struggling to make sense of his captain's condition. He inhaled his breath sharply as the realization struck him.

He truly was a numbskulled, ox-pated fool. The captain had never entered the accursed Maison d'Esprit, but *his lady had.* Wolf shot Remy a glance of mingled compassion and reproach.

"Ah, m'sieur. You should have told me."

"Told you what?" Remy grunted, working off his first boot.

"About your lady. The beautiful and reckless Gabrielle. She went into that cursed house and now something dreadful has befallen her, has it not?"

The captain confirmed Wolf's suspicions by freezing at the mention of Mistress Cheney. Then he gave his boot a hard yank and flung it into the corner.

"She is not my lady and you needn't worry about *her.* She is just fine. If there is one thing the *beautiful and reckless* Gabrielle is good at, it is looking out for herself." There was an acid note to Remy's voice when referring to the lady that Martin had never heard before.

"Begging your pardon, Captain. I don't understand."

Remy lifted his foot, reaching for the heel of his second boot. "It is I who should be begging your pardon. When I sent you off to find the woman for me, I should have warned you. Mistress Cheney is a witch herself."

Mistress Cheney, that loveliest of ladies? A witch. Wolf gaped at the Captain.

"Mother of God!" he exclaimed. "But m'sieur, how do you know this?"

"Because she had me bewitched for years," Remy said, his

mouth twisting bitterly. "But tonight the spell was broken. I am free of her at last."

"Thank the lord," Wolf cried. The room was small and cramped, even more so with the pallet stretched out on the floor. But Wolf managed to pace a few steps, seeking to work off his wonder and agitation at the news.

To think how blithely Wolf had trailed after that deceitful woman, admiring her from a distance, not knowing what an evil creature she was. And him, without a single amulet or charm for protection!

"Oh, Captain," Wolf said, nearly stumbling over the pallet as he prowled the room. "God should make all sorceresses old and ugly hags so that a man might be warned to steer clear of them. It is not right that Mistress Cheney should appear so fair."

"No, it isn't," the captain muttered.

"So tell me what happened. Did her magic finally weaken and you finally perceived her true wicked face beneath that beautiful mask?"

"Something like that."

"All I can say again is, thank God." Wolf flung up his hands dramatically to the heavens. "You have had a narrow escape, m'sieur. We should have a cup of wine to celebrate."

"I suppose we should."

But the captain did not look much in the mood for celebrating. He appeared drained. He removed his second boot and let it fall to the floor. Wolf studied him anxiously. It was not a good thing when the captain became too exhausted. When Remy was particularly worn down, that was when the captain's nightmares came.

Remy seldom spoke of his past glories, but Wolf had heard enough stories of the deeds of the great Scourge. It thrilled him to imagine Remy brandishing his sword, striking terror into the hearts of his foes as he boldly led the charge in countless battles.

But Wolf knew from the things that Remy muttered in his

sleep that it was those selfsame battles that tormented the captain's dreams. That and what had happened on St. Bartholomew's Eve. Wolf had seen many dreadful things himself the night of the massacre, but he possessed the ability to banish anything too grim from his mind. Not so the captain. He felt things too deeply. That was often the way with such quiet men.

Bad enough that Remy was haunted by his memories, but now the evil witch Gabrielle must needs turn up to devastate the captain to the depths of his noble soul. Remy declared he was cured, but Wolf did not entirely believe it. In fact, he suspected that the nature of the captain's bewitchment might have been the worst spell any woman could put upon a man.

Love.

Remy was a proud, reserved man and Wolf had learned a long time ago not to plague him with questions. But Wolf was a shrewd observer and he greatly feared that the captain had believed himself to be in love with that Cheney witch. So what had happened tonight to finally break the spell? Wolf had his suspicions about that as well. They had both heard the tales circulating around town, about the enchanting Gabrielle, the most bewitching courtesan in all Paris. The gossip had made the captain ferociously angry and he had refused to believe it. As for Wolf, he had accepted the rumors with a philosophical shrug. The stories had done the lady no harm in his eyes.

Wolf might fault the lovely Gabrielle for being a witch, but a courtesan? Women had a need to do what they could to survive the same as men. Perhaps even more so, being barred from so many more respectable ways of gaining a livelihood.

In many ways, Wolf thought that he was far worldlier than his captain. Wolf had grown up in the streets of Paris and Parisians tended to take a more liberal view regarding sexual liaisons than did the folk from the provinces. Not only was Remy from the wilds of Navarre, he was also a Huguenot. The captain did not assault Wolf with strictures from the Bible as many Protestants were wont to do. But as a breed, Huguenots did har-

bor sterner opinions about sin. The captain was a deeply honorable man.

Discovering that the lady he adored was a courtesan would
have crushed the captain more surely than acknowledging she
was a witch. Ah, love. Wolf shook his head darkly. At least that
was one misery that Wolf had been spared in his perilous eighteen years of life. Perhaps if he had had some experience of that
dire enchantment, he might be able to come up with some words
of wisdom to comfort his friend.

Remy remained immobile on the edge of the bed, his eyes
clouded as though he was still lost in the dark haze of that
witch's making. Wolf shuffled over to Remy and said gruffly,
"Things will improve for you, Captain. I have heard it sometimes
takes awhile for a man to shake off the full effects of being bewitched. But at least you are finally free of that terrible woman.
Surely that is cause for rejoicing."

Remy angled a look up at him, his grimace a poor substitute
for the captain's usual quiet smile. "I daresay I'll rejoice tomorrow. I am too bloody tired tonight."

Though it appeared to cost him some effort, the captain rallied, straightening slowly to his feet. "You take the bed, lad."

"Oh, no, m'sieur—" Wolf started to protest.

"I *said* take the bed. I never sleep well anyway and one of us
must get a good night's rest, for tomorrow we commence our
mission."

Wolf had opened his mouth to argue further, only to
promptly close it. Their mission. In all this turmoil over cursed
houses and treacherous enchantresses, Wolf had nearly forgotten the reason that had brought him and Remy back to Paris.

The quest to save the Huguenot king of Navarre from his imprisonment at the Catholic court of France. Wolf espoused no
particular religion himself. As far as he was concerned, each man
could go to the devil in his own way. But rescuing the king of
Navarre was important to Remy. Therefore it was important to
Wolf.

Wolf suddenly realized that the captain was staring at him with an assessing frown. "Martin, you do remember my initial reason for seeking out Mistress Cheney?"

"To get her to carry a message to the king?"

"Yes, but she has refused. She will not help us." Remy's jaw tightened. "In fact, she will do her best to hinder the rescue. She intends to bewitch the king and keep him for herself."

"Mon Dieu!" Wolf exclaimed. No wonder the captain was looking so grim.

"Do—do you think she will use her sorcery against us?" Wolf faltered.

"She may use any means at her disposal, but Mistress Cheney will not prove the worst of our enemies. We will face a sorceress of far more formidable and evil power."

Wolf shuddered, realizing full well whom Remy meant. Catherine de Medici, the Dark Queen. One could not live in Paris for any length of time without hearing terrible tales of the Queen Mother of France, cruel, hard, and ruthless. Well, she was after all an Italian and a foreigner and one knew no good could ever come of *that*. The Dowager Queen was said to be especially adept at the dark art of concocting potions and poisons.

Remy placed both hands on Wolf's shoulders, peering intently into his face. "If you have had second thoughts, if you decide you no longer want to be involved in this dangerous enterprise, I will quite understand."

Wolf realized what the captain had been leading up to with all this grave talk. He felt his face flush a hot shade of red. After Wolf's pathetic performance outside the Maison d'Esprit, the captain doubted his mettle. Wolf was so humiliated he wanted to fling himself out the window and dash his useless brains upon the pavement below.

He regarded Remy with a look of mingled hurt and shame. "Oh, m'sieur, I am sorry I failed you before. But I vow upon the graves of all the men who could have been my father, I will never do so again. I will brave the worst of curses, fight the most dread of witches. I will follow you into hell itself—"

"All right. All right, lad. I believe you." Remy gave Wolf's shoulders a bracing squeeze. "I am glad you are still willing to help me, for your knowledge of the ways of Paris is far greater than mine. I am relying upon you, my clever Wolf, to help me find a way to get inside that palace and reach my king."

"I will, Captain. I will. I will lurk outside the gates and snuffle out every bit of information. I will tunnel like a mole beneath the Louvre if I have to or—or scale a ladder to the highest towers."

"Well, just don't break your damn fool neck," Remy said. The captain's expression lightened for the first time since his return.

Wolf grinned back at him. But as Remy strode past him to snuff out the candle, Wolf had to duck his head to conceal how deeply moved he was. No one had ever trusted or depended upon Wolf for anything before. But Nicolas Remy, the great Scourge himself, had said that he was relying on him. *Him,* Martin Le Loup, humble thief and pickpocket, street rat of Paris. Tears pricked Martin's eyes and his chest swelled with such pride, he thought his heart would burst.

As Remy extinguished the candle, Wolf quickly finished undressing and bounded into the bed with a lighter heart. He nestled into the pillow and closed his eyes, his head swimming with visions of glory, all the heroic deeds he would perform fighting at the captain's side, the tales that would circulate over the wine cups in inns all over France. Tales of the great Scourge . . . and his Wolf.

Long after Martin had sunk into slumber, Nicolas Remy lay stretched out on the pallet, his hands propped behind his head, staring at the patterns the moonlight made upon the cracked plaster of the ceiling. As Martin's soft snores filled the room, Remy deeply envied the lad his ability to lose himself in such blessed unconsciousness. Martin slept the sleep of the just and untainted conscience. But then why shouldn't he? Martin's flaws and sins were all minor ones. He had no blood on his hands, no one's death to repent. At least not yet.

One of Martin's gangly legs dangled off the side, his dark hair tumbled across the pillow. At such an unguarded moment, he appeared less like the swaggering man of adventure he fought so hard to portray and more what he was, a boy who had some-how survived his rough-and-tumble upbringing in the streets of Paris. Not only survived, but emerged unscathed with an aston-ishingly romantic and optimistic soul.

Martin had endured enough hardship and peril in his short life and the rescue of Navarre was not Martin's cause, not his king. Remy should do his best to get Martin to clear off. His mouth tightened grimly because he knew he wouldn't. He would make use of Martin in the same hard way he had used countless other lads in the past, marching them into the mouth of cannon-fire to be blown to bits, leading them to die in some furious charge against the enemy's columns and all to claim one more costly victory.

Remy only had to close his eyes, lose himself in sleep, and he knew he would see their faces, battered, bloodied, some of them scarce sprouting their first beard. Many times he had been able to hold his terrible dreams at bay by thinking about Gabrielle, but now—

Remy's lips thinned, fighting to banish her from his mind. But soft as the moonlight that stole through the narrow window, her image came to him. Just as she had been that day in the woods, her sunlit hair tumbling down her back, her graceful white feet whispering across the grass. Gazing up at him with jewel-blue eyes that could at one moment be bright with laugh-ter, the next subdued with melancholy.

His lady fair, the best and brightest of his memories. Now re-membrance of her was only a source of torment because Remy could not stop himself from imagining other men doing what he had been too cursed honorable to ever do. Fondling her full ripe breasts, tumbling her naked body back into the sheets, parting her legs.

Had Gabrielle's eyes blazed with fire? Had she emitted little cries of pleasure? Had she looked at them the same feverish way as she had done Remy after kissing him so passionately tonight? Remy flung one arm across his eyes as though by doing so he could blot out the taunting pictures of Gabrielle in another man's arms. But the names pounded through his head . . . Duclous, Penthieve, Lanfort. How coolly Gabrielle had reeled off the list of her lovers, filling Remy with the kind of black killing fury he'd only ever let loose upon the battlefield. He had wanted to find each one of those bastards, take up his sword, and hack them into bloody ribbons.

And as for Gabrielle . . . Remy had never laid rough hands upon any woman before, but he'd come so close to shaking her until her teeth rattled, while he roared.

Damn you, Gabrielle! How could you do this?

He well understood the poverty, ignorance, and desperation that could drive women into selling their bodies for a few coins, but Gabrielle had no such excuse. She came of a good family, one that loved her. Her father's fortune might have been lost, but she had a generous and wealthy brother-in-law in the Comte de Renard, able to supply her every want. What reason could Gabrielle possibly have for pursuing the life of a courtesan except ambition and greed?

But that simply didn't fit with his memories of the girl he'd known that summer on Faire Isle. Like a golden enchantress Gabrielle had seemed, a faery queen far too fiercely proud to surrender her heart or her body to any man. And yet by her own admission, she had already taken her first lover, even then.

How could the same girl who could paint such a tender portrait of her little sister, who could show such compassion and kindness to a wounded soldier, be the same woman Remy had met tonight? Cold, ruthless, and scheming to become the mistress of a king.

Remy would never have believed it if he had not heard it from Gabrielle herself. What a blind, stubborn fool he was. He wished he could despise her, simply learn to forget, but that was the most damnable part of this whole thing.

Despite everything he still wanted her, still hungered for her in a way that was nigh unbearable, the ache in his heart as well as his loins. Remy gritted his teeth and tossed restlessly from side to side. He sought to divert his thoughts by planning what he would do tomorrow, his first steps toward the rescue of his king.

Dragging himself to a sitting position, Remy stretched out his arm, groping beneath his pile of clothing for the precious pouch he never let far from his side. He cupped the small leather sack in his hands, the feel of it heavy and reassuring, weighted as it was with gold. The funds that Remy had gleaned during the past few years by the sweat of his brow and the steel of his sword.

He loosened the drawstrings and shook several of the coins out into his hand, his heart swelling with a fierce satisfaction. It was not a fortune, but it would be money enough to buy weapons and horses, hire mercenaries or bribe guards. More than enough to plot the rescue of a king.

Or to purchase a woman.

Remy caught his breath at the wayward thought, fighting to suppress it. But the coins gleamed in the moonlight as temptingly as the golden tresses of Gabrielle Cheney's hair. So what was the asking price of a Parisian courtesan these days? How much would it take to possess Gabrielle, keep her for himself?

Remy stared at the coins glittering in his palm a moment longer, then shoved them hastily back in the pouch. The blood rose in his face and he was sickened by his own speculations. Not only was the thought of buying Gabrielle revolting to him, it was impossible as well. No matter how much money Remy acquired, he was certain that no mere captain would ever satisfy her.

No, Gabrielle wanted a king . . . Remy's king, to be precise.

Well, he would be damned before he ever let Gabrielle have Navarre. Remy tucked the sack of coins back under his discarded doublet and then lay back down on the pallet. Despite his resolve, Remy's brow furrowed as his doubts nagged at him. Could Gabrielle succeed in so seducing Navarre that even if Remy did find a way for the king to escape Paris, Henry would not want to go? Remy greatly feared that she could.

After all, Gabrielle had beguiled Remy into forgetting his duty for the length of a summer and she hadn't even been trying. And as for Navarre, well . . . Remy recollected a young prince who could be brave in battle, who even showed signs of being an astute ruler for the Huguenot people except for one fatal weakness.

Women. From the tender age of fourteen, Navarre had found the charms of the ladies as irresistible as they seemed to find him. His fascination with the fair sex had often rendered him lax about more important duties such as pursuing his studies and paying heed to matters of state.

Had the indolent young prince changed at all since he had become a king? Remy could only hope so or Navarre would never be any match for Gabrielle's charms. She'd slay him with but one dazzling smile.

Remy nestled his head deeper into the bolster, reflecting that the sooner he got Navarre out of Paris, the better. He needed to have his wits about him, get some sleep. But even as weariness tugged at him, Remy felt the old sinking dread, knowing that as soon as he closed his eyes, they would come for him, the ghosts of his past. All those enemies that he had slain, the men that he had lost in battle, returning to stare at him with bitter and accusing eyes.

Right beyond them would be those other poor souls from St.

Bartholomew's Eve, stretching out wraithlike hands to pluck at him with their desperate cries. His fellow countrymen, the men, women, and children he had sworn to protect and failed. And if it were a truly bad night, *he* would come, the demon man, his heavy battle sword drenched with blood, his lips pulled back in a death's-head grimace of savage joy at the slaughter.

Remy stirred on the pallet, his brow beading with cold sweat, his thoughts flying instinctively toward Gabrielle. But she was gone, his maiden of the island, his enchantress, his protecting angel. A dream, no more. That was all she had ever been and now she was lost to him forever. Remy closed his eyes, surrendering to the inevitable.

His demons would have him this night.

⊁⊁⊁⊁

GABRIELLE WHIMPERED AND TOSSED ON HER BED, TRYING TO FIGHT against the nightmare, struggle back to wakefulness. But it was of no use. The silken sheets beneath her body vanished, transforming into dried straw prickling against her skin. She was back in the hayloft of the barn, stifling, all but crushed under the weight of Etienne Danton.

"N-no, Etienne," she protested, twisting, trying to turn away from his greedy mouth pressing against her neck. She shivered in revulsion at the flicker of his tongue against her skin.

"P-please stop. I—I don't want to—"

"Oh, yes, you do," Danton panted, his breath hot against her face. "You want it right well enough, you hot little witch. Why else have you so been tempting me?"

"No. I didn't want—didn't mean—" Gabrielle choked on a cry of protest as Etienne pawed at her breast, his fingers clamping down hard.

"Stop! You are hurting me."

But Danton ignored her, his fingers hooking in the neckline of her bodice, the sound of ripping fabric assaulting her ears.

"I said, stop!" Gabrielle shrilled fiercely. Doubling up her fists, she struck out wildly at his face, her heart pounding with a mixture of anger and mounting fear. But Danton seized her wrists, roughly pinning them over her head. This man she had believed she had loved, her knight, her champion using his brutal strength against her.

Etienne leered down at her, his lean handsome features contorting into an ugly mask of lust, transforming before her very eyes into a devil, a monster. Gabrielle felt her gown being shoved up, her legs being forced apart.

"No!" she cried, bucking to get away, straining to free herself, but it was useless. Danton's heavy weight bore down upon her. She panted. She could scarce breathe. She felt something hard thrust at her woman's core, followed by a hot, searing pain.

"No!" But this time her cry came much fainter, tears leaking from the corners of her eyes. Danton's body pounded into her, driving Gabrielle mercilessly against the rough straw, the hard planking of the loft floor.

The punishment seemed to go on and on as though it would never end. Gabrielle lay broken beneath Danton, just praying for it all to be over soon.

"Sweet Jesu, help me," she whispered. "Somebody help me."

Then past Danton's shoulder she caught a glimpse of something that dazzled her eyes. Sunlight glinted off a full suit of shining armor. Gabrielle blinked, slowly bringing into focus the shadowy figure of a man, a tall proud warrior with dark gold hair, trim beard, and eyes the tender shade of night.

"R-remy," Gabrielle breathed, her heart lifting with a surge of desperate hope. "Ah, Remy. Help me, please."

To her horror, Remy merely gazed down at her dispassionately, then his lips curled with scorn, his eyes going cold and hard. He turned away from her in disgust, melting into the sunlight.

"No, Remy. C-come back. Please, come back—"

Gabrielle's ragged sobs woke her at last. Her eyes flew open and she stared wildly about the room, trying to regain her bearings, convince herself she truly was safe here in her bedchamber in Paris, not trapped on the floor of that barn.

Heart thudding, she drew sharp quick breaths, willing the nightmare back to the shadows of her mind from whence it had come. But the dream clung to her like a gritty layer of silt.

Gabrielle sat up, realizing that both her nightgown and the sheets were soaked in sweat. The feel of her own clammy skin revolted her and she fought aside the covers, stumbling in her haste to scramble out of the bed.

She tugged and yanked at her fine lawn nightgown, nearly tearing the damp, clinging fabric as she wrenched it off over her head. Gabrielle staggered over to the washstand and splashed water from the blue-trimmed enamel ewer into the bowl. Snatching up a piece of scented soap and a sponge, she proceeded to scrub herself as vigorously as she had that day after Danton had finished with her.

Her fingers trembled so badly the soap slipped from her grasp, plopping back into the washbowl. She could scarce keep a grip on the sponge either and let it go, bracing her hands along the sides of the washstand, breathing hard in an effort to steady herself.

She had not had that horrid dream for such a long time, Gabrielle had finally hoped she was done with it. The nightmare had always been far too vivid, forcing her to relive every dreadful moment of that day in the barn. But it wasn't what Danton had done to her that left Gabrielle so shaken this time. No, it was Remy's intrusion into the dream, Remy refusing to help her, Remy turning his back on her in disgust.

"Oh, God!" Gabrielle groaned, biting down hard on her lip to still its trembling, hot tears leaking from her eyes, splashing down her cheeks. She sniffed hard, taking a shuddering breath.

"Get hold of yourself, girl," she admonished herself. "It was only a dream, only a bloody dream."

But it wasn't, her heart whispered back. Remy did regard her with disgust. He did despise her now and he likely would not ever lift one finger to come to her aid. Gabrielle swallowed hard to stifle a wrenching sob. All the hurt she had refused to let herself feel over Remy's rejection welled up inside her in such an aching flood, it threatened to bring her to her knees.

She felt chilled to the bone, shaking so hard that her teeth chattered. Gabrielle stumbled about the room until she managed to locate her dressing gown. Somehow she got it on, wrapping the silk folds tightly around her naked body, but still she trembled.

Her gaze lit upon an object left on the window seat, the moonlight pouring through the glass panes glinting off the steely length of the sword, the same one Gabrielle had dropped in the courtyard earlier . . . Remy's sword.

When Bette had come upstairs to clean up the debris of shattered bottles, she must have left the sword for Gabrielle to find. Gabrielle lurched across the room and snatched up the weapon, her fingers gripping the hilt as though it was the last possession of any value left to her.

She clutched it desperately, hoping to feel some of the old protective strength she'd always sensed from Remy's sword. Remy who now hated her, who regarded her with such contempt. Ah, that was because he had finally seen the terrible flaw in her, Gabrielle thought, tears streaming down her cheeks. All the shameful stains on her soul left by her degradation at Danton's hands.

But it had all been her own fault. She remembered sitting there on the rough floor, clutching her torn bodice over her bruised skin. She had confronted Danton with a hurt and dazed look. "How—how could you do this to me, Etienne? I thought you were a man of honor."

"I *am* a man of honor," he'd muttered, avoiding her eyes as he hitched up his trunk hose. "Whatever I did, you made me do. You bewitched me past all bearing."

It had been then that Gabrielle had realized the harsh truth about herself. Beyond the artistry of her deft fingers, her skills with paint and brush, she possessed a far darker magic, the ability to drive a man out of his senses with desire, even to the point of committing unspeakable acts.

And in that moment, Gabrielle had felt that the part of her that could see beauty in every leaf, every blade of glass, the part that could breathe life into unicorns or put fairy lights in a little girl's eyes . . . that part of her had withered and died.

As the hot tears blurred her vision, Gabrielle blinked hard and lifted her head, catching a glimpse of her own reflection in the windowpanes. She saw a wild-eyed woman clutching a sword, her damp hair hanging lusterless about her shoulders, the set of her mouth looking bitter and old.

Lord, Gabrielle sighed. She truly was ugly. She wondered why Remy hadn't seen it sooner. Rubbing the tears from her eyes, she stared down at the sword she had clasped by her side, wondering what she should do with the thing.

She should find out where Remy was staying and have it returned to him, but something inside her rebelled at the thought. No, damn it, why should she return the sword? Remy had obviously wasted no time in acquiring another and Gabrielle might well have need of this one. Considering how Remy had threatened her . . .

Gabrielle raised the blade of the sword before her and laughed, to think of herself proposing to cross swords with the mighty Scourge. But the sound was a little shrill, unable to lighten the heavy ache in her heart.

She had realized that she and Remy could no longer be friends, but never in her worst nightmares had she ever thought they could become bitter enemies. But what else had she imagined would happen, Gabrielle chided herself. After she had so foolishly announced her intentions of seducing Navarre and keeping him in Paris. The king that Remy considered it his duty to rescue. And heaven knows nothing ever came between Nicolas Remy and his duty.

Gabrielle lowered the sword and propped it in the corner. Nothing would ever come between Gabrielle Cheney and her ambition either, she thought, squaring her shoulders. No matter how hard Remy might seek to prevent it, Gabrielle would have Navarre. Had not the great Nostradamus himself predicted it?

Gabrielle sat down on the window seat, and drawing her knees up to her chin, she hugged them close and peered out the glass panes. The sky that had been so misty earlier in the evening was now sharp and clear, the stars themselves seeming to chart the way to Gabrielle's future.

Oh, she knew very well what her mother would have said to such a notion. Evangeline Cheney had been skeptical of Nostradamus's predictions even when the seer was alive. Maman had had even less faith in astrology.

"Your fate is not writ in some distant stars, my dear heart," Maman had once told her. *"It rests entirely in your own choices."*

Gabrielle had made her choice that long-ago day when she had left Remy standing alone on the riverbank. Even before that, she reflected sadly, when she had let Etienne Danton take her by the hand and lead her into that barn.

Once she had accepted the dark magic inside herself, Gabrielle had learned to use her charms and outward beauty, honing her very body into a weapon capable of ensnaring any man, even a king. Never again would she feel so weak and helpless as she had been that day she'd lost her innocence.

She would be powerful and strong, as formidable as the Dark Queen. At least she would tomorrow. But as she stared up at that vast cold sky, tonight all Gabrielle felt was very small and alone.

She ached desperately for someone's strong arms to steal around her, comfort her, hold her close. But those would never be Remy's arms. He would never want to touch her again.

Instead, Gabrielle felt herself longing for Ariane. Her older sister had often driven Gabrielle to distraction with her attempts to mother, to teach and protect. But now Gabrielle wanted nothing more than to be back on Faire Isle, to bury her face in Ariane's lap and pour out her woes while Ariane stroked her hair.

But her older sister despised her as much as Remy did, Gabrielle thought bleakly. As the Lady of Faire Isle, full of a great healing magic, wise, gentle, and good, Ariane was the sort of woman who inspired love in men, not lust. She had the respect of the people on the island and beyond, the admiration of all other daughters of the earth and the adoration of her Comte de Renard.

Gabrielle despondently rested her chin upon her knees. There was no way her older sister could ever understand her. Just like the life she led, Ariane was perfect.

Chapter Seven

THE CHÂTEAU TREMAZAN PERCHED AT THE CREST OF THE HILL like some stone-faced warlord surveying the valley below. The turrets and crenellated battlements bore the aspect of a grim and forbidding fortress. But the bedchamber located on the highest level of the keep more resembled a room in a prosperous farmhouse. The lime-washed walls were as unpretentious as the polished wood floor, the surface scattered with braided rugs.

The furnishings were likewise simple, some sturdy chairs, a few tables, a heavy chest situated at the foot of a four-poster bed curtained in a blue silk the same shade as the cloudless summer sky. A breeze drifted through the open windows, stirring the bed curtains and carrying with it the scents of the world far below, freshly cut meadow grass, a hint of rose petals, and an earthier tang emanating from the stableyard.

The breeze was soft and warm as it whispered over the heated flesh of the two lovers entangled in the sheets. Ariane Deauville, the Comtesse de Renard, lay naked beneath her husband, her chestnut-colored hair fanned across the pillow, her gray eyes narrowed to hazy slits. Her breath issued in quick sighs as Justice Deauville braced himself above her, his mouth blazing a hot trail of kisses along the curve of her neck.

The comte was a formidable figure in all respects, large, well over six feet of raw bones and hard muscle. His face, with his hooded green eyes, lantern jaw, and battered nose was enough to frighten many a brave man, especially when the comte was angered. But as Renard hovered over his wife, taking great care not to crush her beneath his massive frame, his harsh features were softened by a flush of passion and tenderness.

"Ma chère," he said huskily, his sun-streaked light brown hair tumbling forward as he kissed her lips, teasing her with the hot thrust of his tongue.

As Renard settled himself between her legs, Ariane closed her eyes and wrapped her arms about his neck, drawing him close. But Ariane's arousal eluded her, her mind consumed by one thought, one wish, one prayer.

"Oh, please, dear God, let this be the time. Let Renard fill me with a child."

She could feel Renard's hardened shaft teasing against the nest of curls between her legs, prolonging their joining with tantalizing slowness. Ariane reached between them, guiding him in with an impatient upward thrust of her hips. Mouth set in a determined line, she began to rock against him in a pulsing rhythm.

"Chérie." Renard's gasp was part endearment, part protest as Ariane quickened the pace. He stiffened his body in resistance, whispering kisses across her brow.

"Chérie, there . . . is . . . no . . . need . . . for such haste. We have . . . all . . . afternoon."

Ariane only tightened her grip and drove him harder, panting from her efforts. She worked at him with ever-increasing urgency, returning his kisses with something akin to desperation while her thoughts urged him to fulfillment.

Renard kissed her again and again, the heat of his tongue mating with hers as he breathed words of love against her lips. Ariane could tell he was doing his best to slow the pace, to bring her to the brink of arousal. But she refused to allow that, urging him on with a single-minded purpose.

A child . . . a little daughter. Grant me a girl child.

Ariane wrapped her legs tighter around Renard, pressing her heels against his hard, flat buttocks, using them like spurs to drive him on. Showing no mercy until she broke Renard's resistance. With a groan, he pumped harder and harder until at last Ariane felt him shudder with his release. Though he took care not to collapse on top of her, Renard was breathing as hard as a mighty destrier winded after a battle.

"Sweet Jesu, woman!" he gasped, resting his forehead against her shoulder. Her own heart pounding hard, Ariane caressed the damp strands of his hair. She released a shaky breath, torn between triumph and doubt. Had she succeeded this time? Had the miracle of conception occurred?

Renard lifted his head to brush a quick kiss against her lips. He levered himself off of her, collapsing on his back, blowing out another gusty breath.

"Mon Dieu! That was . . . certainly . . . vigorous."

Ariane only smiled, carefully arranging herself, keeping her knees drawn, her pelvis tilted lest one precious drop of Renard's seed escape her. He shifted to his side, reaching out to draw her back into his arms, cradle her close to his heart.

Ariane resisted, pushing his hands away. "No, let me remain like this awhile longer. It might help, give your seed every chance to move deeper into my womb."

Renard flopped onto his back again. "Your pardon, ma chère. I forgot. We were not making love. We were making a babe," he said in a flat, disappointed tone.

Ariane was dismayed to see the frown creasing Renard's brow. "But you know that I have been carefully charting my monthly courses and when the time was right—"

"Yes, yes," Renard grumbled. "It is only that I am starting to feel a bit like a stallion put to stud."

Ariane chuckled, striving to lighten his mood. "And a truly magnificent stallion you are." She skated her knuckles over the hard plane of his sweat-dampened chest.

"I did give you pleasure, did I not?" she demanded.

Renard caught her hand and carried her fingertips lightly to his lips. "But of course, chérie. When have you ever not?"

He released her hand and rolled to his side, raising himself onto one elbow so he could peer intently down at her. "The real question is, did I pleasure you?"

"Why . . . why certainly," Ariane lied, seeking to avoid his eyes.

Renard seized her chin, forcing her to meet his gaze. His frown deepened.

"No. I thought as much." He sank back down on his pillow, flinging one arm across his brow, looking annoyed and frustrated.

Ariane silently cursed the old witch of a grandmother who had taught Justice the art of reading eyes, something that only the daughters of the earth were supposed to know. Renard was far too infernally good at it.

"All right," Ariane said. "So perhaps I did not quite reach my—my usual peak. I was looking for fulfillment of a different sort. My pleasure didn't matter—"

"Didn't matter!" Renard growled, sitting bolt upright. "Didn't matter? Perhaps not if you were some hired wench who was only concerned with the size of my purse. But I would like to think that my *wife* found more satisfaction in my arms than that."

"Oh, Justice—" Ariane cried, but Renard shoved to his feet and stalked over to the washstand, his broad back and hard buttocks toward her. After pouring the contents of the ewer into the washbowl, he splashed the water over his face, using both hands.

Ariane sighed, torn between her need to remain positioned

as she was and her desire to go to Renard and soothe his wounded male pride. For all that he claimed to have the hide of an elephant, her mighty husband was as vulnerable as any man when it came to his prowess in the bedchamber.

She watched as Renard scrubbed himself in terse silence, no doubt preparing to get dressed and return to his afternoon chores. Ariane gingerly rose from the bed. Stealing up behind him, she brushed the damp strands of brown hair away from his neck.

Renard stiffened a little at her touch, but otherwise ignored her, scrubbing the sponge up the long reach of his sinewy arm. A tall woman herself, Ariane still had to stretch a little to press a kiss to the nape of his neck.

"Justice, you know I love you," she murmured. "I feel great joy each time you touch me, even at your slightest caress."

"So you say, milady."

Ariane ducked around him and wriggled in between him and the washbasin.

"Here, let me do that," she coaxed, reaching for the sponge. Renard resisted for a moment, then surrendered the sponge to her.

He stood, legs braced slightly apart, hands on hips, staring fixedly at some point above her head as Ariane lathered the sponge across the broad region of his chest. She worked slowly, lovingly, trying her best to make it up to him for her lack of response before. Her gaze roved admiringly over her husband's large, masculine frame.

Although Ariane found him almost shatteringly beautiful, Renard did not view himself as an attractive man. He was not classically handsome, his skin not white and smooth like many elegant noblemen who seemed like they had been cut from some skilled tailor's silken cloth.

With his half-peasant ancestry, Renard was more like a man who had been fashioned from the earth itself, all flesh and bone and sinew. As Ariane dipped the sponge lower, she felt a responsive quiver in his loins. His male organ stirred beneath her hand and he drew in his breath with a gasp.

"No more of *that*, milady," he said, seizing her wrist to stop her. "I have done my duty by you and I have other matters that require my attention."

Ariane straightened, her cheeks stinging with hurt and embarrassment. "Why—why you talk as if I was some rapacious female out to use you for my own ends."

Renard merely arched one eyebrow in expressive fashion, then stalked away from her, snatching up a linen towel to dry himself. Ariane plopped the sponge back in the washbowl, vexed by her twinge of guilt. Damn it! She was not acting to satisfy some rampaging lust, but for a child, *their* child, a blessing for both of them.

Ariane wrapped her arms across her bare breasts, feeling chilled and exposed. She would bathe and dress after Renard had left, but for now she retrieved the shift from the pile of clothes she had discarded in her eagerness to get Renard into bed. As Ariane tugged the light linen fabric over her head, she was aware of Renard dressing at the opposite end of the room, the distance of a few floorboards and scattered carpets seeming to yawn like a chasm between them.

She watched as Renard yanked on his breeches, quickly doing up the buttons as though he could not wait to be gone.

"I am sorry you find your duty so irksome," she said. "But I thought you wanted a child as much as I do."

Renard paused. "I want whatever will make you happy, ma chère," Renard muttered, digging through the aumbry for a fresh shirt.

"That is an annoyingly evasive reply," Ariane snapped.

Renard pulled out a shirt and slammed the cupboard door closed. "Nothing would please me more than to have a child with you, but you are going at it too blasted hard, Ariane. You will wear us both out, woman."

"You never used to complain of such a thing before. You had much more stamina than that."

Renard paused in the act of unfolding his shirt to glower at her. "So I did. I could make love to you the livelong day. But that is not what we have been doing of late. We have merely been joining our bodies to make a child. Sometimes you seem so far away from me, I wonder if you even remember that I am there, if any other man would serve your purpose."

"That is not true!" Ariane cried hotly. "What a dreadful thing to say."

Renard compressed his lips, then said curtly, "You are right. I apologize."

He attempted to wrench his shirt over his head, but his skin was still damp. The light cotton bunched up around his shoulders where he could not reach to yank it down.

"Damn!" Renard snarled. In another moment he would have the shirt torn in his impatient struggles. Sternly ordering him to hold still, Ariane worked at the knotted fabric until she managed to ease the shirt past Renard's shoulders and down his back.

"Merci, madame," he muttered. As he glanced down at her, the harsh cast of Renard's face softened. Both his eyes and his voice were gentler, more patient as he caressed her cheek.

"I am sorry for behaving like a wounded beast, ma chère. But we have plenty of time for children. We have only been married three years."

His warm touch and coaxing smile eased some of Ariane's tension, but she had to suppress a quiver in her voice as she said, "Most women my age are already mothers several times over. I am going to be twenty-four come next Michaelmas."

"A mere babe." Renard dropped a kiss on the tip of her nose. "Did you not deliver a child only last week to the miller's wife? And she is forty-two, if she is a day."

"But Hortense has already had ten children." Ariane's throat constricted. She had to swallow hard before she could finish. "And I have already failed twice."

Renard caught her face between his huge hands and regarded her fiercely. "Do not talk like that, Ariane. What happened was no fault of yours. You are a wise woman. You should know better. It is often simply the way of nature for a woman to miscarry."

"*Miscarry,*" Ariane echoed bitterly, pushing his hands away. "How I hate that word. It makes it sound as though I lost nothing more precious than a bucket of water I dropped on the way from the well. The first time was disappointing, but I scarce realized I had conceived before it was ended. But the last time—"

Ariane closed her eyes and pressed her hand over the region of her womb. "Oh, the last time, Justice, I could feel the first flutter of life from our babe, like a tiny bird flexing its wings.

"I did not *miscarry,*" she said in a voice tight with anguish. "I lost our child."

"And I nearly lost you!" Renard replied tersely.

"Don't exaggerate, Justice. I admit the pain was bad and I lost some blood—"

"You nearly died, Ariane." Renard grasped her by the shoulders and peered sternly at her as though he would force her to acknowledge the truth of his words.

Ariane tipped her chin to a stubborn angle. "I did not! And even if I had come close to perishing, childbearing always carries a certain amount of risk. But to have such a precious prize, our own babe, does that not make it worth it?"

"No! Not to me it doesn't." The set of Renard's jaw was so implacable, a muscle throbbed in his cheek.

"But you are the Comte de Renard. Surely you must want an heir?"

Renard expelled an impatient breath. "Ariane, you know right well I never particularly cared about inheriting all of this." He gave an impatient jerk of his head in the direction of the castle window, toward the sprawling estate beyond. "And I could care even less who has it after I am gone. All I care about is *you.*"

Renard's eyes seethed with a mingling of love and frustration. He flexed his fingers, trying to massage some of the tension from her shoulder blades. "God's truth, woman! My own mother died giving birth to me. Is that what you want? To leave me with a child who will never see his mother's face?"

"No! I am sure everything will go better the next time. That—that is—" The fear that had dogged Ariane so relentlessly of late caused her lip to tremble. "If there is a next time," she whispered.

"Ah, chérie," Renard groaned. Drawing her into his arms, he held her close and buried his face against her hair. "You will have your babe one day. But you must be patient and wait. Your body has not even had enough time to heal."

Ariane nestled against his chest, drawing some comfort from the warm strength of his arms and the steady beat of his heart. But she quavered, "It has been over a year, Justice, since I lost our babe."

"No, only nine months," Renard corrected her gently.

Only? Ariane thought forlornly. It felt like a lifetime to her of raised hopes every time her courses were a little late, followed by crushing disappointment when her monthly flow began. Her despair was only deepened by the realization that she was alone in her grief. Each time she failed to conceive, she suspected that Renard was more than a little relieved.

But to tax her husband with that would only provoke another quarrel and she feared they had been doing too much of that lately. So Ariane rallied her spirits and lifted her head to offer Renard a misty smile.

"Never mind. I am certain you will feel differently about all of this when I place your son or daughter in your arms. And that may be sooner than we both think." Ariane stole a wistful glance toward the bed. "Perhaps we were lucky this afternoon."

"Perhaps," Renard agreed, but his own smile was forced. He brushed a kiss against her forehead and then released her.

Retrieving his boots and his hose, Renard sank down on one

of the stools by the hearth to finish dressing. Without his arms around her, Ariane felt strangely bereft. She hugged herself tightly and studied his averted face with a dull pain in her heart. Renard seldom spoke about the way his mother had died, but Ariane knew he was haunted by the fear his wife might meet the same fate.

She understood Renard's apprehensions for her. Truly she did. She just wished he could make more effort to understand the fierce ache of her longing for a child. He was usually not even willing to talk about her desperate desire to conceive, which left her abandoned in a very lonely place. To wish and hurt, to grieve and dream all by herself.

As Renard yanked on his boots, he abruptly changed the subject. "When do you leave for Faire Isle?"

Ariane sighed, moving to pick up the rest of the clothing she had dropped on the floor. In truth, she had given little thought to her impending journey or the council meeting of the daughters of the earth that awaited her.

"Tomorrow morning, early, I suppose—" she began, then stopped as the full import of Renard's question struck her. She regarded him with a tiny frown. "Will you not be accompanying me?"

"No, not this time. I have pressing business of my own to attend." Renard stood up to ram his heel the rest of the way into his second boot.

"Oh," Ariane said, quietly concealing her disappointment. She carried her soiled gown over to place it in the woven straw laundry basket.

"But I will send a retinue of men to accompany you," Renard added.

"Faire Isle is not that many leagues away," Ariane protested. "I will be traveling across our own lands, to my own home. I don't need to be escorted by an army."

"Six of my very best men," Renard said in a tone that

brooked no argument. He stepped behind her and caught her by the elbow, pulling her around to face him. He stroked a stray wisp of hair behind her ear.

"I would do anything to protect you, to keep you safe. *Anything*. You do understand that, don't you, Ariane?"

"Why—why, yes," she stammered, a little taken aback by the intensity of his tone, the fierce glitter in his green eyes.

"Good!" Renard pressed a hard kiss to her lips, then strode away from her. In another second he was gone, the bedchamber door closing sharply behind him.

Ariane ran her fingers over her mouth, which felt a little bruised from the force of her husband's parting embrace. When she had first met Renard, he had often seemed intimidating, a stranger who hid many secrets behind his cool smile.

Ariane had always prided herself on her own ability to read eyes, but she had been frustratingly unable to penetrate the thoughts Renard concealed beneath his heavy lids. As she had fallen deeply in love with him, she had finally been able to read his mind as easily as he did hers. But there were still times when Renard's thoughts eluded her and those times were growing more disturbingly frequent.

Ariane brushed her hand back through her hair and cast a despondent glance around the empty bedchamber. She should bathe, get dressed, and start making some preparations for her journey. But Renard's abrupt departure and their ongoing disagreement about the babe left her feeling unsettled and restless.

Ariane drifted listlessly toward one of the open windows. The height of this chamber afforded her an excellent view of the estate beyond the curtain wall of the castle. She could make out the mysterious shadows of the thick wood nearby, the wheat field that was slowly being harvested by a hive of workers wielding their scythes. Off to the left was a meadow dotted with daisies where the foal from Renard's prized mare was gamboling about on spindly legs.

So many times Ariane had imagined herself wandering that same sweet meadow, small chubby fingers clinging to her hand. She would bend down to point out some plant or flower, teaching her daughter all the lore her own mother had taught her. Her child would nod eagerly, absorbing all Ariane said, a little girl with Renard's keen green eyes and sun-streaked hair. Or perhaps a shade more golden like her father's had been.

Or like Gabrielle's.

The thought of her sister only served to further lower Ariane's spirits. Gabrielle was never far from her mind, her fears for her headstrong sister having cost Ariane many a sleepless night. If she had not managed to plant Bette in Gabrielle's household to send back regular reports, Ariane thought she might have run mad with worry.

When Gabrielle had run off, Renard had offered to go to Paris, haul her back by force if necessary. As tempted as Ariane had been by the notion, she had refused. She could hardly hold her sister prisoner and she feared she had already made enough mistakes with Gabrielle.

The brightness of the day dimmed as Ariane was flooded with painful recollections of the last time she'd seen her sister, their bitter quarrel. Ariane had always understood the nature of the injury that had been inflicted upon Gabrielle by Etienne Danton and how much her sister had grieved over the death of Nicolas Remy, although Gabrielle would never admit to either.

As a healer by nature, it had hurt and frustrated Ariane that she was unable to ease her sister's pain. That last afternoon her patience had worn thin. Although she had not confided the fact to anyone as yet, Ariane had suspected she was pregnant with her first child and it was not going well. She had spotted blood only that morning and the sight of Gabrielle stubbornly packing her trunk had caused something to snap inside Ariane.

"You are not going to Paris, Gabrielle." Ariane yanked out the gowns and petticoats from the trunk as fast as her sister was

packing them and flung them back on the bed. "And that is the end of the matter."

Gabrielle glared at her. "No, it isn't. You might be prepared to let a perfectly fine house go to waste, a house that our father paid for, but—"

"A house for his mistress! Will you insult our mother by accepting such a gift from the vile woman who broke her heart?"

Although Gabrielle swallowed thickly, she replied, "Maman is no longer here to care."

"And do you think she wouldn't care that her daughter is prepared to embark on a career as—as a whore?"

"That is what I already am," Gabrielle said, doggedly refolding a gown.

Ariane seized hold of her wrist to stop her. "No, you aren't. What happened with Danton was not your fault."

Gabrielle's cheeks flamed as she wrenched herself free. "You know nothing about what happened and I don't want to discuss it."

"No, you never do, do you? Or your grief over Remy, either."

At the mention of Remy, Gabrielle clutched the gown she was holding almost protectively in front of her, her mouth setting in that thin line Ariane knew all too well, the expression a mingling of suppressed pain and sheer stubbornness.

Frustrated by her inability to reach her sister, to reason with her, Ariane paced about the bedchamber. "Do you think I don't know what you have in mind? You believe if you seduce enough great men, you'll become rich and powerful enough to take your place at court. And that somehow you'll find a way to take your revenge on the Dark Queen for what she did to Remy.

"But it won't work, Gabrielle. You'll never be any match for Catherine. And even if you did succeed in destroying her, you'll destroy yourself as well. Your heart, your very soul will become as black as hers and none of that will bring Remy back."

"I don't have a heart," Gabrielle said, stuffing the gown into

the trunk. "And this has nothing to do with Remy, only my own ambitions."

She jumped back when Ariane slammed the lid down to prevent her packing anything more.

"You can forget your cursed ambitions," Ariane said, losing all patience. "You are not going anywhere. I absolutely forbid it."

"You forbid it?" Gabrielle cried. "Who do you think you are?"

"Your older sister and the Lady of Faire Isle."

"Oh, yes, the great healer who thinks she can fix anything. Well, you can't fix me, Ariane. When are you ever going to understand that? I am not perfect like you and Maman. And maybe if Maman hadn't been quite so saintly, she'd never have lost Papa to that trollop—"

Ariane's hand shot out before she could stop herself, connecting sharply with Gabrielle's cheek. She and Gabrielle regarded each other in stunned silence for a moment, Gabrielle clutching her face.

Ariane had never struck either of her sisters before. She felt sick as she saw the tears well in Gabrielle's eyes.

"Gabrielle, I am sorry. I—"

But Gabrielle blinked fiercely and turned away . . .

Ariane rested her head wearily against the window frame. Gabrielle had vanished from the castle the very next day and they had not seen or spoken to each other for the past two years. She was as much to blame for that as Gabrielle. Hurt that Gabrielle would run off that way, angry that she was now living in that cursed woman's house, overwhelmed by her own problems, Ariane had made no effort to heal the breach.

If she had sent word to Gabrielle when she had had either of her miscarriages, Ariane knew that Gabrielle would have returned to be with her at once. But Ariane had been too proud to do so.

She was acclaimed far and wide as the most learned of wise women. She had helped scores of mothers through difficult conceptions and births, safely delivered countless babes. But instead of a child, the only thing that grew inside her was her fear. That despite all her cleverness, all her learning, all her magic, she might prove barren.

If only Renard could be brought to comprehend how empty, how desolate that made her feel. But perhaps no man could. Perhaps she asked far too much of her husband. The making of a child was supposed to be a joyous, almost sacred thing, drawing a man and wife closer together, Ariane reflected bleakly. Instead her deep longing was driving her and Renard further apart.

✳✳✳

A FINE MIST CURLED ACROSS THE PASTURE, THE GRASS DAMP WITH dew, the sun barely poking its head over the horizon. The early morning stillness was only broken by the twittering of some sparrows and the steady thud of Renard's hammer as he sought to repair a break in the pasture fence.

He hunkered down, one nail held firmly between his lips, while he drove another into the replacement board with hard, precise strokes. Mending fences was scarcely a befitting task for the Comte de Renard.

But Renard feared that the peasant blood had always been stronger in him than whatever thin strain he had inherited from the mighty Deauvilles. He liked the feel of an axe or scythe in his hand, far preferring good honest labor to hunting, hawking, or sipping wine with some fop of a nobleman who reeked of scent like a Parisian whore.

Renard had always felt far closer to his kinsman, Toussaint, a distant cousin of his peasant mother's. The redoubtable old warrior had gone to meet his Maker two springs ago. A peaceful death, a dignified end to what had been a long and full life. Renard still missed the old man who had been like both a father and conscience to him. Especially now that this trouble had arisen with Ariane.

Renard plucked the second nail from his mouth and pounded it into place. At the distant winding of a horn, Renard straightened and shaded his eyes, squinting in the direction of the road that led away from the castle. He could make out the mounted troop of some half dozen of his retainers, clad in the black-and-gold livery of the house of Deauville. Riding in their midst, perched sidesaddle on a richly caparisoned palfrey, was his Ariane. A scarlet wool mantle hung off her shoulders, her chestnut hair falling down her back in a thick braid.

The Lady of Faire Isle. Renard's mouth curved in a smile that was part rueful, part filled with pride. He and Ariane had kissed each other good-bye in the predawn darkness. And a strained embrace it had been, despite their efforts to pretend otherwise.

Renard watched as the troop of riders came closer. When they reached the part of the road that meandered past the meadow, Ariane craned her neck to peer in his direction. She smiled and lifted one hand in a farewell salute. Even at such a distance, Renard could detect the aura of sadness that clung to her.

But he grinned determinedly back and stretched up his arm to wave until the troop of riders and his wife disappeared from view, leaving behind a faint cloud of dust.

Renard lowered his hand, his smile disappearing into a worried frown. "Ah, chérie," he murmured. "You still look much too tired and pale to me." Despite all of Ariane's protestations to the contrary, Renard feared that she had never recovered her full strength since the ordeal of her miscarriage.

Although he found himself missing her already, it was as well that she would be gone for awhile. Perhaps the visit to her old home would do her good, get her mind off the obsession that was fretting her to the bone. Give him a chance as well to clear his head and decide what the devil he was going to do about their problem.

Renard had always been good at masking his emotions, at least until Ariane had entered his life and heart. Now he lived in hourly dread that wise woman that she was, Ariane would read his eyes and uncover his guilty secret, how he had been betraying her for the past nine months. Oh, not with another woman. The woman did not exist who could entice him from Ariane's bed. But Ariane might find that kind of infidelity more forgivable than what he was doing, something that would be perhaps far worse in her eyes.

He was preventing her from conceiving a child.

Digging another nail from the pouch tied to his waist, Renard returned to his task of mending his fence. But every thud of his hammer seemed laden with his nagging guilt.

Ariane was the daughter of a fabled wise woman, the saintly Evangeline, the previous Lady of Faire Isle. But Renard's peasant grandmother . . . well, Renard thought with a wry twist of his lips. There was no gainsaying the fact. Old Lucy had been a witch and often of the most wicked kind. Eschewing the gentle arts of healing, Lucy had become an expert in the dark art of poisons and potions designed to hinder the creation of life, not encourage it.

She had passed on much of her knowledge to Renard, including a certain brew that could render a man's seed temporarily infertile. Renard had been distilling that potion and secretly taking it for months now.

He could imagine what Toussaint would have said to him. Much as the old man had loved Lucy, he had ever deplored her dark magic and all she had taught Renard. But what the hell else could he do? Renard thought. He slammed the hammer into the nail so hard, he drove it crooked and was obliged to pause to pry it out again. He would have loved to have a dozen children with Ariane, but not at the expense of her health, perhaps even her life. Renard had tried to avoid having relations with her after her last miscarriage. But despite his wife's quiet modesty, Ariane could be a damned determined seductress and—Renard reflected with a huge sigh, his flesh was very weak where the woman he loved was concerned.

Ariane had left him no choice but to resort to the cursed potion. She was fairly killing herself in this quest for a child. But he felt like a complete bastard every month when Ariane's courses came upon her and she would be crushed with despair, her heart breaking a little more each time. Renard's guilt only deepened when she would curl up in his arms for comfort, innocently unaware that he was the Judas responsible for her disappointment.

They could not go on this way much longer, Renard thought desperately. He had to find a solution, even if it meant exploring methods Ariane would not approve of. Renard straightened from his labors and rested his arms broodingly atop the fence post. He feared there was far too much of old Lucy's witchy blood in him after all.

But he had made up his mind. He was determined to find some way for Ariane to have the child she craved, all the while protecting her, keeping her safe . . . forever. Renard intended to search out every ancient text of knowledge and spells he could get his hands on. Even, he reflected with a grim set to his lips . . .

Even if it meant resorting to magic of the very blackest kind.

Chapter Eight

MOONLIGHT SHIMMERED OVER THE LOUVRE, THE DANK SMELL of the nearby Seine mingling with the fragrance of roses emanating from the palace gardens. The palace was etched against the night sky like a fairy-tale castle, light and music pouring from the windows of the main salon where the masked ball was being held.

But the soft beauty of the summer night was lost on Remy as he stood frozen in the shadows, his mind hurtling him back across the years to the last time he'd walked away from the Louvre, accompanying old Admiral Coligny and two of his brother officers back to their lodgings. Memories of his own voice echoed in Remy's ears.

". . . *we can't just leave our king there, surrounded by our enemies,*" he had urged. "*We have to get him out of there.*"

"*Get him out?*" *young Tavers exclaimed.* "*His majesty has only been wed a day ago. He's scarce had time to enjoy the pleasures of his marriage bed.*"

"*Marriage bed! It is more likely to be his deathbed and likely the rest of ours as well,*" Remy said heatedly.

"*Ah, please, lad.*" The Admiral regarded Remy with a weary patience. "*No more of that nonsense about Queen Catherine being a witch, plotting to murder us all.*"

"*It is not nonsense, sir. If you had seen and learned what I did this summer on Faire Isle—*"

"*You should never have set one foot there.*" Remy's friend, Captain Devereaux, interrupted, the burly man shaking his shaggy brown head. "*It is said to be a passing strange place, the Faire Isle.*"

"*No doubt our good Remy has been sleeping with the fairies,*" Tavers chimed in.

"*Or was bewitched by some blue-eyed Circe,*" the old Admiral teased.

Remy was annoyed to feel the red sting his cheeks, the Admiral's words perilously close to the truth of what had happened with Gabrielle.

"*I think we need to domesticate our Scourge. Find him a wife,*" the Admiral declared.

"*A wife. The very thing.*" The two others agreed and soon they were all jocularly putting forth suggestions for a possible bride. Only Devereaux seemed to realize the depth of Remy's fear and frustration. He said soothingly, "*You simply need a flagon of wine and a good meal. Come back with me to my lodgings. Claire has not clapped eyes on you for an age and you have yet to see our newest offspring, your namesake. The lad has such a set of lungs on him, he keeps the entire street awake. We've taken to calling him the wee Scourge.*"

Remy attempted to smile, but his heart was far too heavy with apprehension to do so. He allowed his friends to drag him farther away from the palace where he had abandoned his young king, trying to quash his fears, to hope that perhaps the Admiral might be right, that somehow all would be well.

"Remy! Captain?" The low voice whispered close to Remy's ear and someone tugged impatiently at his arm.

Lost in his memories, Remy turned, still half-expecting to find Devereaux, the man's genial face split in a gap-toothed grin. But Dev was long gone, his wife and child as well. Just like young Tavers and the old Admiral. Lost with so many others to the brutality and madness of St. Bartholomew's Eve.

It was Wolf who peered up at Remy out of the darkness. "Captain? Come on, monsieur. We must hurry or we will miss the rendezvous."

Remy nodded. Shaking off the ghosts of the past, he allowed Wolf to lead him away from the main doors of the Louvre, where the guards scrutinized each new arrival. That was the entry for invited guests and Remy hardly qualified as that.

He kept to the shadows, following Wolf toward the older portion of the palace. By the use of one ruse or another, Wolf had spent the last few days learning the layout of the grounds. The lad darted from tree to bush with a speed and cunning Remy was hard pressed to match, hampered as he was by his new suit of clothes.

He wore a pair of stiff satin breeches tied off below his knee, his movements further restricted by a matching doublet with sleeves tapering to a tight fit at his wrists. His feet were crammed into a pair of ankle-high leather shoes, far different from his supple worn boots.

A wide ditch yawned in front of them, the dry remains of the old moat that had once ringed the palace. As Remy scrambled down the slope after Wolf, the short cloak of midnight-blue silk that he wore slung over one shoulder entangled about his arm. Remy shoved it impatiently out of his way.

He nearly lost his footing, his stiff shoes dislodging a hail of pebbles that seemed to resound through the night like gunfire. Remy and Wolf flattened themselves against the rough stone wall of the palace, tensed and listening. Remy groped reflexively for his sword, but instead of his own trusty blade, his fingers closed over the flimsy hilt of a light dress sword. Wolf was armed with nothing more than a dagger. If any contingent of guards came to investigate the disturbance, he and the lad were done for.

As moments slowly passed and no one came to raise the alarm, Remy let his hand drop away from his sword and Wolf emitted a deep sigh of relief.

He leaned closer to Remy to whisper, "Wait here, Captain. I'll go scout ahead."

Before Remy could protest, the lad was off again, stealing along the deep track of the moat. Remy's mouth clamped tightly in frustration, finding it hard to relinquish control of this mission to a mere lad of eighteen. He had been obliged to place a great deal of faith in Wolf and this mysterious maid who had agreed to help smuggle Remy into the palace. But it was not as though Remy had much other choice.

Gabrielle had left him none when she had refused to help. He rested his head back against the wall, his jaw tightening as he wondered if she was even now in the ballroom, her soft smiles and bright eyes bewitching his king.

Very likely she was. In fact, Remy was counting upon it. This masked ball that would enable him to slip into the palace undetected posed a difficulty for Remy as well. With all those disguised faces, would Remy be able to pick out the king he had not seen for this long time?

Remy did not know for sure. But masked or not, Remy was fairly certain he would be able to recognize the woman who had filled his dreams for these past three years. And where Gabrielle was, so likely would Navarre be. The most dangerous part of this enterprise would be finding a way to have a private word with Navarre without rousing Gabrielle's suspicions or attracting the attention of the Dark Queen.

Accordingly he had taken every preventative measure that he could. He had a cap tucked in his belt to cover his hair and when he donned his mask, the black leather would fully conceal the upper portion of his face and as for his jaw—

Remy raised his hand to stroke his chin, disturbed by the feel of smooth, bare skin. He'd worn a beard ever since he'd been younger than Wolf. Without it, Remy felt strangely naked, vulnerable. Gabrielle had never seen him clean-shaven. The absence of the beard might help to deceive her.

And if it didn't? If she guessed who he was, would she seek to betray him? His heart longed to cry out no, that such a thing was utterly impossible. But his head reminded him cruelly of all the other cold facts he had sought to deny about Gabrielle. The bitter truth was he didn't know her at all or what she might be likely to do.

"Monsieur? Captain." Wolf's voice hissed out of the darkness, rousing Remy from his black thoughts.

Wolf beckoned Remy to follow. The lad led Remy farther along the rough track of the old moat, pausing to indicate a window near the corner of the old wing.

"There, Captain," he whispered. "At nine of the clock, Mademoiselle Lysette will signal us with a candle from that window and lower a rope for you. She will lead you as far as the main stair and you will be able to slip down to the ballroom from there."

Remy nodded grimly. It was too late now to be considering the rashness of his actions, but he whispered back to Wolf, "You are sure this maid is to be trusted?"

"Oh, indeed, Captain. Lysette is a good and loyal girl."

"She can't be that loyal. If she is willing to betray her master by helping some stranger enter the palace for a handful of coins."

"Ah, but it was not necessary to pay her anything. She is doing it for me." Wolf's teeth flashed in a broad grin. "When I choose, I have quite a way with the ladies and Lysette, you understand, is a girl with a most romantic nature."

Leaning closer, Wolf confided in a low voice, "I told her you are a poor but honest knight, desperately in love with an heiress whose cruel Papa is doing his best to keep you parted. Lysette believes she is helping you to rendezvous with your lady, so it would be best if you say nothing about your true purpose for being here."

"What a good thing you warned me. While this girl is sneaking me through the palace, I thought I'd confess my plans to help the king of Navarre escape and that I really wouldn't mind slitting a few throats in the process." Remy added in a low growl, "I am not a complete fool, boy."

"I know that, m'sieur. You are a brave and honest man, but—but—ah, please do not be angry with me when I say you are not exactly adept at this sort of intrigue. No offense, m'sieur."

"None taken, lad." Remy reassured him with a light clap to his shoulder. "You are quite right. I am much better at soldiering."

Remy tipped his head to peer ruefully up the night-shrouded walls of the Louvre. "I'd give my soul to be able to mount a proper invasion of this cursed place, rescue my king with cannon and sword."

"Sometimes even the boldest of soldiers must resort to deception, like that story you told me about those old Greeks sneaking into Troy. But instead of a wooden horse, you have a mask and a cape." Wolf tugged at Remy's cloak until the folds settled back over his right shoulder. "Ah, m'sieur. I know you hate the cloak, but you must remember to wear it thus, over one shoulder as all the fashionable gallants do. It makes you look more dashing."

"Like a blasted fop, you mean."

"No, you look like a duke, a grand gentleman. If I had such a fine cape to swagger about in, all the demoiselles of Paris would swoon at my feet."

"When this blasted affair is over, you can have the damned thing."

"Truly, m'sieur?" Wolf exclaimed. Before the lad could express his gratitude in too loud a fashion, Remy clamped his hand firmly over Wolf's mouth.

At that moment, the distant bells of St. Germaine L'Auxerois began to toll out the hour of nine. Remy felt a chill ice through him. It had been the bells of that same church tower that had signaled the beginning of the massacre on St. Bartholomew's Eve.

Remy dropped his hand from Wolf's mouth and swallowed hard, wondering if there would ever come a time when something as innocent as the sound of church bells would not make him want to be violently ill. The hard knot in his stomach didn't ease until the bell stopped tolling. He saw the glow of a candle appear in the window that Wolf had indicated. Remy could make out the silhouette of a girl and his heart sank. If he was not mistaken, his guide upon the rest of this perilous adventure appeared even younger than Wolf.

Wolf cupped his hand to his lips and emitted a few low barks and a soft whine, an eerily accurate imitation of some stray cur. The girl craned her head farther out the window. Perceiving them waiting below in the darkness, she retreated and in another moment Remy saw the thick cord of a rope slowly snaking its way down the wall.

So this was it, then, Remy thought, his mouth going dry. In a few moments, he would be back, entombed within the palace among enemies who believed him dead and rotting in his grave and who would be only too happy to remedy their mistake. Back in the presence of the young king he had failed once and could not afford to fail again.

And back close to the golden-haired woman who had once seemed the best part of his life and was now no more than a cold-hearted stranger to him.

As he tugged free the mask that he'd tucked in his sword belt, Remy was annoyed to feel his palms damp with perspiration. He wiped them on the sides of his breeches, then removed his cap to settle the mask in place. The stiff leather that would shield his identity also hindered his vision, making it all too easy for him to be blindsided.

He was only vaguely aware of Wolf hovering at his elbow as Remy reached out to test the rope. He was relieved to discover that this little Mademoiselle Lysette had been wise enough to anchor it securely and it would bear his weight.

Before Remy could begin his climb, Wolf clutched at his arm. "Monsieur, wait!"

Remy twisted his head to observe Wolf through the slits in his mask. Earlier the lad had been sizzling with excitement, but now Wolf had sobered, his thin, sharp face pale in the moonlight.

"Here, m'sieur," he whispered urgently. "You must take this with you—for protection." He thrust something into Remy's hand.

Remy lifted the object to peer at it more closely. *This* was a small canvas sack containing some sort of dried material and suspended from a leather tie. As Remy drew the pouch too near his nostrils, he grimaced, recoiling at the pungent aroma.

"Damnation! What the devil is this, Martin?"

"A powerful charm, Captain, a special mixture of herbs, dried goat dung and garlic I learned from my Tante Pauline. You wear it suspended over your heart and it will keep you safe."

Remy stifled an impatient groan. "Oh, for the love of heaven, lad—"

"No! No, truly it works. It will ward off witches, m'sieur."

"And everyone else. I need to remain inconspicuous, remember?" Remy shoved the pouch back at him. "I thank you for the thought, Martin, but—"

"Oh, no, please, m'sieur. You must wear it." Wolf sought to close Remy's fingers over the small sack. "To keep you safe from her."

"I assure you that I intend to keep well clear of the Dark Queen."

"No, not *her*. The other one, the sorceress who so bewitched you before, the beautiful Gabrielle."

Remy tensed at the mention of Gabrielle, but he shrugged off Martin's fears. Gabrielle Cheney might endanger his life, betray him to death or imprisonment, but there was one thing he was sure of. She would never weave her enchantment over his heart again.

"No, lad. I don't need this. I am quite impervious to her charms." Remy shoved the small pouch firmly back at Wolf, this time forcing him to take it. "Now you have done your part. Go along with you and wait for me back at the inn."

"But, m'sieur—"

"No arguments, boy. We settled all this before and a good soldier always obeys his captain." Remy gave Wolf's shoulder a bracing squeeze, then a small thrust to send him on his way.

Wolf stumbled back a pace, watching unhappily as Remy started his ascent up the rope, an awkward business for the captain in his slick new suit of clothes, but he managed with his usual strength and dexterity. When Remy had clambered inside the window, he paused long enough to direct one final curt gesture in Wolf's direction.

"Go!" the captain rasped.

Wolf drew farther back into the shadows, waiting until Remy disappeared from view and the window went dark again. Ignoring Remy's orders, he lingered, passing the small pouch restlessly from hand to hand.

The taste of adventure had been sweet in Wolf's mouth up until now, but he was left with nothing but fear for his friend. He would have felt so much better if he could have persuaded Remy to take the amulet. He was *impervious* to Gabrielle's enchantment, the captain had declared. But if that were so why had Remy spent so many of these past nights muttering the witch's name in his dreams?

Sighing, Wolf returned the protective charm to the purse fastened to his dagger belt. He knew what Remy expected him to do. Return to the inn and wait. If Remy had not returned by morning, take what remained of their money and flee to safety.

"And have a good life, lad," Wolf muttered to himself. Remy had not said as much but he knew that was what the captain had meant.

Wolf was glad that Remy was gone and unable to see the mutinous expression settling over his face. A good soldier might obey his captain, but a wolf was not nearly so biddable. He was going nowhere until he saw his captain safely returned.

꙰꙰

THE SALON BLAZED WITH A DIZZYING WHIRL OF COLOR, COURTIERS clad in a brilliant array of silks, satins, and flashing jewels. Pipes, lutes, and tambouras sounded out a lively trill of music. Their faces safely concealed beneath an assortment of masks, the dancers cavorted about the room, smiling and flirting with an air of unrestrained gaiety.

Perhaps because as yet the Dark Queen had not put in an appearance at the evening's festivities. Catherine could produce a marked tension at the most carefree event. Even her son appeared more relaxed in her absence. The king of France lounged upon his throne, the dais surrounded by the throng of perfumed and masked young men, his intimate circle of friends all vying for His Majesty's attention.

But the eyes of most other men were drawn toward a young woman swirling amidst the dancers. Never had Gabrielle Cheney appeared more radiant, her hair swept up into a golden crown on top of her head, her features even more lovely and seductive when partly concealed beneath a silvery half-mask.

Her ivory silk gown was the envy of all the other ladies present. Trimmed with rich embroidery, it flared out over a farthingale, emphasizing Gabrielle's tiny waist, the daringly low décolletage affording a glimpse of her full, firm breasts. A high wired collarette of lace rose up, framing her slender neck like a fairy's wings.

She made a regal, graceful figure as she danced, her delicate hand swallowed up in the grasp of a king. Henry of Navarre promenaded at her side, easily identifiable beneath his mask by his thick curly black hair and satyr-like beard.

As they moved forward and back in the steps of the dance, Navarre's dark eyes glinted at Gabrielle through the slits of his mask, his rapt admiration of her evident for all to see. Gabrielle should have been filled with triumph. Instead she was finding it hard to maintain her bright smiles and Gabrielle knew well who to blame for that. Nicolas Remy. Damn the man. Despite her best efforts he continued to torment her every waking moment. She fought so hard to thrust his image from her mind, but she was sick with fear for him, wondering where he was, what rash action he might be contemplating.

Sometimes Gabrielle felt she had been better off when she had believed him dead. Even the pain of that had been easier to bear than knowing he was somewhere here in Paris, despising her, laying plots that might well get him killed. Nearly a fortnight had passed with no sign of the man and Gabrielle fervently hoped he had abandoned his mad quest to rescue the king. Unfortunately, knowing Remy's infernal sense of duty as well as she did, Gabrielle seriously doubted that.

The sudden pressure of Navarre's hand startled Gabrielle back to her surroundings, made her realize she had stumbled out of position. The steady strength of the king's arm guided her back into the line of the dance.

Henry shot her a quizzical look as he did so, murmuring, "You are very cruel, milady."

"I—I beg your pardon," Gabrielle said, deeply mortified as she struggled to regain the rhythm. "I didn't tread on you, did I?"

"It is far more likely I would step on your toes, ma mie. Great oaf that I am."

Gabrielle cast him a wry smile. Careless Navarre might be concerning his appearance, but he was a good dancer, his muscular limbs treading through the measures with all the grace of a natural athlete.

Hands clasped together, they glided two steps forward, raised up on their toes in perfect unison, then moved two steps back again.

"No, my fairy queen," he continued. "When I said you were cruel, I was complaining about the way your thoughts keep drifting from me. Not to another man, I hope?"

Gabrielle was glad her mask concealed the telltale flush that rose to her cheeks. "Certainly not."

"I am relieved to hear it. I should be devastated to discover I had a rival."

"Who could possibly rival Your Majesty?" Gabrielle replied smoothly.

The intricate weavings of the dance separated them and Gabrielle found herself momentarily partnered with the Chevalier D'Alisard, his hawk-shaped mask doing little to disguise his plump features. His gallantries were as oily as the palm of his hand and Gabrielle felt relieved when the steps of the dance returned her to her original partner.

"So you have figured out who I am," Navarre said, resuming their previous conversation as they circled each other. The king pretended to be chagrined, but it was all part of the game.

To Gabrielle, these masked affairs at court were a bit of a farce. Most of the courtiers here were perfectly well aware of each other's identities, although they furiously pretended otherwise.

Prancing forward and back in tempo with the king's steps, Gabrielle flashed him her most dazzling smile. "Of course, Sire. How could I fail to penetrate your disguise? There is only one Henry."

"You are mistaken, mademoiselle. There are several beside myself. Henry, the handsome duc de Guise, and of course, there is Henry Valois, our noble king of France."

The movement of the dance brought them closer together and Gabrielle murmured, "Perhaps what I should have said is that there is only one Henry of Navarre."

Henry's sensual mouth crooked in a rueful smile. "Only one Navarre, eh? I might take that as a compliment except I know how I am described here at court. The kinglet whose nose is bigger than his kingdom."

Gabrielle slanted him a mischievous glance. "As to that, I could not say, Your Majesty."

"Because you don't find my nose so appallingly large?"

"No, because I have never seen your kingdom to compare."

Another man might have been offended, but Navarre possessed a self-deprecating sense of humor. He flung back his head with a hearty laugh, which caused more than one head to turn in their direction, wondering what Gabrielle had said to so amuse the king.

"Ventre Saint-Gris! What a wicked minx you are, to so tease your poor Navarre," he said in a tone of mock complaint. When the king swore and abandoned his courtly manners, he was at his most engaging. His Bearnais accent grew thicker, reminding Gabrielle of Remy. She had to duck her head to hide the pang that shot through her.

The dance once more obliged them to change partners. Gabrielle cringed when she felt D'Alisard's sweaty hand steal about her waist. The next step called for the man to lift his lady off her feet, swirl her in a circle. Grunting and puffing, D'Alisard barely managed with Gabrielle, nearly dropping her in the process. But at least the clumsy interval gave Gabrielle time to compose herself before she was returned to the king.

Navarre's hand closed possessively over hers as he led her through the next step of the dance. "I called myself '*your* poor Navarre.' Have you nothing to say to that, my lady?"

"I would say that I don't think any king could be described as poor," Gabrielle replied lightly. "I would also wonder if you are truly mine."

"I am and I would show you just how much so, if I ever had the opportunity of being alone with you." As they circled each other, Henry carried her hand lightly to his lips.

Bending closer, he whispered in her ear, "Come to my chamber tonight, Gabrielle, and let me prove to you the full measure of my passion and devotion."

Gabrielle drew back from him, experiencing that cold sick dread that always overtook her when she contemplated going to bed with a man. She would overcome the hollow sensation. She always did, but she wished she might postpone the conquest a little longer. Somehow she did not feel quite ready to yield to Navarre.

But Henry was clearly growing impatient and Gabrielle did not know how much longer she could continue to hold the king at arm's length. She was spared the necessity of immediate reply as the dance separated them again.

Distracted by her thoughts, she scarce noticed her new partner, unconsciously bracing herself to be mauled by D'Alisard again. To her astonishment, she felt her waist seized by a strong arm. She was lifted off her feet and whirled with such force it left her giddy. Her partner plunked her back down again, the impact jarring her off balance.

As she recovered her footing, Gabrielle complained, "By my faith, m'sieur, you scarce know your own strength. The idea is to lift your partner, not toss her like a spear."

"Pardon, milady," he mumbled.

"You should—" The rest of Gabrielle's words faded as she took her first good look at her dancing partner, a tall man with a short cape slung off one shoulder, the dark color of his entire garb rippling blue and black like a storm at sea. Definitely not D'Alisard or any of the other courtiers Gabrielle could readily identify.

She tipped back her head, studying the stranger's features, the lean uncompromising line of his jaw and taut set of his mouth left exposed by his leather mask. He stared back just as intensely, his deep brown eyes piercing her through the slits of his mask, his expression a strange mingling of sorrow and anger.

Remy.

Gabrielle froze, forgetting to move. The other dancers swirling around her became a blur of color like paints on a palette left out in the rain. The music faded, to be replaced by a loud drumming in her ears. For the second time in her life, Gabrielle feared she might be about to faint from shock. But the progression of the dance separated them and her partner disappeared into the circle of dancers.

Somehow she recovered her wits enough to resume her place at Navarre's side. As the king's strong hand steadied her through the next few steps, Henry frowned down at her with concern.

"Are you all right, milady?"

"F-fine, Sire, " Gabrielle lied with a wan attempt at a smile.

"You look pale enough to have seen a ghost."

Navarre's words sent a jolt through Gabrielle, but she did her best to conceal it. Not a ghost, she thought, resisting the strong urge to peer fearfully over her shoulder. Only a phantom of her imagination. Yes, that was it, she sought to convince herself.

The man she had just danced with could not possibly be Nicolas Remy. It was just that she had spent so many of these past days torn between the hope and dread of seeing him again, she was starting to fancy that she did.

As she danced with Navarre, Gabrielle twisted and turned, craning her neck for another look at the man in midnight blue. She caught glimpses of him, but the patterns of the dance frustrated her, preventing her from entirely laying her doubts to rest.

Surely Remy was taller than the leather-masked stranger. Or was he shorter? The stranger's soft-brimmed cap all but covered his hair. Gabrielle's stomach knotted when she fancied she caught a hint of dark gold.

But no, that was only a trick of the candlelight. The stranger likely had brunette hair and he was clean-shaven. Remy never went without a beard. Not that Gabrielle was such a half-wit as to suppose Remy unacquainted with the use of a razor. But shaving was one thing, she argued. Remy had appeared on the brink of poverty only a few weeks ago. Where on earth would a fugitive soldier have gotten the funds to outfit himself in such costly attire? How would he have ever managed to gain admittance to the court? And surely not even the great Scourge would be reckless enough to venture here, unprotected in the midst of so many enemies.

Tormented by her doubts, Gabrielle scarce responded to the words the king murmured in her ear, continuing to urge her to join him in his apartments at midnight. Gabrielle returned some vague promise as she waited with mounting dread and impatience for the dance to bring her back into the stranger's presence again.

When she at last did come face-to-face with the man in midnight blue, Gabrielle managed to greet him more calmly this time, although her heart was pounding harder than the tambouras. She placed her palm against his and they slowly circled each other, completely out of tempo with the music.

It was as though they danced to a rhythm only they could hear, Gabrielle thought. His skin was warm against hers, his palm rough and callused. Not like the silken hand of a courtier at all, but more like a soldier's . . . more like Remy's hand.

Gabrielle felt a tremor course through her and she was afraid to meet his gaze, but she forced herself to do so. His eyes did not appear as hard and angry as before, but he still stared at her with an intensity that caused her pulse to race, those dark velvet depths so like Remy's.

A mask did something to a person's eyes, rendered their expression more mysterious and dangerous. Was this man Nicolas Remy or wasn't he? She would know in a heartbeat if only she could force him to speak. As she moved warily around him in the steps of the dance, Gabrielle murmured, "Monsieur is an excellent dancer."

He acknowledged her compliment with no more than a stiff nod of his head. Moistening her lips, Gabrielle tried again.

"Monsieur seems very familiar to me. Do I know you?"

His only reply was a slight shrug of his shoulders, filling Gabrielle with a mounting sense of frustration. They would be parted soon by the steps of the dance and she could not endure the suspense any longer.

Throwing caution to the wind, she leaned in closer and pleaded, "For mercy's sake, monsieur, who are you? Oh, please, Remy, never tell me it is you."

"Very well. I won't," he said in her ear, the voice unmistakably Remy's.

"Oh, God." Gabrielle stumbled, her hand tightening convulsively on his. She stole a wild glance around her, terrified that someone might have overheard or realized what she had. That the Scourge had returned and was here in their midst.

"Have a care, Gabrielle," Remy murmured. "You almost stepped on my foot."

"Step on your foot," Gabrielle hissed back. "I'd like to—to step on your great thick head. Are you completely insane to come here?"

"Undoubtedly," was his cool reply.

Gabrielle glared up at him, uncertain what she longed to do most. Give him a swift clout to the ears or drag him to the safety of the nearest exit. But before she could think what to say or do next, the music stopped. Not as though the dance had reached its natural conclusion, but abruptly, the lilt of the violins replaced with the sudden hum of voices.

Clutching Remy's hand, Gabrielle was too caught up in her own tangle of emotions to notice at first what was happening. But realizing that everyone else in the salon was sinking into curtsies or bowing, she turned around and her blood ran cold.

With her usual impeccable timing, the Dark Queen had finally arrived.

Chapter Nine

GABRIELLE'S HEART CONSTRICTED WITH DREAD AS CATHERINE de Medici made her entrance into the salon. The queen mother stole upon the masqueraders like a falling shadow, her black gown in sharp contrast to the brilliant array of silks and sparkling jewels. She had adopted the hue of mourning upon the death of her husband years ago and never seen fit to abandon it. She looked deceptively matronly in her somber garb, her silvery hair confined beneath a peaked cap, a modest white ruff encircling her plump throat. Her only adornment was the jeweled cross that dangled over her ample bosom.

She had not bothered to don a mask for the evening's festivities, but she didn't need one. Her face was a smooth, white mask in itself, seldom giving away any of the Dark Queen's emotions, her dark de Medici eyes far more likely to pierce the secrets of another than reveal her own.

Gabrielle had always succeeded in blocking her thoughts

from Catherine. After she had believed Remy dead, Gabrielle's
hatred for the Dark Queen had burned inside her like molten
steel, but over time, before she had ever ventured to court,
Gabrielle had learned to temper her anger into something colder,
more patient, more calculating, as impenetrable as armor.

Unfortunately Remy possessed no such armor. Like everyone else in the salon, his attention had riveted on Catherine, his
jaw clenched to such a hard angle, Gabrielle was astonished that
the bone did not snap, his loathing so palpable even a child could
have discerned it. One look into his eyes and Catherine with her
uncanny perception could not fail to guess his identity.

The courtiers fell back respectfully to clear a path for the
Dark Queen toward the dais where her son awaited her, a sullen
expression on the king's face. Gabrielle seized Remy by the arm
and dragged him behind one of the salon's tall pillars.

"Remy, you have to get out of here. *Now*," she urged him in
a low voice.

Remy whipped his arm away from her. "I am sure you would
like nothing better than for me to cut and run so you can continue
seducing my king. Regrettably I cannot oblige you, milady. I am
not going anywhere until I have accomplished what I came for."

"And what is that? To get yourself killed?"

"You know perfectly well why I am here. To speak to
Navarre."

"You won't have much to say if you're dead."

"Is that a threat?" His eyes glinted at her through his mask,
cold and hard with mistrust . . . the Scourge's eyes. Gabrielle
could tell what he was thinking, that all she wanted to do was
keep him away from Navarre.

Stepping closer, she snapped, "No, consider it a warning. I
am trying to save your life."

Remy's lips thinned, making it clear he did not believe her.
Gabrielle's gaze cut anxiously toward the Dark Queen, each step
bringing her closer to the spot where Gabrielle argued with Remy.

In pure desperation, Gabrielle whipped off her mask, hoping that somehow the sight of her face might convince him of her sincerity.

"Please, Remy—" Gabrielle began, then lowered her voice for fear of being overheard. "You have got to disappear before Catherine notices you. She reads eyes as well as most people crack open a book. It is an old sorceress's trick and she is diabolically good at it. Have you forgotten what she is?"

"I have forgotten nothing about that cursed witch. But tonight may be the only chance I have to communicate with my king. The Dark Queen believes me dead and I am masked the same as the rest of these fops. Odds are she won't notice me unless *you* decide to betray me."

Remy leveled a hard challenging look at her. Could Remy truly believe she would be capable of such a thing? Had his opinion of her really sunk that low? Apparently it had. A mingling of hurt and anger brought a flush to Gabrielle's cheeks.

"Me? Why—you—you pigheaded fool. You betray yourself with every word, every gesture—"

"Mistress Cheney."

Gabrielle broke off as she heard herself being summoned in accents that were all too icily familiar. Her heart dropped to the pit of her stomach as she realized the courtiers surrounding her and Remy had thinned away. It was far too late for him to fade into the background or slip out the salon doors.

The Dark Queen stood but yards away, subjecting them both to her piercing stare. Gabrielle froze, momentarily seized by a sensation of panic. But she fought to quell it. Casting one final warning glare up at Remy, Gabrielle surged forward to intercept Catherine before she could draw any closer.

Gabrielle sank into a deep curtsy, spreading her skirts wide as though that would somehow serve to shield the man who towered behind her. Her heart was hammering so hard, she feared that the queen must hear it. Desperately Gabrielle sought to calm herself. When it came to scenting fear, Catherine possessed all the instincts of a jackal.

She touched Gabrielle's shoulder lightly. "Please rise, mademoiselle."

Gabrielle straightened, keeping her eyes fixed on the floor. But she realized that that would only serve to rouse Catherine's suspicions. Gabrielle lifted her head, forcing herself to meet the Dark Queen's stare with her customary boldness.

Catherine caught hold of Gabrielle's chin, her dark gaze probing Gabrielle's mercilessly. Gabrielle stared back, scarce breathing, willing her mind into a smooth, impenetrable shield.

At long last, Catherine released her with a wintry smile. "Why, my dear Gabrielle, it is nowhere near time for the unmasking and yet you have removed yours."

"It was chafing me." Gabrielle smiled back just as falsely. "Your Grace must have suffered from the same complaint. You are not wearing yours either."

"As I am sure you are well aware, child, I consider myself too old for the lighthearted folly of such masquerading."

"What a pity. Since I am certain Your Majesty would be very skilled at it."

"No more skilled than you, my dear," Catherine shot back.

Gabrielle often fiercely enjoyed her battles of wits with the Dark Queen, but never before had she had so much to conceal. Gabrielle longed to steal a glance back toward Remy, see how he was faring, but she did not dare. Fighting to conceal her nervousness, Gabrielle unfurled her fan and waved it languidly before her face.

"So tell me, child. Are you enjoying yourself this evening?" Catherine purred.

"Oh, immensely, Your Grace."

"Truly? I thought you seemed a trifle distressed. You look so pale."

"It—it is only the heat." Gabrielle fanned herself more vigorously. "It is devilishly warm here in the salon."

"Oh, yes, *devilishly*. You should take great care." Catherine's eyes narrowed slyly. "All that vigorous dancing you were doing earlier. It cannot be good for you."

Gabrielle started in spite of herself. So Catherine had been spying on Gabrielle all evening and she was at great pains to let Gabrielle know it, no doubt hoping to rattle her. Catherine was doing a remarkably good job of it too, Gabrielle thought grimly. She wanted to make some sort of clever reply, but her mouth had gone dry.

With an expression of mock concern, the queen patted Gabrielle's cheek. "Clearly you have overexerted yourself. But I understand the temptation. So many charming men . . . my son-in-law Navarre, the Chevalier d'Alisard, and then, that dashing young gallant in the midnight-blue cloak."

Gabrielle thought her heart would stop entirely as the queen made reference to Remy. Her fingers trembled and she nearly dropped her fan.

"Now where has he got to?" Catherine feigned a sweeping search of the ballroom. "Ah, yes, there he is."

As Catherine honed in on a point just past Gabrielle's shoulder, Gabrielle felt as though her corset strings had tightened to the point where she could scarce breathe. She wished that Remy had used the interval of her conversation with Catherine to make good his escape. But of course he hadn't.

He remained rooted beneath the pillar like an obstinate general determined to hold his position on the battlefield at all costs. When Catherine craned her neck in his direction, at least Remy had the wit to swallow his hatred and accord her a stiff bow.

Catherine frowned slightly, tapping her chin. "How strange. I would have thought I could recognize anyone at court, masked or not. But I confess I find this gentleman most mysterious."

"No!" Gabrielle cried.

When Catherine regarded her with brows upraised in surprise, Gabrielle made haste to recover herself.

"I—I mean no," she said in a more moderate tone. "There is nothing in the least mysterious about him. Surely Your Grace recognizes him."

"No, I don't. Who is he?"

Gabrielle felt a bead of sweat trickle down her neck. Fluttering her fan, she essayed a laugh. "Why—why, he is the Marquis de Lanfort, Your Grace."

It was the most reckless gamble Gabrielle had ever taken. She did not even know if de Lanfort was present this evening. From a distance, Remy could easily pass for the young marquis, but if Catherine were to beckon Remy closer . . .

Gabrielle held her breath as Catherine studied Remy for what seemed an interminable length of time. At long last, Catherine murmured, "Oh, yes. Of course, de Lanfort."

With a dismissive nod toward Gabrielle, the Dark Queen continued her progress down the length of the salon. Gabrielle sank into another respectful curtsy at Catherine's departure, but this time she felt her knees tremble.

Had she managed to deceive Catherine? Gabrielle believed so, but with the Dark Queen who could ever tell? Gabrielle was only certain of one thing. She would not know a moment's peace until she got Nicolas Remy out of the palace tonight. Even if she had to club the obstinate fool over the head to do it.

※※※

THE MUSIC HAD RECOMMENCED, THE DANCERS CAVORTING ABOUT the floor. The king lolled back on his throne, braying with laughter at something one of his painted *mignons* said to him. Hovering near her son on the dais, Catherine suppressed her irritation. She was fond of Henry in her own way, fonder than she had ever been of any of her other children. His effeminate mannerisms and his foppish friends often vexed her, but she had more pressing matters to occupy her tonight.

Beyond the whirl of dancers, far across the salon, Catherine could just make out a lovely golden-haired woman disappearing out the door with a man in a midnight cloak.

Catherine vented a wearied sigh. Gabrielle Cheney. Blast the girl. She was definitely up to something and for once it had nothing to do with Gabrielle's determined pursuit of the king of Navarre.

For perhaps the hundredth time, Catherine questioned her own wisdom in allowing Gabrielle's presence at court. The wise women of Faire Isle had never been allies of the Dark Queen and even less so since that affair of the gloves. Catherine had reached a truce with the Cheney sisters, but it was an uneasy one.

Catherine believed it best to keep one's enemies in close view. However, that was not the only reason she tolerated Gabrielle. The girl was not like her late mother, the saintly Evangeline, or like the present Lady of Faire Isle, the gentle and honorable Ariane. Gabrielle was cunning, ruthless, and ambitious . . . more like Catherine herself. Catherine often wished her own daughter Margot was like Gabrielle instead of the foolish romantic chit Margot was, all passion and impulse. Gabrielle Cheney would never lose her head over any man. The young woman intrigued her. But there could be such a thing as too much intrigue, Catherine thought wryly. Even for one who enjoyed it as much as she.

Slipping down from the dais, Catherine snapped her fingers, summoning to her a gaunt older man with thinning hair and straggling beard. The only other person present at the ball beside herself who was not masked. Bartolomy Verducci was seldom to be found far from Catherine's side.

When asked to define his position in her household, Catherine vaguely spoke of Verducci as her secretary, although she realized no one was fooled. The courtiers referred to him in less flattering terms, spy, informer, dogsbody. Gabrielle had even been heard to mockingly call him "the Dark Queen's whippet."

An apt description, Catherine thought, as Bartolomy slunk toward her, bowing slavishly over her hand. She cut his servile demonstrations short by seizing hold of his ruff and yanking him close so no one else could overhear her words.

"I thought that I had instructed you to keep close watch over Mademoiselle Cheney this evening, *signore.*"

"And—and so I have, Your Grace."

"Then why did you just permit her to slip out the door unobserved? Why didn't you follow her?"

"Well, I—I—" Bartolomy nervously licked his lips. "It is just that I thought—"

"I don't require you to think, sirrah. Just follow my orders. I have made that clear on any number of occasions."

The little man waxed pale. "Y-yes, Your Grace. But you instructed me to observe her behavior with the king of Navarre. Since Mistress Cheney left the chamber with someone else, I saw no harm in letting her go. After all, she is only stealing off for a tryst with her young lover, the Marquis de Lanfort."

"Is she indeed?" With a scathing glare, Catherine released Bartolomy. "How very odd, considering I myself witnessed the marquis fall from his horse this morning and sprain his ankle. Unless my lord has made an astonishing recovery, that man with Mistress Cheney is not de Lanfort."

Signore Verducci's jaw sagged open, his eyes threatening to pop from his head.

"Don't stand there gaping at me like a fresh-caught trout," Catherine snarled. Placing her palm against his scrawny chest, she gave him a rough shove. "Go after Mademoiselle Cheney, you fool and find out what the devil she is up to."

※※※

THE MUSIC AND LAUGHTER FROM THE SALON FADED IN THE DISTANCE as Gabrielle tugged at Remy's hand, urging him across the palace grounds. She risked a desperate glance back toward the steps of the Louvre, half-fearing to find Catherine poised there, like the witch that she was, her dark gaze pursuing them into the night.

But there was no one there and the masquerade continued, the silhouettes of the dancers flickering past the salon windows. No sudden hue and cry, no summoning of the guards, nothing to disturb the peaceful silence of the night except the rustling of the trees, the distant burble of a fountain, and the thudding of Gabrielle's own heart.

She was fairly running across the lawn in her anxiety for Remy's escape. Remy's longer stride matched hers easily, his features inscrutable behind his black leather mask. He had acceded to her demand that he follow her from the salon, far too easily given the man's obstinate pride and reckless courage.

Gabrielle clutched tightly at his hand, fearing that at any moment he might change his mind and seek to go back. The Tuileries loomed in the distance, the skeletal outline etched against the moonlit sky. Catherine's new palace, designed after the Florentine fashion, was as yet incomplete, only the maze, gardens, and grotto finished, quiet and deserted at this time of night.

If she could just get Remy that far, persuade him to keep going, he could make his way back to the city from there. Then she could breathe easier. Then she would know he would be safe—at least for the moment. But to her dismay, Remy balked, his grip tightening on her hand, wrenching her to an abrupt halt.

"No! You mustn't stop—"

Remy clamped his hand over her mouth, smothering her protest. "Careful," he growled in her ear. "Look."

Gabrielle turned in the direction he indicated, her heart going still. Moonlight glinted off the helmets of two of the palace sentries, making their rounds. Remy's clothes might blend well with the night, but in her ivory gown, she stood out like a fairy fluttering through the gardens.

It was obvious they had already been spotted, one of the guards gesticulating to the other. Both men veered off the path, marching in their direction. She would be recognized at once, but if they challenged Remy, obliged him to remove his mask and identify himself, it would be all over for him.

Gabrielle froze in momentary panic, wondering if they should flee back toward the palace or attempt to disappear into the shrubbery. Before she could decide, Remy seized her into his arms. Dragging her beneath the shelter of a towering oak tree, his mouth descended upon hers in a ruthless kiss.

Gabrielle's eyes flew wide in astonishment until it occurred to her what he was doing, pretending they were lovers, merely out for a tryst beneath the moonlight. She wrapped her arms reluctantly around him.

As accomplished as she'd become as a courtesan, she had never truly liked kissing. The mingling of lips, breath, and tongues was far too intimate, demanding that she offer more of herself beyond the mere empty pleasure of her body.

Remy's kiss was definitely asking far too much. His lips gave her no quarter, his fierce heat touching too near her own suppressed desires. Gabrielle tried to remain detached, to remember this was only a performance, to keep a wary lookout for the guards.

But her eyes fluttered closed in spite of herself as she sank deeper into Remy's embrace. His tongue teased the seal of her lips and with a soft, quivering sigh, she parted for him, allowing him greater access to the sensitive hollows of her mouth, to invade her with hot thrusts that melted her bones and turned her blood to fire.

This was far different from the frantic joy of their kiss on the night she'd realized Remy was still alive. This was an embrace born of heat, passion, and danger, perhaps the greatest peril the way her body responded to his. A soft moan escaped Gabrielle. Heedless of the damage to her gown and farthingale, she crushed herself against Remy, desperate to get as close to him as possible.

His hands moved away from her waist, roving over her back, stroking up her side, tantalizingly near the curve of her breast. She could feel the heat of his hands even through her gown and her nipples tightened in aching response. She buried her fingers in the silky hair at the nape of his neck, forgetting all sense of danger, forgetting everything but Remy, the feel, the touch, the taste of him.

She felt flushed, giddy, recklessly drunk on his kiss and wondered how it was possible. To feel as though she were about to erupt into flames and yet so safe in a man's arms all at the same time. When he drew his mouth away from hers, she sighed in protest. She quivered, struggling to regain her bearings, dimly aware that the guards had passed on by, their sniggering laughter echoing to silence as they disappeared.

Gabrielle wondered if Remy had even noticed they were gone. His eyes were dark and liquid behind his mask. There was no reason for him to continue to hold her so close. Yet he made no move to release her and Gabrielle did not attempt to draw away either. It was as though they were held fast by some strange bewitchment, some dark enchantment of the night and moon, their hearts pounding in unison.

Gabrielle was the first to recover her wits, pulling away from him. Remy let her go with some reluctance, she thought, but who could tell with most of his face hidden behind that damned mask? Gabrielle regretted ever having discarded her own. Without it, she felt far too vulnerable, stripped naked beneath Remy's impenetrable gaze.

Embarrassed that her face was suffused with heat, she pressed her hands to her cheeks in an effort to cool them. Good lord, she was supposed to be a woman of some sophistication, not the sort of silly girl who would blush and tremble in a man's arms merely because he'd kissed her.

Gabrielle smoothed back her hair, straightened her collarette, struggling to recover her customary élan. "Well!" she said as soon as she could trust herself to speak. "That—that was quite a performance, Captain Remy. Your acting is much improved."

"I'm learning," he replied. He leaned up against the tree, folding his arms and watching her, looking so blasted calm it irritated her. As though it was nothing to him to risk being caught by the Dark Queen, to narrowly avoid the guards . . . to kiss nearly senseless a woman he regarded as an enemy.

She was suddenly conscious of how quiet and deserted it was here in this part of the grounds, so far from the main palace, the moonlight barely touching where they stood beneath the tree. Never had Gabrielle ever imagined she would become flustered at finding herself alone in the dark with Remy.

Her hand fluttered toward her throat. "The danger of discovery appears to be over, but it is unwise for you to linger here. You should go and—and I need to return to the salon before I am missed."

But when she gathered up her skirts, preparing to sweep past him, Remy uncoiled away from the tree. His hand shot out to grasp her wrist.

"Not just yet. I want to talk to you first."

Talk to her? Gabrielle gaped at him incredulously. The man truly was mad.

"Your pardon, Captain," she said with some asperity. "But this hardly strikes me as the best moment for a chat. I believe we have said all there is to say to one another."

"This won't take long." Remy drew her nearer, his cloak falling between them like a shadow. The fashionable habit of wearing a cape slung off one shoulder gave many of the courtiers a dandified look. But it had a far different effect on Remy, drawing attention to his broad shoulders, a feeling of power barely leashed in his hard, masculine frame. His eyes were no more than dangerous glints through the slits of his mask, but the shiver that coursed through Gabrielle had nothing to do with apprehension.

"Just one question, milady," he said. "Why did you do it?"

"Do what?" she faltered, wondering what he meant to accuse her of now.

"Why did you lie to the Dark Queen, tell her that I was your lover, that de—de Lanfort?"

"*Former* lover," Gabrielle said with a haughty lift of her brows, although she scarce knew why it felt so important for her to correct him. "What would you rather I had told her? Oh, that is only Nicolas Remy, Your Grace. Remember him? The one you used to fondly call the Scourge."

"I would rather you had stayed out of it and let me take my chances," Remy snapped. For the first time Gabrielle realized that far from being grateful for her intervention, Remy was annoyed with her, even a little angry.

"It certainly was not to your advantage to become involved."

"You hardly need to tell me that." Gabrielle grimaced. Even now Navarre was probably back in the salon, looking for her. If the king had noticed her stealing off with another man, she was going to have some clever explaining to do.

As though he'd been able to read her thoughts, Remy's jaw tightened. "So what the blazes did you do it for, then? Why did you protect me?"

"What does it matter why?" She tried to squirm away from him, but Remy's grip on her wrist only tightened.

"It matters to me." When she attempted to avoid his eyes, Remy seized hold of her chin, forcing her gaze back to meet his own. "You claim to be so determined to seduce my king. It would surely have been more in your interest to have me out of the way. So why were you at such pains to save me?"

With a hard yank, Gabrielle managed to free herself. Backing away, she rubbed her bruised wrist and glared at him. "Considering that I am the only one who knows who you are, it would also be in your interest to be rid of me. Perhaps that's why you really accompanied me out here. To strangle me and dump me in the bushes."

"Don't be so bloody ridiculous. No matter how much you infuriate me, you know damned well that I could never hurt you."

"Then you should know equally well that I could never betray you!"

But he clearly didn't or he wouldn't feel the need to ask her such questions.

"Oh, I see how it is," she said bitterly. "You are the great hero, positively stuffed with honor. But I am only a lowly harlot, capable of any base thing."

"I never called you that."

"You didn't have to. Your contempt for me is obvious." Gabrielle was horrified to feel a lump rise in her throat. Before he could see just how badly he'd wounded her with his doubts, she tried to dart past him. But Remy was too quick for her, stepping into her path, his hard muscled frame an impassable barrier.

"I express no contempt," he said. "But I *will* have an answer to my question."

He clearly did not mean to let her go until he had one. Remy's hands closed over her shoulders not roughly, but holding her fast all the same. There was no escaping him, short of engaging in an undignified and probably futile struggle.

"Why did you protect me, Gabrielle?" he persisted. *"Why?"*

"Because . . ." she began.

Because she still cared about him far too much, an inconvenient emotion for a woman who was determined to feel nothing but cold ambition. Gabrielle swallowed hard, glaring helplessly up at him.

"Damn you, Nicolas Remy. You never plagued me with such questions on Faire Isle. You never worried why I protected you from the Dark Queen then."

"I am fully aware of what you did for me that summer, but so much has changed since then. *You* have changed."

"No, I haven't," Gabrielle muttered. "Obviously I am as big a fool where you are concerned as I ever was."

Remy's grip on her gentled, his voice softening as he said, "I am sorry, Gabrielle. But you can hardly blame me for being confused. I find you so altered, so different from the girl I remembered. You are like a stranger to me now."

"You are a fine one to talk about strangers." Gabrielle said. "The Nicolas Remy I knew would never have been such a bully. Holding me prisoner, interrogating me, hiding behind that damned mask like a public executioner."

Remy responded by whipping off his feathered cap. As his fingers moved toward the strings of his mask, Gabrielle was horrified by what she had goaded him into. She cut a frantic glance around her, the shadows of the trees, the shrubbery taking on a sinister aspect, alive with eyes eager to see, to report back to the Dark Queen.

"No, don't—" she cried, but Remy's mask had already fallen away.

A shaft of moonlight picked out the glints of gold in his dark hair and played over his profile. The finely chiseled bones of his cheekbones stood out prominently, the sensitive curve of his mouth starkly defined. His jaw was sculpted on hard, bold lines somewhat softened by the faint indentation in his chin. No longer hidden behind his beard, his features appeared at once stronger and strangely more vulnerable.

Gabrielle forgot her hurt, forgot her anger. She scarce remembered to breathe. She drifted closer, her fingers tingling with the old urge to capture such indescribable masculine beauty on canvas, her heart despairing over the magic that was lost to her. She stroked Remy's face, her fingers sculpting that near-perfect bone structure, the smooth, warm texture of his skin, the faint hint of roughness from the banished beard threatening to reassert its dominance.

Remy's eyes widened at her touch. He made no move to stop her exploration, but he looked self-conscious beneath her avid stare.

"My God," she murmured.

"What?" he asked anxiously.

"You are beautiful. That is what."

Gabrielle could not be certain in the semidarkness, but she thought the man actually blushed. Remy caught her hand and removed it from his face, but he made no move to release her, his fingers engulfing hers.

His lips twitched into a reluctant grin. Remy's own particular sweet smile, the one Gabrielle had never expected him to bestow on her again. Gabrielle smiled tremulously back at him, her heart aching with the realization that this could be no more than a temporary truce between them, his smile all the more precious because of that.

He raised her hand lightly to his lips. "Er—I thank you for your compliments, milady. But beautiful was not exactly the look I was striving for tonight."

"And what were you striving for, idiot?" Gabrielle teased to cover the rush of tender emotion that surged through her.

"I was just trying to pass myself off as a nobleman, one of these court fops. I fear I never was much good at play-acting." Remy's mouth twisted ruefully. "So exactly what was it that gave me away to you?"

His eyes. The sound of his voice. The feel of his hand.

"Oh, nothing in particular," she lied. "Everyone here knows everyone else, even when disguised. You were bound to stand out. A masquerade at court is just another pretense, an intrigue, a game."

"And you enjoy all this intrigue? Are you truly happy in this new life of yours?"

Gabrielle started at his question. Remy had acquired a bad habit of asking the most damned uncomfortable things. Was she happy? That was something she had never taken time to think about in her quest for power. She didn't *want* to think about it.

She shrugged. "Of course, I'm happy. Paris, the court, this is my world now."

Remy shook his head as though he could not quite accept

that. "It's a very treacherous world, Gabrielle, and dangerous. When I watched you with the Dark Queen, it made my skin crawl. I wanted to snatch you away from her."

"You needn't worry for me. I know how to deal with Catherine."

"But why would you want to? How can you endure being near that evil woman day after day, forced to curtsy to her, trading false smiles?"

Gabrielle had wondered the same thing many times herself. She replied hesitantly, "Perhaps because I—I have grown to understand her better whether I wished to or not."

"*Understand* her? She once set witch-hunters after you, tried to destroy your entire family."

"No woman is born cold and ruthless, not even Catherine. She was no doubt as young and innocent as any girl once. Perhaps she even believed in fairy stories until she discovered there were far more dragons than knights in the world. Fiery monsters to reduce your dreams to ashes, to scorch you with betrayal until you wither and die or let your heart be forged into steel. I imagine that Catherine also knows what it is like to be hurt and humiliated by someone she loved, made to feel weak and powerless."

"Also?" Remy frowned, giving her an odd measuring look.

Gabrielle stiffened. She didn't know what had impelled her to defend Catherine. Perhaps because in so doing she was also defending herself. She was straying dangerously near the ugly wounds on her soul she had kept hidden for so long.

"Yes, also—like—like many another woman foolish enough to trust her heart to a man."

"Something you've never done?" Remy asked softly.

"No! Never," Gabrielle denied. Rather too fiercely she realized. She withdrew her hand from Remy's grasp and retreated deeper into the shadows beneath the trees.

To her dismay, Remy followed her, his hands lightly caressing her shoulders.

"Gabrielle?" The tenderness in his voice made Gabrielle fear he had glimpsed too much in her face during those few un-guarded moments.

She stiffened beneath his touch, saying with a forced bright-ness. "How reckless we both are being. It is hardly wise for you to linger on here, or me either. Navarre will be wondering what has become of me. I had to promise him practically every dance this evening. He is growing so possessive of me, His Grace would not have it otherwise."

Remy's hands stilled. For a fleeting moment, she could feel the warmth of his breath stirring her hair. Then his hands fell away from her.

"Yes, Navarre," he repeated, his voice a strange blend of grim resolve and regret.

The mention of the king had put the distance back between them. She felt bereft as Remy stepped back from her, but she rallied, drawing herself up briskly.

"I really must return to the salon."

"And so must I."

"What!" Gabrielle exclaimed, praying she had misunder-stood him, but he was already drawing forth the mask he had tucked into his belt.

"You didn't betray me. You actually provided me with an identity, so I do have to risk going back there."

"Remy! No!"

To her horror, he began to fasten the mask back in place.

"You *are* insane." She ripped the mask out of his hands. "I have never seen a man so determined to get himself killed."

"Gabrielle," Remy said, his voice part plea, part warning. "Give me that."

"No!" Gabrielle whipped the mask behind her back, stum-bling away from him. "What was the point in my protecting you if you are only going to march right back into the witch's lair again?"

Remy stalked after her. "It isn't that I am not grateful for what you did—"

"I don't want your gratitude. I just want you to go away."

He cornered her against the tree, his arms reaching around her for the mask. Gabrielle crushed it desperately between her fingers.

"Oh, Remy, please. You can't—"

"I have to. Now that I have seen my king in this cursed place, I am more determined than ever to have him out of here."

"It is not as though anyone is torturing him."

"No, they are doing something far worse. They are stealing his soul. What little I saw of him tonight, I could tell how he is being seduced by this place, by—"

By *you.* Remy did not come out and say it, but she could read the accusation in his eyes as he sought to wrench the mask away from her, his sinewy frame bearing hard against her. "Navarre is losing all sense of who he is, becoming just another of these court fools, a prancing puppet dancing to the Dark Queen's tune. I see how he is mocked on all sides."

"It won't always be this way for him," Gabrielle pleaded, despairing as she felt Remy's fingers prying loose her grip on the mask. "I know you don't believe in augury, but Navarre is destined to be king of France one day. I swear it's true."

"With you as his mistress?" Remy's lips thinned. "I am sorry, Gabrielle, but he is already a king. The king of Navarre. His people have borne with enough persecution and hardship. They have been left leaderless for three years. He needs to return to his own country and I intend to make sure he does."

With a final tug, Remy yanked the mask from her grasp and levered himself away from her. Gabrielle recognized that obstinate set of his jaw all too well. She stamped her foot with sheer frustration while her heart squeezed tight with fear for him. He truly did intend to charge straight back into the salon. Unless Gabrielle threatened to expose him or render him unconscious, there was no way she was going to stop him.

Except there was a third option.

Gabrielle fretted her lower lip as she considered it, the idea not without a certain amount of risk, to Remy and to Navarre, to say nothing of herself. But blast the man. Even now he was fitting his mask back into place. He left her little other choice.

"All right. All right," she cried. "I will help you."

"What?" Remy had the mask partially fastened, but he shoved it up to frown at her.

"If you will be so cursed stubborn, so insistent upon pursuing this reckless course, it would be better if you waited here until the ball is over." Gabrielle fetched a deep sigh. "I will speak to Navarre and arrange for you to meet him privately in his chambers."

Remy looked thunderstruck by her proposal. He slowly stripped off his mask as though he was actually considering it, then shook his head. "No, it would be far too dangerous, especially for you."

"Dangerous!" She shot him a look of pure exasperation. "No, *dangerous* is that little dance we were doing back in the salon with the Dark Queen. Compared to that, smuggling you up to Navarre's apartments will be child's play. Besides, you were willing enough for me to slip him a note before."

"A note is one thing. But what you are proposing—" Remy raked his hand back through his hair. "How could you possibly bring it off? More importantly, *why* would you? It would hardly be—"

"Yes, I know," Gabrielle interrupted him with a grimace. "It would hardly be in my interest. Let us just say that I will do it because you'll keep turning up at odd moments, giving me heart seizures. Besides, I have faith in Navarre's judgment. I think he is too wise to go along with any reckless schemes you might propose. He would far prefer to remain safely in Paris."

"With you?" A troubled look sifted across Remy's face. "You are that sure of your hold over him?"

Gabrielle was sure of nothing except that she had endured Remy's death once. She was not certain she could survive it again.

"I am willing to take my chances," she said. "But if I agree to help you, there are two conditions."

"Such as?" Remy asked her with a wary quirk of one brow.

"You will put your proposal to Navarre. Escape with you or remain in Paris with me. But whatever His Grace wants, you'll abide by. No further attempts at persuasion, no more reckless attempts to see him. Agreed?"

Remy frowned as he paused to consider her terms.

"Agreed," he said at last. "And your other condition?"

"That you stop plaguing me with so many damned irritating questions."

A wry laugh escaped Remy, but he nodded, holding out his hand to seal the bargain. But as his fingers closed over hers, an odd change came over him. He stared fixedly at some point past her shoulder.

His hand tightened on hers. Although his features remained impassive, she could feel the tension thrumming through him as he leaned toward her.

"Take care," he whispered, his mouth warm against her ear, sending a shiver through her. "We are being watched. Someone is hiding in the bushes behind you."

Gabrielle's pulse lurched. It was all she could do not to react, steal an alarmed glance over her shoulder. Before she could even think what to do, Remy's hand eased between them. Nudging his cape aside, his fingers inched toward the jeweled hilt of a poniard fastened at his belt.

The look that crept into his eyes was one Gabrielle had seldom seen. Cold, hard, somehow more frightening than the prospect of the spy lurking in the bushes. It was the Scourge and not Nicolas Remy who eased the weapon from its sheath, coolly preparing to slit a man's throat.

He backed away from Gabrielle, looking so deadly calm as he bowed, saying in a loud clear voice. "I give you good night, mademoiselle."

Then he whirled about so fast, Gabrielle scarce had time to

draw breath. Darting behind the shrubbery, he pounced on whoever lurked there. An alarmed cry rang out as Remy raised his knife.

Gabrielle pressed her hands to her mouth, not wanting to see, yet unable to look away. At the last possible moment, Remy froze, moonlight glinting off the blade. Then he swore roundly, sheathing the weapon again.

Reaching down, he collared the intruder and dragged him out from behind the bushes. Her heart still thudding from her fright, Gabrielle blinked in surprise. The person that Remy grasped by the neck of his tunic certainly didn't look like anyone the Dark Queen would employ as a spy.

He was no more than a boy, with a tangled mass of dark hair and blade-sharp features. Anyone else would have been cowed by the murderous glance Remy darted his way. Although the boy did appear abashed at being caught, he nonetheless had the impudence to offer Remy a weak smile.

"Good evening, Monsieur le Capitaine."

Gabrielle averted her gaze from the boy to stare questioningly at Remy. "You know this person?"

"Yes, I am afraid I do." Remy shot the boy another dark scowl, then thrust him toward Gabrielle. "Mademoiselle Cheney, allow me to present my Wolf."

Gabrielle was rather bemused to see that the boy appeared far more terrified of her than of Remy. He made a tremulous sign of the cross, clutching at something hidden beneath his tunic, something that smelled truly foul. She wrinkled her nose in distaste.

As Remy cuffed Wolf lightly on the back of the head, obliging him to make his bow to Gabrielle, none of them noticed the other figure slipping out from behind a tree. A gray ghost of a man stealing toward the palace to make his report to the Dark Queen.

Chapter Ten

REMY FOLLOWED GABRIELLE ALONG A BACK CORRIDOR OF THE palace, a sullen Wolf trailing behind him. There had been no getting rid of the boy no matter how Remy had growled at him for not obeying orders. To his astonishment and irritation, Wolf had growled right back. While Gabrielle had returned to the salon to arrange this meeting with Navarre, Remy had spent the interval pacing the garden, locked in bitter disagreement with his young companion.

"Monsieur, you must not trust that wicked sorceress. She is going to lead you into some sort of trap. I knew I should have made you take the amulet. You are falling back under her spell again."

Remy would have roundly rebuked the boy for his impudence except he feared that Wolf could be right. At least about the spell. When he had stolen into the salon and seen Gabrielle flirting with Navarre, he had been seized by a kind of madness.

Jealousy. Pure mindless jealousy over every smile Gabrielle had accorded his young king.

Remy had forgotten his mission, forgotten the peril to his life when he had inserted himself into the dance. He'd tried to tell himself it was the only way to get close to his king, but it was Gabrielle he'd needed to be near. Part of him had wanted her to recognize him, to know he was there. God help him. He was indeed a great fool.

Remy's gaze never left Gabrielle as she led the way down the passage, her skirts swishing against the stone floor. Light from the torches embedded in the wall flickered over her graceful figure. Her lacy collarette rose up from her gown like a pair of wings, emphasizing the slenderness of her neck, framing the golden halo that was her hair.

Once Remy had believed her all that was good and innocent. Disillusioned, he thought he had finally taken her measure as one of the coldest and most ambitious women he'd ever met. But her actions in protecting him tonight had again upended all his opinions of her until he began to despair of ever understanding Gabrielle Cheney.

And he wanted to . . . as badly as he wanted to haul her back into his arms. That heated kiss they'd shared in the gardens had sent the blood surging through his veins, left his body hard, aching for her.

The corridor ended abruptly before a steep set of stairs that yawned upward. Pausing at the foot, Gabrielle leaned closer to Remy, whispering, "This is the back stair that leads up to Navarre's bedchamber, used by the servants and the king's, er, guests."

And exactly how was Gabrielle so familiar with this discreet, private stairway? Remy wanted to demand sharply. He feared he knew the answer to that and it left a cold feeling in the pit of his stomach.

"You wait here until I see if it is safe for you to go up." Gabrielle held a cautioning finger to her lips. "Don't make a move until I signal you the way is clear."

Before Remy could object, she lifted the hem of her skirts and rustled up the stair, disappearing into the darkness of the landing. Wolf crowded close behind him, tugging urgently at his sleeve.

"Monsieur, there is still time. We could—"

"Be quiet," Remy muttered. He grimaced as he caught the pungent odor of the amulet Wolf was nervously fingering. "And if you insist on waving that damn thing about, get back a pace from me."

With a disgruntled sigh, Wolf did so, slinking back a few steps, but not far, looking as wary as though they were both about to get their heads snapped off in the steel jaws of a trap. Maybe they were, but Remy doubted it. Gabrielle could have betrayed him already if she wished to do so. Instead she had taken pains to preserve his life, even at the risk of her own safety. But why? She had never really given him an answer.

He wanted desperately to believe she cherished some sort of tender feelings toward him. But how was that possible in a woman whose avowed ambition was to become the mistress of a king?

Above him on the landing, Remy caught the faint sound of Gabrielle tapping on a door, the creak of it opening. Words were exchanged in low murmured voices, but strain though he might, Remy could not hear what was being said.

Gabrielle was good at all this intrigue. Far too good, able to lie so smoothly, even to the Dark Queen, familiar with every twist and turn of this rambling palace. Remy could not begin to imagine what combination of charm, bribery, and cunning she'd used to get him undetected this far.

"This is my world. I belong here," she had said.

As much as the notion pained him, she did. Dazzling in her costly jewels and gowns, as seductively beautiful as Helen of Troy, capable of inspiring men to fight and die for her. And yet there had been fleeting moments back there in the garden when she had not appeared quite the poised lady of the world. When she had mounted her strange defense of the Dark Queen, that old sadness had crept back into Gabrielle's eyes.

"There are far more dragons than knights in the world. Fiery monsters to reduce your dreams to ashes, to scorch you with betrayal until you wither and die or let your heart be forged into steel."

Those words seemed to have been wrung from her heart and she had no longer been the bold courtesan and seductress. She had looked so young and lost that Remy had wanted to gather her up in his arms and demand, "Who or what blighted your dreams, Gabrielle? What dragon's fire forged your heart?"

But he doubted she would have ever answered him. Gabrielle had always been too skilled at hiding her secrets and it was far too late to ask her anything now. Because he'd promised . . . no more questions.

There was a flutter of movement at the top of the stairs, then Gabrielle reappeared. She came partly down the stairs and beckoned to him. Remy sprang toward her, pausing on the riser just below hers.

"You can go up now. It's safe. Navarre has found an excuse to dismiss his attendants, many of whom are definitely not to be trusted. The Dark Queen plants her spies everywhere. So do be careful, Remy, and try not to remain too long. When you are done, the king will help you to get safely away."

"Then you are not staying?" Remy asked in surprise.

"No, I agreed to let you have your chance to persuade the king to leave Paris." She offered him a wry smile. "If I remained, I think I'd prove a bit of a distraction."

Remy was forced to agree, although he was not sure who would be in greater danger of being distracted, Navarre or himself. As Gabrielle eased past him on the stairway, he breathed in the sweet scent of her perfume. Even as his body tightened in response, his heart sank with a sudden realization.

If he convinced Navarre to escape with him, Remy would soon be leaving Paris. If he didn't, he would likewise be gone. There would be no reason for him to remain in this cursed city. Either way it would be highly unlikely he would see Gabrielle again.

Before she could retreat back down the stairs, Remy caught her hand.

"Gabrielle, I—I just wanted to say—" Remy compressed his lips. He didn't know exactly what he wanted to say, so many conflicting emotions churning inside him toward this lovely woman with her face upturned to his.

At last he muttered, "Thank you for doing this for me, although I still don't know why—"

"Ah, no," Gabrielle admonished him with a shake of her head. "No more questions, remember?"

With her free hand, she reached up to stroke his cheek, her fingers so soft and warm, he had to suppress the urge to bury his lips against her palm.

"You really do look better without that beard," Gabrielle murmured. "If you ever grow it back, I vow I will come after you with a razor myself."

"For the beard or my throat?" Remy attempted to jest even though his heart felt hollow.

"I don't know. It would depend on how angry you had made me at the time." As she gave him her familiar impish smile, she looked much less like Mademoiselle Cheney, the infamous courtesan and more like the Gabrielle he'd once known. Remy curled his fingers tightly around hers as though he could keep that girl from disappearing.

But she had already gently loosened his grasp on her hand. As she rustled down the stairs, she encountered Wolf at the bottom. The boy flattened himself against the wall as though terrified the slightest contact with Gabrielle would turn him to stone.

His fear of her obviously afforded Gabrielle a certain amount of amusement. She tapped him playfully on the tip of his nose. "And so you are Martin Le Loup, the young man who once saved Captain Remy's life?"

"Oui, m-mademoiselle." Although Wolf shrank farther away from her, he tipped up his sharp chin in defiance.

Gabrielle regarded him for a long moment, her face softening. She leaned over and she brushed a kiss against his cheek.

Straightening away from the boy, she looked up at Remy and cast him a tremulous smile that lodged deep in his heart. Then she turned and hurried away down the corridor without another glance back.

As soon as she had vanished from sight, Wolf peeled himself shakily away from the wall. Yanking at his neckline, the boy stole an anxious peek inside his shirt. Despite the leaden feeling bearing down upon him, Remy's lips quirked in a half-smile.

"What's the matter, boy? Have you acquired an extra nipple?"

"N-no." The boy smoothed his shirt back into place. "Although I still fear that lady is indeed a powerful witch. But by my faith, she is a most bewildering one."

"You don't need to tell me that," Remy responded dryly. He had struggled, saved, and plotted for three years to be able to return to his king. The long anticipated meeting was now arranged. Navarre was waiting for him.

But instead of rushing to Navarre's side, he lingered, gazing after Gabrielle, longing to call her back. He should have given Wolf's amulet a try. He clearly needed some protection from the enchantment Gabrielle wove over him, to banish her from his heart. Except that Remy feared there was no magic in the world strong enough to do that.

* * *

GABRIELLE'S FOOTSTEPS ECHOED DOWN THE SHADOWY HALLS OF the Louvre, the great palace settling into silence. The ball long over, the king and courtiers had retreated to their own apartments, even most of the servants retired for the night. Here and there, Gabrielle could hear a door creak, the sound of a whisper, a giggle, that told her that intrigues were afoot of a more amorous nature than the one she had just arranged.

Gabrielle could not help congratulating herself on how she had managed the secret meeting between Remy and Navarre. Although it was an odd thing for her to regard with satisfaction considering she might well have put her own future at risk.

"I must be completely mad to have helped him," Gabrielle told herself ruefully. But how could she have done otherwise? She would have hazarded her own ambitions a dozen times over to keep Remy from harm. And besides, she doubted he would succeed in his mission. Not according to Nostradamus's prophecy.

Yet Gabrielle could not help remembering how little her mother had believed in prophecies. What if Remy succeeded in getting Navarre to escape, the both of them disappearing back into the mountains of their border country? Gabrielle was disconcerted to realize she would not regret the loss of the king so much as she would Remy.

"Confound the man," she murmured. Every time Remy crossed her path, he tangled her emotions into a hopeless snarl, longing, wariness, joy, and despair. He made her feel vulnerable again, the last thing she could afford to be in this court crawling with jackals ready to pounce on any sign of weakness.

Unfortunately one of them was waiting for her near the door where she meant to make her own escape out into the gardens. Signore Verducci melted out of the shadows.

"Good evening, Signorina Cheney."

Gabrielle drew up sharp at the sight of Catherine's favorite spy. The torchlight played over his gaunt features lost behind the straggling gray beard, the flickering light making him appear more cadaverous than ever.

He sketched her a stiff bow. "You are here very late, my lady. Some new conquest perhaps among the king's gentlemen?"

Recovered from her initial alarm, Gabrielle cast him an icy look. "That is hardly any of your concern."

"Perhaps not, but I fear it is of great concern to the queen."

Gabrielle had prepared to make a dignified sweep past Verducci, but she froze, her heart skipping a beat. "The—the queen?"

"Si." The dour little man was rarely given to smiling, but his eyes lit with a certain malicious satisfaction. "It really is most fortunate that you have not yet returned to your own home. It just so happens Her Majesty would like a word with you."

※※※

REMY STOOD BEFORE THE BANK OF WINDOWS IN THE KING'S BEDchamber, as tense as a soldier on parade, his hands locked behind his back. He had never been at ease in the grandeur of the Louvre and was even less so in the apartments of his king. Remy had spent so much time plotting and working toward this reunion with his king, he had never planned exactly how he would go about persuading Navarre to escape from Paris. Gabrielle had afforded Remy this golden opportunity and he found himself unaccountably tongue-tied.

Even in the middle of explaining to Navarre how he had survived the massacre, Remy stumbled to silence, his gaze drawn once more to the moonlit night beyond the windowpanes, as though he half-expected to see a fairy-like creature making her regal way across the grounds. He wondered if Gabrielle had left the palace yet, hoping that she had and was safely back at her own town house.

Remy wished that he could have escorted her. A foolish wish, he knew. Gabrielle would neither have desired or needed him to do so. She was obviously well able to look out for herself, but Remy couldn't help remembering how small and fragile she had appeared as she vanished down the dark corridor of the Louvre.

"Captain Remy?" Navarre's voice wrenched Remy's thoughts back to the king.

As Remy tore his gaze from the windows, one of Navarre's thick brows arched upward in questioning fashion.

"You were telling me how you and this remarkable young man who saved you arrived on the shores of Ireland," the king prompted. "Then what happened?"

"Why, nothing else of note, sire. There is really little more to tell."

Navarre's mouth quirked. "You always were a man of few words, Captain."

And one that Remy knew the king had always found rather dull. Henry had preferred the company of reckless youngbloods like himself who enjoyed carousing and hunting, whether it was deer, wild boar, or women. Remy feared he had had a tendency to quietly remind Navarre he had more pressing matters to attend.

By the pale glow of the candlelight, Remy studied the king, searching hopefully for some new sign of maturity in him. After all, Henry was now what? Three and twenty and he'd been through enough harrowing experiences to age any man, the murder of his mother, the massacre of his subjects, the constant peril to his own life.

Yet on the surface Navarre appeared much as he'd ever been, a wiry athletic young man, his full dark beard framing a face noted for its prominent nose and full sensual lips. He still carried himself with that careless attitude that had ever been the despair and worry of his mother, although he could adopt a regal enough manner when he chose. When he had commanded his pages and Wolf to retire to the antechamber, even the impudent Martin had been awed into obeying without hesitation.

With the servants gone, Navarre moved to pour a glass of wine for himself and Remy. Crossing the room, he fetched the goblet to Remy with a genial smile. Any awkwardness between them, Remy realized, was entirely on his part and not the king's.

Perhaps it was owing to his guilt at having survived the massacre when so many other good and brave men had fallen. Perhaps it was his consciousness of having failed to protect his king and spirit him safely out of Paris that grim night. But as Remy accepted the glass from Navarre, he knew there was a far more basic cause for his tension. The shadow of a woman lay between Remy and his king.

Remy wondered if he had failed to appear this evening, if even now Gabrielle would be tumbled in the sheets of that massive bed that formed the centerpiece of this chamber. The image of her lying naked in Navarre's arms ate like lye at his soul and Remy had to fight hard to thrust the picture from his mind.

It only made it worse that Navarre was completely unaware of the conflict raging inside of Remy. There was no constraint in Navarre's bluff features as he grinned at Remy. "Damn my eyes, Captain, but you've no notion how it gladdens me to have my brave Scourge returned from the grave. So many loyal and trusted friends I lost that terrible night. My poet Rochefoucauld, my good old Admiral Coligny . . ."

Navarre's smile dimmed as he took a sip of his wine. He lifted his head almost immediately, his face lighting with sudden hope. "But if you survived, is it possible any of the others did? What about those officers who were so frequently in your company? Tavers and—and—"

The king snapped his fingers in effort of memory. "What was his name? That huge burly fellow with the quick wit and ready laugh?"

"Devereaux," Remy said softly. After a painful beat, he added, "No, Dev—the captain died trying to protect his family."

"The captain's young wife and the boy he named after you. They too were destroyed?"

Remy nodded, not trusting himself to speak.

Navarre's mouth thinned into a hard line. Suddenly he looked far older and wearier than his twenty-three years. Raising his glass to Remy's, he said, "Let us drink then, to—to the memory of absent friends."

"Absent friends," Remy repeated. It was the bitterest draft

he had ever swallowed. He took little more than a mouthful before setting his glass down.

Navarre all but drained his cup. For a long moment, he stared pensively at the dregs. But the king had never been the sort of man to surrender to melancholy for long. He rallied, giving Remy a hearty clap on the shoulder. "Delighted as I am to see you again, Captain, it is not wise for us to linger reminiscing about the past. So tell me how I may serve you."

Remy blinked. "Serve me?"

Navarre strode across the chamber to refill his wineglass, his smile taking on a more cynical edge. "Certainly. When one requests a private audience with a king, it is usually because one wants something. You are the bravest soldier our country has ever known. You have no small claim on me. I would be only too delighted to grant you any reward in my power."

Remy drew himself up proudly. "I fear you have been here in Paris too long, Sire. You mistake me for one of these fawning courtiers snuffling round Your Highness's boots for favors."

Navarre waved his hand in a placating gesture. "Oh, don't get your hackles up, Captain. It is merely the way of the world, that is all."

"It is not my way, Sire," Remy grated. "I seek no rewards. I never have. Only to be of service to you and my country."

Cradling his wineglass, Navarre sank down on his bed, propping his back against a mound of feather pillows. His lips curled into an expression of self-mockery.

"You may have failed to notice, Captain. But I no longer command an army for you to serve in. If you are seeking a military post, you'd do best to return to seek employ with the duc de Montmorency. He has assumed the leadership of the Huguenot cause."

Remy could not help frowning slightly at the young man lounging upon the bed. "I am sure the duc de Montmorency is a capable man, Sire. But it is your presence that both the Huguenots and your kingdom require. You must return home, my liege."

Navarre lowered his eyes as he sipped his wine, his expression becoming more guarded. "To even speak to me of returning to Navarre is dangerous, Captain. My mother-in-law most firmly wishes that I remain with the French court."

Remy could not choke back his sense of outrage. "Since when does the king of Navarre give way to the wishes of some infernal Italian witch?"

"Since that witch displayed her power in a way neither of us is likely to forget." Navarre fortified himself with a swallow of wine. "Besides, my captivity is not that bad."

"Not that bad!" Remy exclaimed.

"The court is not without its diversions. Spending a night in the arms of a beautiful woman can even make the prospect of attending mass in the morning endurable." Navarre toyed with the rim of his wineglass, avoiding Remy's eyes. "I suppose you have heard. I am a Catholic now."

"Yes, I have heard," Remy replied grimly, remembering his outrage when the tidings had reached him that his king had been forced by the de Medici witch to abandon his faith or else join his subjects in the grave.

A look chased across Navarre's countenance, part shame, part almost angry defiance. "Frankly, I never could see what difference it makes whether one chooses to worship God while fingering a chain of ave beads or reading from the Book of Common Prayer. Certainly not enough difference to be willing to kill or die over."

To a certain extent, Remy could not help agreeing with him. But he also could not help remembering all those men and woman to whom it had made a difference, who had willingly sacrificed their lives in the Huguenot cause, dying for the right to worship as they chose. The massacre at Paris had been cruel enough for the people of Navarre to endure. To have their king desert their cause had been the final blow to many.

Remy tried to keep his features impassive, but some of what he was feeling must have shown through because Navarre said,

"Knowing that your king is a coward, a contemptible turncoat, I am surprised you are still so eager to serve me."

"You had no other choice, Sire."

"*You* wouldn't have done it. You would never have surrendered your honor and principles to save your own neck."

Remy shifted uncomfortably. "It makes no difference what I would have done. I am not a king."

Navarre swung his legs over the side of the bed and sat, peering glumly into his wineglass. "There are those who think I am not much of one either. There are many, even in Navarre, who now despise me. They compare me to my father, say that I am as weak-willed as he was, instead of being strong and wise like my mother."

"Then prove them wrong, Sire," Remy urged. "Escape from here and take your rightful place as the leader of the Huguenot cause."

"But what if they are right? When I made my choice to convert, I was not thinking that I owed any great duty to my subjects to stay alive. My only thought was that I was young and I wasn't ready to die. I found life incredibly sweet."

Some of the darkness lifted from Navarre's face as he added, "I still do and never more so than at this moment. You see, Captain . . . I have fallen in love."

Remy heard the king's words with dread. He had no need to ask with whom. He tried to treat Navarre's confession lightly, forcing a stiff smile to his lips.

"By the rood, Your Grace, I can scarce remember a time when you were not in love with someone."

"True enough," Navarre said with a rueful laugh, levering himself to his feet. "Unlike you, my fierce Scourge, who has never been in love with anyone. I swear I have never known any man so immune to the charms of the fair sex."

Immune to all but one, Remy reflected bleakly.

"Alas, I fear I am all too weak in that regard." Navarre gave a mock sigh. "From the age of fourteen, I have been all too keenly aware that women are the most magnificent creatures God ever put on the face of this earth. And Mademoiselle Gabrielle Cheney is unquestionably the loveliest of them all."

Remy was hard-pressed to remain impassive as Gabrielle's name fell from the king's lips. Navarre strolled past him to the windows and peered out into the night, an expression of dreamy sensuality settling over his features.

"Such golden hair as would put the sun to shame. Eyes that remind me of those clear blue streams in our mountains back home. Soft red lips that promise a man every imaginable pleasure. Her skin is as white as new cream and smoother than silk, her breasts so firm and ripe they positively beg to be caressed."

Remy hitched in his breath sharply. If it had been any other man going on about Gabrielle this way, he would have roared at him to shut his mouth or he would shut it for him. But he could hardly command his king to be silent. All Remy could do was clench his hands into fists so tight his muscles ached and listen in grim silence.

His lack of response must have irritated Navarre. The king interrupted his catalogue of Gabrielle's charms to cast Remy an impatient glance. "You have seen the lady for yourself, Captain. Surely even you must have noticed how exquisite she is."

Remy gritted his teeth. Yes, he had noticed. God help him.

"She is lovely enough, I grant you," he said stiffly. "But I am sure there must be many beautiful women here at court. And back home in Navarre."

"Yes, there are, and for a long time I believed Gabrielle no more unique than the rest. There is at times a haughty reserve about her that puts a man at a distance. But of late, she has allowed me to see past that and I keep catching glimpses of a woman who is warm and vulnerable. I gaze into her eyes and see this trace of some secret sorrow that haunts me long after she is gone."

Navarre broke off with a wry smile. "But of course you would have no idea what I am talking about, Captain."

That was the problem. Remy did know, all too well.

"The man who finally succeeds in winning Gabrielle's heart will have himself a treasure indeed," Navarre murmured. "The lady can be maddeningly elusive. However, beneath that cool exterior of hers burns an inner fire, a passion that a man longs to sample. And I would have done so, but for you, Captain."

Navarre angled a glance at Remy, part teasing but also containing a flicker of frustration. "Your unexpected return from the dead was a little untimely. I thought that I had finally persuaded her to share my bed tonight."

So Gabrielle had not already bedded Navarre? It should not have mattered so much to Remy. It was not as though Gabrielle had not had other lovers. But the thought that she had not yet given herself to the king stirred in Remy a savage feeling of exultation he was hard-pressed to hide. He ducked his head.

Mistaking the gesture, Navarre stalked over and jabbed Remy playfully on the arm with his fist.

"Don't look so downcast, man. I entirely forgive you for disrupting my amours," the king joked. "There will be plenty of other nights."

Yes, there would be. Remy's sense of exultation fled. He clenched his jaw so tight, he was astonished Navarre did not hear his teeth grinding together.

"No matter how intrigued you are by Mademoiselle Cheney, you cannot remain here merely to pursue a woman," he said. "Not while your country cries out for your leadership. You must escape at the first opportunity and return home. Both your honor and your duty demand it."

Navarre's mouth set in a stubborn line. "What if a man's first duty is to the woman he adores? Kingdoms fall, Captain. Wars are forgotten, noble causes fade to dust. What if in the end all that truly matters about one's life is how one loved?"

Remy regarded the king uneasily. He had seen Henry in the throes of infatuation before, but never waxing this passionate. Gabrielle did indeed truly have the king in her thrall. No wonder she had been willing to risk having Remy meet with him. Remy felt a rush of anger, against Gabrielle for bewitching the king, against Henry for letting himself be so beguiled. And most of all against himself for this jealousy he could not suppress.

"There is something you are forgetting, Sire. You are a married man. What of your wife?" Even as he spoke, Remy realized how priggish he sounded and hopelessly naïve. He was not surprised when Navarre laughed in his face.

"Margot? I assure you, Captain, my queen could not care less whose bed I am in as long as it is not hers."

"And what about Mademoiselle Cheney's family?"

"What about them? Has she even got one?"

"Yes! She is the daughter of a French chevalier and an heiress known as the Lady of Faire Isle. Her older sister, Ariane, is the Countess de Renard, a woman of surpassing reputation. She would not approve of your plans to make Gabrielle your mistress."

"It would be a little late for her to voice her concerns about her sister's virtue now, wouldn't it?" Navarre said dryly. "Gabrielle has been a courtesan for some time."

"I am sure that Ariane has been deeply distressed by Gabrielle coming to Paris. She would wish to see her sister abandon this way of life, become respectably settled."

Navarre shrugged. "Tell the lady not to worry. I will make sure Gabrielle's future is secure. I intend to get her a husband. Some minor nobleman perhaps, someone to give her his name and title. A man I could trust to understand the unique nature of our arrangement. That Gabrielle would be his wife in name only while she shared my bed. There are many men who would agree to such an arrangement for the sake of my gratitude, the wealth I could bestow upon them."

Navarre's eyes glinted slyly at Remy. "Or men who declare themselves to be of such unquestioning devotion to me, they would perform any service I require."

Remy turned away to conceal his disgust. The king's mother,

Jeanne, had always feared her son being corrupted by what she deemed the appalling morals of the French court. Remy grieved for the memory of his late, good queen. He grieved over the callous, indolent man her son had become.

Most of all he grieved for Gabrielle, picturing the cold and empty future Navarre had sketched out for her. His mistress until such time as what? That Navarre tired of her, that she grew too old? Then she would be left entirely to the care of a husband of such low principles he'd pander his wife to a king, a man of no honor, no pride . . . no love.

Remy had to rein in his outrage, remind himself this was the future Gabrielle desired. He was not here tonight to try to save her, but to rescue his king. Forcing Gabrielle from his thoughts, Remy paced the chamber, attempting to divert Navarre's mind from the lady and focus on the possibilities of escape.

Although Navarre steepled his fingers beneath his chin and regarded Remy thoughtfully, Remy was not certain if he was even listening.

"Escaping from Paris might be impossible, but the court moves about frequently, does it not? During one of those progresses, surely some opportune moment will be found," Remy argued. "I vow to you I will make sure there is no risk."

When Navarre made no response, Remy demanded, "You do want to return home, do you not, Sire?"

"Lord, yes. There are times I look out on these teeming streets and hunger for the crisp air of my mountains. To cease masking my every thought, every emotion. To be truly a king."

Navarre leaned up against the bedpost, studying Remy through narrowed eyes. "I would give much to see my home again, to escape the Dark Queen's watchful eyes. I will let you go ahead with the plans for my escape, providing you also arrange one thing."

"What is that?"

"You must make certain Gabrielle comes with us."

Remy bit back a sharp oath. Navarre had ever been single-minded when it came to the pursuit of a woman. There was seldom any dissuading him.

"And just how am I supposed to arrange that, Sire?" Remy asked impatiently. "I know little of Mademoiselle Cheney, but it is my understanding that she has no wish to leave Paris. So what would you have me do? Abduct her?"

"No, my good Scourge." Navarre's lips curved in a slow smile.

"I want you to marry her."

Chapter Eleven

THE DARK QUEEN'S ANTECHAMBER WAS MAGNIFICENT, RICH tapestries adorning the walls. The fireplace was carved in scenes of Diana the huntress sporting with fauns, deer, and satyrs, the mantel emblazoned with initials, an elaborate letter H entwined with a C.

Gabrielle felt like a hapless fly that had strayed into the lovely silken web of a spider, although Catherine's greeting of her could not have been more cordial. She dismissed her attendants, forestalling Gabrielle's curtsy, waving her toward a chair.

"No ceremony, child," she murmured. Already attired for bed in a dark dressing gown, a white coif framing her graying hair, Catherine could well have been someone's maiden aunt. At least if that aunt had been a witch with dark, watchful eyes.

Gabrielle supposed that in other countries it would be deemed an honor to be accorded a private meeting with a queen. But most Frenchmen did not regard an audience with Catherine de Medici in that light. Her own children were said to tremble with fear when ordered into her presence.

Gabrielle was one of the few who had ever been able to answer a summons from the Dark Queen with aplomb . . . until tonight. She calmed herself by reasoning that surely if Catherine had summoned her here because she had found out about Remy's return and his secret meeting with Navarre, the queen would be furious. Both Gabrielle and Remy would have been arrested by now, wouldn't they?

Then why had Gabrielle been hauled in for this midnight tête-à-tête? What new game was this to be? Her stomach knotted as Catherine glided toward her, her expression as mellow as the wine she offered. The dark red wine sparkled in the finely cut Venetian crystal.

"Here, my dear. You look as though you could use this."

Never accept anything to eat or drink from the hands of the Dark Queen. It was almost an unwritten law among other daughters of the earth, a saying that Gabrielle scoffed at. If Catherine had poisoned everyone she was accused of, France would have lost half its population by now. Still, she could not help regarding the wine warily.

Catherine's dark eyes snapped with amusement. "My dear Gabrielle, it is not poisoned, I assure you. Would you like me to take the first sip?"

"Of course not. If you decided to kill me, I doubt you'd do it here in your own chambers." Raising the glass to her lips in a display of careless bravado, Gabrielle took a swallow, then added, "After all, it would be a trifle awkward disposing of the body."

"Not as awkward as you might think," Catherine said dryly.

Gabrielle, who had just taken another mouthful of the wine, choked.

Catherine patted her on the back. "There, there, child. I was only teasing you."

Seeking to recover herself, Gabrielle set down the wineglass with a sharp click. Catherine watched her beneath hooded eyes. "Why would you ever imagine I would wish to harm you? You are the daughter of one of my oldest and dearest friends."

Annoyed that she had allowed Catherine to disconcert her, Gabrielle shot back, "Your Grace has a strange notion of friendship. You were the one who set out to destroy my mother's happiness."

Marguerite de Maitland, the courtesan who had seduced Louis Cheney, had been one of Catherine's creatures, part of that group of ladies known as the Dark Queen's Flying Squadron, chosen for their beauty, wit, and skills in the bedchamber. Few men possessed the will to resist these sirens even when they were fully aware who had sent them. It was well known that Catherine used these young women to spy for her, to establish dominance over her masculine enemies. But in the case of Evangeline Cheney, Catherine had merely acted out of spite and jealousy.

Catherine made no attempt to deny Gabrielle's accusation, assuming a mournful expression that was a mockery in itself. "Alas, I did engage Marguerite to, er, entertain your father. But even if I hadn't, he would have strayed from your mother's bed eventually. All men are unfaithful in the end. Your mother should have been more philosophical about it and not allowed it to break her heart.

"But that is all in the past, long forgotten." Catherine dismissed the devastation she had wrought in the Cheney family with an airy wave of one hand. "You certainly must have done so or you would never have accepted the inheritance from Marguerite. You and I are much alike, Gabrielle. We are practical women who never let anything as foolish as sentiment interfere with our personal advantage."

"Yes," Gabrielle agreed, but she found it a bitter reflection. There were times she would have given her soul to be more honorable and untainted. She turned swiftly away before Catherine could read the thought in her eyes. Display any sign of weakness or sensitivity in front of Catherine and one might as well bare one's throat. Or worse still bare one's eyes. If Gabrielle didn't take care, the Dark Queen would get inside her head and discover the truth about Remy and every other secret Gabrielle had sought to hide.

Striving for her usual composure, Gabrielle moved toward the chair Catherine had offered her and sank gracefully into it. "Flattered as I am by this private reception, Your Grace, I am curious as to the reason for it. Especially when it waxes so late."

"I don't intend to keep you long, child." Catherine settled herself opposite Gabrielle, the small table between them bearing a single taper. Catherine inched the silver candlestick closer to Gabrielle so that its glow played over her countenance, leaving Catherine more in shadow. Gabrielle stiffened at this maneuver, but did not betray her tension by so much as the flutter of an eyelash.

"I only wanted a moment to chat with you. I scarce saw you all evening," Catherine said. "You seemed to keep disappearing."

"The salon was very crowded, Your Grace. It was easy to become lost in it."

"Another less striking lady perhaps, but never you, my dear. Your presence or your absence must always be remarked. I never even had a chance to compliment you on how lovely you looked. Exactly who had you attired yourself to be?"

"The queen of the fairies."

"Ah. So tell me, Gabrielle. Are you going to prove to be a bad fairy?"

"No, I believe that is a role better left to Your Majesty."

Catherine gave a throaty chuckle and pinched Gabrielle's hand. The seemingly playful gesture was sharp enough to force Gabrielle to stifle a gasp.

Catherine's smile broadened. "Impudent creature. I wonder why I put up with your insolence. I must be rather fond of you."

Gabrielle rubbed her throbbing hand. "Really? I always thought you tolerated me because you fear the power of my sister."

Catherine's smile vanished. "Don't be ridiculous. I admit that Ariane and I had our differences in the past, made many threats to each other, but we did reach an understanding. I have nothing but admiration and respect for her.

"So pray tell. How is the dear Lady of Faire Isle?" Catherine's mouth took on a cruel cast as she added, "But you wouldn't know, would you? Because Ariane has washed her hands of you."

Gabrielle fought to conceal how painfully Catherine's jab had found its mark. That was the danger of trading taunts with Catherine. She knew well how to draw blood.

"Yes, Ariane and I are estranged," Gabrielle said quietly. "I am sure your spies must keep you well informed about both of us."

"Usually they do. Unfortunately, the denizens of Faire Isle and your esteemed brother-in-law's estate are extremely loyal to the lady and distressingly suspicious of strangers. It is quite annoying really." Catherine toyed with the stem of the silver candlestick as she added softly, "My spies here in Paris serve me far better."

The implications of that remark caused Gabrielle to freeze.

Catherine eyed her slyly and continued, "There is Signore Verducci, for example. A useful creature but at times a bit of a fool. He came to me with such astonishing tales of your doings, I nearly boxed his ears. But if he has spoken the truth, I must offer you my congratulations. I had no idea you had developed your powers to such an extent."

Although her pulse beat quicker with every word that Catherine spoke, Gabrielle replied, "I have no idea what you are talking about."

"And to think I fancied myself skilled in the dark ways," Catherine murmured. "But even I have never managed to conjure up a man from the dead."

Gabrielle felt the blood drain from her cheeks. Catherine's

sharp gaze honed in on Gabrielle like a swordsman closing in for the kill.

"I wonder . . . do you think the Scourge enjoyed the tender reunion with his king?"

Remy! The Dark Queen had discovered Remy . . .

Gabrielle was unable to control her panic. She shot to her feet and slammed her palms down on the table, nearly overturning the candlestick. "Dear God! What the devil have you done to him?"

Catherine reared back in her chair, clearly astonished by the depth of reaction she had provoked from Gabrielle.

"Why . . . nothing *yet.*"

"I don't believe you. Have you had him arrested or—or—is he—" Gabrielle's throat closed up, unable to give voice to her greater dread.

"Calm yourself, child. The captain is quite safe and as far as I know, still enjoying Navarre's hospitality."

Gabrielle searched Catherine's face. For once in her life, the Dark Queen appeared to be telling the truth. Gabrielle sank back into her chair, weak with relief but sickened by the realization of how she had betrayed herself. Remy's return had robbed her of the edge she'd always had in her duels with Catherine, the indifference of a woman who hazarded nothing but her own neck.

Catherine clucked her tongue. "My, my! To think I feared that I faced another tedious evening, just another of my son's absurd masked balls. How diverting it has all turned out to be. Not only do I have the Scourge back from the dead, but I have Gabrielle Cheney, the ice maiden, behaving most unlike herself. Such excess of emotion. You are actually trembling."

Gabrielle gripped her hands together in her lap. *Don't let the Dark Queen think it has anything to do with Remy. Don't give her that power over you.*

She moistened her lips. "Of—of course I tremble. Who would not when caught out doing something which I know must displease Your Grace?"

"Yes." Catherine studied her through narrowed eyes. "Which makes me wonder why you did it. You usually have a greater care for your own interests."

Gabrielle hunched her shoulders. "I share the same apprehension of boredom as Your Grace. There is nothing like a little intrigue to liven things up. When poor Captain Remy came to me, begging me to get him in to see his king, I saw no real harm in it."

"No real harm?" Catherine's brows arched haughtily. "You consider smuggling one of my worst enemies into my palace doing no real harm?"

"Nicolas Remy is no longer any threat to you. He has no army at his back, no powerful connections. He only wanted to see his king one last time, be certain that Navarre is—is well."

"Either you are a fool, Gabrielle, or you take me for one," Catherine said tartly. "The captain wants what so many of these Huguenots desire, to see their king out of my Papist clutches. Remy is not just one man. He is a blasted legend, capable of persuading otherwise prudent people to take foolish risks. Only witness the effect he appears to have had on you."

Gabrielle flushed, but sought to conceal it by stifling a feigned yawn. "Oh, the captain is handsome enough, I grant you, but I always found him a trifle dull. Such honest, incorruptible men usually are."

"Yet you and your sisters once risked everything to protect him. And here you are, still doing it. Why is that, I wonder?"

"I have no idea," Gabrielle drawled. "Force of habit?"

"A very unwise habit, my dear Gabrielle."

"Perhaps it is. But my sisters and I do owe a certain debt to Captain Remy. He helped to protect us the night you sent the witch-hunters to burn down our home."

"Witch-hunters that I only sent to find Captain Remy and retrieve my gloves. If you had not been sheltering him—Oh, never mind." Catherine lifted one hand in a regal gesture. "Let us not rake up that old quarrel again. It was a mere misunderstanding."

A misunderstanding? If that was how Catherine behaved when she had a misunderstanding with you, what would she be likely to do if she really regarded you as an enemy? Gabrielle knew the answer to that all too well. The Dark Queen made you a gift of poisoned gloves. She dispatched dark armies to slaughter you and all your countrymen in the streets of Paris. Gabrielle rubbed the nape of her neck, suddenly wearied of playing this game with Catherine.

"Enough of this fencing, Your Grace," she said bluntly. "It is clear you could have easily stopped Remy's meeting with Navarre. So why didn't you? Why haven't you arrested both of us?"

Catherine scowled. "I have been asking myself that very same thing. Perhaps because there is an uneasy truce existing between my Catholic and Protestant subjects at the moment and I am sick to death of all this civil unrest. Those pious Huguenots mourned the loss of their great hero years ago. If I were to make a martyr out of Captain Remy a second time, I would risk the outbreak of hostilities again.

"War can be a useful thing sometimes. It helps to keep my great nobles occupied when they might otherwise make nuisances of themselves here at court. But it is also costly. I prefer to keep my coin to finish my beautiful new palace and quite frankly, Gabrielle, Captain Remy does not alarm me as much as you do."

"Me?"

"Indeed. I have watched your career at court with great interest. You are not in the least like these other foolish courtesans, content with a few jewels, fancy gowns, a fine house, and a good time. Oh, no, you hunger for much more than that. You want power, the kind of power that comes from holding sway over the heart of a king."

As Gabrielle opened her mouth to reply, Catherine forestalled her. "Don't bother to deny it. You are good at concealing your thoughts, milady. But the merest novice of a witch would be able to read your ambitions. I have been aware for some time of your hopes regarding my dear son-in-law, Navarre."

"So why haven't you sent me away from court?" Gabrielle demanded.

Catherine didn't answer. Instead she rose and stalked over to the fireplace and beckoned to Gabrielle imperiously. "Come here."

Gabrielle approached her with slow, wary steps. Catherine seized her by the wrist and yanked her closer. She pointed toward the magnificent relief carved upon the stone mantel, the enjoined letters done in a fancy scroll.

"Have you ever noticed those initials emblazoned upon my fireplace?"

"It would be difficult not to. They are to be found carved throughout the palace."

"And do you know what they stand for?"

Gabrielle fetched an impatient sigh, wondering what new game this was. "Certainly. The H represents your late husband, King Henry the second. And the C of course stands for Catherine. An ever constant reminder of Your Majesty's presence."

"Not my presence. What you imagine to be a C is actually a crescent moon. The symbol of the goddess Diana, which was the name of my husband's mistress."

Gabrielle's eyes flew wide. The reign of Catherine's husband had been well before her time. She could not have been more than eight years old when Henry II of France had met an untimely end due to an accident during a mock tournament. But Gabrielle had heard the whispers of the king's grand affair with Diane de Poitiers. A name none dared speak aloud before Catherine.

Releasing Gabrielle, Catherine moved closer to the fireplace. She traced the outlines of the letter H, an unusual softness stealing over her features.

"I was only fourteen when I first came to France to be wed to a man I had never set eyes upon. Torn away from my home in

Italy, frightened of the journey to a strange new land, terrified my bridegroom would turn out to be hideous, repulsive."

Catherine gave a low mirthless laugh. "I would have been better off if he had been. Instead my Henry was young, vigorous, and so earnest, not unlike your Captain Remy. I had the misfortune to fall in love with him at first glance."

"Misfortune?" Gabrielle echoed.

"Yes, because his heart already belonged to another. Diane de Poitiers." Catherine's mouth twisted bitterly. "Henry wed me. I bore his heirs. But he made her the uncrowned queen of France. It was her voice that had a say in all his royal appointments and councils. She even had dominion over the nursery, decreeing how my children should be educated and raised. She was flattered and honored by all the court while I was scorned and forgotten."

A rare quiver of emotion crept into Catherine's voice as she continued to caress her husband's initial. "Henry did no more than his duty by me and even that reluctantly. As soon as he rose from my bed, he went straight to her. I had a hole bored in the floor above Diane's chamber so I could watch the two of them making love."

Gabrielle was revolted by the notion of Catherine spying on her husband as he bedded his mistress. But she felt a reluctant pang of sympathy for the older woman.

"How could you endure it?" she exclaimed. "I would have gotten rid of every one of those crescent moon symbols even if I'd had to raze the entire Louvre."

"Would you?" Catherine's hand fell away from the carving on the mantel. "That would have been such an expensive redecorating, and for what? By the time Henry died, it didn't matter anymore. Because *she* no longer mattered. That is the point I am trying to make to you. King's mistresses come and go and are swiftly forgotten.

"I'll admit that Madame Diane's time in the sun was longer than most, but I doubt you will enjoy a similar success with

Navarre. You may have noted that my dear son-in-law has rather a wandering eye."

Facing Gabrielle, Catherine's familiar mask settled back into place. "No, my dear Gabrielle. Never place your dependence upon a king or any man. You would be far wiser to seek service with a queen, one of your own kind, a daughter of the earth."

Gabrielle drew in a sharp breath, any vestige of pity for Catherine vanishing. Feeling sympathy for the Dark Queen was more dangerous than being afraid of her. It tended to make one forget how cunning Catherine could be. Gabrielle knew quite well what Catherine was getting at. This was not the first time Catherine had tried to recruit Gabrielle into the ranks of her Flying Squadron.

Gabrielle backed away from the queen, saying scornfully, "Serve Your Grace? How? By becoming part of the royal bordello? Does Your Majesty propose to become my panderer?"

"Don't be crude, child," Catherine scolded, pursing her lips. "I would have a much higher regard for you than those other ladies who serve me. I could offer you everything that a king could and more. Wealth, lands, titles . . . power."

"Power?" Gabrielle gave an incredulous laugh. "You are offering to share your power with me?"

"Alas, I am growing older, my dear. I would welcome the use of your youthful wits and energy. Just think of what the two of us together might accomplish, Gabrielle, for the glory of France, especially her women. You would become my right hand, more cherished than my own daughters could ever be. I would teach you everything I know, including my most powerful and secret arts. All I would require from you is—"

"My soul?" Gabrielle interrupted wryly.

"Your friendship, your undivided loyalty and devotion. Do not take my offer lightly. It could be the making of your future. Otherwise, I might be obliged to reassess your little role in Captain Remy's intrigue tonight and . . ." Catherine trailed off.

Despite her glinting smile, her meaning was clear. She wasn't asking Gabrielle to become one of her ladies this time. She was issuing an ultimatum, the same one she had once given Henry of Navarre. *Join me or die.*

Catherine's desire to make Gabrielle one of her creatures might give Gabrielle the only bargaining chip she had to save Remy's life. But she was going to have to play her cards very carefully. Struggling to keep her tone cool and indifferent, she asked, "And Nicolas Remy, what do you propose doing about him?"

Catherine frowned, inspecting a rough spot on her finger-nail. "Monsieur le Scourge has been something of a thorn in my side in the past. I have no intention of letting him become so again. A public trial and hanging would be most awkward. How-ever, even vigorous men like the Scourge suffer from . . . acci-dents, mysterious ailments that suddenly carry them off."

Especially if such accidents were carefully arranged by a Dark Queen and there were so many ways Catherine could get at Remy. A subtle poison slipped into his drink at a tavern, the out-break of a fire at his lodging, an assassin slitting Remy's throat in some dark alley. Gabrielle's mind reeled with all the terrible pos-sibilities.

Gabrielle turned away from Catherine to conceal her agita-tion. Thinking furiously, she said, "I have a much better idea. Why don't you let me deal with him?"

"*You?*"

"Yes, I could take him to my bed, seduce him. Could you imagine how that would affect all those stern Huguenots when the word got abroad? That not only did you succeed in making a Catholic of their king, but now their great hero, the Scourge, is in thrall to one of the Dark Queen's most notorious courtesans."

Gabrielle faced Catherine, summoning up her most brilliant and convincing smile. "Far more effective than merely killing the man, you would destroy his legend."

Catherine steepled her fingers beneath her chin, her brow furrowing as she considered. Gabrielle held her breath, wondering what she would do if Catherine rejected her proposal. Fall to her knees before the queen and beg for Remy's life or seize Catherine by the throat and choke the life from her before she could harm him.

Gabrielle actually felt her fingers flexing when a slow smile spread over Catherine's face.

"I have always admired the way your mind works, Gabrielle. Ruthless and devious, so like mine. But do you really believe that even your charms would be enough to tempt our honorable Scourge from his path of duty?"

Her charms hadn't been enough in the past, Gabrielle reflected, but then she had never really tried. She bit down hard upon her lip as she remembered Remy's kiss, the way it had stirred desires in her that she'd believed long dead, the passion she had seen flare in Remy's eyes. But to seduce Remy into forgetting his honor, twisting him to the Dark Queen's purposes, would be the final betrayal, the corruption of everything that had ever been fine and good between them. The thought filled her with despair, but if she didn't succeed, it would be the same as signing Remy's death warrant.

For Catherine's benefit, Gabrielle suppressed the sick feeling in her heart and traced her hand seductively over her ample curves. "Could I manage to seduce the Scourge or any other man?" she purred. "What do you think?"

Catherine gave a throaty chuckle and stripped off a small gold signet ring from her finger. "I do believe you and I have finally reached an understanding, Gabrielle. Take this ring as a token of my good faith. Now come and pledge me yours."

Catherine held the glittering ornament out to Gabrielle. Gabrielle recoiled from the ring as though it were a snake. Then she forced herself to smile. Rustling forward, she sank down gracefully before Catherine and brought the queen's hand to her lips, feeling strangely hollow inside. As though she was about to barter away the last remaining vestige of her honor. That by making this pact with Catherine, she betrayed not only Remy, but her sister as well, Ariane, who had once so fiercely and bravely defied the Dark Queen.

Don't be so melodramatic, Gabrielle, she chided herself. This was only another part of the game, another bit of intrigue, and pacts were made to be broken. Besides, what other choice did she have?

"I pledge myself entirely to Your Majesty's service," she began.

"Oh, no, my dear." Catherine caught hold of her chin, tipped Gabrielle's head back. "Forget the words. Just pledge to me with your eyes."

Catherine's voice was soft and soothing, but her dark eyes bore into Gabrielle's. Gabrielle's heart sped up as the Dark Queen sought to invade her mind. She had to will herself to not jerk away, to remain calm. To stare steadily back, to reveal nothing to Catherine but the ice in her veins, the cold shadows of her heart. Above all else, not to think of Remy, the devastation she would feel if—

Catherine's fingers tightened on her chin, her gaze thrusting hard against Gabrielle's barriers and for one terrible moment, Gabrielle wavered. She made quick recovery, slamming the door to her mind closed. But had she been quick enough? How much of her vulnerabilities, the secrets of her past might Catherine have read?

Gabrielle searched Catherine's countenance anxiously for some sign of triumph. But to her relief, the Dark Queen merely looked bitterly disappointed. She jammed the ring upon Gabrielle's finger, her shoulders sagging as though suddenly exhausted.

"Very well," she said. "I'll consider our bargain sealed. I am suddenly finding myself extremely tired, child. You may leave me now."

Gabrielle was only too grateful to do so. She ducked into a curtsy, which Catherine did not even acknowledge. But as she was on the verge of slipping out the door, the Dark Queen called softly after her.

"Just remember this, Gabrielle. If you are unable to deal with Nicolas Remy, I will."

†††

THE NIGHT CREPT TOWARD THE DARKEST HOURS BEFORE MORNING and still Catherine could not sleep, a problem she experienced more often of late. A troubled conscience, her enemies would say. Catherine merely laughed at such a notion.

No, her lighter sleeping habits were just one more thing to put down to the vagaries of advancing age, a burden even all of her sorcery could not find a way to defeat. She could have summoned one of her ladies to fetch her a sleeping draft, but that would have been a concession to weakness, an admission she was not prepared to make.

Her powers were on the wane. The Dark Queen was growing old.

Catherine preferred to battle the demons of her restlessness by prowling her bedchamber. To and fro until she was at last exhausted. As she took another wearied turn before the chamber's windows, Catherine fidgeted with the empty place on her finger where her signet ring should have been. The same ring that now adorned Gabrielle Cheney's graceful hand. Of course the ring had been much too large for her.

"Just like all your grand ambitions, my girl," Catherine murmured.

A thin smile curled her lips as she thought of her conquest over Gabrielle, but the triumph did not afford Catherine the pleasure she had once expected it would. She had looked forward to her duels of wit with the girl, her attempts to read Gabrielle's eyes that the young woman had always successfully blocked.

The contest had helped to keep Catherine's wits sharp, her

powers well honed. Gabrielle had seemed so clever, bold, and ruthless, a truly worthy adversary. At least until tonight, when Catherine had penetrated her mind at last, uncovered all of Gabrielle's secrets and weaknesses. Those pathetic memories of her encounter with Etienne Danton.

Catherine remembered the young chevalier quite well. He had been a minor hanger-on at court years ago until he'd been dismissed in disgrace for cheating at cards, breaking the law against dueling, and, worst of all, for raping one of Catherine's ladies.

None of the charms of the Dark Queen's beautiful courtesans were to be wasted on some insignificant knight from the provinces. And Gabrielle Cheney had fancied herself in love with such a man? Pah!

Catherine could have forgiven her that. After all, Gabrielle had only been sixteen. Catherine herself had been foolish enough to devote her heart to a husband who had humiliated and betrayed her at every turn. But Catherine had learned her lesson, that love only weakened a woman. Clearly Gabrielle had not and that was what Catherine found truly unforgivable. Gabrielle had repeated the same mistake all over again and she was too stupid to even realize it.

The girl was hopelessly in love with Nicolas Remy.

When Catherine had learned that Gabrielle had smuggled the Scourge into the palace tonight, she had believed that Gabrielle had done it merely to make mischief, to curry favor with Navarre and advance her ambitions to become his mistress. Catherine could have admired her for that, the deviousness of her plans, the coolness of her nerve. But to discover that the girl was merely besotted with that stiff-necked Huguenot soldier—it was nauseating.

Catherine paced the bedchamber, shaking her head in disgust. She was disappointed in Gabrielle, most cruelly disappointed. Now she was obliged to find some way to be rid of a promising young woman who could have been a valuable asset to her. One could not rely upon loyalty or even prudent self-interest from a woman idiotically in love. Gabrielle's agreement to seduce Remy from his mission was not to be trusted. Not that it mattered. Catherine doubted that even a woman as devastatingly beautiful as Gabrielle Cheney could divert the Scourge from his notions of honor and duty. Nothing could do so . . . short of death.

Catherine had realized that about the earnest young soldier a long time ago. She had made many attempts to dispose of him, attempts that had all failed. She would have to proceed more cunningly and carefully this time. Especially with any actions she took against Gabrielle. Catherine had not been entirely truthful earlier when she had declared she did not fear the power and influence of the Lady of Faire Isle.

Catherine remembered far too well that day in the wake of the St. Bartholomew's Eve massacre when she and Ariane Cheney had confronted each other in this very palace.

How tall and proud that young woman had been, her deep brown eyes so like her late mother's, full of Evangeline's searing honesty and indomitable strength.

"I am warning you, Catherine." Ariane had declared. *"I mean to revive the council of the daughters of the earth, the guardians against misuse of the old ways as you have done. Even you cannot fight us all, a silent army of wise women."*

A silent army of women . . . There had been a time when such a threat would not have fazed Catherine. But she no longer felt quite so invincible. She halted before the windows, resting one hand upon the sill. She peered past the glass toward where the moonlight charted its way across the grounds leading to the Tuileries, the Florentine palace Catherine intended to be her legacy. A palace that was destined to remain unfinished and not just because of the necessity of diverting funds to waging war.

The true reason she had halted the construction was far less rational, far more humiliating. She had fallen prey to a prophetic dream, a belief that when the last stone was mortared into place, that would also be the day that Catherine drew her final breath.

How her enemies would have laughed if they had known of this superstitious fear, that Catherine de Medici, the most powerful sorceress France had ever known, the dreaded Dark Queen was afraid . . . of dying.

Death—that ultimate helplessness and loss of all power. Her hand fluttered to her neck as though she could feel the cold brush of its fingers fastening around her throat. She dragged in a lungful of air, taking comfort in her very breath, the strong steady beat of her heart. No, death should not have her yet. But she had to take care. Before she raised her hand against Gabrielle or her Scourge, Catherine needed to ascertain how powerful the Lady of Faire Isle had become, exactly what went on at those little council meetings on the island.

Fortunately, Catherine had finally secured herself a reliable spy. One of the last persons that the Lady of Faire Isle would ever suspect . . .

Chapter Twelve

THE BONFIRE BLAZED IN THE CLEARING ATOP THE CLIFF, THE flames casting leaping shadows over the circle of dolmens, the mysterious ring of standing stones that seemed as old as Faire Isle itself. The massive, timeworn rocks strained upward to touch the night sky with its sprinkling of stars and traces of cloud drifting across the face of the moon.

Beyond the ring of stones and the sparse line of trees, the land fell away into darkness. Far below at the base of the cliffs, the surf pounded against the rocks on this wilder, less inhabited side of the island. But within the ring, the bonfire gave off a cheering light, as did the scattering of torches embedded in the ground. Their glow reflected on the women who had gathered in the clearing, some seated on makeshift benches of fallen logs, others on the ground, feet tucked demurely beneath their skirts.

They chattered amongst themselves, waiting for the meeting to begin, many stealing awed glances in the direction of the flat altar rock where the Lady of Faire Isle sat enthroned. Ariane wished they could have held these councils in a less melodramatic setting, back at Belle Haven, sensibly seated on proper chairs, passing out mulled wine.

That would have likely disappointed many of these wise women, who had traveled so far and were meeting the Lady of Faire Isle for the first time. She studied the sea of faces that surrounded her. Many of these she recognized from right here on the island, women she had known all her life . . . the ribald apothecary, old Madame Jehan, with her straggling gray hair, the stately Marie Claire, abbess of the island's convent of St. Anne's, Marie Claire's lay servant, the strapping Charbonne with her boyishly cropped milk-white hair. Others, like the prim Hermoine Pechard and the buxom Louise Lavalle, were exiles from Paris owing to having run afoul of the Dark Queen.

But word of these council meetings had spread, drawing in daughters of the earth who were entirely new to Ariane. Most were from France, but a handful hailed from as far away as Spain, Portugal, and Italy. There was even a pair of English sisters, Prudence and Elizabeth Waters, and one Irish girl. Hooded in a dark cloak fastened with a brooch of Celtic interlacing, she tapped her foot with impatience for the proceedings to begin.

But there were two daughters of the earth whose presence was markedly absent. Her own kin. Ariane's eyes swept the shadows beyond the ring of stones for the approach of a tall young woman with white-blond hair, a dark cat close at her heels.

But there was no sign of Miri or her pet, Necromancer. It appeared that her youngest sister did not mean to attend. But Miri had always preferred the lone trails of the forest, the company of woodland creatures to the world of men. These days she was more withdrawn than ever. The girl grieved for all the people who had vanished from her life, her mother, her father, and now Gabrielle—

Ariane hitched in her breath, refusing to think of her other sister. The fact that she had not heard from Bette in some time regarding Gabrielle filled Ariane with anxiety. But tonight she could not afford to be worrying about Gabrielle or fretting over the strained way she had recently parted from Renard or despairing over her childless state.

Ariane needed to keep all her own troubles from her mind. These women had risked much to come here to Faire Isle, many of them defying fathers and husbands. Not only did they hazard the usual perils involved in traveling, they also faced the dangers of participating in a gathering that could be misconstrued. They could easily be accused of being a witches' coven rather than what they were, wise women seeking to preserve and share ancient knowledge long forgotten or forbidden by an ignorant superstitious world. These brave women deserved Ariane's respect and her full attention.

The Abbess of St. Anne's glided forward to rest one hand on Ariane's shoulder. Marie Claire's starched wimple framed a face that one exasperated archbishop had described as being too willful for a nun. The friend and confidante of Ariane's mother, Marie Claire had served the same role for Ariane for years.

Although her face was lined with the full weight of her sixty-odd years, Marie Claire's eyes still retained all the sparkle of youth as she smiled at Ariane. "These women will talk themselves hoarse before the meeting has even started. Should we not begin?"

Ariane concluded ruefully that she could not wait for Miri any longer. She nodded her assent to Marie Claire. The abbess signaled to Charbonne, then positioned herself at Ariane's right, folding her hands into the sleeves of her white robes.

Tall and lanky as any peasant lad, Charbonne dressed like one in her loose muslin shirt, coarse breeches, and heavy boots. She strode to the center of the circle, rapping a thick staff of white birch against the rocky ground.

"Let all tongues be still except mine," she called out in her booming voice. When her first request did not entirely meet with success, she shouted louder, "Silence!"

Charbonne's fierce gaze raked the throng of women until the last murmur had died away. Then she continued, "Here upon the sacred ground of these standing stones and in the presence of our Lady of the Faire Isle, let the third gathering in recent memory of the daughters of the earth commence.

"These meetings are intended to promote peace and harmony among all wise women everywhere, to share and preserve our ancient knowledge, to redress grievances, to solve problems, and to seek advice from our learned Lady."

Charbonne extended the birch staff outward. "Let anyone having business to bring before this council step forward and claim the staff of office."

The words were scarce out of Charbonne's mouth when Hermoine Pechard leaped up to seize the staff. Ariane exchanged a dismayed glance with Marie Claire. Madame Pechard was a thin woman with a perpetually soured expression. Caught helping to spy on the Dark Queen years ago, Hermoine had lost everything, her comfortable home and her husband, who had disassociated himself from her.

Hermoine never lost an opportunity to complain about the decline of morals and the depravity of other wise women. A faint hum of conversation had broken out again and she rapped the staff sharply on a stone, quivering with self-importance.

"Milady," she said, with a stiff curtsy to Ariane. "Esteemed members of this council." Hermoine swept her hawk-eyed gaze over the rest of the assemblage. "I wish to address a growing problem that I have observed among many of our sisters. The misuse of our knowledge for the purposes of lewd and wanton behavior."

Hermoine's opening words evoked a few groans from some of the young women present. She drew herself even more rigidly upright. "We daughters of the earth are meant to devote ourselves to the arts of healing and keeping records of history and knowledge for future generations. Instead some among us waste our time on frivolous matters, brewing up perfumes and lotions to tempt and overcome the senses of men."

The woman's words caused Ariane a twinge, calling up

thoughts of Gabrielle. Madame Pechard, however, stared at Louise Lavalle. The courtesan merely laughed, the dusting of freckles on her nose enhancing Louise's mischievous expression.

"I wouldn't say it was a waste of time," Louise drawled. "And you wouldn't either, Hermoine, if you had spent the night I did with that burly young ostler who works at the Passing Stranger."

Old Madame Jehan slapped her knee and cackled. "I know the one you mean, the one with the fine legs on him like a pair of young oak trees. How was he, dearie?"

"A proper stud, Madame Jehan. I rode him to heaven and back again." Louise leaped up and demonstrated with a provocative thrust forward of her hips.

The gesture produced a spate of laughter, even from Marie Claire. But as Madame Pechard looked ready to explode with outrage, Ariane bit back her own smile.

"Ladies, a little courtesy and decorum if you please," Ariane reproved gently. When Louise subsided, Ariane turned with forced politeness to Madame Pechard.

"Now you were saying, Hermoine?"

The Pechard woman's face mottled an ugly shade of red. She gestured furiously toward Louise and spluttered, "That—that is exactly the sort of licentiousness I was talking about, milady. Men are no match for such wicked charms as practiced by strumpets the likes of Mademoiselle Lavalle."

"Better to be a strumpet than a dried-up old prune," Louise shouted.

Hermoine's lips thinned, but she strove to ignore the interruption. "Strumpets using their dark arts to tempt poor weak men into sin and dishonor. It isn't right. Surely you must agree with me, milady. Your own family has suffered in that regard, your father lured into betraying your good mother by that Maitland trollop."

Ariane stiffened. Her father's infidelity was a source of much private pain and she did not care to have the matter aired in such a public setting. She felt Marie Claire's hand rest comfortingly on her shoulder, the abbess drawing breath to rebuke Madame Pechard, but intervention came from another, unexpected source.

The Irish girl leapt to her feet. "By the blessed St. Michael, 'tis you that waste our time with such petty concerns," she snapped at Hermoine. "So what if a few of our sisters are inclined to use their magic for seduction? The men must look out for themselves, which they are well able to do."

There was a chorus of agreement, especially from old Madame Jehan.

Hermoine glowered at the Irish girl. "Why—why, how dare you—"

"Oh, go and sit yourself down, you spindly fool. I've a matter to lay before this council of a far more troubling and terrifying nature." The girl wrenched hold of the staff and shook back her hood to reveal a fiery mane of hair, pale skin, and fierce blue eyes.

She could scarce have been more than sixteen years old and she was not tall. But something in her fierce manner brought to mind the Celtic warrior maidens of old. Hermoine protested, making an effort to snatch the staff back. But the Irish girl's ferocious glare caused her to think better of it.

Madame Pechard appealed to Ariane instead. "Milady, I wasn't finished."

"Yes, you are." The girl thrust Hermoine out of her way. She stalked forward to stand before Ariane. "Your pardon, milady. My name is Catriona O'Hanlon from the County Meath. I've little skill with the French tongue, but it is important you be understanding me. What I have to tell you concerns matters of life and death."

Ariane might have been tempted to smile at such a dramatic pronouncement but for the intent light burning in the O'Hanlon girl's eyes.

"I understand you well enough, Mademoiselle O'Hanlon," Ariane said gravely. "And if you have information that vital, you had better go ahead and speak."

"Milady!" Hermoine howled, but Ariane held up one hand to silence her.

Ariane felt guilty for her eagerness to brush the querulous woman to one side, but Ariane had read enough in Catriona O'Hanlon's eyes to prickle with apprehension. She soothed Hermoine with the promise that she could speak again later and the woman slunk resentfully back to her seat.

"Thank you, milady," Catriona said, then turned to face the throng of women. Her foreboding expression caused an uneasy hush to fall over the clearing.

Catriona's voice held all the lilt of her own country, the brogue a curious blend with the smooth French language. But her words rang out clear and forcefully.

"As I told the Lady, my name is Catriona O'Hanlon. Better known as the Cat to my own people. Like the rest of you, I come from a long line of wise women, stretching back even before the days of the mighty Cuchulainn. I count many of my friends among the daughters of the earth and one of these was Neve O'Donal."

Catriona gripped the staff tighter, her voice vibrating with strong emotion. "Neve was a good woman whose heart was in the right place even though her thoughts strayed in dark directions. But she had cause enough for her anger, as too many of us Irish do."

Catriona paused, compressing her lips tightly. "I am sure you are all aware how my people have suffered under the invasion of the cursed Sassenach."

There was a sharp hiss from the two English women. Marie Claire also frowned.

"Have a care, Mademoiselle O'Hanlon," she said. "Many of our Lady of Faire Isle's ancestors were English, including her mother, our own revered Lady Evangeline."

Catriona cast Ariane a glance, half-angry, half-apologetic. "No offense intended, milady. I am sure none of your ancestors were the murderous English scum that pillage our land, kill our babies, rape our women, destroy our heritage—"

"Please, mademoiselle," Ariane interrupted Catriona, observing the two Waters sisters starting to bristle. "No one doubts that your people have suffered, but it would be as well if you came back to the point you were making about this Neve—"

"Aye, poor Neve. She had more reason than most to be bitter against the English, deprived of her land, all her menfolk slaughtered. Neve vowed she'd drive the Sassenach out of Ireland, no matter what dark methods she had to use."

The muttered protests from the Waters sisters grew louder. Prudence, the elder of the two, half-leapt to her feet, but Catriona waved her contemptuously back down.

"Ah, don't go getting your corsets in a knot, girls. Neve's threat was a hollow one. At least until . . . I don't know how . . . I don't know where, but—" Cat hesitated, then said in clipped accents, "Neve gained possession of the *Book of Shadows.*"

Cat's dramatic pronouncement produced gasps of fear, shock, and amazement from the crowd and one skeptical hoot from old Madame Jehan. Many of the daughters of the earth owned ancient manuscripts that contained snippets of forbidden arts. But there was said to be one masterwork, the *Book of Shadows,* that contained all the blackest secrets of magic ever known to mankind. Evangeline Cheney had been skeptical about the existence of such a book and Ariane tended to agree with her mother.

The crowd hummed with uneasy murmurs and Ariane was obliged to clap her hands and call for silence. Then she addressed the Irish girl. "Mademoiselle O'Hanlon, I know we have all heard rumors of this *Book of Shadows.* But it is a myth, no more true than stories of the devil's Sabbaths and witches flying on broomsticks."

"The *Book of Shadows* exists, milady," Cat said fiercely,

banging the tip of the staff against the ground for emphasis. "I saw it with my own eyes."

"Was it hideous, covered with the skin of dead babies?" Madame Jehan mocked.

"No, mistress." Cat spun around to glare at her. "The book was bound in leather, harmless looking as a Bible. It was the contents that'd make your blood run cold, spells of a most fearsome nature."

Cat prowled the edge of the crowd, thrusting her face so close, her expression so savage, many in the front ranks shrank back. "Spells to make you immortal by drinking the blood of another living creature. Or to preserve your own life by ripping out someone else's beating heart. Potions to keep you young by devouring the livers of wee babes."

"Madre di dios!" one of the Spanish women cried, crossing herself.

Marie Claire bent down to mutter in Ariane's ear. "Mademoiselle Cat is enjoying herself a bit too much, methinks."

Ariane feared the abbess was right. Catriona did seem to be taking a gruesome relish in the alarm she was raising, especially from the two English women. Cat stopped in front of the Waters sisters, raising the staff like a Druid priestess preparing to make a sacrifice. "There were potions in that book telling you how to confound your enemies with bitter poisons to make them drown in their own blood. Or how to inflict diseases upon your foes, making their skin turn black with raw oozing—"

"Mademoiselle O'Hanlon, please," Ariane attempted to lighten the grim mood with a smile. "You will be giving us all nightmares."

Cat reluctantly lowered her arms and stalked back to stand before Ariane. "Your pardon, milady, but that book is the stuff of nightmares. I have not even told you the worst. There were instructions in the *Book of Shadows* for waging war on such a dire scale as has never been seen on this earth. Potions to spread a foul pestilence in the air so thousands at a time will sicken and die. Or directions to brew up a terrible explosion that would level a city, even one the size of Paris."

"Or London perhaps?" Prudence Waters shrilled. Her younger sister clung trembling to her arm. But Prudence shook free of Elizabeth and leapt to her feet, her plump face washed pale. "Milady, it is plain as a pikestaff where all this is leading. This Irishwoman, this—this Neve person means to employ the deviltry in that *Book of Shadows* against my own country."

Cat flung the Englishwoman a sad, angry look. "*Meant* to, God rest her soul. But Neve will be meaning nothing now, because she is dead. She was foully slaughtered by an evil man who wanted that cursed book."

These grim tidings caused everyone to fall silent, even Prudence.

"So who has the book now?" Ariane asked with mounting dread.

"Neve's murderous kinsman, Padraig O'Donal, a nasty little man who fancies himself a sorcerer. Padraig scarce knows how to scratch his own arse let alone perform any magic. He can't decipher a word of the old runic language. But he reckons that the *Book of Shadows* might be worth a pot of gold to the right party. So he killed poor Neve and took the book, hoping to make his fortune by selling it."

"And where is this Padraig now?" Ariane demanded.

"Well, he could scarce peddle the book in Ireland, milady, not with Neve's friends and her loyal kin after him. But Padraig's a wily devil. He gave us all the slip and stole away on a small fishing boat." Cat raked back her wild mane of hair in a frustrated gesture. "I tracked the wretch as far as the coast of Brittany, but I lost him after that."

"Marvelous," Marie Claire muttered. "Just what we need. We are already cursed with the Dark Queen and her poisons. Now we have a mad Irishman running amuck peddling the secrets of the devil amongst us."

"There's even worse to tell," Cat said.

"Isn't there always?" the Abbess grumbled.

"Marie, please." Ariane gently hushed her friend. "Continue, mademoiselle."

Cat placed the staff before her, bracing both hands upon it as though preparing to deliver the final blow. "I am not the only one tracking Padraig to recover that book. There is a witch-hunter after him as well."

The mere mention of a witch-hunter was enough to send a ripple of panic through the gathering. Ariane forced herself to inquire calmly. "A witch-hunter? Who is he?"

Cat gave a rueful shake of her head. "I don't rightly know, milady, but he has been prowling Ireland these last six months, practicing his hellish trade. A tall, gaunt man, with a burning gaze, an ugly, scarred face, his head bald as the devil himself."

"I always pictured Satan as being rather hairy," Madame Jehan objected.

Her remark produced a few nervous titters. Cat arched one eyebrow in contemptuous fashion at the old woman, then went on, "This witch-hunter might as well be the devil. No one seems to know from where he has sprung. He may well be one of your countrymen, milady, because he calls himself Le Balafre."

"The scarred one," Ariane murmured.

A young Frenchwoman near Madame Jehan shivered and started to cry. Madame Jehan gave the girl a bracing hug. "Now, dearie, we've dealt with devils of our own and survived. Remember Le Vis, God rot his soul. He burns in hell and we are all still here."

There was a chorus of assent from many of the other women, but Cat said scornfully, "I have heard of your Le Vis. He was nothing more than a mad monk in his black robes compared to this new man. Le Balafre fights against our kind more like some pagan warrior. He puts anyone he believes is a witch straight to the sword."

Cat's words evoked more wails of consternation, but Ariane

held up one hand for silence, seeking to comfort herself as well as the frightened cluster of women.

"At least if this Le Balafre were to find the *Book of Shadows,* he will surely destroy it," she reasoned. "For once, a witch-hunter may do us all a good turn."

"I wish it were that simple, milady, but there is worse to tell."

Marie Claire groaned loudly and Ariane shifted on her uncomfortable seat, regarding Cat with a hint of impatience.

"What could possibly be worse?" she asked tartly.

Cat shuffled her feet, for the first time looking reluctant to speak. "My good friend, Neve, was not always the most discreet of women. She kept a record of all the daughters of the earth who were known to her."

At Ariane's indrawn breath, Cat went on hastily, "Neve meant nothing but good by her recordings. In gentler, more tolerant times she hoped to write a history of the daughters of the earth."

"And where exactly are those records now?" Ariane asked sternly, although her heart sank because she already knew the answer. She could read the truth in Cat's chagrined eyes.

"The leather cover of the *Book of Shadows* had a small slit in the binding. The records are concealed in that. Not—not all that well concealed so if Le Balafre were able to get his hands on the book . . ."

Cat's voice trailed off, but she had no need to finish. She had said enough. The grove rang out with cries of fear and dismay on all sides. Prudence Waters leapt back to her feet, shaking one meaty fist in Cat's direction.

"You Irish are a race of idiots! No wonder you need the English to come in and sort your country out for you. A pox on all stupid Celts, I say!"

A hot tide of color surged into Cat's cheeks as red as her hair. Bellowing out a Gaelic curse, she charged at Prudence with the staff upraised. But Prudence caught the end of the staff in her wide palm as the blow fell. The two women went at each other in a flurry of skirts, kicking, shouting, and fighting for control of the staff.

Ariane shot to her own feet to call the women back to order, but the entire meeting erupted into chaos. Charbonne darted forward to intervene in the fight. She jerked the staff away from both women and flung it aside. Then she knocked Prudence and Cat's heads together. Unfortunately this caused both the combatants to turn on Charbonne, and a fresh melee ensued of gouging, scratching, and biting. Caught up in the excitement, Hermoine and Louise Lavalle renewed their quarrel, slapping and pinching.

The other women thronged round, some calling out encouragement to the fighters, while others cried, "Shame, shame!" Still others sank down, weeping hysterically.

Ariane rushed from one group to another, struggling to restore calm, shouting until her voice was hoarse. She staggered back, overcome with sheer frustration.

Marie Claire, who had kept well back from the uproar, merely rolled her eyes. "Well, so much for understanding and harmony among the daughters of the earth. And just think, my dear Ariane, so far, only two of them have had a chance to speak."

¥¥¥¥

HOURS LATER THE CIRCLE OF STONE WAS SILENT, EXCEPT FOR THE crackle of the dying fire and the distant roar of the surf far below. Ariane sagged wearily on the flat altar rock, resting her head upon her hands. The other women had melted away or, more accurately, had *limped* off to seek shelter for the night before departing for home in the morning.

After Catriona O'Hanlon's dire tidings, the rest of the meeting had been mercifully uneventful. Ariane had succeeded in restoring order when she had lost her temper and snatched up the staff, threatening to crack a few heads herself. The rare sight of the Lady of Faire Isle in such a fury had persuaded even Cat O'Hanlon and Prudence Waters to resume their seats. If Renard could have seen Ariane brandishing that staff, her husband would have been proud of her, she thought with a tired smile.

She toyed with the ring on her finger, the strange metal band with its runic markings that insured that Renard was never more than a thought away from her. With the burden of that missing *Book of Shadows* weighing heavily upon her, Ariane longed to employ the ring's magic to call out to Renard. *"My love. Come to me. I need you."*

And he would saddle up his fastest mount and thunder through the night until he reached her side. But Ariane feared she had disturbed her husband's peace enough of late between her fits of melancholy and her insistent demands upon him to give her a child. There was little that Renard or anyone else could do tonight about recovering the *Book of Shadows.* Better to let him have his rest while he could. None of them were going to know much ease in the coming days until that cursed book was found.

Ah, but Ariane would have welcomed the strong feel of Renard's arms around her at this moment. She stole one last wistful glance at the ring, then sighed, resisting any further temptation by burying her hands in her lap.

The soft swish of skirts alerted her to Marie Claire's return to her side. The abbess and her servant had been making a final inspection of the grove, checking for any articles that might have been left behind, making certain the torches were extinguished.

"Charbonne has gone to fetch our horses from that fisherman's shack. When she has them saddled, she'll whistle for us to join her on the path," Marie Claire informed Ariane.

Ariane gave a weary nod and shifted to make room for the

abbess beside her on the rock. Marie Claire sank down beside her and produced a small leather flask.

"Here, my dear," she said thrusting it toward Ariane.

Ariane accepted the flask gratefully. Her throat was parched from all the talking, shouting, and arguing she had done. She tipped the flask to her lips, but instead of the cool water she'd expected, she got a fiery mouthful of a very potent brandy.

Ariane bent forward, spluttering and gasping. "M-marie Claire!"

The abbess only smiled and urged her to take another swallow. "Go on. After all we've endured tonight, you and I could both use a stiff drink."

Ariane winced, but obeyed, taking a more careful swallow. As the brandy spread its welcoming warmth through her veins, she handed the flask back to the abbess.

"Thank you," Ariane murmured.

Marie Claire took a long pull at the flask herself, then recorked it, daintily wiping her mouth with the back of her hand. She studied Ariane's face with approval.

"That's better. You were looking very peaked before. Mistress Cat and all her tales of horror would be enough to drive the blood from anyone's veins. Unless you have some other reason for appearing a trifle pale?"

Ariane's hand flew reflexively to the region of her empty womb. "No, no other reason that I know of yet," she said sadly.

Marie Claire gave Ariane's hand a comforting pat. Ariane ducked her head. She found her barren state difficult to talk about even with an old friend like Marie Claire, but she confessed forlornly. "Lately, I have started to wonder if my childless state is a judgment from God because . . . because I was not content with just desiring a child. I so badly wished for a daughter."

"Tush, child. I don't think God punishes people for their wishes." Marie Claire gave Ariane's fingers a light squeeze before drawing her hand back into her own robes. "But He does tend to answer prayers after His own fashion and in His own time."

"Meaning I should be more patient. You sound just like Renard."

"And how fares your very mighty and large husband?" Marie Claire inquired affectionately.

"Well enough, I hope. I was tempted to send for him immediately after Catriona's tidings. But Renard would nigh kill himself getting here, and there is scarce anything he could do tonight."

"No, but in the days ahead, the comte and his retainers might prove useful in searching for this Padraig O'Donal."

"What do you think our chances are, Marie?" Ariane asked dispiritedly. "Of finding O'Donal before he sells that book or the witch-hunter gets to him first. That Irishman could be anywhere by now. It will be like looking for a needle in a haystack."

"Surely not as bad as all that," Marie Claire protested. "After all, there cannot be that many people wealthy or mad enough to want to purchase this *Book of Shadows*. Unfortunately, the most likely one is—"

"Catherine," Ariane filled in with an involuntary shudder. "I have been trying not to think of the possibility of the Dark Queen acquiring that book."

Catherine had already accomplished enough evil between her poisons and the miasma she had brewed up to foment the madness of St. Bartholomew's Eve. What more havoc might the Dark Queen wreak with the powerful spells Cat had described?

"But Catherine is already well versed in the ways of dark magic and—and perhaps the *Book of Shadows* would not even interest her," Ariane said, seeking to convince herself as much as Marie Claire. "Since we reached that truce after St. Bartholomew's Eve, she has not employed her black arts on anyone."

"That we know of," Marie Claire said dryly. "Unfortunately, since Louise Lavalle and Madame Pechard were exposed, our spy system is not what it once was. A pity since Gabrielle is so much at court, she could not be persuaded to keep an eye on Catherine and provide us with information."

Ariane shook her head vehemently. "Even if Gabrielle were willing, I would never allow that. I worry enough about my reckless younger sister being in such close proximity to that evil woman and what mad risks Gabrielle might already be taking. It seems like forever since we have had any reports from Bette."

"Well, as to that, I had no opportunity of telling you earlier. My little hawk has finally returned from Paris."

Among her gifts as a daughter of the earth, Marie Claire possessed the ability to train birds to carry messages over long distances. A gift that Ariane had found a great boon in the past, even more so since Gabrielle had run off to Paris. Without the regular reports from Bette, Ariane thought she would have run mad with worry for her sister. Although sometimes, she feared she was better off not knowing exactly what Gabrielle was up to.

She regarded Marie Claire with a mingling of eagerness and apprehension. "So what did Bette have to say? How is Gabrielle? Is—is she well?"

"Well enough, but you had best brace yourself for some tidings of an extraordinary nature."

"Dear God! What—what is it? Tell me, Marie."

To her astonishment a slow smile spread over the abbess's face. "Nicolas Remy is still alive."

"What!"

As Marie Claire told her about Remy's startling resurrection, his arrival in Paris, Ariane could not contain herself. She leaped to her feet and paced excitedly, tears of joy stinging her eyes. Not just because of her affection for the solemn captain, but because of what this could mean for Gabrielle. For the first time in years, Ariane saw a glimmer of hope for her wayward sister.

"Thank you, God," she cried, clasping her hands together. "Oh, Marie, this is wonderful. I never recognized it at the time, but I believe Remy was the one man who could have healed

Gabrielle, restored her magic. When she learned of his death, the last, best part of her seemed to die with him. But now—"

Ariane broke off, realizing that Marie Claire was not sharing her enthusiasm.

The older woman stared into the dying embers of the bonfire, avoiding Ariane's eyes.

"Remy's return is a good thing, is it not?" Ariane faltered. "Surely it could mean Gabrielle's salvation."

Marie Claire sighed. "It might have done, except that Bette reports Gabrielle appears to have done her best to—to end their friendship, to drive him away from her."

The hope that had flared inside Ariane died with painful swiftness. She groaned. "Oh, of course Gabrielle did. I might have known. Was there ever anyone better than my sister at pushing away anyone who might love or care for her?"

The abbess fingered the small wooden crucifix suspended around her neck. Gazing into Marie Claire's eyes, Ariane read enough to realize that Marie Claire was holding something back from her.

"What is it?" she asked. "What else did Bette have to say about Gabrielle? What aren't you telling me?"

"Forgive me, my dear. But you are already so overburdened." Marie Claire fluttered her hand in a helpless gesture. "You have quite enough to worry about."

"I fear that I do, but you had better tell me all the same."

When Marie Claire remained reluctant, Ariane sank back down beside her and pressed the older woman's hands. "Tell me, Marie."

"It may be nothing to worry about at all, but apparently Gabrielle has befriended another wise woman living there in Paris . . . one Cassandra Lascelles."

When Ariane regarded Marie Claire with a puzzled look, the abbess asked, "You have not heard of this woman?"

"A little." Ariane frowned, wracking her memory. "Cassandra is some sort of recluse, is she not? A poor, helpless blind woman whose entire family was destroyed by witch-hunters years ago."

"Blind, Cassandra may be. But helpless?" Marie Claire grimaced. "If the rumors I have heard about Mademoiselle Lascelles are true, the woman dabbles in many of the black arts. She is supposed to be especially adept at necromancy."

Ariane squirmed, avoiding Marie Claire's eyes, because at one time Ariane herself had dabbled with the dangerous art, raising her mother's spirit from the dead. There were times that Ariane still longed for Evangeline Cheney's wise counsel, but Ariane had made her mother a solemn promise to leave all such dark magic well alone.

"A cloud of suspicion hangs over this young woman," the abbess said gravely. "There are many daughters of the earth who wonder: How, out of all the Lascelles women, was Cassandra the only one to survive the witch-hunters' attack? Some even wonder if Cass herself had something to do with that raid."

Marie Claire shrugged. "Of course, all these tales about Cass might be nothing more than gossip and innuendo. All the same, Gabrielle ought to be cautioned."

"You know Gabrielle will never heed anything I have to say." Ariane sighed.

"You are not Gabrielle's only sister. Miri has also worried much about Gabrielle. In fact—" Marie Claire hesitated. She drew in a deep breath before finishing, "In fact, Miri has made up her mind to journey to Paris and see Gabrielle for herself."

Ariane stared at Marie Claire, dumbfounded at the notion her shy younger sister would even think of such a thing. Her initial surprise was instantly replaced with alarm. "Miri shall do no such thing! Bad enough that Gabrielle has run off on her own. I'll not have two sisters swallowed up in Paris, so close to the Dark Queen's grasp."

Ariane leaped to her feet and stalked away from Marie

Claire, demanding, "Where is Charbonne with those horses? I shall find Miri at once and tell her that I forbid her to set one foot off of Faire Isle."

But Marie Claire sprang up and took hold of Ariane's arm. "My dear child, you cannot forbid Miri anything. This is what I have dreaded telling you. It is too late.

"Miri has already gone."

Chapter Thirteen

GABRIELLE LIFTED THE HEM OF HER SKIRTS TO AVOID THE MUD, horse droppings, and other offal that clogged the street. The passageway threaded through buildings crowded close together, three- and four-story timber frame houses and shops. Some of the structures were so old, they sagged against their nearest neighbor.

The wide brim of her straw hat shielded Gabrielle's face from the late morning sun as she sought No. 14 rue des Cartelles. There it was. The last house but one before the corner. A newer building of whitewashed stone, a prosperous ironmonger, had the lower level, the horizontal shutter folded down, making a counter to display the shop's wares. The second floor was the shopkeeper's dwelling place, the third reserved for apprentices and servants, while the attic was let out as accommodations to travelers.

Gabrielle squinted as she studied the fourth story's narrow window, where the shutters were forbiddingly closed. This, according to Catherine's spies, was where Captain Nicolas Remy had taken his lodgings, living under the name of Jacques Ravelle.

Most of the people who brushed past Gabrielle in the street were working people, apprentices, shopkeepers, artisans, housewives, a few beggars. Clad as she was in her oldest gown, with her hair tumbling loose about her shoulders, Gabrielle realized she could have passed for a humble tradesman's daughter herself.

Exhausted by the events of last evening, Gabrielle had passed a sleepless night. She had simply felt too tired this morning to be decked out in the corset, farthingale, and petticoats required for one of her elegant and costly gowns. Never had she looked less like the infamous courtesan she was reputed to be, a woman capable of carrying out the promise she had made to the Dark Queen, to betray Remy, to seduce him from his duty.

The ring she had been forced to take from Catherine was already locked away in a drawer and Gabrielle had lain awake for hours, trying to think of some way out of the devil's bargain she had made and still manage to keep Remy safe. One did not lightly break faith with the Dark Queen and Gabrielle silently cursed Remy for putting them both in this difficult position.

Still, she was eager to see the man if only to find out how he had fared with Navarre last night. She waited impatiently for a grain cart pulled by a stout mule to lumber past. Darting across the street, she hastened toward Remy's lodging, dismayed to feel her heart begin to trip faster. Who was she trying to fool? she wondered.

She was quite simply . . . eager to see him.

Stealing inside the workshop, Gabrielle was accosted by the harsh clanging of hammers pounding hot iron into shape. The forge bellowed out a fiery blast of heat like a dragon's breath, rendering the shirts of the young apprentices damp with sweat. She had no difficulty charming one of the gangly youths into showing her the way up to Remy's chambers.

She felt an unaccountable flutter of nervousness. Her knock was more timid than she intended. Curling her knuckles tighter, she rapped harder. No one answered. Gabrielle frowned. The apprentice had told her that Wolf had gone out, but the ironworker was certain that Monsieur Ravelle was still within. Gabrielle started to knock again, then tried the door handle. To her astonishment and consternation, it turned easily.

Was Remy quite mad, to not even bother locking his door? Never mind about the dangers of the Dark Queen. This was Paris, for heaven's sake, not some rustic village in Navarre. The city teemed with robbers, pickpockets, and cutthroats.

Gabrielle shoved open the door and peeked cautiously inside. "Remy?"

The room was so shrouded in gloom, it took Gabrielle several moments before she was able to discern anything. Not that there was that much to see in the sparsely furnished chamber. Someone was stretched out upon the cot underneath a thin blanket. She caught the gleam of dark gold hair tumbled against the pillow.

Remy was still abed at this hour? It seemed so unlike him, Gabrielle's stomach knotted with apprehension. She tiptoed over to the bed.

"Remy? Are—are you—" She broke off as a guttural cry breached Remy's lips. A cry so horrible that Gabrielle jerked back in alarm.

Remy writhed on the mattress, dislodging the blanket. It fell to his waist, exposing the contours of his chest, his skin glistening with perspiration. With another low moan, he tossed on his pillow as though he was locked in the delirium of a fever.

Fear shook Gabrielle that Catherine had already broken her word, found some way to get at Remy and administer one of her deadly poisons. Gabrielle dropped to her knees by the cot, groping frantically for Remy's pulse. She captured his wrist for a few fleeting seconds before he wrenched away from her, but it was enough to assure her his pulse was strong, although thundering rapidly.

He groaned again, muttering, "Sword . . . damn you. Give

me . . . sword. Need to fight . . . need to save." He shuddered with a deep sob that wrenched at Gabrielle's heart.

No fever held Remy in its grip. He was trapped in the throes of a nightmare . . .

ϟϟϟ

THE CHURCH BELLS PEALED OUT AN INCESSANT CLANGOR THAT REMY *thought would drive him mad. He clutched his hands to his ears as he staggered through streets that twisted and turned. Madness erupted around him, the toll of the bells punctuated with the screams of women, the wails of children, the guttural cries of men. Paris was washed in ashen gray, the houses, the cobblestones, the faces of the dead and dying. The only color left was the crimson tide of blood, splashed upon the walls, pooling beneath the bodies sprawled on the pavement.*

His sword . . . Remy needed to retrieve his sword before it was too late. But every step he took, another massive wall reared up before him. He ran down one alley after another, his desperation mounting. The ground was so thick with bodies, he could scarcely move without stumbling. Losing his footing, he crashed to his knees by the lifeless form of a burly man, his beard spattered with blood.

"Dev," Remy choked.

The dead man's eyes flew open to stare accusingly at Remy. "Why didn't you save us? You should have saved us. You are our Scourge."

"Dev, I—I am sorry. I lost my sword. I—" Remy clutched at Devereaux's hand. But the man's flesh melted away until Remy gripped nothing but skeletal fingers.

Remy recoiled, his breath coming in ragged gasps as he heard the tramp of feet, the strike of boots against stone. They were coming for him now, the demon army that had murdered his people. And he had no armor, no weapon. He braced himself.

But only one man emerged from the ashy shadows at the

end of the street. Tall and powerful, his features were obscured beneath the half-visor of a steel helmet, his tunic and hands soaked in blood. The demon bore down upon Remy, a cold smile curling his lips. He raised one bloodstained hand toward the visor, preparing to shove it back and reveal the rest of his hideous features.

"No!" Remy tried to escape, not wanting to see. But he was held fast by soft warm hands, the voice of an angel calling to him from some far-off place . . .

"REMY! REMY."

Gabrielle hovered over him, not wanting to make things worse by brutally snapping Remy awake. She shook his shoulder gently, called his name in soothing tones, but to no avail. Remy thrashed on his pillow, ranting about lost swords and demons. Gabrielle took his face firmly between her hands, straining to hold him still.

"Remy! *Wake up.*"

With a loud roar, Remy opened his eyes. He surged upward and launched himself at Gabrielle, her straw hat flying off her head. Before she could draw another breath, he had her pinned beneath him on the bed, his muscular body bearing down upon her.

Damp strands of hair tangled across his eyes, his expression so wild, Gabrielle's throat clogged with fear. Remy growled, drawing back his fist.

"No! Remy," Gabrielle cried. "S-stop. It's me."

She flinched, bracing herself for the blow. Remy checked his hand, bare inches from her face. Blinking in confusion, his gaze traveled from her to the gloom-ridden surroundings of the bed-chamber.

"Gabrielle? W-wha—"

"You were having a nightmare." She wriggled one arm free.

With trembling fingers, she stroked the hair back from his brow. "Only a nightmare."

Panting, he shifted his gaze back to her. She thought herself familiar with all of Remy's expressions, proud, stern, tender, even the darkness of his temper. But never had she seen this strong, silent man look so broken and vulnerable. Gabrielle wrapped her arms around him, drawing his head to her shoulder. He buried his face against her neck, his breath still ragged.

"It's all right," she crooned, seeking to comfort him as she would have her little sister, Miri, who was frequently prey to bad dreams. Gabrielle caressed the back of his head, burying her lips in his hair.

"It's all over and I am here," she murmured. "Just hold on to me."

His arms closed so tight about her, Gabrielle thought she would be crushed to the very bone. But she hugged him just as fiercely until she felt the mad race of his heart begin to slow. She stroked her fingers down the curve of his spine, over his warm, bare skin, trying to ease the tension she felt in the taut muscles of his back. As her hand trailed lower, she was startled by a fact that had escaped her before.

Remy was completely naked.

Muttering something incoherent, he levered himself off her. Springing from the bed, he groped about the floor until he found a pair of breeches. Gabrielle struggled up more slowly, trying to do the modest thing and avert her eyes. She had had many lovers and never any desire to look at any of them.

But their bodies had been weak and soft compared to the hard frame of a man who had spent his life soldiering. Remy had his back to her as he eased the fabric up over his sinewy thighs and the taut curve of his buttocks. Gabrielle could not help staring.

Remy darted a furtive look back at her. He finished doing up his breeches, then stalked over to the washstand, splashing so much water over his face, it was as if the man was trying to drown himself. Slicking back his hair, he wrenched the shutter open, letting the morning breeze play over his face and bare chest.

The eruption of sunlight into the room caused Gabrielle to blink. She shaded her eyes with her hand to peer at Remy. He braced one arm against the window frame, his face half-averted from her, but she noted the dark stain of red that began at his neck and crept all the way up into his cheeks.

An awkward silence ensued and Gabrielle sought for something to say. She was supposed to be capable of coming up with a witty rejoinder to cover any situation. Not just sit here, blushing like some foolish virgin.

Nervously twisting one strand of her hair, she said, "G-goodness, Remy, there is no need to be so embarrassed. It is not as though I have never seen a man naked before."

She winced as soon as the words were out of her mouth, realizing that was not the best thing to remind him.

"I know that," he replied. "And it is not as though I have that much modesty. It wasn't you seeing me naked that bothers me. It was . . . the other thing."

"What other—" Gabrielle began, only to break off as the realization struck her. It was her bearing witness to his vulnerability in the wake of his nightmare. That was what shamed Nicolas Remy to the depths of his proud warrior's soul.

She understood all too well that raw feeling that came from exposing too much of one's heart to a stranger. But she wasn't a stranger. Despite everything that divided them, she was still very much his friend. Gabrielle followed him to the window. He tensed at her approach, presenting her with the rigid line of his back.

She rested one hand on Remy's shoulder with a gentleness she rarely displayed. "Remy, everyone has bad dreams."

"Soldiers don't." He added, in a voice laced with self-disgust, "At least if they do, they are not supposed to quake like a mewling boy."

"No one would ever mistake you for a boy." Gabrielle tugged at his arm, coaxed him round to face her. Remy shifted reluctantly and Gabrielle's breath caught in her throat, the sunlight revealing to her what she had not noticed before.

Remy's chest was a mass of scars, some only faint streaks, others jagged lines of white flesh that marred the smooth surface of his skin. Gabrielle clapped her hand to her mouth to smother her cry of horror.

Remy's mouth tightened, but he attempted to jest. "Not a pretty sight, is it? I expect I look a lot better from the rear. If you'll just hand me my shirt?"

Gabrielle scarcely heard his request. Remy was a man who'd fought in many battles and he'd always borne a few scars to prove it. But nothing like this. She traced the outline of one that was crueler than the rest, a harsh ridge that began at his shoulder and ended perilously near the region of his heart. She was able to picture too clearly the sword that had left this harsh mark upon him, tearing through skin and muscle. She could almost feel the cold sharp bite of the weapon piercing her own shoulder.

"Oh, Remy," Gabrielle whispered, splaying her fingers over his chest, needing to feel the strong reassuring beat of his heart.

"It's nothing to get so distressed about, my dear," he said gruffly. "Just marks from a few old wounds."

"The scars are from that night, aren't they? St. Bartholomew's Eve. And that is what you were dreaming about."

"Perhaps. I don't remember my dreams after I wake."

He was lying. The memory of that nightmare was still etched in the lines that bracketed his mouth, in the shadows that haunted his eyes.

"You kept muttering something about a demon. A man whose face was hidden from you. A man you didn't want to see. Who was it?"

"I have no idea. It was only a dream, a foolish dream."

"But—"

"Just forget about it."

Gabrielle recognized the note of finality in his voice, like a door being slammed closed in her face, because she had done it so often herself, fiercely guarding the raw places in her heart. She had just never experienced before how hard it was to be the one shut out.

She caressed his chest with both hands as though somehow she could rub out the scars, smooth away the painful memories as well. Remy's flesh quivered as she continued her reckless exploration, becoming less aware of the scars and more aware of the man, the bold contours of his chest and arms, the powerful sculpting of muscle, the fine dusting of golden hair that disappeared beneath the band of his breeches.

She heard Remy's breath quicken, realized the heat that surged into his face no longer had anything to do with embarrassment.

"I could take him to my bed, seduce him," she had told Catherine.

Gabrielle was dismayed to realize it had not been an empty boast. How easy it would be to carry out that pledge, the more so because Gabrielle wanted Nicolas Remy in a way she had no man for a long time. Perhaps ever. The thought filled her with the familiar panic, made her afraid to meet his eyes.

She forced herself to do so and discovered him staring at her, the faint stubble of beard that roughened his jaw making him look lean and dangerous. But it was his dark, brooding expression that took her aback. His arousal was readily apparent but tempered with wariness.

He seized hold of her wrists and held her hands away from his chest, demanding, "What are you doing here this morning, Gabrielle? And how did you get in?"

This was hardly the greeting she had anticipated after helping Remy to see Navarre last night. She didn't expect Remy to be grateful, but she thought they had reached a truce of sorts, that Remy might have come to trust her a little. Although—she winced as she remembered the bargain she'd made with Catherine—there was not the least reason why he should.

Gabrielle yanked her hands free, whipping them almost guiltily behind her back. "I came in as one usually does, through the door. The door that you failed to lock."

"I did lock the damned thing, but it's broken. It doesn't always catch."

"Then I suggest you have it fixed. Because I noticed you haven't asked me the most important question yet."

"And that would be . . ."

"How did I know how to find you?"

"How did you?"

"Catherine very kindly furnished me with your address, even the false name you used to rent your lodgings. She had you followed when you left the palace last night."

Remy received Gabrielle's information with astonishing aplomb, his agitation only betrayed by the muscle that tightened in his jaw. Retrieving a discarded shirt, he dragged the white linen over his head.

"Then the Dark Queen knows—"

"Pretty damned near everything," Gabrielle told him tersely. "She had us spied upon and is fully aware of the little meeting I arranged for you with Navarre."

Remy eased his arms into the sleeves and then shrugged. After the hellish night she had spent fretting over him, terrified for his life, the man's calm was maddening. Storming in front of him, Gabrielle placed her hands on the flat of her hips. "Remy! Did you hear what I am telling you? Catherine *knows.* You can't risk staying here in Paris another day. It would be better if you were miles away from here."

"Better for who?" Remy retorted. "If the Dark Queen knows everything, then why am I not dead? Or at least arrested. And you too."

Because I pledged my soul to the woman and yours as well.

"I—I am not really sure," Gabrielle hedged. "I believe I managed to convince her that you no longer pose a threat to her interests."

"That must have taken some damned clever convincing." Remy eyed her suspiciously. "Exactly how did you manage to do that?"

"I am a good liar. Besides, if she martyred you a second time, it would only add fuel to tensions between the Catholics and Huguenots. Catherine is finding civil war a costly business. She will likely want you back at court where she can keep an eye on you. You will be safe enough, but only for the moment."

As long as she convinced the Dark Queen that she had Nicolas Remy under her spell, beneath her control and in her bed. But Gabrielle could well imagine Remy's reaction if she told him that.

Instead she stretched one hand out to him in a pleading gesture. "Oh, Remy, please. Even you must see it is too dangerous for you to remain. You have to leave. Now."

"I appreciate your concern," he said tersely. "But I'll stay and continue to take my chances."

Ignoring her outstretched hand, he stepped around her, continuing to dress, tightening the drawstrings of his shirt. Gabrielle let her hand fall awkwardly back to her side. When she had parted from Remy on the backstairs of the palace, there had been something approaching the old warmth between them.

But there was an edge to Remy this morning, even a hint of hostility, and Gabrielle believed she knew the reason for it. He must have failed in his efforts at convincing Navarre to try and escape. She wasn't that surprised. Despite his indolent manner, Henry was shrewd, a pragmatist who had only survived this long by never taking unnecessary chances.

Henry remaining in France was exactly what Gabrielle desired to further her own ambitions. But she found she could not rejoice over Remy's failure. She suspected that Remy wanted Navarre to be a second King Arthur, imbued with all that legendary monarch's courage and ideals, a man that Remy could serve and follow to the death. Just as Remy had once imagined her to be perfect, flawless and chaste.

It was astonishing that a soldier like Remy, who had seen so much of the ugliness in the world, the brutality of war, could still retain his own impossibly high standards of honor and expect others to do likewise. It was his most endearing and exasperating trait and made her long to wrap him in her arms and shield him from the disappointments he was doomed to suffer.

Although she doubted he would welcome any sympathy from her on the subject, she said softly, "So I am guessing from your grim demeanor that your meeting with Navarre did not go well. You weren't able to persuade him to attempt the escape."

Remy inspected his unshaven jaw in the small cracked mirror above the washstand. "No, he agreed."

"What!" Gabrielle gasped.

"Navarre consented to let me arrange his escape, but only under certain conditions. All of them, of course, concerning you." He turned from the mirror long enough to cast a bitter look at Gabrielle. "Congratulations. You have the man completely bewitched. He won't return to Bearn unless I find a way to fetch you with us."

Recovering from her initial shock, Gabrielle said tartly, "*That* is never going to happen. I told you before that my future is here in Paris. And Henry's as well."

"It seems that *Henry* has his own plans for your future. He intends to find you a husband."

"A husband!"

"Yes, he's got some damned notion that it will make your liaison with him more respectable if he gets some poor sot to wed you. A lawful lord and master to help keep control over you and insure you do exactly as the king wishes. Navarre believes a husband could order you to leave Paris with him."

Gabrielle swore roundly and took an agitated turn about the room. As if her life wasn't already complicated enough between trying to keep Remy from getting himself killed and steering her own way through the treacherous vipers at court and the Dark Queen's wiles. Now Henry must get this fool idea into his head.

It was not unusual for some lord to accept the charge of a king's mistress in wedlock, the man being well rewarded with lands, wealth, and titles. But Gabrielle had no wish to be burdened with some simpering ass of a courtier as her husband.

"Marvelous," she muttered. "And did Henry happen to mention exactly what poor sot he has in mind for me?"

Remy picked up his razor from the washstand, although from the way he looked at it, Gabrielle wasn't sure if he was contemplating shaving or slitting his throat.

"Me. The king wants me to marry you."

Gabrielle listened in stunned silence, certain Remy could not be serious. But he obviously was. She had to stifle a mad urge to break into hysterical laughter at the sheer irony of it. At roughly the same time Gabrielle had been promising the Dark Queen *to seduce him,* Navarre had commanded Remy *to marry her.*

But one glance at Remy's grim expression robbed her of any desire to laugh. No wonder he was so tense around her, looking like someone had flung mud at his family escutcheon. He would have found the idea of marrying a soiled woman like her an intolerable insult. That it should be so hurt Gabrielle more than she would admit.

But she gave a proud toss of her head. "You marry me? How utterly ridiculous. No doubt you refused with the proper amount of moral outrage."

Remy said nothing, his gaze sliding away from her.

"You did refuse, didn't you?"

When he continued silent, she prodded, "Remy?"

He flung the razor down and snapped. "No. I said I would do it. I pledged to marry you."

Gabrielle's jaw dropped. She was speechless for a moment,

then cried, "Are you quite mad? You do understand the nature of the arrangement Navarre is proposing?"

"Oh, yes, I understand *that* all too well."

"Then why on earth did you ever consent?"

Remy regarded her with a mix of frustration and some other emotion she couldn't read. "Why the devil do you think I would agree?"

"I have no idea."

"Because—" Remy whipped away from her, studying his reflection in the mirror, the set of his jaw rigid. "Because my king commands me. That's damned well why."

Gabrielle swallowed hard. Perhaps at one time Remy might have had a far different reason for wanting to wed her, before he had learned the truth about her and knew what she was. But now— What else had she expected him to say? Still, the thought that he would accept her out of his infernal sense of duty hurt and angered Gabrielle more than if he had rejected her outright.

"Well, what a loyal subject you are, Captain," she said icily. "Ready to fall on your sword for your king or wed his mistress. It's all one to you, isn't it?"

Remy flinched at her sarcasm, but he replied, "You were the one, Gabrielle, who insisted that I abide by whatever he decreed."

"I was talking about his decision regarding your escape plans. Not some absurd matrimonial arrangements."

"There is no need for you to get so perturbed. After all, it does take two people to consent to a betrothal."

Gabrielle glanced at him sharply. So that was what Remy was hoping for, that she would refuse and he would be freed from a duty he obviously found distasteful. But she would be damned before she made it that easy for him.

"Well, why not?" she said, pasting a brittle smile on her face. "It sounds like a good idea to me."

She waited for Remy's reaction to her agreement, expecting shock and dismay. But he maintained a posture of stoic resignation, his spine so rigid it could have been made of iron instead of bone. No doubt that was how the man looked right before a battle when he stared into the mouth of enemy cannons.

Determined to provoke a response from him, Gabrielle continued, "It is always good to have a little additional security in case the king should tire of me. Not that I will ever allow that to happen."

She took a savage satisfaction in the way Remy's lips tightened. "The marriage will be good for you as well because Navarre is certain to reward you handsomely. Marrying me should be good for an estate and a title at the least. Would you settle for a knighthood or are you hoping for a barony?"

"Gabrielle . . ." The dangerous note in Remy's voice should have silenced her, but it only made her more reckless.

"Just think . . . all those years of devoted service, risking your neck on the battlefield and the most you acquired was a captaincy. But all you really needed to do was give the king's whore the honor of your name."

"Gabrielle, stop it," Remy growled and she knew if she had any sense, she'd heed his warning. She'd witnessed the Scourge's temper before.

But she was too angry and hurting to care. She sashayed closer. "How would you like to seal our betrothal, Captain? With a handshake like two merchants signing a contract? Or would you prefer a kiss?"

She wound her arms around his neck and gazed defiantly up at him. His gaze darkened and he gave a low curse. She expected him to fling her from him, but Remy's mouth crashed down on hers with a fury that drove the breath from her body. She tensed before his assault before she responded ferociously in kind until they were not kissing so much as making war upon each other, a fierce battle of lips, a heated duel of tongues.

Remy offered her no quarter, his body hard and unyielding. He forced her back toward the bed. Gabrielle scarcely knew whether he flung her onto the tangled blankets or she yanked him down with her. They tumbled to the cot, grappling in a fiery volley of kisses and roving hands. Remy tugged ruthlessly at the lacings of her gown and wrenched the fabric down her shoulder, baring one of her breasts, cupping it with his callused palm. Gabrielle countered by thrusting her hands beneath his shirt and scoring her nails over the smooth skin of his back.

With a low growl, Remy blazed a path from her neck to the swell of her breast, his unshaven jaw abrading her tender skin. His mouth fastened over her nipple, suckling her, tugging with his teeth until a low moan escaped Gabrielle, her anger spilling into the darker currents of desire. The kind of passion she'd long been afraid to experience, strong, aching, out of control.

Remy pressed himself between her thighs. Even through the folds of fabric, she could feel the hard evidence of his arousal bearing down on the soft core of her sex and the familiar flutters of panic took hold. She stiffened.

"Remy, please. Sto—" Her words were smothered beneath the heat of his mouth as he kissed her again, his mouth both coaxing and demanding her surrender. He shifted his weight and started to ease up her skirt. Gabrielle's panic flared to full-blown terror.

Suddenly it was no longer the rugged planes of Remy's face hovering over her, but the leering countenance of Danton.

"No," she shrilled, thrashing wildly to get away from him. "Stop it!" Not giving him a chance to respond, Gabrielle lashed out frantically, clawing to be free.

Her heart pounded as she braced herself to feel her arms pinioned ruthlessly above her head, followed by the searing pain of his conquest. But the man braced above her froze for a second, then wrenched himself off her. His blurred features cleared, resuming the clean, hard lines of Remy's face, his eyes roiling with frustrated desire and confusion. He backed away from her, his chest rising and falling rapidly as he sought to subdue his passion.

Gabrielle sat up slowly, her cheeks burning with shame over her bout of near hysteria. Remy was not Danton. In her heart she knew that Remy would never seek to take any woman by force and that only made her response all the more irrational.

Her fingers trembled as she worked her gown back up over her shoulder. She could not bring herself to look at Remy, realizing he must find her the most contemptible of jades, teasing, tempting a man to the brink, only to thrust him away. What was it Danton had called her that terrible day? A dishonest little slut.

Remy must be furious with her and he had every right to be. But his voice was more raw with despair than anger. "I don't understand you at all, Gabrielle. Am I that repulsive? You seem willing to make love to any other man in Paris. Why not me?"

"Make love? Is that what you think I do?" Gabrielle gave a hollow laugh. "I survive. I endure. The only way I can ever tolerate bedding a man is to go through the motions, while I pretend that I am somewhere else."

And she knew she would never be able to do that with Remy. He was not the kind of man any woman could pretend away. He'd make her want, ache, and burn for him, but in the end she would shatter with her brutal memories of Danton.

Remy studied her with frowning intensity as though waiting for her to explain further. But Gabrielle feared she'd already said too much. She fumbled with her lacings, getting them in a hopeless snarl. When Remy stepped toward her, she tensed.

"I was only going to help you do up your gown," he said, drawing back.

"Well, don't. We are both in danger of forgetting that our betrothal is to be in name only. I will belong to your king, so it is far better if you never touch me again."

"Very well. I—I promise. I won't."

Rather than reassuring her, his promise inspired her with an unreasonable urge to burst into tears. The sooner she got herself out of here the better. Haphazardly finishing with her laces, she looked about for the straw hat she had lost earlier. She found it wedged between the foot of the bed and the wall, along with some of the garments Remy had discarded last night. She retrieved the crimson-lined cape, smoothed out its folds of midnight blue, and handed it to him.

"You really ought to take better care of this. Satin doesn't clean easily and that cape must have cost you a pretty penny. Where did you—" Gabrielle broke off as a horrified thought occurred to her. "My God, Remy. You and that Wolf friend of yours, the thief— You—you haven't been . . . been . . ."

"Picking pockets and waylaying innocent travelers? No." Remy's gaze still rested broodingly on her face. He tossed the cape down on the bed as though he could not care less about how expensive the garment was.

She pressed him uneasily. "Then where did you get the money?"

"I hired out my sword to some English barons."

"You were a mercenary. For the *English.*"

Remy had always claimed that he loathed war, that he only ever fought in defense of his countrymen. Discovering this compromise of his ideals troubled Gabrielle more than the loss of her own innocence.

"I see. So I am not the only one who has been selling myself."

Remy flushed. "I never looked at my activities in that light. I needed funds to help my king and unfortunately soldiering is the only thing I am good at."

"Just as seducing men is the only thing I—"

"Don't say that. Don't you ever say that." Remy started to grasp her shoulders, staying the gesture as he appeared to remember his pledge. Eyes dark with frustration, he fisted his hands and held them rigid at his side.

"Damnation, Gabrielle, can you not forget all this bloody

nonsense about becoming Navarre's mistress? Let's leave Paris. Now. Let me take you back to Faire Isle."

This unexpected offer astonished her more than anything else had. She did not think he could possibly be serious, but never had Remy appeared more in earnest.

"But why—why would I ever want to go back to Faire Isle?" she faltered.

"Because that's where you belong. That is your home."

Home . . . Remy had no idea the images he evoked with that simple word, of the snug manor house nestled in the valley, smoke rising in lazy whorls from the chimneystack. Of the breeze that crept past her bedchamber window, stirring the bedcurtains and carrying with it the distant tang of the sea and sweet scents of Ariane's herb garden. Of romping with Miri through the cool, mysterious shadows of the wood. Or sitting before the fire while Ariane patiently worked the tangles out of her hair.

These pictures were so vivid, so real, it was as though Gabrielle had painted them on her memory when her magic was at its strongest. Preserved them in the leaves of her sketchbook, a book that she slammed closed.

"I can't go home," Gabrielle said hoarsely. "Ariane—she—she wouldn't want me there. She'll never forgive me for coming to Paris, the things I've done."

"Of course she will. She's your sister. She'll forgive you anything."

"And what about you? Could you forgive me?" Gabrielle peered searchingly up at him. "If you whisked me away to Faire Isle, would you stay there with me?"

Remy hesitated over his reply, but he didn't need to answer. The regret in his dark eyes told Gabrielle everything she needed to know. She turned away from him, gathering up the tattered ends of her pride.

"Never mind. Thank you for your kind offer, Captain, but I

must decline. I am not looking for absolution or a way home. I am quite happy where I am."

"Gabrielle . . ."

She ignored him, fearing that one word more might overset the icy grip she had on her emotions. Jamming her hat on her head, she strode toward the door.

"I must be going." She managed to toss Remy a cool parting smile. "And you really should see about finding a good lock-smith."

❦❦❦

REMY LEANED OUT THE WINDOW, CRANING HIS NECK FOR THE LAST view of Gabrielle as she made her way down the crowded street below. Even clad in that old gown and straw hat, she carried her-self like a duchess and other women moved instinctively aside to let her past, while the men— They fairly snapped their necks, staring at her with naked appreciation and lust-filled glances.

Much as all that ogling made Remy want to crack a few skulls, he could scarce blame other men for their reaction to her sensual beauty. Not when his own body still throbbed with such aching need, he could have pounded his fists against the wall in pure frustration. Or better yet, his head. Why had he just stood there like a bloody fool and let her walk out on him that way?

Why hadn't he been quicker to answer her questions? Could he forgive her? Would he have been willing to take her back to Faire Isle? Could he have forgotten the quest that had brought him to Paris and stayed there with her?

Ah, that was the hitch. The part he'd stumbled over and still did. Ever since St. Bartholomew's Eve, the only thing that had sustained him, kept him sane, was his mission to rescue Navarre. He'd been a soldier all of his life, no home, no family. His duty and honor had been all he'd ever really had and he feared he had compromised the latter.

It had stung when Gabrielle had accused him of selling himself, but she'd been right. He'd bartered his honor for English gold and now he was parceling off the rest of it by consenting to Navarre's nefarious command. To be a husband to Gabrielle, but no husband. To don cuckold's horns before he was even wed.

As he watched Gabrielle vanish into the crowd, he could still hear the echoes of her astonished demand. *"Why on earth did you ever consent?"*

Remy sagged wearily against the sill. His duty. That was what he'd told Gabrielle and he even managed to convince himself that was the reason before he wakened this morning to find her in his bedchamber.

Remy gritted his teeth. If Gabrielle had to descend upon him unannounced, why couldn't she have come in one of her fancy gowns looking all high and mighty? Why'd she have to go all soft and gentle on him, soothing away the nightmare and his ravaged pride? When she had caressed his ugly scars without flinching, her blue eyes so sweet and sad, she had reminded him of the girl who had fashioned his dreams for so long, the Gabrielle of their days on the island, the one she insisted didn't exist.

He'd known right then and there that it was no sense of duty that had made him promise to marry her. He'd agreed because he wanted Gabrielle more than he'd ever wanted any other woman in his life. If he hadn't consented, he feared the king would have given her to someone else. And he couldn't endure that—the thought of Gabrielle being another man's wife, some unscrupulous bastard who'd only wed her for the sake of his own advancement. Who'd stand up with her before God and pledge to love, honor, and cherish her, never meaning a word of it.

And you would? a voice inside him mocked. The way you tried to cherish her earlier? Remy's gaze flicked to the rumpled bed and he flinched with shame at the memory of how he'd flung Gabrielle to the mattress and all but ripped off her gown. He'd never had a great deal of finesse as a lover. His couplings had always been with camp women, hot, hard, and quick, a swift satisfying of a mutual lust.

He'd imagined that he'd be different if he had ever been fortunate enough to have Gabrielle in his bed, slow, tender, and patient, carefully overcoming her maidenly modesty.

Modesty? Remy's lips curved wryly as he remembered how hotly she'd kissed him, digging her nails in his back, just as fiercely passionate. At least in the beginning, until that sudden look of fear had descended over her face. Nay, more like terror when she shrieked at him to stop, then struck out at him as though she feared he wouldn't. As though she actually thought he might try to force her.

Remy frowned, picturing the way her hands had shaken as she'd dragged her gown back up over her shoulder, the tremor in her voice.

"Make love? Is that what you think I do? The only way I can ever tolerate being in bed with a man is to go through the motions and pretend I am somewhere else."

She had looked nothing like an accomplished courtesan in that moment. The bleak expression in her eyes triggered a memory. Of the devastation he'd seen on other women's faces in the aftermath of some battle or siege that had spared their lives but taken their souls. Women brutally ravished by soldiers drunk with bloodlust.

Was it possible that Gabrielle had ever been— The mere thought of such a thing was enough to make him sick with rage. Because if he ever got his hands on the bastard, he'd cut him apart by inches until the miscreant begged to die.

His hands clenched as though he already had his hands around the villain's throat. Remy had to force himself to relax. For all he knew there was no such man and nothing had ever happened to Gabrielle. He might well be letting his imagination run wild.

But one thing he was sure he hadn't imagined. No matter

what Gabrielle declared, she was deeply unhappy with her life as a courtesan and this so-called glorious future as a royal mistress she had planned for herself. The woman needed rescuing even more than his king.

But there would always be a major impediment to helping Gabrielle and that was Gabrielle herself. How the devil did a man even begin to play knight-errant to a woman who swore she didn't want to be saved?

Chapter Fourteen

GABRIELLE WANDERED DOWN THE BUSTLING STREET, STILL REEL-ing from her encounter with Remy. The stubborn pride that had enabled her to walk out the door with her chin held high had long since deserted her. When she blundered headlong into a stout matron, the woman jabbed Gabrielle with the corner of her marketing basket.

"What's the matter with you, young woman?" she snarled as she skirted round Gabrielle. "You'd best get your head out of the clouds and heed what you are doing."

"Sorry," Gabrielle mumbled. Heed what she was doing? It already seemed a little late for that. She had just agreed to marry Nicolas Remy out of sheer defiance.

But it would never happen, she assured herself. The next time she saw him, she would tell him she had no intention of going through with such a farce, that he and his king could both go and be damned. Except that some wistful part of her kept wondering what it would be like to be Remy's bride if things had been different. If there had never been any Danton, any Navarre, any Dark Queen. If she was still an innocent girl . . .

She would have been married on Faire Isle, wearing a simple gown, fashioned of soft blue cloth by weavers on the island. Ariane would have lovingly arranged a circlet of flowers in her hair while Miri danced around them, unable to contain her excitement. Even though Gabrielle was the daughter of a Catholic knight and Remy a Huguenot, differences of religion would not have mattered on Faire Isle. They would have exchanged their vows in the glade behind Belle Haven, sealed with a tender kiss.

She would have given Remy a wedding gift, a scabbard that she had etched with fire-breathing dragons to remind him of the day he had pretended to be her knight in the woods. And that night when she surrendered her virginity, Remy would have been so patient and gentle. Their desire for each other would have been beautiful . . .

"Oh, wake up, Gabrielle, and stop this idiotic dreaming," she told herself fiercely. Damn Nicolas Remy! Before he exploded back into her life, she had at least been sure of her ambitions and her destiny. But he had confused her, made her long for things that were lost to her; her home, her innocence, her magic . . . her love.

Her love? Remy?

Gabrielle came to a dead halt in the middle of the street. A merchant clattering by on horseback cursed out a warning. Gabrielle leapt to one side to keep from being trampled, flattening herself alongside one of the shops. Her heart beat wildly, but not so much from her narrow escape as from the thought she could no longer suppress.

She was in love with Remy.

No, she cared about him. She considered him a friend, that was all.

What a terrible liar you are, a voice inside her mocked. *You've been in love with that man ever since the day he knelt at your feet and vowed to protect you forever.*

Gabrielle shook her head, still wanting to deny it. How could she possibly be in love with a man who . . . who was only every woman's dream of valor and chivalry? Who was so confident in his own strength, he was not afraid to be gentle. Whose honesty shone as bright as polished armor among the corruption she had found at court. A man who did his best to keep the promises he made, a man, who, unlike her father, would always be there for his wife and family.

Unless, of course, it happened to conflict with Remy's duty to his king. It was good to remind herself of that, otherwise she would be crushed by regrets for what could never be. She was no fit bride for Remy, not the sweet, patient, kind lady he deserved. She was sharp-tongued and quick-tempered, cynical and devious, her virtue tainted beyond any hope of redemption.

But even knowing that hadn't been enough to stop her from falling in love with him. Gabrielle closed her eyes, giving way to despair before rousing herself with a brisk shake. There was only one thing she could do for Remy, and that was to keep him safe, which meant driving him as far away from her as possible.

In the meantime, she was going to have to convince Catherine she had succeeded in her seduction. God forbid the Dark Queen should ever guess how Gabrielle, the noted courtesan, absolutely shattered at Remy's touch. And she was going to have to work on Navarre. While usually the most easy-tempered of men, occasionally Henry did remember he was a king and could be cursed stubborn when he took an idea into his head.

Gabrielle was going to have to charm Henry out of his notion to marry her off to Remy, stop him from participating in Remy's dangerous escape plan, persuade him to order Remy to leave Paris. Of course then, Remy truly would hate her.

"Oh, lord, Ariane," Gabrielle thought bleakly. "How did my life become such a tangled-up disaster?"

More than ever did Gabrielle wish she could go to Ariane and pour out everything to her. Her sister had such a calm, clear-eyed way of seeing things, a wisdom that Gabrielle had never fully appreciated until now. But there was no sense longing for the impossible, whether it was Ariane's love and forgiveness or Remy's.

Gabrielle heaved a deep sigh, feeling more alone than she ever had been in her life. She desperately needed to talk to someone, preferably another wise woman. And there was only one person she could even come close to calling a friend here in Paris.

THE MAISON D'ESPRIT WAS A DIFFERENT HOUSE BY THE LIGHT OF day, not nearly so dark and sinister as much as sad and neglected. This time it was not the dog, Cerberus, who greeted Gabrielle with a snarl, but Finette.

The maidservant pounced upon Gabrielle as soon as she set foot in the decaying hall. Arms locked over her scrawny bosom, she barred the way with a fierce scowl.

"What are you doing here? Mistress Cass don't like unexpected callers."

Gabrielle struggled to contain the dislike she felt for Cass's servant. Finette was a sharp-faced, slatternly woman with sly eyes. Her stringy blond hair looked as though it had not been washed this past twelve-month and her skin as well. The creases at her wrists and neck were permanently ingrained with dirt and her stained brown frock emanated a sour smell of sweat and unwashed flesh.

"I know Cass doesn't like surprises," Gabrielle said. "But if you would just go and tell her that I am here—"

"No! I got into enough trouble blabbing to you about the necromancy. I won't be risking her anger again. Besides, mistress is in no fit state to see anyone."

A sound carried up to Gabrielle from the chamber below the house, an unmistakable groan.

"What is the matter with her? Is she ill?" Gabrielle asked sharply.

Finette shrugged, scratching her neck beneath her lank fall of hair, but her smirk told Gabrielle all she needed to know. Cass had been at her bottle again.

"Oh, Cass," Gabrielle thought, torn between pity and frustration over the woman's destructive habit. Another moan sounded, louder this time, followed by a whine from Cerberus. Thrusting the bony maidservant out of her way, Gabrielle headed toward the aumbry that concealed the hidden doorway. Finette grabbed her elbow.

"Now you just stop right there. Mistress Cass will have my hide if I let you—" Finette broke off with a howl as Gabrielle smacked her hand away.

She fumbled until she found the lever that worked the door. When the aumbry creaked to one side, Gabrielle didn't hesitate. She plunged down the dark narrow stair with Finette hard after her, scolding furiously. As Gabrielle emerged into the underground chamber, the light of a single torch revealed Cass slumped on the floor by her bed. Her legs curled under her, her head lolled against the mattress, her features hidden beneath her tangled fall of black hair. Cerberus pressed close to her side, pawing at her skirt, attempting to nuzzle her face.

When he saw Gabrielle, he bounded toward her, emitting several barks, but not of menace. Pacing between Cass and Gabrielle, he whined. He could not have solicited help for his mistress any more clearly than if he had asked for it. Gabrielle nearly tripped over the empty bottle as she rushed over to Cass and knelt down beside her.

"Cass?" she called gently. She had to nudge Cerberus aside as she struggled to lift the woman's head and brushed back her heavy fall of ebony hair. Cass reeked of strong spirits. Her face was deathly pale, deep hollows gouged beneath her sightless eyes.

Before Gabrielle could stop him, Cerberus lunged forward and licked Cass's face. Cass muttered an oath, twisting her head to one side.

"Down!" The command was slurred, but Cerberus obeyed, settling back on his haunches with another low whine. Although it appeared to cost her great effort, Cass jabbed clumsily at Gabrielle in an effort to discern her features. "Helene? Is zat you?"

Finette hovered sulkily behind Gabrielle. But at Cass's question, she emitted a shrill giggle. "Oh, lord. She thinks you're one of her dead sisters."

Gabrielle caught hold of Cass's fingers. "No, Cass. It's me. Gabrielle."

"Gab—gabbyelle?" Cass sagged against Gabrielle's shoulder, becoming a dead weight.

Struggling to keep Cass from tumbling flat on her face, Gabrielle glowered at Finette. "How could you let her get into such a state?"

Finette's sneer twisted to become a pout. "No one *lets* Cassandra Lascelles do anything and if you were her friend as you claim to be, you'd know that."

"Help me to get her up onto the bed," Gabrielle snapped.

"When mistress gets this dead drunk, she don't much care where she lies." But after another fierce glare from Gabrielle, Finette shuffled to obey.

Even a woman as slight as Cass was hard to lift. The task was made more difficult by the dog renewing its efforts to rouse its mistress. But with Finette's help, Gabrielle wrestled Cass onto the bed. Finette gave another of her irritating giggles.

"The other day mistress made her own way off to the tavern and she thought she found herself a fine specimen of a man, a real prince charming, but Mistress Cass was so dead drunk when she went to bed with him, she didn't realize that she was tupping some skinny pot boy from the kitchens who was missing half his teeth."

Gabrielle could imagine too clearly the loneliness that must have driven Cass out of hiding, seeking comfort in both the bottle and a strong pair of arms, only to be taken advantage of by some randy male. Finette's callous mirth at her mistress's expense made Gabrielle long to slap the woman. Her disgust must have penetrated even Finette's thick skull because her laughter subsided.

"You needn't look at me that way." She squared her shoulders defensively. "Even Mistress Cass thought it was amusing when she realized her mistake. We both had a good laugh over her prince of the pots and pans."

Gabrielle eyed her coldly. "Fetch me a basin of water and some cloths. Clean ones."

Finette bristled at the command, but she slunk off to obey. Cerberus leaped onto the bed beside Cass and Gabrielle feared the dog might turn protective, growling at her to keep away. But with a low whimper, the mastiff curled up at Cass's feet. Gabrielle settled herself gingerly on the bed beside Cass and began to loosen her gown.

Cass stirred at her touch, her eyes fluttering open. As Gabrielle bent over her, Cass prodded her cheek, but she still didn't seem to recognize Gabrielle.

"Helene?" she faltered in a broken whisper. *"Forgive me."*

※※※

GABRIELLE HAD NO IDEA HOW MUCH TIME HAD PASSED DOWN IN THE underground chamber. She surmised that the afternoon had waned into evening before Cass felt well enough to rise from the cot. Even then she was astonished by Cass's power of recuperation. If she had rendered herself that drunk, Gabrielle feared she would be moaning in her bed for a week.

Cass groped her way over to the rough-hewn table. As she located her chair and drew it back, she winced at the rasp of the wooden legs against the rough stone floor. She seemed sensitive to the least sound. Perhaps that was why she had dismissed both her dog and her maid, sending Cerberus upstairs to guard the house and Finette off on some errand. Gabrielle hoped that it wasn't to purchase more whiskey.

Cass eased herself down onto the chair and indicated that Gabrielle should join her at the table. Gabrielle did so reluctantly, feeling she ought to go as well. Despite her insistence that Gabrielle stay, Cass looked as though she belonged back in her bed, her face haggard, her eyes puffy, the white rims bloodshot.

She propped her elbow on the table and held the cold compress that Gabrielle had fashioned to her forehead. She was clearly embarrassed that Gabrielle had found her in such a pitiable state, her voice gruff as she said, "Thank you. It has been a long time since anyone took care of me so—so kindly. Not since . . ."

"Since you lost your Maman?" Gabrielle filled in gently.

Cass grimaced. "No, my mother was not exactly a nurturing sort of female. I was thinking more of—of one of my sisters, Helene."

Helene, one of the Lascelles wise women who had been tortured and burned by the witch-hunters. The sister that Cass had mistakenly believed Gabrielle to be. The one whose forgiveness she had begged. But for what?

Cass didn't seem inclined to pursue the subject. Putting the compress down, she rubbed her eyes and leaned back in her chair. "It has been over a fortnight since you have been to visit me. I thought maybe you had forgotten all about your poor old friend."

Gabrielle felt a twinge of guilt. "No, of course not. I have been a little distracted of late, that is all. Something—something truly unexpected has happened. But this hardly seems like a good time to bore you with my difficulties."

"Nonsense." Cass said. "I am perfectly sober now. Tell me what is going on." She winced and massaged her temple. "Just do it softly."

Gabrielle still felt reluctant, but a rare gentleness had stolen over Cass's gaunt features. Gabrielle began slowly, then found herself pouring out the entire story of Remy's return, their quarrel, the events of the masquerade ball, the devil's pact that had been forced upon her by Catherine, the demand that Navarre had made of Remy, the impossible position Gabrielle found herself in.

Cass listened without comment. She did not even register surprise when she learned the reason for the failure of their séance, that Remy was still very much alive.

When Gabrielle finally fell silent, she prompted, "And?"

"And—and that is all. There is nothing more to tell."

Cass stretched one arm across the table, groping until she located Gabrielle's hand. She probed Gabrielle's palm with her fingertips.

"There is something more," she insisted. "What is it that is really troubling you?"

Gabrielle tried to draw her hand away, but Cass's grip tightened around her wrist.

"Tell me."

Gabrielle sighed, then admitted in a low voice. "I—I might be in love with Remy. I—I don't want to be, but I just can't help myself."

A choked sound escaped Cass. She released Gabrielle, her hands flying to her brow as though she feared the top of her head was going to come off.

"Oh, please," she moaned. "Whatever you do, don't make me laugh."

"I have just bared my heart to you and you find it amusing?"

"Very." Cass started to chuckle, then stopped, groaning. "Good lord, Gabrielle. Even a blind person could *see* how you feel about that man."

"But I don't want to be in love with Remy. It—it is quite impossible." Gabrielle buried her face in her hands. "Oh, what a disaster."

"Is it? I fail to see the nature of your problem. You are fated to become the mistress of the king of France and you get to marry the valiant captain you adore. I would say the sun shines very brightly on your pretty little arse, Gabrielle Cheney."

Gabrielle thought she detected a hint of envy and rancor in Cass's voice. But when she glanced sharply at the other woman, Cass smiled at her so benignly, Gabrielle felt she must have imagined it.

"But, Cass, I can't be Remy's wife and still share the king's bed," she protested.

"Why not? Men do it all the time, have both a wife and a mistress. Why should it be any different for a woman?" Cass arched her brows, then flinched as if even that small gesture aggravated her headache. "You surely aren't thinking that your affection for Captain Remy changes anything? You are destined for greatness. Nostradamus himself has told you so."

"Isn't it possible he was mistaken?"

"No, the old master is never wrong. Especially not since he has passed over. If he says that Navarre will be king of France and you his uncrowned queen, that is what will come to pass. There is no way of undoing one's fate. Besides, why would you want to avoid such a glorious future?"

Why indeed? Gabrielle sagged back in her chair, her mind filling not with images of palaces, kings, and power, but a soldier with sun-streaked hair and soul-wearied eyes. The destiny that had once stirred in her such fierce excitement filled her with weariness and despair. She made no answer to Cass's question, but the other woman seemed able to read her silence all too clearly.

"Gabrielle Cheney! Would you even consider for a moment sacrificing your future for a man who will never love you as much as he does his duty? A man who would never besmirch his honor by marrying a woman like you if his king had not commanded him to do so?"

Gabrielle flinched, Cass's harsh words biting all the more deeply because she knew they were true.

"You know the folly of love," Cass insisted. "It is a fleeting emotion at best. Nothing compared to wealth, position, and power. Those are the things that matter, the things that last. If you don't wed the captain, the king will only seek to saddle you with someone else. Use Remy as you would any other man. Stay strong and ruthless, Gabrielle. It is the only way for a woman to survive. Besides, look at it this way. Your Scourge strikes me as being rather rash. The more powerful you become, the better you will be able to protect him."

Cass could scarce have hit upon a more compelling argument. Losing Remy again, something terrible happening to him had become Gabrielle's greatest fear.

But she said, "I don't see how pursuing my ambitions with Navarre will protect Remy, especially from Catherine. I am far more likely to provoke her. Despite the agreement we reached, I don't trust her."

"Nor should you. But I might be able to give you some help in that regard."

"What do you mean?"

"Conjuring the dead is not the entire extent of my magic. I also have considerable skill in other areas." Cass gave her a sly smile. Splaying her palms on the table, she thrust herself to her feet. A little too quickly. She winced and swayed, gripping the back of her chair. When Gabrielle rushed to her aid, Cass thrust Gabrielle away impatiently.

She felt her way over to the cupboard, running her fingers over the wooden shelf until she located a small box. Her back to Gabrielle, she huddled almost protectively over the small chest's contents. Gabrielle could hear the chink of items being sorted over. Cass turned, thrusting something in Gabrielle's general direction.

"Here. Take this."

Mystified, Gabrielle accepted the object and examined it. It was a small five-sided medallion suspended from a tarnished metal chain.

"Cass, what on earth—"

"It's a protective amulet. Give that to your Scourge. Make him wear it always. It will help keep him safe."

Gabrielle tried to think of a way to refuse without insulting Cass or hurting her feelings. "Er—thank you. I appreciate the gesture, but Maman taught all of us girls not to set much store by such things as charms and amulets."

"She also taught you to leave black magic alone, but you've seen for yourself what a powerful tool necromancy can be in my hands. That is no gypsy's trinket I have fashioned. Examine it more closely and tell me if you have ever seen its like before."

Gabrielle carried the medallion over to the torch and studied the charm in the flickering light. It was molded from no metal she could identify, neither copper, nor iron, nor silver. The amulet's dull surface was etched with strange runic markings.

Gabrielle's brow creased into a faint frown. Actually she had seen something similar to this charm before. It looked very much like the metal and the markings that comprised the strange ring that her brother-in-law, Renard, had given her sister, linking their thoughts no matter how far they were separated. Gabrielle would never have believed that to be possible either if she herself had not witnessed the proof of it.

She dangled the medallion before her eyes, still a little skeptical. "Exactly what does this charm of yours do? You claim it could protect Remy?"

"Not exactly. But if he wore it, he would be able to feel malice directed toward him, sense impending danger. Forewarned is forearmed."

"Incredible," Gabrielle murmured.

"Believe in the charm's power or not, just as you choose. But what harm could it do your captain to try it?"

"None, I suppose. But what would you want for something like this?" Gabrielle asked uneasily, remembering the last bargain she had made with Cass.

Cass felt her way forward until her fingers curled around

Gabrielle's arm. "Consider it a gift, a token of our friendship. You remind me of a part of myself I have lost. My sisters . . ." She trailed off, her face pensive and sad.

Cass could be a strange, intense woman at times, but Gabrielle felt a tug of kinship with her. Perhaps because she too knew what it was to lose her sisters. But she at least had the hope, however slim, of someday seeing Ariane and Miri again.

Cass trailed her hand up Gabrielle's arm and shoulder, until she rested her fingers against Gabrielle's cheek. "Perhaps you will be my sister now. We have already made an unbreakable pact between us. You pledged to do a favor for me. You do remember that, don't you?"

Gabrielle caught Cass's hand and squeezed it gently. "Let me redeem my pledge now by getting you out of this dismal place. No wonder you are seized by these bouts of melancholy, living alone with just your dog and that wretched servant girl for company. There is no need for you to keep hiding here in this horrid house. The pack of witch-hunters who attacked your family has long been destroyed."

"Ah, there will always be more witch-hunters, my dear Gabrielle. They are as certain as death and taxes." Cass eased her hand away. "I do not stay hiding at the Maison d'Esprit out of fear, but by my own choice. I am waiting."

"Waiting? For what?"

"For my own destiny to take shape. I will know when the time has come for me to emerge, to make my presence known to the world," Cass said softly. Her mouth curved in an odd smile that sent an inexplicable shiver through Gabrielle.

She wondered if all this seclusion or the amount of drink Cass consumed was starting to drive the woman a bit mad. But Gabrielle's unease was forgotten in the wake of a disturbance from upstairs, an outbreak of fierce barking from Cerberus.

"An intruder," Cass muttered, tensing. "Gabrielle, you were careful that you were not followed when you came here?"

"Of course," Gabrielle said. After the incident with Catherine's spy, Gabrielle had been doubly cautious wherever she went. Yet despite her assertion, her stomach knotted with alarm as the commotion above them increased. Cerberus's barking waxed even louder, interspersed with the sound of footsteps.

"Never mind," Cass said tersely. "No one can find the entrance to my secret room and Cerberus will soon make whoever it is regret—"

Her brave words choked to a halt as Cerberus went still. Not a bark, not even a low growl. The silence was far more frightening than the disturbance had been.

Cass's face washed white. "My dog. Something has happened to my dog."

She lurched forward, banging into the table in her haste to reach the stairs. Gabrielle intercepted her, catching hold of Cass's shoulders. "No, stay here. Let me go."

If Gabrielle had brought any sort of danger down upon the house, she was determined to shield Cass at any cost. But Cass was so frantic for the safety of her dog, it was all Gabrielle could do to persuade her to remain below.

Gabrielle looked about her for anything that might serve as a weapon. She glanced down at the charm she clutched in her hand. So much for Cass's protective amulet, she thought wryly. She had not felt so much as a tingle of approaching danger.

She shoved the charm in the pocket of her gown and seized upon Cass's stout walking stick. Gripping the gnarled wood in her hands, she crept up the narrow stair.

Cass hovered below her, whispering anxiously, "Be careful."

Gabrielle did not reply, her concentration focused on making her way through the darkness that enveloped her, finding the lever that controlled the door to the hidden chamber. Following Cass's instructions, Gabrielle twisted the handle a few degrees to the left, just enough to barely shift the cupboard.

The creaking of the mechanism sounded infernally loud to Gabrielle's ears, enough to alert any intruder. She waited a few seconds before cautiously poking her head out the opening. The great hall was shrouded in the gloom of evening, the dust thickening on the floor appearing undisturbed. But the sound of a ferocious hiss caused the hairs on the back of Gabrielle's neck to rise.

She muffled her startled cry and tracked the sound to its source. A black cat with snowy paws had taken refuge atop the high table. Back arched, it spat furiously. Gabrielle released a tremulous breath. Was it possible the dread intruder was no more than this cat? But then where was Cerberus? Why wasn't he baying his head off and threatening to make a meal of the feline?

As the cat hissed again, Gabrielle realized its venom was not directed at her. Those golden feline eyes glared at something out of her range of sight. Tightening her grip on the walking stick, Gabrielle inched from behind the aumbry until she spotted Cerberus. The dog flopped over on his back, but not because he had taken any harm.

Cass's hellhound groveled shamelessly at the feet of a slender youth obscured beneath a long gray cloak, a hood pulled forward over his face. All Gabrielle could make out of the lad were his dusty boots and shapely legs encased in a pair of dark trunk hose. He crouched down, scratching Cerebus's stomach, subduing the fierce animal with no more than a touch and a few soft words. Gabrielle had only ever known one person in her life who had such a magical way with animals. But no. It could not possibly be.

She stepped forward and the floor creaked beneath her feet. The lad glanced up at her and then calmly rose to meet her. He thrust back his hood and revealed—not a lad at all, but a tall young woman with straight moon-gold hair and eyes of silvery blue.

"Hello, Gabby," she said with an impish smile.

"Miri?"

At least now Gabrielle knew why Cass's amulet had failed to signal danger. Recovering from her shock, she gave a glad cry and gathered her sister into her arms.

✶✶✶✶

GABRIELLE RUMMAGED THROUGH HER WARDROBE, INSPECTING GOWN after gown only to discard them, the chair in her bedchamber disappearing beneath a rainbow array of silks. As she considered each garment in turn, her gaze traveled to the figure curled up on her bed, fearing that Miri might vanish just like the fairy child she had always been.

Perhaps she only imagined the girl lying propped on one elbow, teasing her cat with a bit of ribbon, conjured her up out of her lonely ache for her home and family. Except this was not the Miri of Gabrielle's memory. This was a girl on the verge of womanhood, her figure blossoming with soft curves that her boyish garb could not quite conceal. Her high cheekbones and winged brows combined with her moon-gold hair and unusual silvery-blue eyes to give her a dreamy, ethereal appearance.

When had this happened? At what point during the past two years had her scapegrace little sister been transformed into this serene young beauty? The changes in Miri brought a bittersweet ache to Gabrielle's heart and filled her eyes with tears. When Miri lifted her head and regarded her gravely, Gabrielle was swift to turn away. Blinking hard, she dove back into her wardrobe and hauled out one of her simpler gowns with a modest square neckline and tiered sleeves.

"This one might do." She held up the green silk folds. "Come here and let me see."

The cat had draped itself over Miri's lap. When she shifted him off her, Necromancer let out a yowl of protest. Miri approached Gabrielle reluctantly. "There is no need for you to be going to so much bother, Gabby."

"No need? It is bad enough you have been running all over

the countryside garbed as a boy. You cannot possibly continue to do so here in Paris. Now stand still."

Miri fetched a heavy sigh, but obeyed. Gabrielle bit back a smile. At least one thing about her little sister had not changed. Miri still preferred the freedom of doublets and trunk hose to feminine lace and frills. But as Gabrielle held up the gown to Miri's shoulders, she made another startling discovery.

"Great heavens. You—you are taller than me."

"So I am." Miri lifted her chin proudly. "I am a bit taller than Ariane too."

The mention of their other sister caused Gabrielle to stiffen. It was as though a shadow fell between them. Miri must have felt it too because she said softly, "Ariane misses you very much, Gabrielle."

"Does she?" Gabrielle's heart lifted with sudden hope. "Is that why you have come to Paris? Did Ariane send you here to act as peacemaker?"

"No, she didn't even know I was coming."

"Oh." Gabrielle concealed the depth of her disappointment, berating herself for a fool. She should have known her older sister better than that. If Ariane had the least interest in mending their quarrel, she would have come herself.

Lifting the lid of the trunk at the foot of her bed, Gabrielle hunted for petticoats and chemise to go with the gown. "So then how the devil did you get all the way here to Paris?" she demanded of her younger sister.

"I, er, borrowed one of Renard's horses and outfitted the saddle with a basket for Necromancer. Neither Brindel—that's the horse—nor Necromancer were fond of the arrangement. But we managed by taking the journey in easy stages."

Gabrielle paused in the act of unearthing a shift to gaze at her sister in consternation. "Miribelle Cheney! You—you traveled all this way alone?"

"I wasn't alone. I just *told* you. I was with Brindel and Necromancer."

"A horse and a stupid cat!"

Necromancer perched on the end of Gabrielle's bed, haughtily licking his snow-dipped paws. As though he understood her, he paused to shoot Gabrielle a baleful look.

Slamming the lid to the trunk closed, Gabrielle straightened and scolded. "Damnation, Miri. I would have thought you would have acquired more sense by now. That is a journey most men would have feared to make alone."

"Ah, but I am not a man. Nor some ordinary woman." Miri's air of unruffled serenity only added fuel to Gabrielle's outrage.

"Do you even realize what could have happened to you? You could have been set upon by brigands, robbed, attacked, even worse." Gabrielle's blood ran cold as she imagined the horrors that could have been visited upon her innocent young sister, injuries that might have made death welcome by comparison.

But Miri replied with infuriating calm, "Nothing could have harmed me. Necromancer would have warned me if there was peril nearby and I have my own sixth sense for danger. It is not as though I stayed overnight at public places like inns. Thanks to Ariane's council meetings, I know where other wise women reside. I merely traveled from one safe house to another."

"I don't care!" Gabrielle fumed. "It was still a reckless and irresponsible thing to do. Ariane must be frantic. You do realize that she will blame me for you running away and hate me more than ever."

"Ariane doesn't hate you. And she knows that I make my own decisions. She understands that I am no longer a child."

"Then she must be a great deal different from the Ariane I remember. I never thought she'd willingly allow either one of us to grow up."

"Ariane has changed." Miri's remarkable eyes darkened, clouding to a hue of gray. "She has not been the same since the babe—"

"Babe? Ariane has had a child?" Gabrielle's anger faded in

the face of this new staggering information. "I—I am somebody's aunt?

"Well, what is it?" she asked eagerly. "A boy or a girl?"

"Ariane lost the child before we could tell. She has had other miscarriages as well and seems unable to conceive again. It grieves her deeply. I think it is tearing her all to pieces inside."

Ariane, all to pieces? Gabrielle could not even begin to imagine it. Her older sister had been a pillar of strength for as long as she could remember. The Lady of Faire Isle, the wise one, the great healer. It was frightening somehow to think of her being beset by the sort of woes that afflicted other, lesser mortals. All this while Gabrielle had been fancying Ariane's life so perfect, Ariane had been suffering from some of the worst kind of pain any woman could know.

"I should have been there with her," Gabrielle berated herself. "Why didn't she send word to me, let me know? She should have realized nothing would have kept me away if I thought she was in trouble. I don't know what I could have done, but at least I might have offered her some comfort."

"You know what Ariane is like, Gabby. She always felt she had to be strong, never burdening anyone else with her sorrows. Infernally independent, not unlike someone else I know."

Miri dropped a kiss on Gabrielle's brow. Gabrielle wrapped her arms about her little sister and they hugged each other close. The sunshiny scent of Miri's hair reminded Gabrielle poignantly of the sweet scents of Ariane's herb garden, carrying her back to those days on Faire Isle when it had been just the three of them, she, Ariane, and Miri. The Cheney sisters. Despite their differences and disagreements, there had been a unity among them, sisterly bonds that Gabrielle had brutally snapped when she'd fled to Paris.

She feared she had cost Ariane enough grief. She could not let Miri do so as well. Much as she might wish to, there was no way Gabrielle could permit her younger sister to remain in Paris.

Not with all the dangerous currents and intrigues swirling about Gabrielle, threatening to engulf her at any time. Not when there was so much about her that her innocent sister didn't know and Gabrielle would just as soon Miri never did.

But for the moment she held her sister close, stealing precious moments of warmth from her presence. Miri leaned her head against Gabrielle's shoulder with a deep sigh. "I have missed you, Gabby. When you went away, you never even said good-bye to me." Miri's voice was not so much accusing as hurt.

Gabrielle knew full well why she had played the coward's part and avoided bidding farewell to her sister. Miri would have cried and clung to her, asking too many awkward questions. How could Gabrielle have possibly told Miri she was running off to Paris to make her fortune by seducing powerful men, that she was going to be living in the house purchased for their father's lover? Miri had been closer to her father than either of the other Cheney girls. If Miri were to ever find out the full extent of his betrayal . . .

Gabrielle's gaze skated uneasily over the lush trappings of the bedchamber once owned by Louis Cheney's mistress. "I am sorry, Miri. I never meant to hurt you, but when I left there was so much you were too young to understand."

Miri raised her head from Gabrielle's shoulder. "Such as your determination to become a courtesan, the same as the woman who used to own this house. The woman who seduced our father."

Gabrielle stared at her in shock. "Then you—you know about Papa—"

"I have known for a long time. I overheard you and Ariane the night you quarreled, about you coming here to Paris and accepting this house."

"Oh, Miri." Gabrielle groaned. She tried to hug her again, but Miri slipped out of her reach, standing beside the bed. She managed to smile but the expression in her eyes appeared far too sad and wearied for her years. "I truly am not a child anymore. I know that there aren't unicorns and elves hiding in the woods. That my Papa was not perfect and my sister isn't either."

Gabrielle recalled how often she had been vexed with Miri for her whimsical imagination and longed to shake some sense into her. But hearing her renounce those childhood beliefs was almost enough to break Gabrielle's heart. She had never allowed herself to be ashamed of the path she had chosen, but Gabrielle felt her cheeks burn. She lowered her head, unable to meet Miri's eyes.

"Oh, Miri. How you must despise me."

"Don't be foolish, Gabby." Her sister cupped her chin, forcing Gabrielle to look up at her. "I am often disappointed and made unhappy by the choices that the people I care about make, but that has no effect on the way I love them."

Gabrielle felt a lump rise in her throat. Unable to speak, all she could do was press Miri's hand.

"I have even managed to forgive Simon," Miri added.

Simon Aristide, the young witch-hunter who had once taken part in the raid against Belle Haven? Miri had persisted in believing that Simon was her friend until he had betrayed her trust most cruelly.

Gabrielle regarded her sister with a troubled frown. "You still think about that boy? I hoped you would have forgotten about him by now."

Miri drifted away from her to stare out the bedchamber window where twilight had deepened into night like a heavy warm mantle being drawn over the city of Paris.

"I don't grieve for Simon as I once did. But I do think about him from time to time," Miri admitted. "I hope that wherever he is that he overcame his pain and bitterness, that somehow his spirit managed to heal."

Necromancer padded over to the window, pawing at Miri's skirt as though sensing his mistress's sorrow. She scooped the cat into her arms and buried her face in his fur. "No matter what Simon did, I loved him, Gabby."

"Miri, that was three years ago. You were little more than a child," Gabrielle protested faintly. "It was but your first infatuation."

"No, I loved him. And when I love someone, it is forever."

Gabrielle was both awed and disconcerted by how sure Miri sounded. She couldn't help envying her sister this ability to love so simply and with such conviction. Especially when Gabrielle's feelings toward Remy were so complicated. She had told Miri nothing about Remy as yet, his miraculous return or the peculiar nature of their betrothal. She winced, wondering if Miri would be able to be quite so accepting of that. But there was time enough to broach that subject tomorrow.

Miri's head drooped and she started to look fatigued. Gabrielle bustled over to her and gave the girl's shoulders a light squeeze. "We have much more to talk about and catch up on. But you have to be exhausted. I will summon Bette to draw you a bath and fetch you a light supper. Then straight to bed, young woman. As delighted as I am to see you, you do realize that I am going to have to find a way to send you home."

Miri snuggled her cheek against her cat, but her lips thinned into that stubborn line Gabrielle knew all too well. "I have no intention of going anywhere until I am sure you are safe and happy."

"You mean to stay in Paris the rest of your life?" Gabrielle asked wryly.

"It is nothing to jest about, Gabby. It is not a whim that brought me all this way to find you. I have been having my bad dreams again. This time about you."

Gabrielle's smile faded. Her sister's dreams certainly were nothing to laugh at. From the time she had been very young, Miri had been afflicted with recurring nightmares of a prophetic nature. She had dreamed about both their mother's death and the St. Bartholomew's Day massacre long before either event had occurred.

"What sort of dreams have you been having?" Gabrielle asked.

"You know what my nightmares are like, never clear until it is too late for me to do anything about them." Miri shuddered and cuddled her cat closer. "I keep seeing this grand palace with endless halls and galleries. The air is full of voices whispering about you. I hear your name over and over again. Gabrielle, Gabrielle.

"And then I see a blond-haired woman in a lovely gown, drifting through the halls. I can never see her face, but I am certain it is you and you keep moving closer to these doors. Somehow I know where they lead. To the bedchamber of the king. I keep calling out to you, trying to stop you, get you to come back. But you never hear me. Each time I have the dream, you get closer to those doors."

Gabrielle felt a hot flush creep into her cheeks. How was she to explain to Miri that what her sister regarded as a nightmare was the very goal Gabrielle had been pursuing these past months? Miri's dreams only confirmed what Nostradamus had predicted. Gabrielle would become the king's mistress. This was her fate, her dazzling future . . . and she felt as though someone had just hammered the final nail into her coffin.

But she forced herself to rally with a brittle smile. "Your dream doesn't sound so alarming. Some regard sharing a king's bed as an honor, a great opportunity."

"I know that. But I still have this suffocating feeling of danger. The same feeling I had when I tracked you to that house today where that strange woman hides."

Miri cast Gabrielle a worried look. "There is something very troubling about your new friend, Gabby. Something dark and disturbing."

"Cass? I'll admit she can seem a little . . . disconcerting sometimes. But she has had a very hard and tragic life. You only exchanged a few words with her. Aren't you being rather quick to judge?"

"It is not my judgment. It is Necromancer's." Gabrielle solemnly hefted the cat a little higher in her arms as though fully expecting the feline to confirm her words. "He thinks Cassandra is very dangerous."

Gabrielle did her best not to roll her eyes. She had never shared Miri's fixed belief in the wisdom of animals. "Er—don't you think Necromancer is being too harsh? Cassandra's dog obviously adores her. That ought to count for something."

"Necromancer doesn't have a great opinion of dogs either. He thinks they are notoriously undiscriminating."

"Perhaps being a cat, he is a trifle prejudiced on that score."

"Perhaps," Miri said with a rueful laugh. "Just be a little careful around Mademoiselle Lascelles, all right?"

"I am always careful, little sister." Gabrielle gave Miri another hug, then went to summon Bette.

Amid the flurry of joyous greetings between Miri and the former housemaid from Belle Haven, Gabrielle quietly gave instructions to another of the servants regarding which bedchamber should be prepared for her sister. Then, before Bette bore Miri away to tend to her, Gabrielle thought she had better mention Remy's return from the dead. She didn't want her sister fainting from shock the way she had done.

But when she informed Miri as gently as she could, her sister's lips merely curved into one of those odd little fey smiles of hers.

"That is excellent news, Gabby, although . . . even when I grieved for Remy, it was more because I missed him. Somehow I always knew he wasn't dead."

Toting her cat, Miri walked off with Bette, leaving Gabrielle gaping after her.

There were times, Gabrielle thought, when her younger sister could be a bit unnerving.

Chapter Fifteen

THE GOSSIP SPREAD FROM THE CORRIDORS OF THE LOUVRE TO the lowest taverns in the city. There had not been tidings of such startling and scandalous nature since France's beloved Princess Margot had been married off to that Protestant oaf, Navarre.

During the next few weeks nothing else was talked of but the miraculous return of Nicolas Remy. The man known as the Scourge, enemy to all loyal Frenchmen and devout Catholics everywhere, had somehow survived the St. Bartholomew's Eve Massacre.

But as wondrous as that was, it was completely eclipsed by the more startling fact that upon his return, the Scourge had not been arrested. He was to be welcomed back at court under the blessing of no less a personage than Queen Catherine herself. The matter was much discussed in the shops, the streets, and the marketplaces. The wiser of the Parisians shook their heads over it, muttering that the ways of the Dark Queen were very devious.

The general consensus was that Monsieur Le Scourge had best watch his back.

Attired in her usual somber black, Catherine lingered by the windows of the king's antechamber. She had an excellent view of the hive of activity taking place in the courtyard below, the rasp of saws, the banging of hammers as carpenters labored nonstop to construct the lists and the stands in time for the morrow's festivities. Pennants already fluttered in the breeze, stirring in Catherine unwelcome memories of another tourney held long ago to honor the marriage of her daughter Elizabeth to Phillip of Spain. Three days of costly celebrations, culminating in that fatal joust on the last day.

Despite the fact that his hair had turned to gray, Catherine's husband had cut a fine figure in his armor, sporting the colors of his lady. Not her colors of course, Catherine reflected grimly, but those of Henry's beloved mistress, Diane. Powerful and strong as ever, Henry had defeated each opponent, one by one, until he faced the young Comte de Montgomery.

If Catherine closed her eyes she could still see that last terrible charge, the two horses thundering toward each other, the two armored figures coming together in a mighty clash, lances breaking against shields, the wood splintering. Henry reeled, slipping over the pommel of his saddle, and tumbled to the ground, blood spilling from his visor where the shard of lance had pierced his brain.

A freak accident, no one to blame, but the king of France was dead. Catherine remembered weeping until her eyes were red. It was the last time she ever recalled crying for anyone. Her tears had owed as much to guilt as grief. Nostradamus had warned her. The great seer had predicted Henry's death long before the event and Catherine herself had had a dark premonition only that morning.

So why had she not tried harder to stop Henry from entering the lists? Had some dark secret part of her welcomed the death of her husband, the chance to finally seize the power so long denied her? Catherine still didn't know, but she supposed it hardly mattered now. Henry and his mistress were both long dead.

Catherine was no longer a shadow queen. But that was the damnable thing about attaining power, she thought with a wearied sigh. One had to strive to keep it and of late, Catherine had begun to find the struggle wearisome.

Her spy still had not arrived from Faire Isle. She had no idea what was going on at those secret council meetings of Ariane Cheney's. And as for Gabrielle, the girl had made no effort to carry out her promise to seduce Nicolas Remy. As near as Catherine could discern, Gabrielle had not even been near the man since the night of the masquerade. Not that Catherine had truly expected anything different. She would have to deal with the Scourge herself and she had already laid her plans.

A commotion at the other end of the hall drew Catherine's attention from the window. The double doors were flung wide with a flourish to announce the arrival of her son. His Royal Majesty, the king of France. Though she had named the boy for her husband, Henry was certainly nothing like his stalwart father, Catherine thought with a slightly scornful curl of her lip.

His entourage of painted mignons trailing after him, her son toted one of those annoying little dogs of his. Catherine had nothing against dogs, at least not proper-sized ones that served useful functions such as guarding and hunting. But Henry's whippets reminded her of half-starved rats and did nothing to enhance her son's masculinity.

Which could have used some enhancing. His braided and pinked peascod doublet set off his slender waist to advantage, but gave him a slightly effeminate look. As did the pearl earrings that dangled from his shell-like ears, and his long black hair swept back from his brow. Still Catherine couldn't help taking a certain amount of pride in him. His dark Italian looks and total lack of scruples made him seem more of her blood than any of her other children had ever been.

Henry handed off his whippet to one of his lackeys and with

a dismissive gesture to the rest of his entourage, he made his way alone to where Catherine awaited him by the windows. She sank into a curtsy, then angled her head to offer him her cheek to kiss. An invitation that Henry pointedly ignored. He stared out the window, pulling a sour face as he observed the progress of the construction for the tourney. Catherine sidled close enough so that she could speak without being overheard by the courtiers at the other end of the hall.

"Still sulking, Your Grace?"

Henry shot her an irritated glance. "If I am, I have reason to be, Madame. It seems that everyone here at court down to the lowest page knew of the Scourge's return before I did. And all because my mother who had the earliest intelligence of anyone did not see fit to tell me."

"I saw no reason to disturb you with the information."

"Disturb me? I am the king. I should have been told that one of my greatest enemies was slinking about Paris. Good God, Madame. You may have forgotten how Nicolas Remy and his ragtag troop of Huguenot rebels once defeated my forces on the battlefield. But I have not."

"Everyone loses once in a while, Henry dear. Do try to get over it."

The muscle in her son's cheek twitched, an unfortunate facial tic that only increased as he grew more agitated. Catherine laid her hand soothingly over his heavily bejeweled fingers resting on the windowsill.

"I was slow to inform you of Captain Remy's return because I feared you might do something rash."

"Like finish what we started on St. Bartholomew's Eve?"

"Yes, precisely. Except for some minor skirmishing, we have achieved a delicate balance of peace with the Huguenots that I intend to preserve. You already created more than your share of martyrs that night."

"At your urging, Maman," Henry growled. "Sometimes I

don't think I would have participated in the slaughter at all if I hadn't breathed in that strange incense you burned."

"Don't fool yourself, my son. All men are violent by nature. They require no spell being laid upon them in order to kill. And there was nothing in the least magical about my incense. Anyone would think you had begun to lend credence to those absurd rumors that your mother is a witch."

Henry said nothing, merely arched his plucked eyebrows and cast her an odd look. Drawing his hand from beneath hers, he drummed his slender fingers on the sill, sunlight striking rainbow patterns off his rings.

"Very well. I will admit it might be less than politic to kill the Scourge. But do explain to me why you felt it necessary to honor the wretch by inviting him to participate in *my* tourney."

Henry looked as petulant as a child being forced to share his toys and Catherine had to resist the urge to give him a sharp smack. Her son was ostensibly the king of France. An inconvenient fact but one that Catherine needed to remember. Curbing her impatience, she explained in the careful tones of one reasoning with a backward child.

"Ever since the death of your dear father, jousts have become much more controlled, tamer affairs. But tourneys are often full of surprises, Your Grace. It is still possible for a dreadful accident to occur."

Henry regarded her through narrowed eyes. "Ah, so that's your game. Well, it won't be as satisfying as taking the bastard's head myself, but I suppose whatever accident you've arranged for the Scourge will have to serve."

Henry thrust himself away from the window. His dark de Medici eyes so like her own glinted down at her. "However, I do want to make something clear to you, Madame. You've had three sons who were king. My brother Francis was sickly and weak. Charles was just plain mad. I am neither. I intend to rule without my mother constantly intriguing behind my back.

"And as for this tourney, I may have a surprise of my own to offer." With a sly smirk and a mocking bow, Henry left her to rejoin his entourage.

Catherine watched him go with a heavy scowl. She had always been able to easily read all her children's eyes. This was the first time she had ever been stymied by one of them and it left her more than a little unsettled.

A surprise? At the tourney? He intended to rule without his mother's intrigue? Exactly what did Henry mean by all that? If Catherine didn't know better, she might fancy that her son had just had the impudence to threaten her.

Chapter Sixteen

T HE GROUNDS OF THE LOUVRE HAD BEEN TRANSFORMED INTO
something out of the tales of Camelot, colorful tents erected,
pennants snapping in the breeze. Knights sprouted instead of
flowers, stalwart young men in various stages of donning armor
called greetings and taunts to one another while their squires
flew about polishing weapons.

The sun beating through the canvas promised that it would
be a warm day's work. Remy paused to wipe a drop of sweat
from his brow. Hunched over his king, he fastened the straps of
Navarre's arm harness. No easy task, as the king was not inclined
to stand still and Remy felt more than a bit edgy himself.

Crowds continued to pour through the palace gates, mounted
horsemen mingling with the throngs of the more common folk
arriving on foot. Coaches drew up to disgorge silk-clad nobles
and their ladies. At the glimpse of each gown spread over a farthingale, each veiled headdress, Navarre strained forward only
to slump back with disappointment.

Remy feared he was just as bad. It did not help his tension in the least to realize that he and the king were both eagerly awaiting the arrival of the same woman. Remy wrenched the straps holding the plate of armor into place with a fierce jerk, eliciting a gasp from Navarre.

"Damnation, Captain. What are you trying to do, batter me before I even take to the lists?"

"Sorry, Your Grace," Remy muttered.

"And why so blasted glum, man?" the king demanded. "Your expression could curdle milk. This is a tourney we are attending, not a funeral."

"Let us hope not, Sire." Remy gritted his teeth as he concentrated upon fitting the king's spaulder into place on his shoulder. "I confess I do not like the thought of your hazarding your person in the joust."

Navarre barked out a laugh. "What hazard? *Combat à outrance* has been outlawed in France for a long time. The most I will risk is a few bruised ribs. The rough and tumble days when a tourney meant real sport are long gone, more's the pity. Now it is all mere prancing and showing off for the ladies."

His dark eyes twinkling, Navarre teased. "I am sure there is many a lady here at court who would swoon to see your stalwart physique in action, Captain. Shall we see if we can find you some armor so you can run a course or two?"

"I thank you, Sire, but no."

Navarre chuckled. "I forgot. You never were one for games. Even during my youth when you helped to train me, you were always so deadly earnest."

"That is because war is a deadly business." Remy shifted position to fasten the armor plate to Navarre's other shoulder. "I could not participate in the tourney in any case. I am neither a noble lord nor a knight."

"Oh, I can take care of that fast enough. Just kneel before me. A knighthood is the very least I could confer upon you for the service you have done me."

"I have not helped you to escape yet," Remy said in a low voice.

Navarre smiled and replied just as softly, "I was referring to your other service with regards to the lady, Gabrielle."

Remy's mouth tightened. He focused on the armor fastenings to avoid making eye contact with the king. Navarre had been mighty pleased with Remy when he'd told him he'd secured Gabrielle's promise to wed. His Grace still had no idea of the turmoil that raged within his loyal captain, that Remy was consumed with finding a way to keep Gabrielle from the king's bed.

Several of Navarre's gentlemen in waiting approached to display an array of lances and swords for the king's selection. Remy welcomed the respite to put some distance between him and Navarre. He was finding it more and more difficult to play his part in this farce, to keep his own feelings regarding Gabrielle firmly in check.

Remy stalked out of the tent, taking refuge beneath the welcoming shade of an enormous oak. All around him a festive atmosphere prevailed but the excitement left him untouched. He leaned back against the trunk of the tree, arms locked across his chest, observing the bustle with a scornful eye.

Navarre was right. The time was long past when a tourney served any useful function such as training for combat or an outlet for the energies of warriors between battles. Now it was not much more than a spectacle. The day of the knight and his bold charger was gone. Remy watched two young pages struggling with a recalcitrant mount. A glossy brown gelding, obviously not trained for this sort of nonsense, yanked back on its lead. Ears flattened, it snapped, strenuously objecting to being draped in yards of elaborate trappings of gold and purple velvet.

Remy scarce blamed the poor beast as he reached up to tug at the modest starched ruff that encircled his own neck. He was trussed up in another set of fine new clothes, his doublet and trunk hose of deep forest green. But at least this time he had the comfort of a proper sword strapped to his side.

He needed to be properly attired to dance attendance upon his king, but he still begrudged the cost of all this finery. At least his own. He hadn't minded what he'd spent to outfit Wolf as his manservant. Despite his tension, Remy couldn't help smiling as Wolf swaggered toward him, clad in his new livery. A far cry from the ragged street thief who had come to Remy's rescue on St. Bartholomew's Eve.

Wolf munched on an apple, his dark eyes darting about him, eagerly drinking in all the colorful sights of the men preparing to play at war. He strutted, carrying his head high as though he fancied he was a noble knight himself. An effect that he ruined as he fetched up in front of Remy and wiped his mouth on the back of his hand.

"Ah, monsieur, I have been over to look at the tourney field. You should see the lists and the golden throne built for the king. There is even a mock tower painted to look like stone but fashioned out of wood. And so many beautiful ladies." Wolf kissed his fingertips. "Such display of wealth. Such fat purses worn so carelessly it would take but the flick of a knife to sever the drawstring—"

"Martin," Remy growled warningly, interrupting the lad's excited flow of chatter.

"I was only jesting, monsieur. Even though the temptation is very great. As my Tante Pauline used to say so often, old habits die very hard."

"You are supposed to be my respectable page."

"Oui, monsieur." Wolf fetched a deep sigh. "But respectability can be so infernally boring."

Remy gave the lad an affectionate cuff to the ear. "I think you had best go see if you can help the king's squire with the horses. That will keep you out of trouble."

Wolf groaned. "Ah, monsieur, you know I have never been good with horses."

"Go!" Remy said sternly. Wolf grumbled under his breath, but stalked off to obey. As he disappeared around the side of the tent, a fine carriage approached pulled by a team of glistening black horses. The curtains at the windows were drawn back, revealing Gabrielle's lovely profile.

The coachman pulled on the reins and a footman flew forward to open the door. Gabrielle paused in the opening, her golden hair curled beneath a bongrace, the stiff, heart-shaped bonnet framing the ivory perfection of her face. Dainty brocade shoes peeked out from beneath the gold-trimmed hem of an azure blue gown the same hue as her eyes. The neckline was more modest than what Gabrielle usually wore, but the soft silk hugged her bosom tight enough to arouse a man's hungriest fantasies.

Remy strode forward, intending to hand her down from the coach, but the king was already there before him. Despite the encumbrance of his armor, Navarre had shot from beneath the flap of tent. Grinning up at her, Navarre's hands spanned Gabrielle's waist, and he lifted her down. His dark head bent toward hers, engaging Gabrielle in some intimate conversation, perhaps arranging some tryst for after the tourney. The mere thought was enough to make Remy feel like he'd swallowed live coals. It was all he could do to restrain himself from charging forward and dragging Gabrielle away from the king, his duty to Navarre be damned.

Remy's attention was focused so grimly on Gabrielle and the king, it took him a moment to realize two other women had alighted from the coach as well. One was Bette. The other was a young woman in a simple green gown who drew many admiring glances, the girl's beauty like the silvery moon in contrast to Gabrielle's sun.

She was a great deal taller, her once boyishly flat figure rounded with a woman's curves. But her straight fall of pale blond hair and unusual otherworldly eyes were just as Remy remembered them.

"Miri?" Remy called in disbelief.

Miri spun round at the sound of her name. Gabrielle had

been on the verge of presenting her younger sister to the king, but Miri's face lit up as she spied Remy. Ignoring Navarre's outstretched hand, Miri gave a glad cry. She rushed toward Remy and flung herself into his arms with a force that made him stagger back a pace. Moved by the unrestrained joy of Miri's greeting, Remy hugged her as fiercely in return as if she had been his own little sister.

Far from being affronted by Miri's snub, Navarre let out a booming laugh. "Well, it appears our bold Scourge has made himself a conquest."

⁂

MIRI CHENEY HAD BEEN PAINFULLY SHY AS A CHILD AND SHE STILL retained traces of that bashfulness as the king of Navarre engaged her in conversation near the tent. But Navarre had a gift for charming women and putting them at their ease. He soon had Miri smiling up at him. Remy hovered at a discreet distance, keeping a wary eye on his king. He was relieved to see that Navarre's manner toward Miri bordered on the avuncular.

Despite his initial joy at seeing Miri again, Remy fervently wished the girl back home on Faire Isle. She was an added complication in his life that already seemed overfull of them, just one more thing to worry about. Remy heard the soft rustle of a silken skirt and out of the corner of his eye, he saw Gabrielle approaching him. Her ladyship deigning to take notice of him at last, Remy reflected bitterly.

"Good morrow, Captain Remy."

The coolness of Gabrielle's greeting made an almost painful contrast to the warmth of Miri's welcome. Gabrielle's distant manner stung him into rounding on her.

"Damnation, Gabrielle. What the hell were you thinking of to let Miri join you here in Paris? The French court is no place for an innocent child."

Gabrielle arched her neck in haughty fashion, but a hint of color stained her cheeks at his rebuke. "I didn't let Miri do anything and as you may have noticed, she is no longer a child. She has grown into a rather willful young woman. But you needn't worry. I expect that Ariane will come roaring into Paris very soon to snatch Miri away from my evil influence. Were you afraid that I meant to keep Miri with me, encourage her to become a courtesan? Teach her the tricks of my trade?"

"No," Remy snapped. "You know damned well I never thought any such thing. I know right well how protective you've always been of your younger sister."

Gabrielle tried to maintain her icy manner and failed. Her shoulders suddenly slumped. "Remy, please, let's not quarrel today. I have already had enough of that with Miri."

Beneath the lovely façade she presented, Remy detected signs of strain, traces of shadows beneath her eyes as though she had not been sleeping well. He longed to reach for her hand, but he had promised to never touch her again. A pledge he heartily regretted. He kept his hand fisted at his side. "What have you and Miri been arguing about?"

"Oh, everything. About her accompanying me to the tourney today. About her remaining in Paris. I even threatened to have her trussed up and carted back to Faire Isle. She just says that she will escape and come straight back. She is so determined to look out for me. Can you imagine that? My little sister." Gabrielle lifted her gaze hopefully to Remy. "Can you talk to her? Make her see reason?"

"I can try," Remy said dubiously. "But none of you Cheney girls have ever been what a man would term biddable women."

His remark provoked a reluctant laugh from her. "I don't suppose that we are."

"Lord, I'll be glad when I have the lot of us safely away from this cursed city."

"Yes," Gabrielle murmured, but there was little enthusiasm

in her voice. She was still not keen on his plan to free Navarre and spirit them all out of France, but since he had persuaded the king, Gabrielle had little choice but to acquiesce.

An awkward silence fell between them. Remy became aware of the curious stares trained in their direction, the whispers behind hands. He pulled himself up to his most erect, staring rigidly ahead. But Gabrielle behaved with all the noblesse oblige of a princess, nodding, murmuring greetings to the other ladies, and wishing the various armed combatants good fortune in the upcoming tourney.

One knight in particular paused to bow to her as he passed by. He appeared to be no more than a lad with his blond waves of hair and smattering of freckles, but he was as solemn as if he were off to slay a dragon or set out on a quest.

His face softened at the sight of Gabrielle and he raised one gauntlet in a shy salute. But it was the sweet way Gabrielle smiled and waved back that pricked Remy.

"Yet another of your admirers?" he asked tersely.

Gabrielle didn't answer at first. As she slowly lowered her hand, she finally said, "That—that was Stephen Villiers, the Marquis de Lanfort."

De Lanfort. The name sent a jolt of recognition through Remy like a kick in the gut. He twisted his head, craning his neck for another look at the young man as he vanished into the crowd. "That was de Lanfort, your former lover? The one you had me pose as at the ball? That puppy? Damnation, does he even shave, Gabrielle?"

"Stephen is older than he looks. He cannot help that his face looks so young and sweet. The other courtiers, especially his own brothers, tease him cruelly for it. Consequently, he has always been shy and awkward, especially with the ladies. He badly needed some experienced woman to notice him, to give him a little confidence."

"So you took this young man for your lover merely to be kind to him?" Remy asked incredulously.

"No! But after Georges . . . my duke decided to quit Paris and return to his country estate, I—I was rather lonely. And Stephen was so gentle and attentive."

Remy frowned. "You implied that you cared nothing for any of your lovers. You told me that you had to pretend you weren't even with them."

"Only in bed. The rest of the time—" Gabrielle met his gaze levelly. "I know you think me the most calculating of harlots, but I have never given myself to any man that I did not esteem. I have been fond of every one of my lovers after my own fashion."

"But you didn't love any of them? You were never in love?" Remy asked, hating himself for the fierce desperation behind his demand.

"No," Gabrielle replied quietly.

"Not even the first time?"

"The first time? I—I don't know what you mean."

"You gave me to understand that you had taken a lover before you'd ever met me. Did you believe you loved him?"

"I—I, no, of course not." Gabrielle forced a laugh. "He was so insignificant, I don't even remember his name."

She looked quickly away, but not before Remy saw that haunted look creep into her eyes. She remembered all too well. So who the devil was he, the bastard who had first claimed her innocence? Remy was convinced that he had hurt Gabrielle. How cruelly, Remy could only guess. Enough to shatter her faith in love and herself. Enough to blunt her desire and daunt her heart so that by the time Remy had ridden into her life, he'd never stood a chance with her.

Remy found himself hating an enemy whose face he'd never seen. Burning to kill a man whose name he didn't know. As he clenched his fist, the frills attached to his sleeve fell forward over his wrist. He'd been battling the damned lace all morning. With a low curse, Remy shoved it back again.

"Don't do that," Gabrielle scolded.

"Cursed stuff," Remy muttered. "Makes me look like a blasted peacock."

"There is a reason why peacocks flaunt their feathers. To attract a peahen. There is something rather seductive about the contrast between lace and the bold contours of a man's hands. Especially hands as strong as yours."

She took hold of his arm, smoothing out the trim, her fingertips brushing the back of his hand. The touch, light as it was, sent a powerful current through his veins. Remy longed to seize her hand and bury his lips against the silken warmth of her palm. It took all his will to resist.

"Do *you* find it seductive?" he murmured.

Gabrielle lifted her head reluctantly and their eyes met. Remy felt the tug of desire as though they were bound together by a cord, knotting tighter and tighter. What was more, Remy was convinced that Gabrielle felt it too.

There was only one difference between them. She didn't want to feel it. She even seemed frightened by it. She snatched her hand back from him as though the frills of his shirt had suddenly caught fire.

"Gabrielle, you don't have to be afraid of me," he said softly. "I promised I wouldn't touch you again. I meant it."

"I know you did and you always keep your promises." Why did that make her sound so sad?

"I wish you would promise me one thing more," she said.

"And what would that be?"

"That you will not let yourself be persuaded to take part in this tournament today. These jousts are only supposed to be mock affairs, but an event such as this would be an easy place for—for accidents to happen."

"You think the Dark Queen might be planning one for me?"

Gabrielle shrugged. "Who ever can tell what is on Catherine's mind?"

Or Gabrielle's either. She looked so uneasy Remy couldn't help wondering if more had passed between her and Catherine at their midnight meeting than Gabrielle had ever told him. Catherine was skilled at intrigue, but so was Gabrielle. Remy hated having to remind himself of that. He wanted to trust Gabrielle. He wanted everything to be straightforward and honest between them.

"Just promise me you will stay out of the tournament," Gabrielle insisted.

"But I might enjoy the chance to accidentally break a few heads myself."

"Remy!" Gabrielle glared at him, but mingled with the reproach, he saw the worry that darkened her eyes. She was afraid for him. It was a far cry from the depth of emotion Remy wished he could inspire in her, but at least it was something.

"Don't fret yourself, my dear. I have no intention of giving anyone an excuse to put a sword between my ribs today. You know how I feel about games and that is all this tourney is. All flash and nonsense."

"Dangerous nonsense," Gabrielle murmured, nervously flexing her fingers. "Remy, there—there is something I have been meaning to give you."

To his surprise, she tugged at his sleeve, drawing him to a relatively secluded spot behind one of the tents. With a furtive glance to be sure no one was looking, she dove into the small velvet purse she had attached to the golden girdle about her waist. She drew forth a metal object and pressed it into the palm of his hand.

Remy's brow furrowed as he examined the medallion suspended from a tarnished silver chain. It was smooth, five-sided, and etched with queer symbols. "What is this?"

She tugged the drawstrings of her purse closed, looking a trifle sheepish. "It's a protective amulet to help keep you safe. I am not sure exactly how it works or even if it does. It's supposed to enable you to feel the presence of malice, warn you if someone is planning to hurt you."

"I hardly need an amulet for that. The sight of a big, pointed sword in the other fellow's hand is usually warning enough."

But Gabrielle didn't smile. She looked so astonishingly earnest, Remy abandoned his teasing tone. He turned the amulet over in his hands, studying it more closely. Despite all the strange things he'd witnessed on Faire Isle that summer, Remy knew that there were some elements of so-called magic that were only chicanery, superstitious folly like much of his young friend Wolf's beliefs.

This medallion with its odd symbols was very different from the crude and aromatic charms Martin fashioned for himself. As Remy fingered the strange piece of metal, it rendered him inexplicably uneasy. Out of all the Cheney sisters, Gabrielle was the one who had the least belief in magic. At least not until she'd come to Paris. He hoped she hadn't been paying any more visits to that eerie abandoned house with its disturbing history. Or calling upon that recluse who claimed she could conjure the dead.

Remy held up the medallion. "Gabrielle, exactly where did you get this?"

Was it his imagination or did she hesitate a beat before answering? "Ariane. It was something she gave me a long time ago. Here. Let me help you put it on."

Gabrielle reached up to drape the chain over his head. She was so close, he could feel her breath on his cheek, the warmth of her fingers against his skin as she tucked the medallion out of sight beneath his shirt. It settled like a cold weight over his heart, but he scarcely noticed. Her hands lingered on his shoulders, her eyes blinking up at him like two bright jewels. She astonished him by straining closer until her lips touched his in a kiss that was sweet, warm, aching with promise and over all too soon. His mouth still clung to hers even as she drew away.

"I—I am sorry," she faltered. "I shouldn't have—"

"Why not?" Remy demanded, struggling to repress both his desire and his frustration. "We are betrothed to be married. Surely that calls for some modicum of affection between us."

"No, we would be ridiculed for it. Marriages are arranged for wealth, title, or political alliance. Only fools wed for love, Nicolas Remy."

She gave him an odd wistful kind of smile. Before Remy could reply, she turned away. As he followed her from behind the tent, her words echoed in Remy's head.

"Only fools wed for love."

Then he had to be just about the biggest fool in all of Christendom.

⚜⚜⚜

NAVARRE TOOK THE SILK SCARF GABRIELLE HAD GIVEN HIM AND carried the lightly perfumed fabric to his lips. "I shall wear this upon my sleeve and joust in your honor, milady. I am deeply honored that you would bestow your favor upon me and not some other bold champion."

The irony of the king's tone was not lost upon Gabrielle. She summoned a stiff smile to her lips. "Why would Your Grace believe I would favor anyone else?"

Navarre arched his brows quizzically. "You have been maddeningly elusive of late, Gabrielle. I wonder if I have done something to offend you."

"Of course not, Sire." A telltale blush stole into Gabrielle's face. She was fighting hard to keep her gaze from constantly moving in Remy's direction, but it was a losing battle. She stole a glance toward where Remy stood fierce guard over her younger sister. If any man present was tempted to make Miri the object of any dubious gallantries, Remy's dark glare made him think better of it. He had no armor, but he looked more of the knight than any of these other strutting fools.

She was all too aware of the stir that Remy's presence at the tourney was causing among the courtiers. The ladies raked him over with appreciative glances while most of the men scowled. Some simply stared. Remy fingered the chain Gabrielle had draped about his neck, toying with the medallion hidden beneath his doublet. She wondered if the amulet was working, if he sensed treachery.

If he was, he didn't have much farther to look than in her direction, Gabrielle thought miserably. She had lied to him about the medallion, but if she had told him the truth, she doubted that Remy would have accepted the charm.

He would have deplored her friendship with Cassandra Lascelles, in full accord with Ariane's view that anyone who practiced dark magic was to be avoided. Perhaps Cass's ability to conjure the dead was unnerving. But how could any woman be accounted evil who grieved so for her lost sisters, who so loved her dog she'd been willing to risk her life to rush to his rescue?

Cass was merely another sad instance of a woman who had been brutalized by the tragedies in her life, who struggled to conquer her weaknesses and survive the best she knew how. And that was something Gabrielle understood all too well.

The lie she had told Remy about the amulet was actually the least of her sins. She was practicing upon him a far greater deceit. Remy assumed that because she had consented to marry him, she was resigned to the plan.

But later after the tourney when Navarre was mellowed with wine, Gabrielle meant to work her charms on him, dissuade him from returning to his country. His destiny lay here in France and hers as well. No matter how much Gabrielle might despair over the fate she had once been eager to embrace, there was no avoiding it.

She could not save herself. But she could save Remy. She would get Navarre to force Remy to leave Paris, to return to the tiny border kingdom in the vastness of the mountains where he would be far out of reach of Catherine and any other enemies at court. How Remy would despise her when he discovered the full extent of her betrayal, but perhaps his hatred would help put an end to her own desperate yearnings for what could never be. His absence would enable her to encase her heart back in ice, return to that blessed numbness that had permitted her to endure for so long.

"Gabrielle?"

She turned back to Navarre to discover he had taken her hand in his. His dark eyes regarded her tenderly. "You look so sad, ma mie. Tell me what is troubling you."

A lump formed in Gabrielle's throat and she was unable to speak. She could scarce have answered his question in any event. How could she tell Navarre that fate had played a cruel jest upon her? That she was destined to be his mistress while her heart belonged to the very man the king had unwittingly selected to pose as her husband.

Fortunately Navarre's attention was diverted by the flourish of a herald's trumpet. The king of France approached, his entourage following him like the tail of a comet. Unlike Navarre, it was obvious that Henry Valois had no intention of taking part in the joust. He strutted in a doublet of rich purple velvet trimmed in ermine, preceded by one of his obnoxious little dogs on a lead. The whippet barked and growled at everyone in sight, a fact that clearly afforded the king much amusement.

But as Valois neared Navarre's tent, the whippet broke free. The little dog streaked straight for Miri and leaped, all but springing up into her arms. With a delighted laugh, Miri bent and gathered the dog to her. As she crooned soft words in his ear, the whippet wriggled with canine adoration, his tail lashing back and forth. His tongue lapped at every portion of Miri's face he could reach.

Valois's mouth thinned with outrage. As the king of France bore down upon her sister, Gabrielle hastened to intervene. But Remy was already there. With a wry smile at Miri, Remy eased the whippet from her arms and handed it back to the king. When the little dog whined, straining to get back to Miri, the king impatiently handed the whippet off to one of his attendants, his annoyance palpable.

Miri sank into a curtsy. Remy managed a stiff bow, but his

spine appeared so rigid, Gabrielle marveled it did not snap in two. The king shook back his mane of dark hair, accorded them a sullen nod, then pointedly ignored them.

It was another voice that exclaimed, "Ah, Captain Remy. Welcome back from the realms of the dead. You grace us with your presence at last."

The folds of Catherine's black gown swept the grass as she approached. Remy made no response or move to offer her even the most token bow. His jaw might well have been carved from stone.

"Come, my dear Captain. Let all past misunderstanding between us be forgotten. It pleases me greatly to receive such a noted hero at our celebration today. I offer my hand in friendship. Let me see some sign of your own goodwill and regard."

She held out her hand to him. Catherine's smile was all that was amiable, but the sly cast of her eyes told Gabrielle that the Dark Queen knew full well what it would cost Remy to pay homage to the woman responsible for the slaughter of his people. A muscle twitched in Remy's jaw, his deep brown eyes unable to disguise his loathing of the Dark Queen. He'll never do it, Gabrielle thought, not even if it should cost him his life. Her heart constricted with dread, wondering how Catherine would react to the insult.

The Dark Queen extended her hand even more imperiously. An air of hushed expectancy seemed to have fallen over the entire gathering near the tent. The king of France watched, smiling wolfishly.

Catherine stepped closer, murmuring. "Come now, Captain. If you will not accept my friendship for your own sake, then do it for the sake of your dear friend, Mademoiselle Cheney." Catherine smiled and nodded in Gabrielle's direction. Her voice was soft, even caressing, but her implied threat was more than clear. If Remy did not bend before Catherine, he risked her displeasure falling upon Gabrielle.

Remy hesitated but a moment more, then slowly bent until he knelt before the Dark Queen. Gabrielle bit down hard on her lip to keep from begging him not to sacrifice his pride, at least not on her account. Remy took Catherine's hand. His face ashen, he pressed his lips to the Dark Queen's fingertips. A deep sigh of satisfaction echoed through the watching crowd. The king of France actually laughed as the proud Scourge who had rarely known defeat on the battlefield was obliged to humble himself before his enemies.

Remy bore it stoically, only his eyes revealing the full depth of his misery and shame. Gabrielle felt her own eyes sting with furious tears. And in that moment, she hated Catherine more than she ever had before. The Dark Queen kept Remy on his knees until Gabrielle could endure it no longer.

"Enough!" she cried. She thrust Catherine's hand away from Remy and tugged at his shoulder, urging him to his feet. Catherine arched her brows and regarded Gabrielle quizzically. Her outburst drew many a stunned look, not least of all from Navarre. Gabrielle gritted her teeth and sought to recover behind a cool smile.

"Forgive me, Your Grace. But the captain has promised to be my escort today. It vexes me to see him pay homage to any other lady, even a queen." She met Catherine's eyes levelly. "And one never knows what a jealous woman might be provoked to do."

"Oho, that sounds like a challenge, Your Grace," the king of France called out. "Fetch the ladies swords. I will wager ten sous upon my maman."

His mocking words sent a ripple of laughter through the tent, easing the tension in everyone but Remy. Even Catherine smiled. "Mistress Cheney and I prefer a subtler form of jousting. We shall leave the cruder and rougher passage of arms to the gentlemen. Such as our bold captain here, who must be itching to take to the field."

The queen shifted to address her son-in-law. "My dear Navarre, why have you not outfitted your bold Scourge with some armor?"

Navarre shrugged. "My bold Scourge is a serious man, Your Grace. He has no taste for sport."

"Nor do I lay claim to the title of knight," Remy added.

"Then we shall make one of you, at least for the day," Catherine purred. "You shall be my own special champion. I myself shall provide you with horse and armor."

"No!" Gabrielle cried, clutching at Remy's arm. She moistened her lips and forced a more playful tone into her voice. "What, Your Grace! Will you deprive me of my gallant escort? I am determined to have the captain watch the joust with me."

"Tied to the lady's petticoats, monsieur?" the king asked. His sneer brought a dark surge of blood into Remy's cheeks.

Gabrielle squeezed his arm warningly. She was terrified he would forget all prudence and let himself be goaded into entering the lists. The sidelong glance Catherine exchanged with her son made Gabrielle more apprehensive than ever for Remy's safety.

The king of France drawled, "How very disappointing. We were hoping for a sample of the Scourge's famed valor and skill at arms."

"I would have thought Your Grace had already sampled plenty of that on the battlefield," Gabrielle said too sweetly.

When Valois flushed and glared at her, she reflected that it was less than wise to remind the king of his defeat at Remy's hands. This situation was charged enough.

To her relief and great pride in him, Remy kept his temper. He addressed both Catherine and the French king with quiet dignity. "Loath as I am to disappoint anyone, this mock show of arms has never held any interest for me. I don't play at war."

The king looked vexed, but Catherine continued to coax, "Surely you might oblige us this one time. Your reputation as the

Scourge is known throughout France. So many of our young nobles long to challenge your skill, especially one in particular."

She shaded her eyes with her hand, gazing out across the field of tents. "Now, where has he gone? Ah, yes, there he is."

Smiling in a way that sent a shiver of apprehension through Gabrielle, Catherine stepped away from the shelter of Navarre's pavilion. Raising her arm, she beckoned to a distant figure that appeared to have been waiting for her signal to approach. He was already outfitted with armor for the joust, except for his gauntlets and helmet, but the sun striking off his breastplate made it impossible to discern his features.

Gabrielle clutched at Remy's hand, casting him a look both plea and warning. But Remy wasn't even looking at her. Like everyone else, his attention was focused on the approaching figure, a deep frown etched between his brows.

If this man turned out to be the duc de Guise or any of the other great Catholic lords who had taken active part in the massacre, Gabrielle feared that nothing would stay Remy from accepting the challenge.

Her pulse beating anxiously in her throat, she watched the armor-clad figure march closer, his features still indistinguishable until he bowed stiffly to Catherine and then slowly lifted his head. Gabrielle's breath left her entirely. She felt the blood drain from her cheeks as she stared at the lean, saturnine countenance of Etienne Danton.

She was dreaming, Gabrielle told herself desperately. Lost in the throes of one of her nightmares. If she blinked or shook herself hard enough, she would surely wake up and Danton's hateful face would disappear.

But it didn't. The chevalier summoned forth his squire and presented the Dark Queen with a single bloodred rose. Danton's every movement was imbued with a careless arrogance, a mocking image of the true knight she'd once believed him to be.

Gabrielle recoiled a step, swaying slightly on her feet, the only thing steady and solid Remy's hand. He caught her just beneath the elbow, bracing her.

"Gabrielle? Are you all right?"

Gabrielle glanced up to find Remy's eyes clouded with concern. She tried to answer him, but her lips had gone too numb to form any words. She turned her head, avoiding the sight of the man clad in such brilliant armor.

Danton here in Paris. How was that possible? Ever since that terrible day in the barn, she'd dreaded encountering him again, but she had felt safe enough at the French court. She'd heard the rumors that Danton had done something to land himself in disgrace, banished back to his estates in Normandy.

Then why had he been allowed to return and—and what did it even matter? Nothing mattered beyond the fact that he was here and with a few more steps he'd be close . . . close enough to touch her again.

"Gabrielle?" Remy's voice prodded at her again, but she pulled free of his gentle grip, consumed by one thought, one urge. To flee. To run as far and fast as she could. Even all the way back to Faire Isle.

She'd actually staggered a few steps back when her gaze collided with Catherine's. The queen's expression was as bland as ever, but her eyes were dark with calculation and a hint of triumph. The realization slammed into Gabrielle like a mighty fist. If she had not been blindsided by shock and panic at the sight of Danton, she would have arrived at the truth at once. It was Catherine who had arranged Danton's return to court, Catherine as ever weaving some dark web of her design.

Her steady gaze mocked Gabrielle, her faint smile letting Gabrielle know the Dark Queen was fully aware of her past relationship with Danton. It was as Gabrielle had feared that night she had met with Catherine after the masked ball. Catherine had finally managed to read her eyes. She was now in possession of all Gabrielle's vulnerabilities, her fears, her memories of that shameful encounter with Danton.

The thought made Gabrielle feel ill, but she realized if she did not take hold of herself, Catherine might not be the only one privy to her humiliating secret. Others might possibly guess, perhaps even Remy. Gabrielle could not endure that.

Danton's insolent gaze swept toward her. The bile rose in her throat and she swallowed hard. Although her heart beat wildly, Gabrielle gathered up her courage and surged forward to confront her worst nightmare.

Chapter Seventeen

NICOLAS REMY'S EYES NARROWED AS HE STUDIED GABRIELLE and the knight in the costly armor. The newcomer had drawn her away from the tent, the two of them lost in some low, intense conversation. In spite of the crowd milling past her, Gabrielle was oblivious to everyone but the stranger. Except that Remy doubted this man was a stranger to Gabrielle. She had tensed at the sight of him, with an expression Remy had never seen on her face before, not even the day her home had been attacked by witch-hunters.

Fear. Such terror that Remy had expected to see her run away as though the hounds of hell were after her. But she had recovered herself and stalked forward to greet the man. She was pale but so composed Remy wondered if he had imagined the fear.

He saw nothing about the man to terrify any woman. The unknown knight was a handsome enough fellow, Remy grudgingly conceded. Dark hair waved back from a face defined by high cheekbones and an aquiline nose. But his features were stamped with that look that Remy had always despised. An arrogant the-world-is-mine-and-I'll-do-just-as-I-damned-well-please expression.

So who the devil was he? And more important, what was he to Gabrielle?

As though he had spoken his question aloud, a soft voice said, "Mademoiselle Cheney seems to be eagerly renewing her acquaintance with Danton."

Remy glanced down to find the Dark Queen close by his side. Her smile seemed to taunt him with some secret knowledge. "I was not even aware that our dear Gabrielle knew him. But they appear to be rather intimate. One of her conquests, do you suppose?"

Remy knew well what she was getting at, that this Danton had been one of Gabrielle's lovers. Remy's gaze flicked back to Gabrielle. The fellow was whispering something in her ear. Remy felt a savage bite of jealousy, but he sought to contain it.

It would be less than wise to display any undue interest before the Dark Queen, let alone any hint of his feelings for Gabrielle. Reveal no weaknesses before Catherine. Never gaze straight into her eyes. Gabrielle herself had warned Remy of that. But he found himself staring into the Dark Queen's eyes as though mesmerized. Those hooded dark eyes that promised the answers to his questions, answers he had a feeling he wasn't going to like. But he could not seem to look away.

"So who the blazes is he? This Danton?" Remy asked.

"The Chevalier Etienne Danton is a scion of one of our oldest and noblest families in Normandy. He has been unwelcome at our court for many years due to—er—a past indiscretion."

"Then how could he be one of Gabrielle's conquests? She has only been in Paris for two years."

"True. I wondered about that myself. She must have met him

during her girlhood on Faire Isle." Catherine clicked her tongue softly. "I cannot imagine what her mother was thinking of. But alas, I forgot. Evangeline was dead. Otherwise I doubt she'd have ever permitted a man like Danton anywhere near her innocent daughter."

"A man like Danton? What do you mean?" Remy demanded.

"The chevalier has an unfortunate reputation with the ladies. It is whispered that no woman can say no to him." Catherine leaned closer to Remy, lowering her voice to a more intimate timbre. "But perhaps that is because Danton will not allow a woman to say no. What is not willingly surrendered to him, he takes."

Remy blinked, a strange sensation sweeping over him. He swayed on his feet, feeling as though he was falling into the dark pools of Catherine's eyes. Like bursts of lightning, pictures of Gabrielle flashed through his mind. Skirts shoved up past her hips, trapped beneath a man who drove himself brutally into her. Tears streaking down her cheeks, biting her lips to contain her sobs. Dazed and bruised, clutching the torn bodice of her gown over her bared breasts.

Inhaling sharply, Remy snapped his gaze free of Catherine's, grinding his fingertips against his eyes to dispel the harrowing images. Every pore in his body tingled with an awareness of danger. Perhaps it was the amulet working or only some instinct of his own that warned him. The Dark Queen was practicing her witchery on him. He fought to clear his head, but his thoughts seemed to collide and tumble over one another, fragments of his conversation with Gabrielle.

"You were never in love? Not even the first time?"

"Of course not. I don't even remember his name."

The memory of Gabrielle's haunted face swam before Remy and it didn't matter what Catherine might be plotting, what the Dark Queen was doing to him. Nothing mattered except the hatred that swept through his veins, so icy that it burned.

His shadow enemy now had both a face and a name . . . Danton.

✦✦✦✦

"GABRIELLE, YOU ARE AS BEAUTIFUL AND BEWITCHING AS EVER."

Although her heart hammered against her rib cage, Gabrielle forced herself to look at Danton. The lines of dissipation were carved a little deeper about his mouth and eyes, but Etienne still appeared handsome. Dark hair waved back from his forehead, his face all lean angles from his aristocratic cheekbones to the aquiline cast of his nose. He'd completely dazzled the naïve sixteen-year-old girl she had been, with his charm and smooth good looks. She was no longer naïve or sixteen, Gabrielle reminded herself fiercely, but she had to fight hard not to quail as he moved closer.

"It has been far too long since I have had the pleasure of your company."

"Not long enough," she retorted.

He flung back his head and laughed. The manner she had once thought so charming struck her as being affected. When he tried to secure her hand, she whipped her fingers out of reach. If he so much as touched her, she feared she might be sick.

Danton assumed a look of deep hurt. "Gabrielle. Have you not missed me?"

"No. I have not given you a single thought all these years."

Danton smirked. "You lie. A woman never forgets her first lover, although—" His gaze swept insolently over her. "From what I have heard, you have dispensed your favors generously since our little tryst."

Gabrielle curled her hands into fists to resist the urge to rake her nails over his mocking face. She and Danton were the object of far too many curious eyes. Not the least of all Remy's scowling gaze. Keeping her voice low, Gabrielle demanded, "What are you doing here, Danton? I understood that you had been banished from court."

"All is forgiven. I have been welcomed back by no less than the Queen Mother herself. So you should be nice to me, Gabrielle. With the queen's patronage, I am likely to become a very important man."

"You are more likely to become a fool if you trust any promise of Catherine's. But then you never were all that clever."

Something ugly flashed into Danton's eyes to be quickly smoothed away behind his smile. He seized hold of both her hands in a painful grasp and drew her closer. Gabrielle stifled a gasp. Without causing an obvious scene, she could not work herself free. Still smiling, Danton dipped down to whisper in her ear. "You have no idea the sort of plans the queen has for me, especially if I am declared champion of this tourney. She will give me anything I want . . . including you."

Gabrielle glared at him, but even the threat of such a thing was enough to make her feel weak and trembling. As Danton raised first one of her hands to his lips, then the other, she experienced a dizzying rush of that helplessness she'd known that day in the barn. The brush of his mouth against her skin brought it all back to her, every painful memory of the things that Danton had done to her.

"Let her go."

The voice was low, but cold and sharp as a steel blade. Remy had stolen upon them so silently that both she and Danton started. Danton loosened his grasp on her hands enough that Gabrielle was able to pull away from him.

Remy hooked his arm about Gabrielle's waist and hauled her protectively to his side. Gabrielle resisted an overwhelming urge to melt against his strength. The situation was too fraught with potential for disaster for her to give way to any weakness now.

Remy and Danton squared off, each man taking the other's measure. Danton quirked his brow at Remy in a haughty fashion and said, "Mademoiselle and I were enjoying a private conversation, monsieur. Who are you to interrupt?"

"The man who is going to kill you," Remy said softly.

Danton's eyes widened. He gave an incredulous laugh. "Pray tell me, monsieur, what have I done to cause you offense?"

"You are still breathing."

Gabrielle stared up at Remy in astonishment and alarm. During the brief interval since she had left him by the tent, Remy seemed to have taken leave of his senses. His rich brown eyes were so chilling, it frightened her. She tugged urgently at his arm. "Remy, please. Let us go back and rejoin the others."

Remy didn't even seem to hear her, his dark gaze fixed on Danton.

"Ah, Captain *Remy*." Danton's eyes swept contemptuously over him. "So you are the famous Scourge. We have a great deal in common. It looks to me as though you must be our sweet Gabrielle's latest lover. I had the privilege of being her first."

A muscle twitched dangerously in Remy's jaw. Gabrielle's heartbeat quickened. She tightened her grip on his arm. "Remy . . ."

He shook her off and took a step nearer to Danton. "I understand from the Dark Queen that you hoped to challenge me to a bout in the lists."

"Remy. No!" Gabrielle pleaded.

Before Gabrielle could stop him, Remy wrenched free one of the leather gloves from his belt. He struck Danton full force across the face with it.

"Consider your challenge accepted," he said tersely.

Danton clapped his hand to the red welt on his cheek. Glaring, he groped for the hilt of his sword and Gabrielle feared he meant to fly at Remy then and there. But Danton seemed to think better of it. With a stiff bow, he turned and strode away.

Gabrielle released a tremulous breath, her mind reeling with how rapidly the situation had slipped beyond her control. She became aware of the sensation that the scene between Remy and Danton had caused. There were audible gasps, murmurs, and whispers from the throng gathered outside Navarre's tent. The king of France could be heard complaining to his mother. "Damned Huguenot. One challenges a man to joust by striking his shield, not his face. Captain Remy does not know the rules for gentlemanly engagement."

"Precisely," Catherine replied.

Gabrielle glanced sharply back at them. The king's outrage did not alarm her nearly so much as the Dark Queen's thin smile.

※※※

GABRIELLE PACED THE TENT, FUMING TO COVER HER FEAR. THE other ladies had already gone to find a place in the stands, most of the knights to mount their horses, including Navarre. Gabrielle had pleaded with the king to forbid Remy's joust with Danton. But the king had merely shrugged with his charming smile. Navarre did not know the cause of Remy's quarrel with Danton, but one could not interfere. It was a question of honor.

Honor, Gabrielle reflected furiously as she took another turn about the tent. That wretched excuse men used for hazarding their lives and bashing away at one another. It so infuriated her, she longed to box the ears of every man she came across, beginning with the obstinate one stripping down to his shirtsleeves, preparing to fight.

Deaf to her every argument and plea, Remy shrugged into a gambeson, easing the padded undercoat over his shoulders while Wolf laid out the armor. Gabrielle's heart sank with dismay. Even she realized it was not of the best quality and certainly never designed to fit Remy with the precision Danton's armor did him. The helmet still looked rough from the hammer, crude and unpolished.

Remy was entirely indifferent to the fact. He snapped his fingers at Wolf. "Fetch that cuirass here and be quick about it."

When Wolf gave him a blank look, Remy said impatiently, "The breast and back plates. Make haste."

"Leave them where they are, Martin," Gabrielle commanded. Wolf had picked up the breastplate, only to hesitate.

"Bring it here. *Now,*" Remy snapped.

Wolf took a step forward but froze when Gabrielle said, "No! Don't move."

Remy cast him a dark scowl. "Damn it, lad. Whose orders are you bound to obey? Mine or hers?"

Wolf angled an uneasy glance between them. "Hers. Because she might turn me into a three-eyed toad if I displeased her. And in any case, I agree with milady. I think—"

"I don't give a damn what you think." Remy wrenched the breastplate from Wolf's hands. "Never mind. You have no idea how to help me with the fastenings anyway. You are pretty much useless here. Go find one of Navarre's men to assist me and then make sure my horse has been saddled."

A look of deep hurt chased across Wolf's sharp features. He drew himself up with dignity and accorded Remy a curt bow. "As you wish, m'sieur."

He stalked out of the tent, his shoulders slumping as he disappeared from view. Gabrielle rounded on Remy. "Oh, that was well done. That boy only worships you as if you were Hercules sprung down from Mt. Olympus. He is so proud to serve you, but he considers himself your brother-in-arms, not your lackey."

"I'll apologize to him later."

"You might not be here later."

When Remy ignored her, Gabrielle planted herself directly in front of him. "Have you not listened to one word I have been saying to you? Are you so pigheaded or so blind you can't see the truth? The confrontation between you and Danton has been arranged by Catherine. It is a plot to get rid of you."

"That doesn't matter."

"Doesn't matter!"

Remy laced up the front of his gambeson. "You appear to place very little faith in my ability to defend your honor."

"What honor? I don't have any. I am a courtesan."

Remy grimaced at the reminder, but kept doggedly at the lacings. Gabrielle covered his hands with hers to stop him. "Don't you understand? This is a fight you can't win. Dueling and combats to the death are forbidden in France. If Danton kills you, they'll likely pretend it was an accident. If you kill him, they'll have an excuse to arrest and execute you. Not even Navarre could declare it unjust. Will you throw your life away because of some sneering remark that Danton made?"

"No, not because of what he said today, but what he did to you years ago."

"I—I don't know what you mean—"

"Danton raped you, didn't he?" Remy demanded fiercely.

Gabrielle flinched from both his bluntness and his steely, probing look. She snatched her hands away, no longer able to meet his gaze. Remy *knew*. He knew the pathetic shameful secret she had struggled to deny for so long, even to herself.

She moved away from him, hugging herself tightly. "This—this is obviously some ridiculous story Catherine concocted in order to make you—"

"No, it isn't. Do you think I haven't been able to figure out certain things for myself, from the way you behaved the day I tried to make love to you? From what you said about Danton, the way you looked at him? I have never seen you that afraid of anyone, not even a witch-hunter."

Gabrielle winced. Bad enough she had let Danton make a whore of her, but she had permitted him to make her a coward as well. She stiffened as Remy placed his hands on her shoulders.

"Why didn't you ever tell me?" he asked in a gentler tone.

"About Danton? How would that have changed anything?"

"I could have avenged you much sooner."

Gabrielle shook her head, realizing that Remy still didn't fully understand what had happened that day in the barn. Danton had forced himself upon her, but it had been her fault because she—

When Remy tried to turn her around to face him, she resisted, not sure if she would ever be able to bear looking into his honest brown eyes again. He stole his arms around her waist instead, her back pressed to his chest. He rested his cheek against the side of her head, his breath warm against her ear.

"Gabrielle, I made a vow to you once, don't you remember? That day you taught me how to play at knights and dragons, I knelt at your feet and I pledged . . ." Remy paused and went on hoarsely. "Milady, my sword is ever at your service. I vow by my life's blood to serve and protect you forever."

"That was a game, Remy. Only a game."

"Not to me it wasn't. I made you a solemn vow and then I allowed myself to forget it. Today I intend to redeem my promise."

Gabrielle pulled away from him and choked out. "My God, Remy, you are unbelievable. After everything you know about me, you still refuse to see me for what I am. You talk about avenging my honor and you just don't comprehend."

She faced him at last, hot tears raining down on her cheeks. "I am not worthy of it. I have never been. Remy, don't you understand? I am simply not worthy."

With a muffled sob, she turned and fled from the tent. Remy watched her go, torn between wanting to go after her and the need to finish donning his armor. Gabrielle's tears only added fuel to his hatred, his determination to rip out Danton's black heart and feed it to him before the sun set on this day. He strode over to examine the motley collection of armor assembled for him, wondering what the devil was keeping the squire he had sent Wolf to find.

"Remy?" A timid voice called his name.

He spun about to see Miri silhouetted in the opening of the tent. He had all but forgotten her presence at the tourney. The girl had always had an ephemeral quality about her, an ability to come and go like a whisper of mist.

Miri regarded Remy with wide eyes that reminded him of the child she had once been. He swore softly, raking his hand back through his hair. Dealing with another of the Cheney sisters was the last thing he needed right now. Before Miri could say another word, he commanded, "Miri, you should be over in the stands with the other spectators or find Bette and go back to the town house. This never was any place for you—"

"I saw Gabrielle." Miri cut him off. "She was crying."

"Then you ought to go comfort her."

"No, *you* should."

"I have something else I need to do. You don't understand what is going on."

"Oh, yes, I do. I witnessed your encounter with Etienne Danton." Miri's lashes swept down, veiling her remarkable eyes. "I didn't recognize him at first. I was little more than a child that summer he came to Faire Isle. We were still grieved over the death of our mother and Papa had disappeared on his voyage of exploration to Brazil."

Miri had to swallow before she could continue. "Danton was—was like a knight out of the stories Papa used to tell us and he appeared to fall in love with Gabrielle at first sight. Who could help doing that? She is strong, so bright, so beautiful. We thought that Danton meant to woo her for his bride, but instead—instead—"

When she faltered, Remy filled in harshly. "Instead the bastard ravished her, a fact Gabrielle seems determined to deny."

"She always did. Gabrielle would never talk about what happened, even to Ariane. But I knew my sister had changed. Gabrielle was never the same after that man came to our island. She and I used to roam the woods together, having wonderful adventures, conjuring fairies, unicorns, and dragons out of the trees. But it was as though Gabrielle left me behind that summer while she moved on to some dark place I didn't want to follow."

Miri bit down on her lower lip. "Gabrielle had a great magic. You saw for yourself some of the wondrous pictures she painted.

But after Danton, she left her palette and sketchbook to gather dust. She spent more and more time in front of her mirror, brushing her hair, applying poultices to her face, but it was as though whatever she did, she could not make herself beautiful enough. And there were the nightmares. Gabrielle would cry out in her sleep, awake sobbing. When I tried to comfort her, she would only roll on her side, snap at me to leave her alone. It hurt my feelings very much and we grew further apart."

Miri's voice quavered. "I was very young, you see. It took me a long time to understand what—what was wrong—" Her eyes brimmed with tears, one escaping to trickle down her cheek. Remy brushed the droplet aside with the back of his knuckle.

"Danton's blood shall pay for Gabrielle's tears . . . and yours."

"I did not tell you all this to make you more vengeful. I told you so that you can better understand Gabrielle."

Remy's jaw hardened. "I understand quite well what I must do."

"You intend to kill Danton? It will not change what happened to Gabrielle."

"No, but she'll never again have to look upon his face, endure him to—" Remy grated his teeth, clenching his fist. "By God's blood, that bastard thinks to have her again. I could see that in his eyes, the way he leered at her—"

"Then take Gabrielle away from here. Let us all go back to Faire Isle." Miri placed her palms flat against Remy's cheeks in a gesture she often used to calm a restive steed. But the muscles in Remy's face felt hard and unyielding beneath her touch.

"Remy, you must listen to me," she pleaded. "Your sword will not avail Gabrielle anything. Only your love can heal her."

Remy shook his head, his eyes dark with a mingling of anger and anguish. "She doesn't want my love, Miri. My sword is the only thing I have to offer her."

Remy held up the weapon, the glint of the steel reflected in his eyes. Miri shuddered at the sight of both the sword and

Remy's grim expression. She had never understood the need of men to resort to violence, the dark urge to take life and spill blood, no matter in how noble a cause. She had, however, learned to her sorrow that when a man was determined to strap on his sword, there was no deterring him, not even a man as good as Nicolas Remy. There was little more that she could do than brush his cheek with a kiss of resignation.

"May God go with you, Nicolas Remy," she murmured. "And all the spirits of mother earth protect you."

THE SOUND OF PIPES AND DRUMS BEATING OUT A MARTIAL AIR MIN-gled with the applause of the crowd. As she hurried behind the tent, Miri shaded her eyes with her hand and squinted toward the cavalcade of knights parading before the stands. The sun flashed off the suits of armor in a glittering display, the horses as magnificently turned out as their masters, the mounts draped in silk blankets and rich caparisons.

Only one horse remained in the open area behind the tents, resisting all efforts to be saddled. The brown gelding, draped in gold-trimmed purple velvet, wheeled away from the squire who dropped the heavy, high-backed saddle. A pair of young pages idling beneath the trees mocked and jeered the squire's efforts. Their raucous laughter and catcalls did nothing to ease the situation, further exacerbating both the nerves of the horse and the temper of the squire.

Flushed with frustration, his long dark hair tumbled across his eyes, the lad swore roundly. "Bloody, stupid brute. Cursed spawn of Satan."

The squire yanked on the leading reins as though he thought if he cursed loudly and pulled hard enough, he could force the gelding to stand still. The horse was quick to show him other-wise. Flattening its ears, it snapped and kicked, tossing its head.

Miri's spirits sank even lower. If this was Remy's horse and his squire, the captain was in greater trouble than she'd imagined. The witless lad was now engaged in a futile tug-of-war with the massive beast and there was little doubt in Miri's mind as to who was going to win. The gelding reared up, pulling the young man off his feet. Amid the hoots of the watching pages, the squire lost his grip on the lead and fell flat on his face, landing in a pile of horse droppings. Emitting a loud snort, the gelding bolted toward the passage between the tents.

Miri was ready for it. Flinging her arms wide, she positioned herself in front of the runaway horse. Horrified shouts came from the pages, who clearly expected to see her trampled. The gelding veered off at the last possible moment. Miri moved just as quickly to corral it. The horse shifted edgily away from her.

Hands held out in a supplicating gesture, she crooned low in her throat, weaving her own kind of magic until the great beast stood trembling, blowing out frightened breaths.

"Easy, easy, my handsome friend," Miri soothed him. "I am a daughter of the earth. I would never harm you."

Cautiously she reached for the dangling reins. When she had the horse secure, she stroked his nose and murmured more comforting words. When the gelding tossed its head and began to shy away again, Miri realized the squire was storming down on them.

Covered in grass, dirt, and horse manure, his black hair tumbled wildly over his face, he snarled, "Damnation, mademoiselle. What were you thinking to charge into the path of that stupid brute that way? You could have been—"

"Shhh!" Miri laid her finger alongside her lips and cast the disheveled squire a stern look. At least the lad possessed enough wit to come to an abrupt halt before he spooked the gelding all over again.

Miri laid calming hands upon the horse, patting and stroking him. She addressed the squire in a quiet voice. "This creature's name is not stupid brute or spawn of Satan. He is called Bayonne."

"He ought to be called devil," the squire grumbled. "He is going to get my captain killed with his bad-tempered ways and cowardly tricks."

The horse twitched his ears as though he understood the squire's insults. Mournful equine eyes regarded Miri through the openings in the velvet mask banding his head. Her degree of communication with other creatures did not equal what she had with Necromancer. The bond between her and the cat was extraordinary. But she comprehended the horse's thoughts well enough to discern what troubled him.

"This horse does not lack heart, monsieur. Nor is he stupid." Miri gestured indignantly toward the mask and fancy velvet blanket. "It is these foolish garments you have draped over him. You have offended his dignity."

"How on earth would you know that?"

Miri gave the boy a look of lofty scorn. "Because Bayonne told me."

The lad's mouth fell open so wide Miri thought he was in danger of catching flies. He finally managed to ask, "And just who are you, mademoiselle?"

"My name is Miribelle Cheney."

"Cheney? You—you are the sister of Mademoiselle Gabrielle?"

"Yes, but we have no time for this idle chatter. Help me get this velvet nonsense off Bayonne and then I am sure I will be able to persuade him to carry Remy through the joust bravely and true."

The squire made no move to obey her command. He stared at Miri through the wild tangles of his hair, a dazed expression stealing over his dirty face. Perhaps the poor lad was a bit dimwitted.

Not waiting for the squire's help, she began removing the trappings from Bayonne herself. As she stripped away the offending mask, the horse quivered, stamping restively. Miri cradled his nose between her hands and sang to him, weaving her greatest magic in words of an ancient language created by wise women long before knights ever roamed the earth.

Martin Le Loup blinked, knowing he should reclaim the captain's horse from this girl who seemed to have taken charge of it. But Wolf couldn't seem to move. He couldn't think. He felt lost in a haze as he stared at Miri Cheney. Where had she come from so suddenly? It was like she had dropped from the sky, fallen from the moon itself, her cascade of hair the color of moonlight, her skin as translucent. Her eyes were as blue as—No, they were gray. No, they were as silvery as her song.

A song that was at once strange and beautiful in some language he did not comprehend, but the notes vibrated through him, plucking at his heart. Her music was not only calming that great brute of a horse, but in some fashion taming him as well.

If Miri was Gabrielle's sister, then she was also a witch. Wolf feared he should cover his ears, not listen to her, but her lovely melody curled through him, making him want to weep and cry out for joy all in the same breath.

Wolf had entirely new empathy for the captain for being in thrall to Gabrielle. As he gazed spellbound at Miri, Wolf finally understood what it was to be bewitched, enchanted. And he did not have the slightest wish to be saved.

❈❈❈

"Rene de Chinon . . . Pierre de Foix." The herald intoned the names of the knights who maneuvered into position at opposite ends of the lists. The king of France strode toward the front of the stands, beaming as two among his favored mignons prepared to run the course. Visors were lowered, shields were raised, and lances steadied. The king raised a scarf aloft, then released it, the red silk fluttering to the ground.

Amid cheers from the crowd, the two knights charged, horses galloping at full tilt, their lances leveled to strike . . . and missed, thundering harmlessly past each other. The spectators in the gallery groaned in disappointment. The knights veered round for a second charge. This time Rene de Chinon's lance struck feebly off his opponent's shield.

"Oh, well done, Rene," the king applauded as heartily as if his favorite had performed some brilliant feat of arms. Desultory cheers rang out from the rest of the crowd, but the sights and sounds were all a blur to Gabrielle.

She perched on the edge of her tabouret with mounting desperation, dreading that at any moment she would see Remy assume his place at the end of the lists. Her eyes still felt raw from her recent bout of weeping and she despised herself for it. Of all the foolish weaknesses. As if her tears could be of any avail to Remy. Nothing could.

Gabrielle cast a baleful glance at the woman she held responsible for his present peril. Catherine stood behind the king's throne, watching the tourney with such a serene air, Gabrielle longed to strangle her. As the next two opponents ran their course, Gabrielle could bear the suspense no longer. She edged her way to Catherine's side.

"You have got to put a stop to this," she hissed in Catherine's ear.

Catherine's gaze never wavered from the field. "The tourney? My son went to a great deal of expense arranging this little amusement and I doubt he would—"

"You know perfectly well what I am talking about," Gabrielle interrupted her furiously. "The joust between Remy and Danton."

"Ah, that. It was Remy who accepted the challenge. Such a hot-blooded man. I always mistakenly believed our good captain to be rather phlegmatic. Who would have ever suspected him of possessing such a temper?"

"You goaded him. You poured your poison into his ear."

"Actually it was more into his eyes," Catherine said with a sly smile, then shrugged. "The captain asked me who Danton was. I merely answered his question."

"Because you wanted this combat to take place. You are seeking to destroy Remy." Gabrielle regarded the implacable older woman with a mingling of anger and despair. "But why? I thought we had made a bargain. You agreed to leave Remy alone if I seduced him and kept him from creating mischief with Navarre."

"A promise I'm sure you meant to keep," Catherine said dryly. "Frankly, I doubt your ability to do so."

"You've scarce given me a chance. I could control Remy if you would just—"

"Control him?" Catherine's gaze swept scornfully over her. "My dear Gabrielle, I fear your charms are on the wane. You don't even possess enough influence with the man to keep him from fighting."

Gabrielle flinched as Catherine's barb found its mark. What the queen said was true. There was nothing Gabrielle could have said or done to turn Remy aside from the ruinous course. He was determined to fight, to risk his life, and for what? For *her*. A dishonored woman, a harlot, a whore. Before Gabrielle could think of a reply to Catherine, the herald intoned the names she had been dreading to hear.

"The Chevalier Etienne Danton . . . Captain Nicolas Remy."

"You had better resume your seat, my dear." Catherine's dark eyes mocked her. "You are about to miss the best joust of the day."

Gabrielle whirled about, heartsick, as she saw the two mounted figures taking up positions at the opposite ends of the lists. Danton was gleaming in costly engraved armor from head to foot, plumes waving off his helmet, the scarlet feathers matching the surcoat that draped his white stallion. By contrast, Remy's brown gelding appeared plain, outfitted with no more than reins and the high-backed jousting saddle. Remy had not bothered to don a full suit of armor. He wore little protection beyond his breastplate and rough iron helmet. He looked more like a common soldier riding into battle than a knight and his appearance elicited a few jeers and catcalls from the crowd.

But for the most part a hushed air of anticipation had fallen over the spectators, even the most foolish of the courtiers sensing the difference in this contest, the deadly intentions masked by the visors of the two combatants. With a smug smile, the king leaned out over the edge of the gallery and raised the scarf. Gabrielle knew a mad urge to rush forward and snatch it away from him. But it was too late. The red silk fluttered downward. Remy and Danton charged.

Gabrielle stumbled to the edge of the stands and gripped the railing. Her heart thundered in time with the horse's hooves churning up the earth. Danton had often boasted of his skill in the joust. With little effort, he managed both reins and shield, his lance supported by the pouch placed on the bow of his saddle.

But Remy was clearly not trained for this sort of combat. This was not his kind of fighting. Though he guided his horse well enough, he gripped his lance freely, unsupported by anything but his own strength. As the two men came together, it was all Gabrielle could do to not close her eyes. Remy's lance glanced off Danton's shield. Danton's lance struck at Remy's helmet and missed. As the two horses thundered past each other, Gabrielle's palms were slick with sweat.

She clutched the rail until her knuckles were white, but there was no respite, no relief from her suffocating fear. Remy and Danton galloped to the end of the lists. Danton brought his mount around in a caracole. Remy wheeled purposefully, he and the gelding seeming to move as one. Lances leveled, the two men charged again. The tip of Remy's lance struck Danton's shield. To Gabrielle's horror, Remy lost his grip on the weapon and it tumbled to the ground. He barely managed to deflect Danton's blow with his own shield. Danton's lance splintered and snapped in two.

The crowd cheered lustily. Gabrielle pressed her hand to her mouth to stifle a moan. Oh, please, she prayed. Let that be the end of it. Her heart sank as the two men galloped to the end of the field, their squires scrambling to fetch fresh lances. Danton's horse appeared restive. Perhaps it would refuse to do the course again. Gabrielle's hope swiftly died as Danton brought his mount back under control. A new lance gripped in his hand, Remy guided his horse into place.

A hush once more enveloped the crowd as the two men careened toward each other, gaining in momentum, as though all their rage, all their hostility was honed into this final charge. They came together in a furious collision of lance and shield. Danton's horse reared back. Jarred from the saddle, Danton struck the ground with such force his helmet flew off of his head. Remy reined in, drawing his horse up short while Danton's stallion galloped to the end of the course, riderless. Any joy Gabrielle might have felt at Remy being unharmed was dimmed by the sight of Danton sprawled on his side, not moving. A collective gasp rippled through the crowd, many of the courtiers rising to their feet.

Oh, God, Gabrielle thought. Please, for Remy's sake, don't let the wretch be dead. Don't let Remy have killed him. Time seemed to slow to a crawl, the seconds inching by before Danton emitted a groan, then struggled to a sitting position. The crowd broke into a smattering of applause. Gabrielle trembled, her relief so great she nearly sagged to her knees.

She closed her eyes. Thank God. It was over and Remy was safe. So much for the Dark Queen and all of her clever plotting. Gabrielle was tempted to shoot Catherine a look of sheer defiance and triumph. But when Gabrielle's eyes fluttered open, her heart all but stopped as Danton struggled to his feet, bellowing for his sword.

Remy dismounted. He stripped off his helmet, likewise calling for a weapon. Looking mighty unhappy, Wolf scurried forward to hand Remy a broadsword while another page led away the gelding. Danton's squire was equally as quick to arm his master. Remy and Danton marched toward each other. Their swords came together in a horrible clang of steel.

"No!" Gabrielle's cry was lost in the shouts of excitement from the other spectators.

This duel was in flagrant violation of the statutes against *combat à outrance*. Surely the king must stop it. Even Henry Valois could not stand idly by and watch as his own laws were ignored. But when Gabrielle glanced desperately at the king, Henry hunkered down feeding tidbits to his whippet, feigning not to notice the fierce duel being waged. Her hands folded primly before her, the Dark Queen watched with an air of bored detachment as though in little doubt of the outcome.

Gabrielle was jostled as other courtiers left their seats, peering eagerly over the edge of the gallery. She was sickened by their faces, their expressions reminding her of jackals scenting blood. There was no one to intervene, no one to bring a halt to the deadly combat . . . no one but herself. She shoved her way out of the crowd and darted for the steps leading down from the gallery.

※※※

REMY HAMMERED HIS SWORD AGAINST DANTON'S BLADE WITH blows that reverberated up his arm. But Remy scarce noticed any more than he heard the distant roaring of the crowd. His own blood drummed in his ears, the familiar dark rush he'd experienced on so many battlefields taking control, surging through his veins.

His lips pulled back in the grimace that had always struck terror into the hearts of his enemies. Remy bore down on Danton, slashing, driving him back. His mouth tightened in grim concentration, Danton parried the blows. Feinting to the left, Danton slipped past his guard. The tip of his blade pierced Remy's padded sleeve. He felt his arm burn as his flesh was scored by steel. With a snarl, he went at Danton harder, raining down blow after blow.

Danton staggered back, nearly lost his footing. His lack of armor might make Remy more vulnerable, but Danton's was weighing him down. The man's movements grew more labored, sweat trickling down his handsome face. Remy's arm was tireless, his muscles more accustomed to the long hours of fighting required of a soldier, flesh transformed into steel until it almost became an extension of his sword.

As Danton parried his blows, Remy saw the man's arrogance begin to fade. Danton's eyes flickered with his first inkling that he might lose, that he might be about to die. Panting, he fought with increased desperation. Remy smelled his fear, savored it. He arced his sword down in a vicious swing that nearly sliced off Danton's ear. Danton emitted a shrill cry, blood spurting down his cheek.

He backed away from Remy, gasping. "A—all right. Enough."

"Oh, no, not nearly enough," Remy replied. He slashed again, Danton barely responding in time to block the blow.

"Damn you! I said enough." Danton's eyes widened with a mixture of pain and fear. He scrambled farther away. "I yield. I beg you stop."

"Just as Gabrielle begged you to stop?"

"Yes. No . . . I mean, she didn't. She wanted me—"

Remy struck again, his sword coming within a whisper of laying open Danton's cheek. "Wanted you to rape her, you bastard? I'll take you apart piece by piece."

His breath issuing in a ragged gasp, Danton frantically beat back Remy's blade. Their weapons locked, Remy glared into the other man's eyes. His face streaked with blood and sweat, Danton actually attempted an ingratiating smile.

"For—for heaven's sake, man, why all this fuss? She—she is only a whore."

The cold dark river coursing through Remy's veins erupted into a molten fire, a red haze passing over his eyes. He shoved Danton back and brought his sword down brutally, smashing Danton's hand, disarming him. Danton staggered and fell flat on his back. But Remy no longer saw the man cowering at his feet, begging for mercy. His mind blurred with images of Gabrielle's haunted eyes, the memory of her broken sobs. Standing over Danton, Remy raised his sword—

"Remy! No!"

He was dimly aware of someone rushing at him, clutching at his sword arm. He almost flung her to one side until he realized who it was. Even then he fought to shake her off, growling, "Gabrielle. Get the hell out of my way."

Her face white with fear, Gabrielle clung to him with strength born of desperation. "No, you can't kill him. Remy, please. Don't."

"You'd seek to protect this bastard? After what he did to you?"

"No, you damned fool. It is you I am trying to protect."

Remy scarcely seemed to hear her, his expression dark and frightening, his pupils mere pinpoints in eyes that held nothing but blood and vengeance. The Scourge's eyes—

Gabrielle caught his face between her hands. "Don't you understand anything? It is only you I care about. You I don't want to come to harm." She half-sobbed. *"I love you, you great bloody idiot."*

The words seemed so futile, not enough to check such a killing fury. She expected Remy to hurl her out of his way. But he froze, blinking down at her.

"What? What did you say?"

"I s-said I love you," she whispered.

Remy stared at her for what seemed like an age, that terrifying look fading. The Scourge's eyes disappeared, to be replaced with Remy's rich brown eyes, wide with wonder. His sword arm went slack, the weapon slipping from his fingers.

With the aid of his squire, Danton had struggled to his feet. Hand clasped to his ear, the knight slunk off the field. Remy scarce noticed or cared. At the moment nothing mattered except that Gabrielle had spoken words he had never expected to hear, miraculous words he could still not believe.

He stripped off his leather gauntlets and reached for her hands. "Say it again."

She lifted her face to his, her jaw set at a defiant angle, but her eyes were soft and luminous with tears. "I love you. I always have."

He gripped her hands. The feeling that spiraled through him was unlike the thunderclap of emotion he might once have anticipated. Joy stole upon him more quietly, like warmth and sunlight pouring through his veins, banishing the last of the cold, the darkness that had so recently gripped his heart.

The entire world faded away, time itself stopping to allow them this one precious moment. A moment that was over all too soon. Gabrielle was the first to snap to her senses, drawing her hands away from Remy. Becoming aware of the cries and hum of voices from the spectator's gallery, she realized the uproar she must have created by interfering in the duel, but she didn't care. She'd examine the wisdom or folly of confessing her love to Remy at some later date, but right now nothing seemed important beyond the fact that Remy was safe.

Gabrielle turned defiantly, preparing to face the displeasure of the Dark Queen, along with all the curious looks and pointing fingers. To her surprise, she saw that neither the stares nor the gestures were directed at her and Remy. All heads swiveled toward a mounted troop of men that approached from the Louvre's courtyard.

Gabrielle tensed with the fear that she had not succeeded in saving Remy. She had stopped Remy from killing Danton, but the king must have sent for his guard, intending to have Remy arrested after all. She glanced up at Remy, who scowled at the approaching troop. She would have given him a brisk shake, begged him to run if she thought it would have done the least good. All she could do was step protectively in front of him, a move that Remy thwarted by hauling her back.

He swiftly retrieved his sword, the tender lover of a few moments ago replaced by the stern commander. "Gabrielle, go find Miri and Wolf. Then the three of you—"

"I am not going anywhere," Gabrielle snapped.

Remy glared at her, but the rapid approach of mounted men made any further argument futile. He gave a low curse, then thrust her behind him, bracing himself. Gabrielle leaned to one side, peering around his stalwart frame at the arriving troop.

This was no segment of the palace guard she had ever seen. The men were clad in crude helmets and coats of mail, covered with black tunics emblazoned with white crosses. They resembled a party of knights of yore about to embark upon the Crusades.

As they approached the lists, the leader raised his hand and the entire troop came to a halt, wheeling to take up position opposite the spectator's gallery. Gabrielle could just barely make out the faces beneath the raised visors, but she thought them the most ill-favored bunch she had ever seen. They looked like a pack of ruthless mercenaries.

"Now what the devil is all this?" Remy's brow creased with an expression of mingled confusion and apprehension.

"I don't know. A part of the tourney perhaps?" Gabrielle ventured out from behind him. Remy immediately locked his arm about her waist and hauled her close to his side as though he feared one of these men might be tempted to make off with her. Most of them certainly looked capable of it.

Bewilderment was reflected in the faces of the other spectators. Only the king of France showed no astonishment as he stepped to the front of the gallery and signaled for silence.

"Good friends. Ladies and gentlemen of the court," he called out in a booming voice far different from his usual peevish tones. "I had planned to present a surprise to you at this evening's banquet, but it has arrived a little sooner than I expected."

A surprise? Gabrielle and Remy exchanged an uneasy glance. She pressed closer to Remy, feeling as though she had already had enough surprises today to last a lifetime.

The king brushed back his long mane of hair, his rings glittering as he attempted to adopt a solemn expression. "There is a growing threat to the peace of our realm that has long required our attention. Forces of darkness far too great to be dealt with in our ecclesiastical courts or halls of justice. I all but despaired of combating such evil until I heard of the work of these men you see arrayed before you. Soldiers devoting their life to a single cause, the destruction of a plague that has spread through all of Europe."

The king paused for dramatic effect, then hissed, "The foul practices of sorcery."

Witch-hunters. The grim troop of men were witch-hunters.

This had to be more of Catherine's doing, her treachery, Gabrielle thought angrily. It would not be the first time the Dark Queen had resorted to the use of witch-hunters to deal with her enemies. Such practice was considered the worst sort of betrayal one wise woman could inflict upon another. Her lips tightening, Gabrielle sought out Catherine's face in the stands. She was disconcerted to see that Catherine had turned pale, her impassive face gone rigid with shock and another expression Gabrielle had never thought to see on the Dark Queen's face . . . fear.

Catherine clearly had nothing to do with this. Whatever intrigue was afoot was none of her devising, the situation beyond her control. The realization caused Gabrielle to shiver, making her feel strangely even more afraid.

Catherine's son paraded along the front of the stands, the hint of a smirk about his mouth, obviously enjoying the sensation he had created. "Too long have my people been forced to submit to the terror and intimidation of those godless women given over to the use of dark arts," the king intoned piously. "Let me present to all of you the man who will drive out the devil and rid France of her witches once and for all."

The king raised his hand in a dramatic gesture. "Monsieur Le Balafre."

One horseman edged out of the line, wheeling his mount

closer to the stands until he was positioned just below the king. He removed his helmet, the sight of his countenance eliciting gasps from the crowd.

Gabrielle could see why. He was an ugly brute, his head close shaven, and a vicious-looking scar bisecting his right cheek. As he bent forward in the saddle, according the king a stiff bow, Gabrielle was also struck with how surprisingly young he looked. Far too young to be the leader of this hardened troop of men.

In fact . . . Her breath hitched in her throat. She wriggled away from Remy, her eyes narrowing in an effort to study the witch-hunter more closely. To see beneath that scar, to traces of features that struck her with disturbing familiarity.

"Oh, dear God," she groaned.

Remy was hard at her heels, pulling her back. "Gabrielle, what is it? Do you recognize that man? Who is he?"

"It's Simon," Miri's quiet voice spoke up.

Gabrielle whirled around to find her little sister behind them. Miri's face was pale and unhappy, her eyes filled with anguish.

"Simon Aristide," she whispered.

Chapter Eighteen

THE SUN SET OVER THE ROOFTOPS OF PARIS, THE LIGHT FADING on a day Gabrielle was glad to see end. She lingered by the windows of the bedchamber she had assigned to her younger sister, watching the shadows descend over the city beyond her town house walls, the gathering darkness fraught with new menace.

Simon Aristide. That wretched boy whose betrayal had once nearly cost the life of Ariane's beloved Renard, whose treachery had all but broken Miri's trusting heart. Gabrielle wondered what perversity of fate had conjured up so many ghosts of the past all within the same day. First Etienne, then Simon.

Turning from the window, Gabrielle stole a worried glance at her sister. The green gown discarded over a chair, Miri huddled in her shift in the center of the bed. Her knees drawn up, she rested her head against her legs, her shimmering curtain of hair falling forward over her face. Miri seemed to have dwindled back into a child and a hurt one at that.

Miri had scarcely spoken two words since Remy had hustled

them all away from the tourney and back to the safety of
Gabrielle's town house. At least it had seemed safe to Gabrielle
once. Now these walls felt like scant protection from whatever
dark forces might be plotting against them. She crossed over to
the bed and sank down beside Miri. Necromancer rubbed his
head against her legs, purring softly, but Miri ignored him, an action very unusual for her. Gabrielle sifted her fingers through
Miri's silken hair, brushing it back over her shoulder.

"Miri?"

Her sister lifted her head and managed a wobbly smile.
"Don't look so worried, Gabby. I'm fine."

"You don't seem fine, dearest. You're very pale. In fact,
Necromancer's paws have more color than you do," she teased
gently.

Necromancer stretched up on his hind legs and patted Miri's
cheek with his snowy paws as if to emphasize Gabrielle's point.
Miri sighed and gathered the cat in her arms.

"I've had a bit of a shock, that's all. I keep remembering the
first time I met Simon, that night in the ring of stone giants
where those wicked girls were planning to offer Necromancer up
as a sacrifice. They fled when the witch-hunters came and Vachel
Le Vis—" Miri shuddered at the memory of the evil Grand Master of the Order of Malleus Maleficarum. "He thought I was responsible, but Simon knew better. He tried to defend me, and I
thought he was the most beautiful boy I'd ever seen. His hair was
so black and lustrous, his complexion white as milk, his dark
eyes so kind."

"And now his exterior finally matches the ugliness of his
heart," Gabrielle said tartly.

"If only you would have let me approach him, speak to
him—"

Gabrielle shook her head vigorously. She had many reasons
to be grateful to Remy but none so much as for his prompt actions today. He had spirited her and Miri away before that
treacherous Aristide even had a chance to notice her sister.

"When did it ever do any good trying to talk to a witch-hunter?" Gabrielle demanded.

"But Simon was different. There was much that was good in him. Or at least I once thought so." Miri pillowed her cheek on the top of Necromancer's head. "Perhaps this scheme to rid France of all wise women is more the king's doing than Simon's."

"It doesn't matter who is behind it because we are not staying around to find out."

At least you are not, little sister, Gabrielle thought.

When Miri lifted her head, a rebellious light springing to her eyes, Gabrielle said, "Surely even you must see the need to return to Faire Isle. Unless you want to risk finding yourself on trial for witchcraft again?"

Gabrielle felt like a shrew for stirring up such a painful memory for her sister. But she was determined to use any argument at her disposal to get Miri to leave Paris.

Miri sighed, her shoulders slumping. "Perhaps you are right. It was such a jolt seeing Simon again, realizing what has become of him. I can't think clearly right now."

"Of course you can't." Gabrielle soothed. "It has been a long, exhausting day for all of us. Everything will seem clearer in the morning. I will send Bette to fetch you a bit of supper, then I recommend an early bed."

"Never mind about the supper. I have little appetite."

Gabrielle started to protest, but Miri was already struggling with the covers. The sight of her sister's wan countenance caused Gabrielle to hold her tongue. Perhaps a good long sleep was the best remedy for Miri's heartache. Tucking the counterpane up round her little sister, Gabrielle brushed a kiss on Miri's brow. Her sister's eyes were already closed as Gabrielle tiptoed quietly from the room.

No sooner had the door closed behind Gabrielle than Miri's eyes fluttered open. She grimaced to find herself staring straight into Necromancer's amber eyes. Front paws braced on the edge of her pillow, the cat loomed over her, his gaze full of reproach.

I know what you are thinking, Daughter of the Earth. Forget about it.

"I have no idea what you are talking about," Miri muttered.

This meek compliance may have fooled your sister, but it does not fool me. You still want to see that miserable Aristide. You must stay away from him. He is a predator.

"You are a fine one to talk of that. No matter how well you are fed, you persist in preying upon poor defenseless mice."

Necromancer sank back on his haunches, complacently licking his paws. *It is in my nature to hunt, just as it is in his.*

"It also appears to be in your nature to constantly disturb my sleep," Miri grumbled. "Good night."

She tunneled farther beneath the covers, where Necromancer could no longer read her expression. It was possible that Gabrielle and the cat were correct in their judgment of Simon. Perhaps what Miri planned to do was both rash and foolish. But it was not in *her* nature to give up so easily on those whom she loved.

⁂

THE CANDLES HAD BEEN LIT IN HER BEDCHAMBER BY THE TIME Gabrielle returned to it. She froze on the threshold, startled by the sight of Remy bending over her washbasin, stripped down to little more than his trunk hose. The candlelight played over the rippling muscles of his bare back and broad shoulders. Gabrielle's soft gasp alerted him to her presence. He straightened from the washstand.

"I am sorry. I didn't mean to startle you. Bette said you would not mind if I washed away some of the grime of the day and tended to this." He crooked his right elbow, indicating an ugly red cut down his forearm.

"N-no, of course not," Gabrielle stammered. With the advent of the witch-hunters and her concern for Miri, she had forgotten Remy's wound. Stricken with remorse, she hastened to pluck the damp cloth from his hand.

"Here, let me take care of that."

Catching hold of his wrist to hold his arm steady, she dabbed gently at the slash. She was relieved to see that it had congealed over. Six inches in length, the wound did not appear deep enough to require stitches. All the same, she bit down hard upon her lip as she cleaned the wound. But her distress had not escaped Remy's notice. He stroked a tendril of hair gently back from her cheek.

"It's only a scratch, Gabrielle."

She knew that. It was the thought of what could have happened to Remy today that made her want to melt against his chest and dissolve into tears. She focused on the cut instead. Although Remy protested it was not necessary, she insisted upon applying the witch hazel Bette had provided. Remy sucked in his breath sharply at the sting, but otherwise bore her fumbling with the linen bandage patiently.

Her hands were not as steady as she would have wished and she had difficulty meeting his eyes. She had never told any man so bluntly that she loved him before. Her confession left her feeling self-conscious and vulnerable. The fact that Remy was half-naked did nothing to add to her ease. Her gaze strayed to the powerful contours of his scarred chest, Cass's medallion resting against the crisp mat of his dark gold hairs. The charm had proved to be completely useless. What good was an amulet that warned of danger if a man was too obstinate to take heed of it?

She was tempted to lift the chain over his head and simply throw the talisman away, but the contrast of the metal gleaming against Remy's bare skin was in some odd way very masculine and strangely seductive. Such thoughts did nothing to steady her hands. She made an awkward job of wrapping the bandage around his forearm. Remy didn't complain, but he winced when she pulled it too tight.

"Sorry," she muttered. "I have never been as good as Ariane at this."

"You are doing just fine."

She risked a glance up to find his gaze resting warmly upon her, the expression in his eyes tender and passionate enough to make any woman go weak in the knees. When she had confessed her love to him on the tourney field, for one brief moment everything had seemed possible, any happiness within their grasp. But Gabrielle had come to her senses.

She loved Remy. She had finally told him so, but that didn't change anything, none of the peril they faced from the Dark Queen or witch-hunters, the awkward situation with Navarre. It especially did not change the kind of woman Gabrielle was, make her any more worthy of Remy's love.

Gabrielle finished tying off the bandage. Then she moved to dispose of the bloodied water in the basin, summoning one of the servants to fetch a fresh ewer of water so Remy could continue bathing. As Gabrielle refilled the basin, she was aware of Remy watching her every move. The heat of his gaze made her heartbeat quicken, her skin tingle. She had never realized it was possible for a man to make a woman want him simply through the stillness of his eyes.

The silence that stretched out between them was not an easy one. It was far too fraught with unspoken desires. As Gabrielle laid out a linen towel for Remy, she sought to lighten the tension by asking with false brightness, "I don't suppose you'd care to borrow some of my perfumed soap?"

"And end up smelling like some of the French king's petit amis?" Remy replied dryly. "No, thank you. You'd best save the soap for Miri. Perhaps she'd like to try it."

After the fraction of a pause, he asked, "How is your sister?"

"Well enough. I am sure she'll be fine once she's recovered from her shock. But I will feel better when she is safely on her way back to Faire Isle."

"When both of you are," Remy said firmly.

Gabrielle folded and refolded the towel. The moment had come that she could no longer avoid. She avoided looking at Remy instead as she said, "There is only one place I am going and—and that is back to the palace tonight."

"What! Are you quite mad?" Remy growled.

She clutched the towel, crumpling the linen she had just so carefully folded. "I have to seek out Navarre and explain things to him. You must have noticed him mounted near the end of the lists as we were all hurrying away. The stunned look on his face."

"Yes, I did. But it is my duty to explain to him about us—not yours."

"Remy, there is no *us.* I don't want Navarre misinterpreting what I did today and being angry with you. Fortunately, he was not close enough to hear what I said to you. I should still be able to smooth things over with him and make amends."

"What sort of amends?"

Gabrielle could not bring herself to answer him. She sought to refold the towel. Remy snatched it away from her and flung it to the floor. Catching her hard by the shoulders, he dragged her around to face him.

"You still plan to become his mistress, don't you?" he cried. "To share his bed even after what you told me today? Damn it, Gabrielle! You said you loved me. Didn't you mean it?"

It would be better if she could lie, pretend that she'd only said what she had in order to put a stop to the duel. But Remy's eyes clouded with such hurt and self-doubt, she could not bear it.

"Yes, I meant it," she said. "I do love you, but I must never tell you so again."

"In God's name, why?"

"Because . . . don't you see? Because it makes no difference."

"It makes all the difference in the world to me." He hauled her closer, bending to claim her lips. Gabrielle averted her face so that his mouth only grazed her cheek.

"Remy, no matter what I feel for you—"

"What we feel for each other," he insisted, brushing his lips against her hair, his breath warm upon her ear. "I love you, Gabrielle. I need hardly tell you that. You must have always known."

He kissed the sensitive hollow behind her ear, his mouth trailing lower down the column of her neck. The warm rasp of his lips sent a shiver through her, his kisses by turns soft and fierce, tender and passionate. It took all of Gabrielle's will to resist.

"Remy, please don't," she begged. She thrust herself away from him. "Can you not see that any love between us is as hopeless as it ever was?"

Remy's face darkened with a mingling of desire and frustration. "Why? Because of a vision some cursed witch conjured up for you? Some damn fool prediction that Navarre will be king of France, that you will be his mistress and rule by his side. Is that what you really want? Is such a thing so important to you?"

Gabrielle backed farther away him, her hand fluttering to her neck, her skin grazed and flushed from the heat of Remy's kisses. "I made a vow to myself long ago that I was not going to be helpless like other women, without power in a man's world."

"And what the devil will you do with all this power after you get it? I doubt power ever kept anyone warm at night, made them feel any less lonely or happier."

"I never looked for warmth or happiness," Gabrielle said in a small voice. "But if I was mistress of all France, I promise you one thing. No witch-hunter would ever cross our borders again."

She added more fiercely, "And I would put a stop to all fighting. No woman would ever have to grieve for the loss of a husband or son in some stupid, pointless battle."

"Do you really think it would be that easy, Gabrielle? To banish evil by royal decree? That a mere command will turn swords into plowshares? If so, you know very little of the dark nature of men, my dear. But I don't think your attempts to push me away have anything to do with a hunger for power or being a king's mistress. This is about that bastard Danton. Since I realized what he did to you, you have been scarce able to look me in the eye."

Gabrielle tried to refute his claim by staring boldly at him, but she found she could not. Remy closed the distance between them. Crooking his fingers beneath her chin, he forced her to look up at him.

"Gabrielle, when a man behaves like a beast, it is his shame, not the woman's."

Gabrielle could only gaze at him in disbelief. Rape was always accounted to be a woman's ruin, a woman's shame. Her worth diminished, despoiled goods. Yet Remy continued to look at her with such tenderness, such understanding, such—such love Gabrielle found it unbearable. She shied away from him.

"If you only knew," she choked. "You have never seen me for what I am. You are trying to make some sort of wronged angel out of me. What happened in the barn that day *was* my fault."

Her throat tightened so painfully, it was a moment before she could continue. "I was infatuated with Danton. When he led me into that barn, I didn't even try to resist. I had never been kissed by a man before and I longed to know what it would be like. When Danton drew me into his arms, it was exciting at—at first.

"I had never felt such a strange warm rush. I didn't even protest until he—he wanted to do more than kiss me." Gabrielle hung her head, her cheeks burning. "I tried to ease away from him, but he became rougher, more aggressive. I grew frightened and begged him to stop, but it was too late.

"I had enticed him past all bearing. He—he—hurt me." Gabrielle drew in a deep breath. "I had been foolish enough to think he'd loved me, that he might want to marry me. But after he had done with me, he said that all I was fit for was to be a whore."

"The son of a bitch," Remy growled. "You should have let me kill him."

Gabrielle shook her head bleakly. "As much as I hated Danton for what he'd done, I hated myself even more. Because I realized he was right."

"Oh, Gabrielle," Remy groaned. Before she could resist, he gathered her up in his arms, cradling her head beneath his chin. "Of course you would be excited by your first kiss. You were a passionate young girl, but a maiden still. Any man of decency would have been the first to draw back. Instead of respecting your innocence, Danton took advantage of it to satisfy his own selfish lust."

"That may be true," she said sadly. "But it was my own choice to continue down the path he set me upon, to become exactly what he accused me of being."

"Because he'd robbed you of your self-respect."

"He said that he couldn't help himself. That I bewitched him."

Remy's savage oath showed exactly what he thought of that notion. "Sweetheart, you have bewitched me for years. No man could have been more inflamed than I was that afternoon in my bedchamber. But when you asked me to stop, I managed to do so."

"But you are extraordinary. I have never in my life known any other man so honorable, so chivalrous, so gentle."

"Oh, yes." The bitterness of Remy's laugh surprised Gabrielle. She drew away, troubled to find his eyes filled with a dark self-mockery.

"You claim I have never seen you for what you are. I might say the same of you. You have built me up into this impossible image. The great hero. The *Scourge*." Remy pronounced the sobriquet with deep loathing. "What did you think of me today when I was preparing to take Danton's head?"

"Well, I—" Gabrielle stammered, disquieted by the memory of that frightening look on Remy's face. "You were seeking to defend my honor. You were angry—"

"I was beyond angry. There is a darkness that gathers like poison to surge through my blood. I've felt it before. Every time I set foot on a battlefield. When I first gaze out across the field, over a sea of brave faces, many of them lads who haven't yet sprouted their first beard, the thought of the slaughter and loss of life to come revolt me.

"But once the fighting begins, I am as much a beast as the next man. Lusting for blood, filled with a dark hunger to destroy my enemy. And I am good at the killing, Gabrielle. Far too good. Why do you think I have such blasted nightmares?"

"Because of—of St. Bartholomew's Eve. All the friends you lost—"

"Those faces haunt me right enough, the people I failed to save. But there are other specters as well, the ghostly images of the men I slaughtered, the lives I cut short with my blade."

Remy turned abruptly away from her, bracing his arms against the washstand. "You have told me your worst secret. Now I'll tell you mine. You asked me who the man is in my nightmares, the demon whose face is hidden behind the visor. If I am lucky, I wake before I have to see. But the nights I am not so fortunate, I yank up the visor and that hideous demon is me. It is the brutality of my own face that I see, my hands and sword that are drenched in blood. My soul is far more stained than yours."

Remy fell silent. Gabrielle realized this confession had been as difficult for Remy as her own about Danton. She longed to wrap her arms comfortingly around him, but she was held back by the remnants of the past, old fears that had dogged her for so long.

The risks involved in giving way to love and desire were great, opening one up to pain, disappointment, and heartbreak. It was far easier not to feel anything, to place faith in the prophecy of some long-dead astrologer. Let the stars dictate your destiny and there were no difficult decisions, no mistakes to make. Gabrielle gazed out her bedchamber window at a moon just shy of being full, surrounded by a scattering of those small mysterious satellites. She was once more reminded of her mother's words.

"Your fate is not writ in some distant stars, my dear heart, but rests entirely in your own choices."

Looking back on her choices of these past few years, there were very few Gabrielle could regard without regret. She was aware of him anxiously watching her now as though trying to discern her thoughts. When she turned toward him, he offered her a wearied smile.

"Perhaps you are right after all and it is hopeless. Perhaps our separate demons are too great to be conquered."

"But Sir Nicolas, you have always been very good at fighting dragons." Though her heart beat wildly, she gathered up her courage to approach him. "We both are flawed people, stained by our regrets of the past. But maybe it is possible, we—we could wash each other clean."

Picking up a clean cloth, she dipped it into the water, then wrung it out. Her fingers trembled as she turned to Remy and began to wipe it over him, starting at his shoulders, working down to the broad span of his chest. Remy quivered at her touch, his breath quickening. But he held himself still, as though she was some wild creature and his slightest move would be enough to frighten her away.

It very well might have. There was nothing of the bold courtesan about her now. She felt as timid and tentative as a bride on her wedding night. Easing the medallion aside, she caressed the cloth over his golden mat of hair, stroking more gently each time she came to a scar as though those cruel marks must still cause him pain.

It hurt her to look upon them, those harsh reminders of all that he had suffered. Nicolas Remy was a brave soldier who had fought as he had been trained to do, and fought well. Other men might be able to leave the horrors of the battlefield behind them, but Remy carried those dark memories in the weariness of his eyes and in his dreams. He was far too sensitive, this man who had been so misnamed the Scourge. She lingered over the worst of his scars, the jagged raised line just below his shoulder. She cleansed it with the cloth, then bent, pressing her lips to his damp flesh.

Remy hissed between his teeth, catching her shoulders to ease her gently away. "Ah, please. Don't do that, Gabrielle. My wounds are far too ugly for that."

"My scars are as harsh as yours, just not as visible," she said. "Yet you do not cringe away from me."

"I love you. How could I possibly—"

Gabrielle silenced him with a kiss. "Then you must allow me to love you, too. All of you."

Slowly, she proceeded to kiss all of his scars one by one, her mouth lingering as though she could draw out all his painful memories, take them into herself. How she wished that she could. Her eyes blurred, the salt of her tears mingling with the tang of Remy's skin. His chest rose and fell more quickly with each kiss. He caressed her hair, stooping to drop a kiss on the top of her head. He plucked at her hairpins until her hair tumbled loose about her shoulders. His fingers moved on to the fastenings of her gown, his hands no more steady than hers.

Somehow he fumbled through the layers of her clothing and worked the apparel off her shoulders, baring her to the waist. He took the cloth from her and moistened it again. He bathed her, beginning with her face, wiping away her tears, then trailed the cloth down her neck in a sensual path that caused Gabrielle to shiver. Down, down to the valley between her breasts, Remy worked the cloth in slow circles around each breast.

The circles getting smaller, tighter until Gabrielle felt her body tightening in response, her nipples hardening at the faint abrasion of the cloth. A trickle of water escaped from the scrap of linen and Remy bent swiftly to catch it with his lips. His mouth and tongue flickered over her bared flesh, moving up the globe of one breast.

His mouth fastened over one nipple, laving it with the warm heat of his tongue. Gabrielle gasped, clinging to the broad strength of his shoulders. Like someone who had been lost too long in a frigid winter landscape, she felt as though her numbed flesh tingled painfully back to life.

She sighed, burying her fingers in his hair as he suckled her breast. Her fingers roved over his back with a mounting urgency. The washcloth dropped unheeded from Remy's fingers. He straightened to gather her into his arms, the soft sensitive globes of her breasts flattening against the hard wall of his chest. Cass's medallion came between them, the cool feel of the metal striking an odd shiver through her.

Remy tugged the chain over his head and discarded the amulet before drawing her back to him, skin pressed to skin, beating heart to beating heart. His mouth captured hers in a kiss that was fiery and tender, his tongue coaxing and stroking hers in a heated mating. Gabrielle clung to him, kissing him back just as eagerly. Somehow, she scarce knew how, Remy stripped away the rest of her garments.

She stood naked and vulnerable in his embrace. His lips wooing hers, he ran his fingers down her back, his large callused hands settling over her buttocks. He cupped her to him. Despite the barrier of his trunk hose, he left her in no doubt of the extent of his arousal, his hunger for her. Though she fought to quell it, she experienced that old familiar flutter of panic.

This was the point where she always beat a retreat, her mind detaching to flee to some safe distance. But she was held fast by Remy, his kiss, his touch, his adoring eyes weaving gentle, unbreakable bonds about her, allowing her no escape.

She pulled her lips from his and turned away, trembling. At least she could douse the candles and find some small measure of security in darkness. Grabbing up the snuffer, she moved toward the tapers burning atop the mantel.

Remy stepped quickly after her, his hand closing over hers.

"No, Gabrielle, don't. I have waited far too long. I need to see you."

Gabrielle reluctantly surrendered, setting the snuffer down. Facing Remy again, fully exposing herself to him, was one of the hardest things she had ever done. She raised her arms instinctively to cover her breasts, but Remy caught her hands. Gently holding her arms away from her body, his gaze roamed over her. Never had any man's eyes combined so much tenderness with desire.

"You are beautiful," he said hoarsely.

She had been told how lovely she was so many times. She was fully aware of the perfections of her own body in a detached sort of way, cataloguing them as a soldier might take stock of his weapons. But until this moment, she had never actually *felt* beautiful, not until Remy worshipped her with his eyes. She blushed and trembled and suddenly was consumed by the need to see all of him as well.

Her fingers felt wooden and clumsy as she struggled with the fastenings of his trunk hose. With his help, she managed to get him undressed. Her gaze traveled shyly over him, the bold contours of his chest, his narrow waist, his lean hips, the hard muscles of his thighs. She skimmed over the size of his erection, unable to still a small shudder.

Remy must have noticed her response. He cradled her face between his hands, brushing her lips with a kiss. "It will be all right, Gabrielle. I would never hurt you."

"I—I know that," she said, but she trembled all the same. Her apprehensions had no basis in reason, but were far too real, nonetheless. Danton's legacy.

"We'll take this very slowly. You can stop me whenever you wish," Remy promised, kissing her again. He led her over to the bed as tenderly as any bridegroom could have ever coaxed his virgin bride. Drawing back the covers, Remy stretched himself out on the sheets, easing her down beside him.

They lay side by side, her forehead nestled against his shoulder while he breathed kisses against her hair. Remy had ever been a man of few words. He was not the sort of lover to whisper pretty declarations or endearments. He spoke with the intensity of his eyes, the warmth of his touch, the heat of his kiss.

He tipped her face up toward him, kissing her brow, her eyelids, the tip of her nose, his mouth settling over hers in a kiss that was long, deep, and slow. Despite the nervous thudding of her pulse, Gabrielle could not help but respond, parting her lips for the bold thrust of his tongue, warmth spreading through her veins.

Patient . . . he was so very patient. She could only marvel at his forbearance when his own need was so evident. She could feel the brush of his hardened shaft against her thigh, a sensation that both stirred her own desire and alarmed her at the same time.

Kissing her again and again, Remy's hands roved over her, fondling her breasts, teasing her nipples until they ached, sending spirals of heat through her. But when Remy's fingers skimmed downward over the plane of her stomach, inching toward the nest of curls between her legs, she tensed anew.

She clamped her knees hard together, easing his hand away. Mouth clinging to his, she began to stroke him almost feverishly. She had learned the tricks of pleasing a man, how to satisfy him without surrendering anything of herself. It was even possible to bring a man to climax without his ever being inside her.

Almost desperately, she began to practice those wiles on Remy, scoring his chest with her fingertips, her mouth. Her hand closed over his shaft, teasing him with her fingertips. Remy emitted a sharp gasp, his fingers tightening around her wrist. "No, Gabrielle. Not—not so fast. Not until I have pleasured you."

She shifted on her back and stared up at the canopy of her bed, not wanting him to see her doubt, her fear that no matter how much she loved Remy, it would never be possible for her to feel the ultimate pleasure in any man's touch. He took several deep breaths as though fighting to stem the tide of his own arousal. He braced himself above her, renewing his tender assault upon her senses, striving to stir her to passion. Her body ached to respond to his kiss, his caress, to blossom into full-blown desire, but the old fears clung to her, getting in the way. The dark memory of Danton seemed embedded beneath her skin.

The faint stubble of Remy's beard abraded the tender flesh of her stomach as he kissed her, his mouth moving dangerously lower. His hand sought to part her thighs. Gabrielle's breath snagged in her throat. In spite of all her best resolve, she felt her mind struggling desperately to slip away. None of her other lovers had ever noticed before.

But his breath warm upon her thigh, Remy suddenly stilled. The bed creaked as he shifted position. Laying his hand alongside her cheek, he said in a ragged voice. "Ah, Gabrielle, don't. Please don't pretend me away."

"I—I am sorry," she whispered. "This first time, could you just take me quickly and—and—"

"But I am not going to *take* you." Remy stroked the hair from her brow, his smile at once tender and mysterious. "You are going to take me."

Before she could ask what he meant, he shifted on his back and tugged her with him until she rested on top of him, his powerful body pinned beneath hers. Gabrielle's eyes widened when she realized what he was prepared to let her do. As a courtesan, she should have been familiar with any sort of lovemaking. But she had never had a partner who had not preferred the dominant position with the woman submissive beneath.

She was embarrassed to confess, "Remy. I have never—I am not sure I can please you this way—"

"This is not just about my pleasure, but yours as well. Do you not trust me, Gabrielle?"

"With my life."

"Then trust me with your heart as well." Remy kissed her, positioning her legs so that she straddled his powerful body. She could feel the heat pouring off his flesh, arousing her in spite of all her fears.

His hands moved over her arms, her breasts, and the curve of her waist as though he was a sculptor, lovingly molding every inch of her. When his fingers eased between her legs, caressing her most intimate places, she squirmed at the sheer pleasure of it, feeling herself grow hot and moist. Desire like a dark tide threatening to engulf her. Remy caressed her hair back over her shoulders, clearly needing to see her face.

"Don't fight it, Gabrielle. Don't be afraid. Your desire is safe with me."

His breath came quick and hard, his body trembling with need, but he made no move to thrust himself inside her. His fingers continued his gentle probe, coaxing and stroking until her ache for him outweighed any fears.

"Remy, please," she panted. "I—I want you inside me."

"Then take me there," he rasped.

Gabrielle shifted until her fingers closed around his hardened shaft. She positioned herself, easing down until her body stretched like a sheath around him. She drew in her breath sharply at the feel of Remy inside her, awed by the power of his body, of a man so secure in his own strength he could surrender control so completely to her.

He spanned his hands about her hips, helping her rock against him, but letting her set the pace. As her need intensified, she thrust herself against Remy harder and quicker. When her hair fell across her eyes, she tossed her head back, wanting to see. Reveling in the sight of the man straining beneath her, the hard muscles glistening with a fine sheen of sweat, his rugged features suffused with passion. She felt pulled into the rich, warm darkness of his eyes, their ragged breathing coming as one.

The tension coiled inside her until she could no longer bear it. She emitted a low cry as her body shuddered with a burst of pleasure stronger, hotter, and sweeter than anything she had ever imagined. Remy's own control broke at last. He bucked upward with a low groan, his hands gripping her hips as he buried his seed deep inside of her.

The force of the release left Gabrielle weak and trembling. She leaned forward, grateful for the support of Remy's strong hands bracing her arms, reluctant to end the joining of their bodies. Her breasts rose and fell as her racing heart stilled to a more steady rhythm. She closed her eyes briefly as she issued a slow, deep sigh.

She opened them to discover Remy peering up at her, his mouth crooked in that boyish half-smile of his she'd always loved. The expression was tender but also held an element of purely masculine triumph. He knew how well he'd pleasured her, but his knowledge did not shame her. With an unsteady laugh, she tossed her hair and smiled back at him. Shifting her weight off of him, Gabrielle searched for the words to describe how he'd made her feel. Not like a prize to be taken, a body to be used or possessed, but the way a daughter of the earth was meant to feel. Strong and beautiful, a giver of life and love. Her lips parted helplessly as she tried to tell him all that he had restored to her.

But in the end, all she could do was collapse into Remy's arms and whisper, "Thank you."

Chapter Nineteen

THE CANDLES BURNED OUT ONE BY ONE, ONLY THE TAPER IN THE brass holder by the bedside remaining lit. The light flickered over Remy and Gabrielle entwined beneath the sheets, bathing them in a soft glow that seemed to hold the darkness at bay. Remy rested on his back, scarcely moving, not wanting to disturb the woman sleeping at his side. Exhaustion had claimed Gabrielle at last. She nestled her head against his shoulder, her golden hair spilling across his chest. He could feel the soft warm weight of her breasts, the light stir of her breathing, her skin still damp from their coupling.

His body hungered with need of her. He could have buried himself inside her again and again, but that might be more than Gabrielle was ready for. She had actually thanked him for the tender way he'd made love to her. That spoke volumes about the brutality she'd suffered at Danton's hands and the emptiness of her life as a courtesan, the compromises she'd made, the things she'd done to survive. The battle to survive—that was something he understood all too well, because he had done a fair amount of compromising himself these past years when he'd sold the use of his sword to the highest bidder.

He brushed a light kiss against her hair. It was more the future that worried him now, one that seemed fraught with the peril of witch-hunters, the malice of the Dark Queen, and perhaps the anger of his own king. Remy wondered how Navarre would react when he realized that Remy meant to marry Gabrielle, but that he had no intentions of sharing his wife with any man, not even a king. Navarre might be one of the most easy-tempered and congenial men that Remy had ever known, but kings were notoriously unaccustomed to having their desires thwarted.

There certainly would be no royal rewards, no estates, no titles in Remy's future. He had never cared about such things for himself, but Gabrielle had grown accustomed to rich clothes, fine jewels, and the elegance of this town house. It chafed his pride to think he'd never be able to give her such things.

Even before she had come to Paris, she had known a very comfortable life at her family's manor on Faire Isle and then her brother-in-law's château. Remy was hard-pressed to imagine this beautiful woman sharing some mean cottage or farmhouse with him. Or enduring the privations of life at camp, the mud, the cold, the poor rations as she trailed after him on some military campaign.

The bitter truth was he had no more to offer her than he had ever had, but considering the other dangers that threatened them, how he was to provide a home for Gabrielle should be the least of his concerns. Cradling her closer, he rested his chin atop her head, thinking what an ungrateful dog he was. He ought to be simply glad for the moment, rejoicing that he had what he had long desired.

Gabrielle here with him, safe and warm in his arms. He did not want to surrender to sleep, fearing he might wake to find it all no more than a dream. But despite his best efforts the events of the day caught up with him. His eyes fluttered closed, but troubled thoughts made for troubled dreams. Not his familiar one of staggering through the dark streets of Paris on St. Bartholomew's Eve, searching for his lost sword. This time he wandered desperately through the corridors of the Louvre and it was Gabrielle he could not find. No matter how many doors he flung open.

Muttering, Remy tossed on his pillow and wrenched himself awake. His first impulse was to reach for Gabrielle and gather her close to him. But when he groped for her, he found the space on the mattress next to him empty. Heart thudding with an unreasoning sense of panic, he sat bolt upright. "Gabrielle?"

"I'm over here," she replied.

To his immense relief, he saw her silhouetted against the window, her nose all but pressed to the pane. Gabrielle was attired in another of her costly dressing gowns, but this one enveloped her like a cloud of blue silk, making her appear soft and accessible.

Flinging the covers aside, Remy swung his legs out of bed and shrugged himself into his discarded breeches. He demanded anxiously, "What is it? Is something wrong?"

"No, I woke up and couldn't get back to sleep, but I didn't want to disturb you. Come here and look at this." She reached out for his hand and drew him toward the window. He squinted into the darkness. A burst of light flared in the distance, reminding him uncomfortably of the far-off flash of ordnance on the battlefield.

"What the devil is that?" he asked, tensing with the urge to go for his sword.

"A shooting star? Perhaps that is what happens when one defies destiny. The stars fall from the sky."

When he started at her strange words, she laughed and squeezed his hand. "I was only jesting. It is only fireworks, no doubt coming from the palace grounds."

Leaning closer to the window, Remy saw that she was right. A larger burst of light erupted against the night sky, this one exploding into a cascade of red and gold sparks that shimmered down and vanished behind the rooftops of the neighboring houses.

"So what do you think they are celebrating, the arrival of the witch-hunters?"

Gabrielle spared a smile for his wry humor. "They often have fireworks at the Louvre. It is likely just part of the entertainment at the feast after the tourney."

A costly entertainment in Remy's opinion, a foolish waste of black powder, but Gabrielle flattened her hands against the panes as she enjoyed the spectacle. He could not help reflecting that but for his return to Paris, Gabrielle would have been at that feast, radiant in one of her loveliest gowns, her arm linked through Navarre's, watching the fireworks with him. If it had been possible for Henry to marry her, what a queen Gabrielle would have made. A role she was far better suited to than a soldier's wife.

The thought lowered Remy's spirits considerably. "Gabrielle, you—you do not regret what happened between us tonight?"

She looked at him, her fine brows arching in surprise. "No, of course not, Remy. How can you even ask me such a thing?"

"It is only that I do want to marry you—"

"I hope so. You have bedded me. It would be a shocking thing if you were to jilt me now." She draped her arms about his neck, smiling warmly up at him, her lips still tantalizingly red and full from all the kisses they had shared earlier.

He stole his hands about her waist. "That is exactly what I mean. I want to be truly married to you, your husband in every sense of the word."

"And you've made an excellent beginning." Gabrielle pressed herself seductively closer to him, making him all too aware that only a thin sheen of silk separated him from her warm lush curves. When she nuzzled her lips along his jaw, his body stiffened in the inevitable response. But his doubts were too troubling to be pushed aside.

Shifting her away to a safer distance, he said, "I'm not a king, Gabrielle. Hell! I'm not even a knight."

"I don't want a king," she insisted, attempting to nestle back in his arms.

But she had wanted one. And only what seemed a few hours ago. Gabrielle must have read the thought in his eyes, for she stepped back, her hands falling away from him.

"All right. I—I admit it. I have been thinking about Navarre."

Remy grimaced. This was not what he had wanted to hear.

She rushed on, "But I have only been thinking about him because I feel a trifle guilty. I did my best to enchant him, to make him fall in love with me. Beneath his carefree manner, he is a good man, Remy. I have no wish to hurt him."

"Nor do I." Remy recollected uneasily how Navarre's face had glowed when he had spoken of his love for Gabrielle. Of course he had seen his young king in love many times before and he fancied Navarre would get over her quickly, find consolation elsewhere. And yet . . . if there was any woman capable of inspiring a lasting devotion in a man, even one as peripatetic as Navarre, it was Gabrielle.

Even as he considered this possibility, Remy shook his head. "Navarre could not be that much in love with you or he would never have proposed such a dishonorable arrangement, marrying you to me so you would be secure when he tires of you."

"Kings have different standards of conduct than the rest of us mere mortals."

Remy's jaw jutted stubbornly. "A king should have an even higher code of nobility than the subjects he rules."

Gabrielle caressed his cheek, smiling tenderly up at him. "You ask far too much of people, most of all yourself. But I daresay that is why I love you as much as I do."

Her words sent a glow through him, dispelling some of his niggling worries and doubts. She loved him. He did not think he could ever hear her say that enough. He drew her into his arms and their lips met in a kiss that was deep and lingering.

They clung to each other for a long time, Remy resting his brow against her forehead. He sensed a tiny shiver work through her slender frame.

"It is almost frightening to be this happy," she whispered.

Remy's arms tightened around her, knowing exactly what she meant. He feared as though at any moment some jealous gods might find a way to snatch Gabrielle from him. Or perhaps a jealous king . . .

"I don't even want to think what tomorrow might bring, but I suppose we must." She sighed and lifted her head to peer up at him. "What are *we* going to do, Remy?"

"Well, to begin with, I must go through with my rescue of Navarre as I planned because—"

"Because it is your duty," Gabrielle finished, pulling a face.

Remy started to apologize, but she stopped him with a wry shake of her head. "No, it is quite all right. I understand. Have you come up with a plan for carrying out this duty of yours?"

"I believe so, but my first priority is to engage a troop of armed men to escort you and Miri back to Faire Isle, as far away from these witch-hunters as possible."

"That will do well enough for Miri. But I am not going."

"Gabrielle—" he began.

She covered his mouth with her hand. "No. And don't be giving me one of those stern commanding officer looks, Nicolas Remy, like you expect me to snap to attention. There is no way I intend to flee to Faire Isle and leave you here in danger."

He kissed her palm and thrust her hand away from his mouth. "I will be in far less danger if I can concentrate on my mission without your safety to worry about."

Gabrielle drew away from him, rolling her eyes. "Oh, lord, that is such a *man's* argument. You'll never be able to rescue Navarre without my help. Remember? He only agreed to leave Paris because he thought that he would get to have me."

"Well, he is not having you, so that's an end to the matter," Remy snapped.

Gabrielle drifted away as though she had not even heard him. She steepled her fingers beneath her chin, musing, "It was selfish of me to try to keep Navarre with me in Paris. I can see that now. Perhaps he still will be ruler of France one day, but for now he would be better off restored to his own kingdom. Unfortunately, he may not see what is in his best interest, especially if he becomes angry with you and me for betraying him."

"Betraying *him*?" Remy choked.

"We will have to pretend that I still wish to be his mistress."

"No! Absolutely not."

"It will only be for a little while. Once we have him safely out of France and across the border, then we can tell him—"

"Damn it, Gabrielle. Are you listening to me?" Remy seized her by the elbow and swung her around to face him. "I said *no*. I have had a bellyful of all this dissembling and deceit. I don't want you going anywhere near Navarre again."

"Why? What are you so afraid of? That I will end up in his bed?"

"Frankly, yes."

"I have managed to stay out of it this long. Have you no faith at all in my love for you? Do you not trust me?"

"It is Navarre I don't trust." Remy shuffled his feet and admitted gruffly. "And myself. My own ability to hold on to your heart."

"Oh, Remy." Gabrielle melted toward him. "My heart, such as it is, is yours and always will be. I hate having to employ this deception as much as you do, perhaps even more. But Catherine already made one effort to destroy you. She clearly suspects your plans to free the king from her grasp. The arrival of these witch-hunters may prove a distraction to her for a while. I don't think she expected their arrival any more than we did. But you are running out of time. You cannot afford to have a rift with Navarre over me. If you truly want to rescue your king, this is the only way."

Remy understood her reasoning, but he did not like it. But

he could no more stand firm against her arguments than he could the kiss she pressed to his mouth.

"Very well," he conceded with a bitter sigh. "But once we have Navarre out of Paris, you must promise me one thing. That this will be the end of all deception and intrigue. Everything will be straightforward and honest, especially between us."

"If you promise me something in return. Say that you will never frighten me again as you did today. I died a thousand deaths when I watched you risk your life on the tourney field."

"I am a soldier, Gabrielle. I can hardly promise you never to fight again. Especially when I have a king to rescue and there is this new threat of witch-hunters."

"At least swear you will not hazard your life in some foolish cause as you did when you fought Danton."

Remy tensed at the mention of the man's name. "I did not regard that as foolish. In fact, I still wish I had destroyed the bastard."

She cupped his cheek, forcing him to look at her. "But don't you see, Remy? You *did* destroy him. His death would not have freed me from his power. What we did here tonight, the tender way you made love to me, is what conquered him."

If that was true, Remy was mightily glad, but it only slightly mollified his wrath against Danton. "This is not the sort of conquest I am accustomed to. So in other words you are telling me that this afternoon I wielded the wrong kind of sword."

"Nicolas Remy!"

Her outraged gasp made him laugh in spite of himself. When she gave his shoulder a poke of mock reproof, he retaliated by tickling her. Gabrielle responded in kind. Danton was completely forgotten as Remy collapsed back onto the bed, hauling Gabrielle down with him. They tussled in the sheets, engaging in a playful bout of wrestling until both of them were breathless with laughter. Remy braced himself above Gabrielle to avoid crushing her under his weight, his heart feeling lighter than it had for a long time. Her golden hair fanned against the sheets,

Gabrielle's face was still flushed with laughter, but her eyes shone with a rare softness.

"It's so good to hear you laugh, Remy. You carry far too much of the weight of the world on your shoulders. When you laugh, it makes you look years younger."

"Have I grown to be such a graybeard then?"

She sifted her fingers through the hair at his temples and made an impish face at him. "I believe I do spy a few strands of silver, monsieur."

Remy grinned and retorted, "If I do have any gray hairs, you put them there, milady. You are a fine one to talk to me of being reckless, taking risks. If I live to be a hundred, I'll never forget the day you stole my sword to fight the witch-hunters. When you are my wife, I warn you. I won't tolerate—"

He was cut off by an exclamation from Gabrielle. "Oh, lord! I nearly forgot."

Pushing against his chest, she squirmed out from beneath him, kicking the covers away in an effort to get out of bed. Remy wrapped his arm about her waist to restrain her. "Whatever you forgot, can it not wait until the morning?"

"No, I have something I want to give you."

He started to assure her there was only one thing he desired, but when she continued to pull free, he reluctantly let her go. Gabrielle shook back her cascade of hair and stepped to the foot of the bed. She bent down and tugged open the heavy lid of the chest positioned there. Rummaging through the contents, she impatiently tossed aside linens, petticoats, and other garments.

Remy sat up, his curiosity aroused. "What the blazes are you looking for?"

"You'll see." She emerged from the trunk, lifting out a long object wrapped in velvet. Coming around the side of the bed, she tugged away the fabric to reveal a sword. Remy's breath caught in his throat, but not so much at the weapon as Gabrielle herself. The light of the candle picked out the gold in her hair, cast a warm sheen over her creamy skin, rendered her eyes jewel-bright.

Poised with the hilt in her hands, the blade pointing downward, she was like a creature of legend, the sorceress who had risen from the mystical depths of the lake to present King Arthur with his sword. Except this was no Excalibur she brought him, the hilt as plain and unadorned as the length of naked steel. It was his old sword, the one he'd believed lost to him on St. Bartholomew's Eve, the object of his desperate search in so many of his nightmares since then.

Gabrielle rested the heavy blade across her arm, presenting the hilt to him. He hesitated to reach for it, fearing the sword would be too full of dark memories of the last time he'd wielded it, the night of the massacre. But as his fingers closed over the worn hilt of the weapon, so familiar to him, down to every nick on the finger guard, he was seized by a far different memory, of the day he'd first acquired the sword.

He could not have been much more than ten years old. Although Remy had been tall for his age, his father had loomed over him. He had difficulty bringing up a clear recollection of Jean Remy's rugged features and gray-flecked beard. But he well recalled his father's hands, large, callused, and leathery, his knuckles a little gnarled from the number of times they had been broken.

"Think you are strong enough to handle a weapon like this, lad?"

"Oh, yes, sir," Remy had replied, although he could feel the strain in his shoulder muscles as he'd hefted the blade.

"Take care of it. Treat this sword with respect, learn to use it well, and it will serve you. With the grace of God, may it always keep your enemies at a safe distance." Jean Remy's mouth had quirked in one of his rare smiles as he'd ruffled Remy's hair.

His father had been a gruff man of few words, not the sort to bestow random words of praise and affection. But the day his father had given him that sword, Remy had felt the full force of Jean Remy's love and pride in his only son.

"My old sword. You've kept it all this time?" Remy marveled. He shifted on the bed, holding the sword nearer to the candle so that he could inspect the weapon better. Gabrielle had obviously cared for it, keeping the blade finely honed and polished.

"What did you think I would do with your sword?" she demanded as she settled herself beside him on the bed. "Toss it into the Seine?"

"Considering the way I treated you when I returned to Paris, all the harsh things I said, I would hardly have blamed you."

"I said and did a good many things myself that I regret." She placed her hand over his atop the hilt. "For a long time, this sword was all I had left of you, Remy. No doubt you will laugh when I tell you this, but I felt as though your strength and courage had infused this weapon with a kind of magic. If I was ever lonely or frightened, wearing your sword made me feel safe and protected."

Remy did not have the least inclination to laugh. Lowering the weapon to the floor beside the bed, he returned to gather Gabrielle up in his arms.

"I wish I did have that kind of magic, to keep you safe," he said huskily. "But St. Bartholomew's Eve taught me the futility of promising to protect someone forever."

"No one can ever make such a pledge. It will be more than enough if you just promise to love me."

"That I do swear. Now and until I die." Remy sealed his vow with a kiss.

Gabrielle's lips parted beneath his, tenderness giving rise to something more urgent with need. Remy tugged at the buttons of her dressing gown, laying it open. His hands delved beneath the parted fabric, exploring the enticing curves, the smooth warm skin laid bare to him. As he kissed her hungrily, he relished the sound of her sighs, her soft moans of pleasure. Gabrielle fumbled with the flap of his breeches, and they yanked and pulled, wrestled with garments until they were once more naked in each other's arms.

Remy tried to be as gentle and patient as he'd been before, but Gabrielle would not allow it. She wrapped her arms around his neck, pulling him down on top of her, kissing and caressing. Remy rejoiced to see her grow bolder, as eager for him as he was for her. She opened herself to him, inviting him in, with a sultry smile and eyes hazy with desire, as passionate and undaunted a woman as nature had always meant her to be. Losing himself in her loving, Remy let her take him to a place where nothing else mattered. Not the pain of the past, nor the perils of the morrow.

The candle at the bedside burned out, leaving them in darkness except for the flare of light at the window where another distant burst of fireworks lit up the night sky.

⸭⸭⸭

THE FINAL SKYROCKET HISSED SKYWARD AND ERUPTED IN A SHOWER of sparks that elicited applause and gasps from the courtiers seated at the banquet tables beneath the trees. Many of the participants of the tourney were more than mellow from the wine served at the feast. Bursts of raucous laughter mingled with the sounds of delight evoked by the fireworks display.

Swallowed up by the darkness in her own apartments, Catherine hovered near the windows grimly observing the distant scene. The flare of the torches, the occasional shout or sound of rough voices, stirred in her an unpleasant memory. Of a night when she'd been scarce more than twelve years old, an orphaned heiress, the young Duchess of Florence, a city in rebellion against its de Medici rulers. The mob had surrounded the convent where she'd been sheltered, thundering at the gates.

"Give us the girl. Surrender the young witch. We want no more de Medicis lording over us. We'll hang her from the city walls."

"No! Give her to the soldiers to sport with first, then we'll execute her."

Even after so many years, Catherine shuddered at the memory of the obscene threats, the outpouring of hatred that had been directed at her. By some miracle, she had survived unscathed and the rebellion had eventually been put down. But that night had taught her that not even one's high birth or noble name, or a convent's holy walls could be counted upon for protection. One had to rely upon one's own dark magic and wits.

But her wits felt unaccountably dulled this evening. Her mind still reeled from the realization that her son, the one she had always regarded with most affection, had turned on her, mounted what was tantamount to rebellion. Henry had actually had the impudence to smile at her after the initial uproar over the witch-hunters' arrival.

"Was this not an excellent surprise, Maman? Are you not proud of me for taking such an initiative? Le Balafre and his men will certainly make any witch, no matter how powerful she might be, think twice before meddling with my kingdom."

Catherine had been far too angry and alarmed to give him the sort of sharp answer he deserved. Instead she made a stiff curtsy and retreated to the palace. Dismissing her ladies, cowering in the darkness of her own apartments like some frightened rabbit gone to ground, she thought with a surge of self-contempt.

And why? All because of the arrival of this Le Balafre. She'd recognized him almost at once. This terrifying Monsieur Scarface was none other than that young person who had attended upon the grand master of witch-hunters, Vachel Le Vis. Simon something or other. That had been his name, and he'd seemed no more than an insignificant boy. But even then Catherine had glimpsed something in the lad's eyes that had made her uneasy. Le Vis had been a madman and a fool, easily tricked into serving Catherine's purpose, never realizing he was serving a far greater witch than those she had sent him to find. Simon, however, had stared at Catherine as though he saw straight through her, recognized her for what she was. He seemed possessed of an intuition far beyond his years.

After Le Vis had outlived his usefulness, Catherine had disposed of him. She should have done the same with the lad, but she had allowed the boy to go free, a mistake for which she might now be about to pay dearly . . . perhaps with her life.

"Stop thinking like such a fool," she admonished herself with disgust. When all was said and done, this Le Balafre was still no more than a pipsqueak boy the same as her own son.

She would crush him like that. Catherine gave a scornful snap of her fingers. But Simon was not as foolish as his former master had been. He had refused Henry's offers to quarter him and his troop of witch-hunters here at the palace. She'd already learned that Le Balafre had commandeered the use of an inn, turning it into a miniature fortress. It would make getting at him more difficult, but not impossible.

All she had to do was wait and be patient, although she was not sure she had that luxury. She tried to convince herself that Henry was using these witch-hunters as a bluff, an attempt to intimidate her into retiring from her position of power behind his throne.

Her son would not dare allow these creatures to charge his own mother with witchcraft, would he? Even if he did, what evidence would there be? Except for that matter of the poisoned gloves, Catherine had always been most careful. She had never shared the secrets of her magic, not even with her own daughters, as other wise women did.

Very few knew of the hidden room behind her chapel where Catherine kept all her darkest secrets. She experienced an urge to clear out the chamber, destroy all potions and ancient parchments, but she quelled it, refusing to give way to panic. She was not a terrified girl of twelve, she reminded herself fiercely. She was the dowager queen of France. Yet she could not help recalling that that august title had not been enough to save another queen of not so distant memory.

The English queen, Anne Boleyn, had been brought to trial by her husband, Henry VIII. Among the charges of adultery and treason, there had also been included one of witchcraft. And Anne Boleyn, queen though she had been, had lost her head.

Catherine's hand crept involuntarily toward her own throat and she trembled, momentarily giving way to her dark, secret fear. Death . . .

"Your Majesty?"

The voice sent her heart leaping into her throat. Catherine whirled around to confront the man who had dared creep into her presence unannounced. Enough moonlight filtered through the windows to enable her to make out Bartolomy Verducci's skeletal frame.

"Verducci!" Catherine clutched her hand to the cross suspended over her bosom. Her fright gave way to fury. "Sirrah! What do you mean by coming upon me this way unbidden? Did I not leave orders I had no wish to be disturbed?"

The little man bowed deeply and backed away from her like a whipped cur. "P-pardon, Your Grace. I would not have bothered you had I not thought it important. There is someone who craves a private audience—"

"If it is that idiot Danton, I will not see him. I have already told him so. I have no use for those who fail me. Besides, the doings of Mademoiselle Cheney and her Scourge are the least of my worries at the moment."

With a crisp snap of her skirts, Catherine rustled angrily back to the window. Verducci made no attempt to approach again, but his timid voice trailed after her. "It—it is not the Chevalier Danton who desires admittance into your presence, my liege—"

"I don't care who it is. Send them away."

"It is your emissary, Majesty. From—from Faire Isle."

Catherine had started to rebuke him again, but clamped her mouth shut. Her emissary? How like Bartolomy to put the matter so discreetly. Her spy had arrived at last to make report on the Lady of Faire Isle and her council meeting. This could prove the most heartening tidings Catherine had had all day.

"Very well. Show the woman in, but light some of the candles first."

As Bartolomy hastened to do so, Catherine drummed her fingers against the windowpane. As soon as she realized what she was doing, she checked the motion. It had never been her habit to give way to nervous gestures that revealed any weakness. By the time Bartolomy returned with her visitor, Catherine had composed herself.

Bartolomy stepped forward to present his companion, but Catherine cut him off.

"Leave us," she commanded.

The scrawny little man bowed and slunk away, leaving Catherine alone with her spy. Bartolomy had lit several candles and left them burning atop Catherine's escritoire. She beckoned to the woman to join her in the pool of light. Despite the fact that the night was warm, the woman was swathed in a long brown cloak, the hood drawn forward to hide her face. Catherine extended her fingers to be kissed as the woman knelt before her. But when she made no move to fling back her hood, Catherine withdrew her hand.

"It is not my habit to receive those who hide their eyes from me, madam," the Dark Queen said coldly.

Reluctantly, the woman threw back her hood and revealed the pale pinched features of Hermoine Pechard. Catherine deigned to offer her hand again and Madame Pechard saluted it. The woman's touch felt unpleasantly clammy and cold.

Catherine curled her fingers away in distaste. "Well, Madame Pechard. So you are come to Paris at last. I had all but given up on you, you have taken so long."

"That—that is not my fault, Your Grace," Hermoine whimpered, but Catherine silenced her with an imperious gesture.

She could not abide women who whined or squealed like frightened vermin. Such pitiful creatures ought to be sewn up in sacks and drowned, a fate that Catherine had once planned for Madame Pechard when she had caught the woman and the courtesan Louise Lavalle spying on her for the Lady of Faire Isle.

Catherine had little patience for other people's spies, but if Hermoine proved of use to her now, Catherine would be glad the woman had been spared. If not . . . there were still plenty of sacks to be had. Realizing she might gain more information from the foolish woman if she did not terrify her out of what few wits she possessed, Catherine graciously bid her rise. She suppressed her irritation as Madame Pechard resumed making excuses for her delay in that annoying querulous tone.

"It is a long journey from Faire Isle. And I almost turned and fled straight back again. He is here." Hermoine huddled her arms beneath her cloak and shivered. "Oh dear lord, he is right here in Paris. That evil man."

"I thought you were hoping to be reunited with your husband," Catherine said dryly.

"I am not talking about my Maurice," Madame Pechard replied with an indignant squeak. "But that—that devil." She darted a nervous glance about her, then lowered her voice to a whisper. "*Le Balafre.*"

"You know of this witch-hunter?"

"He was much discussed at the council meeting."

"Tell me."

To Catherine's annoyance, Hermoine shrank back biting her pale, thin lips. Catherine would have liked to have seized her by her bony shoulders and pinned her to the wall, ruthlessly probing her eyes. Hermoine's gaze darted every which way, like a terrified mouse hunting for a place to hide. Curbing her impatience, Catherine strove to put Hermoine at her ease, offering to send for a glass of wine, inviting her to be seated. But Madame Pechard refused all refreshment and eyed the proffered chair as though it was an iron maiden where Catherine proposed to torture her.

"Before I tell you anything more, you must understand. I

have no wish to betray the Lady of Faire Isle. She was good to me when—when you had me arrested and then when I had to flee Paris." Hermoine actually achieved a modicum of dignity as she said this, her voice holding a faint hint of reproach.

Catherine felt a flicker of grudging admiration. Not for Hermoine but for Ariane, that she could inspire loyalty and courage even in this wretched excuse for a woman.

"My arresting you was all an unfortunate misunderstanding, as I explained in my letter when I approached you to work for me. It was all owing to Louise Lavalle, her wicked behavior, that implicated a virtuous woman such as yourself in her misdeeds."

Catherine realized she could not have hit upon a more efficacious argument. Hermoine nodded, her lips tightening in self-righteous indignation.

"Mademoiselle Lavalle is indeed a wicked, licentious creature, just as so many of these young wise women are today. But the Lady of Faire Isle is possessed of great wisdom and virtue."

"Of course Ariane is and I wish to be her friend as well," Catherine said soothingly. "But until I can get her to trust me, I must rely on you for information, my dear Madame Pechard. I assure you I can be generous to those who serve me."

The absurd creature clutched her hands together, her eyes filling with tears. "All I want is the return of my comfortable little house, my good name as the respectable wife of a doctor at the university. My life back as it was before I got involved with that wretched Lavalle woman and her schemes to spy on Your Grace."

And what a small pathetic life it had been, of value to no one. Catherine could not imagine any woman wanting such an existence back, but she patted Hermoine's hand.

"I will make sure everything is restored to you, my dear. Now tell me all about the council meeting and what was said of this man, Le Balafre."

"Well, there was this mad red-haired wise woman come over from Ireland, Catriona O'Hanlon. Quite rude she was. She interrupted my turn to address the council to tell us about this Le Bal-afre and the missing book that brought him to France . . ."

Catherine fast realized that once one got the woman talking, it was all but impossible to shut her up. Hermoine waxed far more eloquent about her grievances with the behavior of the other women at the council than she did on the subject of Le Bal-afre. After the first ten minutes, Catherine scarcely paid attention. She had already heard all she needed to hear.

A missing book. The *Book of Shadows,* the stuff of legends and a daughter of the earth's darkest fantasies. Catherine paced over to the window, hard-pressed to contain her excitement. If she possessed such a thing, she need never fear anything again. Not the Scourge or Huguenot rebels, not witch-hunters, not even death itself. She would become in truth a Dark Queen and nothing or no one would be able to stand against her.

She needed to get her hands on that book.

Chapter Twenty

DAWN HAD BARELY CREPT PAST THE ROOFTOPS, THE DARKNESS of night surrendering to the gray light of morning. Miri pulled the hood of her cloak forward to shield her features as she scurried across the courtyard carpeted in mist. The damp seeped into the soles of her shoes and she shivered as she stole a glance over her shoulder.

The town house was enshrouded in silence, not a sign of anyone stirring. No one peered anxiously out the windows, no one burst through the door in frantic search of her. She had eluded them all, Gabrielle, Remy, Bette, even the vigilance of Necromancer.

With any luck, Miri might complete her errand and return before she was missed. If not . . . she breathed a faint sigh. She had no wish to worry or grieve any of these people who cared so much about her, but they could not understand. She realized herself the danger in what she was about to do. She had risked everything once before to save Simon Aristide from the dark influence of the dread witch-hunter, Le Vis, and she had failed. The beautiful boy had been transformed into Le Balafre, the man with the scarred visage and soulless eyes. And still Miri could not give up on him.

Stealing through the gardens, Miri moved as swiftly and quietly as she could. Only a few more steps and she would be out the wrought-iron gate and gone. But then what? Paris was an overwhelming place with its endless maze of streets and sea of rooftops. Without Necromancer's uncanny senses to guide her, Miri had no idea how she was going to locate the inn where Simon was staying.

She would be obliged to ask directions of someone and the city beyond the garden wall still seemed fast asleep. She heard little beyond the distant creak of wagon wheels, the far-off clatter of horse's hooves, and . . . and the snap of a twig.

The sharp crack originated from the recesses of the garden behind her. Miri froze, tensed and listening. A pair of larks twittered in the branches of an elm tree, but beneath their joyous song, Miri detected the light pad of a footfall, the faintest whisper of grass. The sound might have gone undetected by others, but Miri's senses were as finely tuned as any fox or badger.

The nape of her neck prickled with the awareness she was not alone in the garden. She was being stalked and she feared that she knew by whom. Spinning around, she sought to pierce the whorls of mist obscuring the pathways.

"Necromancer?" she whispered fiercely.

"No, mademoiselle. It is me." A shadowy form bounded out of the bushes.

Miri's heart did a wild somersault. She staggered back, clapping her hand to her mouth to stifle a startled cry. A young man loomed before her, a mane of rich sable-colored hair flowing back from his sharp, angular features. Heavy brows and thick dark lashes accented green eyes that stared at her with a hungry avidity.

"Do not be alarmed, mademoiselle. I did not mean to startle you. It is just that I have spent most of the night gazing up at your bedchamber window."

Miri hardly found that information reassuring. She wondered what would be her best course. To bolt back to the safety of the house, which was much farther away, or out through the gate in the hope of finding some refuge in the street. He seemed to divine her thoughts, for he stalked closer. "Please don't run away. I have been waiting for you."

"You—you have?" Miri stumbled back several paces.

"All my life."

Miri doubted that his life could have been of that long of a duration. It was difficult to guess his age. His smooth skin indicated he was not much older than she was and yet the hard, lean angles of his visage suggested a lifetime more of experience. His clothing was fine enough, his sleeveless brocade jerkin fastened over a gleaming white shirt. His breeches tied off neatly below the knee were the sort that might have been worn by the servant in a wealthy household. But the short midnight-blue cloak that swirled so jauntily over his right shoulder was more the attire of a nobleman.

Despite his elegant apparel, there was far too much of the rogue and scoundrel about him, the flash of his smile far too intimate. When he tried to approach her again, Miri held up one hand to ward him off. "Stop. If you come any closer, I'll scream."

It was a hollow threat. Alerting the household to her disappearance was the last thing Miri wanted to do, but this interloper didn't know that.

"If you are a thief," she went on. "You have sneaked into the wrong garden. I don't have so much as a sou on me."

Her words brought him to an abrupt halt. He looked thunderstruck, then deeply injured, flinging his hands up as though appealing to the heavens. "Mon Dieu! She thinks me a thief and she is the one who has robbed me."

"I never did any such thing."

"Yes, you did, mademoiselle." He clutched his hands dramatically over his chest. "You have completely stolen my heart."

Oh, lord, Miri thought. He was far worse than a thief. He was an escaped lunatic. She darted behind a stout oak, seeking to put the massive frame of the tree between them. He peeked round the trunk at her with wide, wounded eyes. "How could you be so brave yesterday when facing that great brute of a horse and then be so afraid of me? Don't you remember me at all?"

Remember him? How could she remember someone she'd never met? And yet there was something familiar about him. Although Miri could readily identify every bird, every fur-bearing creature that inhabited Faire Isle, she had never been as good at distinguishing the face of one man from another.

It was his reference to her dealing with that "great brute of a horse" that jarred her memory. As she scrutinized the stranger's features, she thought she might be pardoned for not recognizing him. The last time she had seen him, he had been coated in dust and horse dung, his face streaked with dirt.

Miri stepped warily out from behind the tree. "Oh, I do know who you are. You are the squire who struggled to saddle Bayonne yesterday."

"Then—then you did notice me? You remember me?"

She nodded. To Miri's consternation, he shot his fist into the air and let out a joyous whoop. "The lovely goddess of the moon remembers me. She noticed me. I must wake all of Paris to share in my joy."

Awake all of Paris? Miri was more concerned about him waking the household behind her. He sprang toward the gate and leaped up onto the bottom rung, drawing in his breath. Miri flew after him and seized the ends of his cape. She yanked hard, the ties fastened around his neck choking off his shout to a gurgle. He lost his footing and flailed backward, landing on his rump. Miri cast an anxious glance at the house.

"I am sorry," she hissed. "But please. No shouting. You must be quiet."

He struggled onto his elbows and beamed up at her. "For you, mademoiselle, I shall be as silent as the grave."

Miri doubted he was capable of keeping his mouth shut for more than a second at a time. "You are in the employ of Captain Remy, are you not? You are his squire?"

"His squire, his lieutenant, his brother in arms, his friend. Ah, but for you, mademoiselle, I am your slave."

"Thank you, but I am not in the market for a slave."

"You have one nevertheless." He bounded to his feet, swirled his cape, and swept her a deep bow, all in one astonishingly fluid motion. "Martin Le Loup, mademoiselle. Forever at your service."

"Martin the wolf? Yes, the name suits you."

"Indeed it does. I have the courage, the intelligence, the cunning, and the—"

"And the modesty," Miri interrupted dryly.

He cast her a look of faint reproach. "I was going to say the heart of a wolf. Did you know that wolves mate for life once they have found the right female?"

"Then I wish you good hunting, monsieur."

"I need hunt no further. I have already found my mate." He prowled closer. "I knew it yesterday from the moment I saw you. Your eyes brighter than a full moon, your hair softer than its light—"

"And my face as round as the moon, no doubt. With you being a wolf, small wonder you are so attracted to me."

He pulled up short, looking deeply hurt. "You mock me, mademoiselle."

"Forgive me, monsieur. But I am a plain and simple girl from a very small island. I do not simper over compliments and flirt the way your ladies of Paris do."

"Flirt!" he exclaimed. "Perhaps I express myself a bit too—

too exuberantly, but my devotion is a true one. I love you so much I don't even care what you are."

Miri frowned in puzzlement. "What I am?"

He leaned closer, lowering his voice to a conspiratorial hush. "You are a witch, are you not? Not that it matters to me in the least. I have many faults of my own."

Miri made a choked sound of outrage. "I am not a witch. I despise that term. I am a daughter of the earth."

He was instantly contrite. "Forgive me, mademoiselle. I did not mean to offend you. Of course you are a daughter of the earth and the heavens as well." Seizing hold of her hand, he covered her fingertips with fervent kisses.

Miri gasped and snatched her hand away. "Stop that at once."

"I am too bold. I am sorry, but I cannot help myself. I—I am enchanted by you. I am dazed. I am bewitched."

"You are also completely insane. And I don't have time to stay here bandying any more words with you. I suggest you go back to wherever it is you call home and lie down for awhile with a cool cloth on your head."

"What good would that do me when it is my heart that is on fire?"

"Then put one there as well." Miri's lips twitched with amusement in spite of herself. She ducked her head to hide the expression but Martin was too quick for her. He tipped all the way to one side in his efforts to peer into her face.

"Aha!" he crowed. "She does not take me seriously, but at least I have finally made her smile. That is a beginning."

Miri tried to reassume a poker-like expression. "Monsieur—"

"Just call me Wolf. Your own Wolf, now and forever."

Miri sighed, realizing that the sky was growing lighter. The household might begin to stir at any moment. "Wolf, then. As interesting as it has been renewing our acquaintance, I need to be going."

She gave him a dismissive nod, then hastened toward the gate. But Wolf loped after her, falling into step beside her. "Where would you be planning to go at such an early hour, my beloved? Quite alone and in such stealthy fashion. Paris can be a dangerous place. You had better let me escort you on this secret errand of yours."

Miri's step faltered. Despite his flamboyant mannerisms and way of talking, Wolf was shrewder than he appeared. He had obviously guessed she was off on some mission that she did not want known. She studied him from beneath her lashes. She truly did require a guide, but she would have preferred someone a little less volatile.

"Wolf, can I trust you?"

"Can you trust me? I vow by every last drop of my blood—"

"No, please." Miri placed her hand hastily over his mouth to silence him. "Just answer yes or no."

"Yes," he mumbled beneath her fingers, then seized advantage of the situation to press his lips to her palm.

"And are you familiar with Paris?"

Wolf shifted her fingers away from his mouth and brushed a kiss against her wrist. "Oh, like the back of my own hand. I will take you anywhere you wish to go, show you the finest shops, where the best bargains are to be had. Or what about Notre Dame? No one should visit Paris without seeing the majesties of the cathedral."

"Well, I—" Miri was distracted as Wolf proceeded to kiss each fingertip in turn. The sensation was not entirely unpleasant. "I would like to go to the Charters Inn."

Wolf paused in mid-pucker, his eyes widening. "What?"

"The Charters Inn," Miri repeated more firmly. "I have heard that is where Le Balafre and his men are quartered."

Wolf let go of her hand and barked out a single word. "No."

"No?" Miri echoed.

Wolf barred her path, shaking his head. Miri regarded him

with rising indignation. "What happened to—'Oh, mademoi-selle, I am your wolf. Your slave. I will take you anywhere you want to go'?"

Wolf leaned back against the gate and folded his arms with a deep sigh. "I sense we are about to have our first lover's quarrel."

"We are not lovers! I just met you yesterday."

"Then I would like to keep you alive to lengthen our ac-quaintance." Wolf seized hold of her hands, squeezing them. "Miri, this Le Balafre, this scarred devil is a witch-hunter and you propose to just saunter over to the inn where he is staying? What do you want to do? Make his job easy for him?"

"I don't believe he would hurt me. I knew him before he was a scarred devil, as you call him. His name is not Le Balafre. His real name is Simon Aristide."

Wolf scanned her face with narrowed eyes. "You knew him. How well?"

Miri felt a hot tide of color wash into her cheeks. "Very well, or so I thought. It was only three years ago when he came to Faire Isle, but it seems so much longer than that. I was much younger then, but so was he. We—we were friends."

"What sort of friend brings such a blush to your cheek? Never tell me you are in love with this man." Wolf let out an an-guished groan. He flipped back his cloak and reached for the dagger strapped to his side. "I might as well plunge this into my heart right now and be done with it."

"You will do no such thing." Miri clamped her hand over his to prevent his drawing the weapon. "Wolf, please strive to be sensible and attend to me for at least two minutes. I was but thir-teen, little more than a child, when I knew Simon.

"We were not lovers and I doubt we ever shall be," she added sadly. "But I have seen firsthand the sort of misery witch-hunters can cause. If I still possess any sort of influence at all with Simon, I must try to use it before a good many innocent women are harmed. Will you help me?"

Wolf shook his head. "You don't understand. If I were to escort you to see this witch-hunter and anything were to happen to you, I wouldn't have to slit my own throat. My captain would oblige me by doing it for me."

"Nothing will happen. If we leave now and go swiftly, we can be back before Remy or anyone else has a chance to know we've gone. I swear it. Of course, if you are afraid to accompany me, I quite understand—"

"*Afraid?*" Wolf swirled his cape behind his back, planted his hands on his hips, and struck an aggressively masculine pose. "For but one of your smiles, I would fight a hundred tigers, take on a horde of brigands, or do battle with Lucifer himself."

"I only want one small thing, to see Simon. Will you take me?"

Wolf scowled at her and muttered, "A man would have to be a complete fool to escort the woman he loves into the presence of a rival. And a dangerous one at that."

Miri rested her hand gently on his sleeve. She pleaded with the full force of her eyes. "Oh, Wolf, please. You have no idea how important this is to me."

Wolf stared at her for a long moment, then issued a sound somewhere between a sigh and a moan. "Alack, it would seem I am a fool where you are concerned."

He smoothed his cloak back over his shoulder, then gallantly offered her his arm.

THE CHARTERS INN WAS SITUATED JUST INSIDE THE CITY GATES, A large hostelry comprised of three wings surrounding a courtyard. Le Balafre and his men had completely taken over the inn, turning it into an armed encampment. It was not even possible to get anywhere near Simon Aristide without being cleared with the sentry.

As much as Miri had appreciated Wolf's escort, she was relieved when he was refused admittance, and only Miri was permitted to enter. Wolf's fierce determination to protect her and his flamboyant nature could only cause trouble and this meeting with Simon could prove difficult enough. She left Wolf swearing and prowling the courtyard, vowing if she hadn't returned in an hour's time, he was coming after her.

She followed a grizzled old guard inside, blinking to adjust her eyes to the darkened interior from the courtyard's bright flood of sunlight. The inn's main parlor was crowded with Simon's men, some of them playing at cards, some dicing. One even dandled a serving wench on his knee.

This was clearly a different breed of witch-hunters from Vachel Le Vis's troop of hooded monks. Not a pair of rosary beads or a Bible in sight. It was a well-known fact that those who helped successfully prosecute a witch were entitled to a share of the condemned's worldly goods. Simon's men were hardened adventurers motivated by profit rather than a fanatical belief they were acting upon divine orders from God. Miri shuddered, unable to decide which motive for destroying innocent women was worse.

Many hard assessing stares tracked her progress across the room as the older guard led her up a stair to the inn's second floor. Miri held her head high, her calm demeanor a foil for the way her heart had begun to pound. After all these years, a corridor, the mere span of a door, was all that separated her from Simon.

At thirteen, she had been far slower than other girls with regards to paying heed to the opposite sex. But a girl would have had to be dead not to have noticed Simon. He had been breathtakingly handsome with dark lustrous eyes and a cap of ebony curls. His smile had been far too kind for a witch-hunter, his eyes too apt to twinkle with good humor and hints of boyish mischief. And his hands . . . Miri especially remembered the long elegance of his fingers as he'd scratched Necromancer behind his ears and set him purring. Back when her cat had still trusted Simon as much as she had done herself.

The old guard came to a halt before a door at the end of the hall, the way barred by two more sentries. After a few low remarks exchanged with the sentries, the older guard beckoned to Miri. He held open the door for her and with a jerk of his head, indicated she was to precede him inside.

Being near Simon had always stirred a queer fluttering sensation in the pit of her stomach. Miri thought she had grown too wise for such foolishness. But as she stepped over the threshold, she felt as though the butterflies inside her were going crazed.

The guard did not follow her into the room, but closed the door quietly behind her. The chamber was one of the inn's more modest rooms, furnished with little beyond a narrow bed and a washstand. But a large table had been moved into the room, the surface littered with documents, quills, and inkpots.

Miri clasped her hands tightly together to still their trembling. She glanced around the room for Simon, hoping to find some sign of the boy she'd once known, whose tender lips had bestowed upon her her very first kiss. But the person she spied silhouetted against the windows was a stranger. Simon Aristide had not grown so much as hardened into manhood. He had always been tall, but slender. His shoulders had filled out in the intervening years, his chest broadened. He was clad simply in dark breeches and a linen shirt, the sleeves shoved up past his wrists. The shirt was open at the neckline, revealing a steel jacket he wore beneath for protection.

The black crown of curls was gone, his hair shaved so close as to be no more than a shadow on his skull. An angry scar bisected his cheek, disappearing beneath the patch he wore over one eye. The other eye that fixed itself upon Miri was dark and cold. It was hard to believe that scarcely four years separated them in age. Simon could not be more than twenty and yet he looked so much older.

The silence that settled between them was so profound Miri was uncomfortably aware of the thud of her heart, the soft sound of her own breathing. She leaned back against the door for support, unable to speak a word. Simon gestured to her to come forward. One thing about him had not changed and that was the grace of his hands.

"Mademoiselle. I am afraid I can accord you no more than a few moments of my time, so please state your business with me."

"M—mademoiselle?" Miri faltered. "Simon, you pretend not to remember me?"

"Of course, I remember you, Mademoiselle Cheney."

"*Miri,*" she insisted.

"Miri." Something softer flickered in his eye that gave her hope, even though the expression was quickly shuttered away again beneath his hard façade. As she approached him, his gaze raked over her. "You have changed a great deal."

"So have you," she said sadly.

"As you may recall, I had a little help." Simon flicked the back of his fingers against his scar, his voice dark with accusation.

An accusation that was unnecessary to wrack Miri with guilt. But she replied quietly, "I am sorry, but you had attacked Renard. I only wanted to stop you from fighting when I grabbed your arm. I didn't want either of you to be hurt. He didn't want to injure you either. His sword slipped."

She touched Simon's cheek softly. "It broke my heart when you just ran off and disappeared into the streets of Paris after you had been so badly wounded. You should have stayed, Simon. Ariane is a great healer. She could have helped you."

"I wanted no help from a witch. And as for your brother-in-law, I attacked Renard because I thought him little better than a demon."

"And me, Simon? What did you think of me?"

A muscle worked in his jaw. "That all was a long time ago. What I thought is of no more consequence than my scar."

Miri continued her tentative exploration, lifting her fingers to his head. Surprisingly, Simon made no move to stop her. She ran her fingertips over his scalp, disturbed by the feel of bristle where there had once been lustrous waves of hair.

"Your beautiful hair," she murmured. "Why did you shave it all off?"

He shrugged. "It was a cursed nuisance, always falling across my face. When a man only has one good eye, he must guard what sight he has."

"Or perhaps you were trying to make yourself look as grim as possible?"

Her suggestion must have struck far too close to the mark. Simon thrust her hand away. "My hair encouraged my conceit. Master Le Vis always said I was far too vain."

"I would not have called you vain. But I would say you were aware of how handsome you were, how capable of pleasing a lady's eye."

"That's not something that need concern me anymore, is it?" He peeled back his eye patch. The jagged scar continued up to his brow, his eyelid sealed closed beneath the puckered flesh. Miri could tell that he thought to repulse her.

He clearly did not expect what she did next. She strained on tiptoe and lightly brushed her lips across his scarred lid. Simon reared back, the expression in his good eye wild with a kind of longing and despair. He moved swiftly away from her, settling his eye patch back into place. But Miri had seen enough in that brief moment to give her hope, that the real Simon Aristide still existed, trapped beneath Le Balafre's hardened exterior. Even when he addressed her brusquely, "As I said when you first came in, I don't have a great deal of time to spare. Will you please take a seat and state your business?"

Before Miri could respond, they were interrupted by a light knock at the door.

"Come in," Simon said.

The door opened and the gray-haired guard who had escorted Miri appeared, bearing a tray containing a roll, a bowl of porridge, and a glass of wine. "Your breakfast, monsieur, and you need not worry. I have made sure everything has been tasted."

"Thank you, Braxton. Just set the tray over there." Simon gestured toward a small table close to the bedside.

The man called Braxton did as ordered. As soon as the door had closed behind him again, Miri turned to Simon and exclaimed, "You—you have your food tasted?"

"A rather wise precaution, don't you think? For a man who has come to hunt witches in a city controlled by a Dark Queen with a particular skill in poisons." Simon regarded her coldly. "And as you well know, I have made other enemies besides."

Miri's chin bumped up a notch. "I am not one of them, Simon."

"I never said that you were." He drew up a chair close to the table that served as his desk and again gestured to her to sit down, this time with a shade more impatience.

Miri sank down, sadly shaking her head. "Having to have your food tasted, wearing armor beneath your clothes, guards at your door. What a dreadful way to live."

"It is not by my choice." His hands lingered on the back of the chair, his voice once more rife with accusation.

Miri did not bear it quite so meekly this time. She twisted round to frown up at him. "Yes, it is. Partly. I once gave you a chance for something far different. I offered you my friendship, my trust, and you used it to help your master Le Vis capture my brother-in-law."

"The Comte de Renard is one of the most evil sorcerers I ever had the misfortune to meet. I had hoped to free you and your sisters from his dark influence. If I had to betray your trust, if I hurt you, it—it was necessary. I make no apologies."

Despite his fierce assertion, Miri perceived something else in his gaze, shame and remorse. It softened some of the hurt she'd long felt over his betrayal.

"It is all right, Simon. I forgive you." She smiled gently at him, but he shrank back as though she had slapped him.

"I don't want your forgiveness. Is this why you have come to see me?" He sneered. "To reminisce over old times?"

"No." Miri fetched a deep sigh. "I was at the tourney yesterday when the king announced your crusade to rid Paris of witches. I realize it is likely futile, but I hoped to dissuade you before a number of innocent women come to harm. Unless you truly have become like your late master and believe there is no such thing as an innocent woman."

"Monsieur Le Vis was good to me. He took me in after my village was destroyed and gave me a home. But I concede there was an unfortunate strain of madness in him. I don't hate all women or think they are evil. In fact, I am not entirely immune to the charms of your sex . . ." Simon paused, his gaze lingering over her in a bold manner far different from the sweet teasing glances he'd once given her. He'd often caused her heart to trip over itself with a girlish flutter, but this look stirred in her something more elemental, primitive. A rush of heat that both excited and alarmed her.

She flushed, folding her arms protectively over her breasts. The gesture seemed to snap Simon back to his senses. "But you ladies can prove a distraction when a man has weightier matters on his mind."

"Such as accusing innocent women of being witches?"

"And sorcerers like the Comte de Renard. I have no bias as to gender when I am on the hunt and I assure you I have never persecuted anyone who was innocent."

Miri tried to relax. Or at least she might have been able to do so if he hadn't taken to prowling about the room in a manner reminiscent of Wolf. What was it about men, she wondered with exasperation, that they could never simply be *still*?

"Anyone can be tortured into being guilty, Simon," she said. "That time your master threatened me with the ordeal by water, I was almost frightened into confessing things I hadn't done."

"I don't use torture. I prefer to offer rewards for information."

"You mean bribing citizens to come forward with accusations. Is that any more reliable than torture for obtaining honesty?"

Simon paused in his restless movements long enough to scowl at her. "People are often so terrified of witches they need some inducement to come forward. But I don't take anyone's word for anything. I investigate each charge carefully."

"How does one investigate statements such as 'Oh, that woman put the evil eye on me and now my hens no longer lay eggs, and my ancient cow no longer gives milk'?"

"Not all statements are that absurd. I have a matter that was brought to my attention only this morning." Simon strode to the desk and snatched up a document. "The case of one Anton Deleon, an unfortunate kitchen boy at an inn who made the mistake of sleeping with a dark-haired witch. She subsequently cursed him."

Simon held the document out to her, inviting her to read his notes. Miri shook her head, refusing to look at it. "That is completely ridiculous."

"You would not think so if you had seen the Deleon boy. He is afflicted with a horrible disease the like of which I've never seen. His flesh is eating itself away."

"If that is so, I am sorry for the poor lad, but the onslaught of illness often defies reasonable explanation. Monsieur Deleon would do far better to seek out the services of some healing wise woman than make baseless accusations of witchcraft."

Simon tossed the document back on the desk with an exasperated look. "You have acquired all the graces of a woman, Miri Cheney, but you still are as naïve as a child. You never could see the evil that exists in the world."

"You are quite mistaken," Miri replied sadly. "I have seen more than my share of the evil that men do, the violence. I have simply never understood it."

"That is because your heart has not yet been touched by darkness. You have never learned to feel anger, to hate."

Gazing at Simon's hardened features, Miri shivered. "I hope that I never do."

"I hope you never do either," he astonished her by saying in a softer tone. "I have seen things these past years that would shatter your rainbow-colored visions of the universe. Men and women who have sold their souls to the devil a thousand times over. Many of them for the mere sake of a book."

"A book?"

"Hunting witches is not the only thing that has brought me to Paris. I am also seeking an evil book that has made its way to our shores . . . the *Book of Shadows*."

Miri tried not to smile, but she could not help herself.

"You find that amusing?" Simon demanded.

"Yes, I am afraid I do. Tales of some evil masterwork have been around as long as there have been daughters of the earth. The *Book of Shadows* is a myth and if you have been wasting your time trying to track it down, then you are the one who is naïve."

"I am not the only one searching for it."

"Then these others are being as foolish as—" Miri checked herself. She had come here to reason with Simon, not to quarrel with him.

She tensed as he circled round the table. He seated himself on the edge so that he loomed over her, so close that she had to draw back to keep her skirts from brushing up against him. Dangling his booted feet, he leaned slightly forward to rest one arm across his knee, making her keenly aware of the supple power of his fingers, the thick muscle of his wrist and forearm. The pose was both disturbingly masculine and intimidating. What was more, she was certain that Simon intended it to be.

"Unfortunately, Miri, I think you may possibly know more of these matters than you pretend. A certain council of witches recently took place on your island."

Miri started at the mention of Ariane's council meeting, but she said nothing, gripping her hands together in the folds of her skirt.

"I captured one of the witches who attended, a high-strung Portuguese girl who was easily persuaded to tell me what went on at that meeting."

"Persuaded or terrified?"

Ignoring her reproachful interruption, Simon continued. "This book that you claim does not exist was the main topic of discussion and since that night a mighty search for it has been organized by your sister's coven."

"Ariane does not have a coven—"

"And the foremost searcher is reputed to be the demonic Comte de Renard." Simon leaned closer so that Miri was obliged to shrink back in her seat. "Now what do you suppose your brother-in-law wants with such an evil book?"

"I don't know. Nothing—I mean, there is no such book." Flustered by the manner of Simon's questioning as well as the things he was telling her, Miri squirmed out of the chair. She had fled Faire Isle before Ariane's council meeting. Caught up in her concern for Gabrielle, Miri had made no effort to contact her eldest sister other than dispatching a note to assure Ariane of her safe arrival in Paris. It had never occurred to Miri that there might be trouble brewing at home.

She still did not credit Simon's assertions. Seized by his band of ruthless witch-hunters, who knows what the poor little Portuguese girl might have been frightened into saying? The thought of Simon, once so kind, terrorizing anyone made Miri feel ill.

She moved behind her chair, gripping the back of it. She was not about to admit the existence of Ariane's council meetings, but she said, "If Ariane and Renard heard rumors of such a book, they would investigate just to set everyone's mind at rest. But neither of them, I assure you, would have any interest in acquiring a *Book of Shadows*."

"Truly?" Simon slid off the edge of the table, landing on the balls of his feet as lightly as Necromancer would have done. "My men and I found the one who brought the book over from Ireland. Unfortunately, Monsieur O'Donal was fatally wounded in his attempt to elude us. He spit out some Gaelic curse before he died, and I learned nothing more from him. He had little in his possession beyond a saddlebag stuffed with gold coin and rare jewels. Now where do you suppose some filthy bog trotter would have acquired such a treasure?"

"I have no idea. Perhaps he was a robber."

"Or perhaps he was a sorcerer, just like your brother-in-law, and they struck a satisfactory bargain between them."

"That is arrant nonsense."

Simon yanked the chair from her grasp, shoving it out of the way. Miri stumbled back as he stalked after her, his movements slow and predatory. Miri was reminded of what her cat had often said about Simon.

"Beware of him, daughter of the earth. He is a hunter."

She backed away until the panels of the wall cut off her retreat. Simon cornered her, bracing his hands on either side of her, leaning close enough that the hard wall of his chest just barely brushed the front of her bodice. His eye was soft, dark, and merciless.

"If you know who has acquired that book, Miri, you would be wise to tell me."

Her heart thudded against her rib cage. But she tipped up her chin, refusing to be frightened by Le Balafre. No matter what he called himself, this was still Simon.

"How can I tell you who has acquired something that I am not sure exists?"

"You were always ready enough to believe in anything else. If you believe in unicorns, you have to believe in dragons too."

"There is nothing wrong with dragons. They only breathe fire when they are trapped and forced to defend themselves from idiotic knights . . . or hunters."

Simon's teeth flashed in a brief smile, but it was not a pleasant one. He captured a strand of her hair and wound the golden skein around his finger. "What did you really come here for, Miri?"

"Because I foolishly supposed I might do some good and—and God help me, I wanted to see you again."

"God help you, indeed. You have the misfortune to be connected with a family steeped in witchcraft, through your own mother and now your sister's unfortunate marriage to the devil, Renard. I do have to warn you. I mean to find that book and root out the evil in France once and for all. You would do well to stay far away from me."

"Or what? You'll charge me with witchcraft? Burn me at the stake?"

"I don't burn witches, Miri. I hang them or put them straight to the sword. It's quicker and far more efficient." His hand still entangled in her hair, Simon removed a knife from his belt.

Miri's breath snagged in her throat. As Simon lifted the blade, for one terrified moment she expected to feel its sting at her throat. Instead she felt a sharp tug as Simon sliced off a lock of her hair. She could not mistake it for any sort of romantic gesture. It was clearly a warning because he crushed the lock in his fist and said with chilling softness, "Now . . . I think you had better leave. Go home, Miri. Go back to Faire Isle."

Raising trembling fingers to her severed strands, she gazed up at him. The dark eye that regarded her was empty and cold, forcing her to accept the truth. If anything did indeed remain of Simon Aristide, he was buried too deep for her to ever find him.

Without another word, Miri eased away from him and groped for the door. Yanking it open, she hurled herself across the threshold and fled. The sentries, the stairs, the men in the taproom below were all a blur. She did not stop until she staggered into the courtyard.

It was only then that she realized how badly she was shaking.

She gripped her own arms tightly in an effort to regain command of herself. For so long she had worried about Simon, wondered what had happened to him. She had been better off not knowing. Necromancer and Gabrielle had both been right. She should never have come here.

All she wanted to do was slink back to her chamber in Gabrielle's house and curl up in her bed like some wild creature gone to ground to lick its wounds. But across the inn's yard, she spied Wolf close to getting into an altercation with one of the guards as he prepared to come and look for her.

Miri's heart sank. As kind as Wolf had been to accompany her here, she wished she could have avoided him. She did not feel up to all the questions he was bound to ask, or to listening to his dramatic declarations of love.

As she trudged toward him, Wolf broke off his heated dispute with the guard. His eyes lighting up, he pounced upon her. "There you are at last, my love. I was just about to—"

He broke off, regarding her sharply. Something he perceived in her face must have silenced him. His green eyes softened with such unexpected compassion, it was nearly Miri's undoing. Wolf asked no questions. Nor did he seek to say another word. Before she could embarrass herself by bursting into tears in front of all these rough-hewn men, Wolf took her by the hand and gently led her away.

۴۴۴۴

SIMON HOVERED BY THE WINDOW, KEEPING WELL TO THE SIDE SO that he could not be spotted by anyone in the inn yard below. He watched Miri slip her fingers into the grasp of some dark-haired lad, as trustingly as she had once held Simon's own hand. The sight had a strange effect on Simon, filling him with an ache of envy and longing.

He fought to quell it as he did any emotion that did not

contribute to his ruthless efficiency. He dropped his gaze to his fist instead and slowly unfurled his fingers to examine Miri's lock of hair. It rested against his palm like a silken curl of moonlight. He ought to force open the casement, toss the strand out of the window and be rid of it, along with the memory of her.

Instead he carried the lock closer to his nostrils, the skein of hair carrying a faint, indescribable scent, like the sweet wild essence of Miri's spirit, taking him back to their brief days together on Faire Isle. Despite her connection with other witches, he'd felt so protective of her, so convinced of her innocence. He'd regarded her with affection, but almost that of a brother to a sister. She had reminded him poignantly of his own little sister. Marie, like the rest of his family and most of his village, had been destroyed when that old hag had poisoned their well.

Miri Cheney certainly did not remind him of a younger sister anymore. She had grown, filled out, and yet despite all her lissome curves, her aura of innocence had not changed. Nor had those peculiar silvery-blue eyes of hers, that fey gaze that seemed capable of illuminating corners of a man's soul best left in darkness, probing paths in his heart he no longer wanted explored.

Why the devil did she have to be here in Paris just now? Why did she have to come to see him? Miri had always made him too soft, sentimental, and tender when he could not afford to be any of those things. After his duel with the sorcerer Renard, Simon had gone to ground like a wounded beast. His master dead, his entire world in chaos, Simon had once more felt lost and abandoned. But with the cache of hidden coins he'd retrieved from Le Vis's house, he'd managed to survive.

More than survive . . . he'd grown stronger, tougher. Once filled with doubts about his abilities as a witch-hunter, he'd discovered in himself an extraordinary gift for detectiving evil and for commanding men as well. When Simon had fully embraced his dark profession, he had resigned himself to the dangers of his choice, to the solitary existence such a role must entail. He had never let himself harbor any regrets . . . until now.

But as he watched Miri and her escort vanish into the crowded streets beyond the inn, Simon could not help reflecting on the irony of it. He was here in Paris, one of the most populous cities in Europe.

And never had he felt so alone.

Chapter Twenty-one

THE MORNING BREEZE STIRRED TENDRILS OF GABRIELLE'S HAIR as she sat curled on the window seat. She had much to do, arrangements to make for the closing of the house, the pensioning off of her servants, final accounts to be settled before she and Remy fled Paris. Yet she could not seem to bestir herself. She yawned and stretched with all the languorous contentment of a cat, her body still aglow and replete from Remy's most recent lovemaking. During the past two days, Gabrielle had experienced a sense of peace rare to her restive nature, despite the continued threat of witch-hunters and the Dark Queen looming on the horizon.

She leaned against the casement, peering dreamily out into a world that seemed reborn, from the verdant greens of her garden to a sky so fiercely blue it made her ache to look upon it. She felt as though she had been viewing life through a veil these past years and it had been suddenly torn away. She could *see* again all the vivid colors, all the intricate details down to the dew on the velvet petals of the smallest rose.

Her fingers tingled with the familiar itch to reach for a paintbrush. The thought that her lost magic might be returning to her filled her with both hope and fear that it might not be true, that she would face that blank wall of canvas only to fail again and be crushed with disappointment.

Now was not the best time for making the attempt, not when she and Remy still had so many difficulties to surmount, chiefly the rescue of Navarre. Remy had been much occupied seeking out other loyal Huguenots, engaging men at arms who could be trusted. To Gabrielle had fallen the task of acting as go-between, conveying messages from Remy to Navarre.

It had taken a great deal of persuasion on her part, but she had discouraged Remy from returning to the Louvre. It was far too risky and not only because of the danger to his life. Remy posessed so little ability to dissemble, Gabrielle feared that one look at his face and Navarre would guess how matters stood between her and Remy.

Gabrielle had had difficulties enough schooling her own features when she had encountered Navarre at court yesterday. She had managed to excuse her sudden departure from the tournament, attributing it to her younger sister being taken ill. Her intervention in Remy's duel had been far harder to explain.

Gabrielle frowned as she recollected the conversation, still uncertain whether Navarre had entirely believed her . . .

". . .and I could see quite clearly how the duel was intended to trap the captain so I made haste to put a stop to it. I—I know how much Captain Remy means to you."

"To me?" the king asked softly. Despite his languid posture, Navarre's eyes appeared far too shrewd.

Gabrielle willed herself not to blush. "Why, yes, he is your Scourge, your most loyal supporter, your best hope of attaining your freedom."

"Perhaps," Navarre murmured. "The captain is indeed a good, trustworthy man, but it is possible that he might deal me a blow without ever having meant to do so."

"What—what do you mean?"

"Only that I believed that Nicolas Remy's return was a great blessing. Now I am no longer so sure. I have done my best to play the buffoon for this court, convince Queen Catherine I do not in the least mind my captivity. I fear all Remy's presence here has done is fix suspicion upon me again. I am more closely watched than ever."

The king's hand closed over hers, an unusually somber expression stealing over him. "I couldn't endure another failed escape attempt, Gabrielle. I think it would be best if we sent our Scourge away, perhaps to look out for my interests in Bearn, while you and I remain here in Paris, continue to watch and wait, throw dust in the eyes of the Dark Queen. Eh, ma mie?"

Gabrielle was hard-pressed to conceal her dismay as Henry carried her hand to his lips, his steady gaze never leaving her face . . .

Gabrielle winced at the memory of that awkward moment. How much of the king's wish to dispatch Remy to Bearn was due to his unease over the escape plot, and how much to the desire to be rid of a rival? She still was not entirely sure. It had taken all of her charm and wit to retain Navarre's faith in Remy, to convince him to go forward with Remy's plans. Parisian gossip being what it was, Gabrielle only prayed that the king did not find out that Remy was now sharing her bed.

She did genuinely like and respect Navarre. Deceiving him was hard, almost as hard as concealing from Remy that his king was having doubts about him. But Remy already had enough to worry about, dealing with the practical aspects of the escape.

Peering out her bedchamber window, she observed him entering the garden from his early morning errand to gather his belongings from his lodgings. She had persuaded Remy to move into her town house. It only made sense, she had argued, but practicality had nothing to do with it. With all the dangers swirling about them, Gabrielle could scarce bear to let the man out of her sight.

As Remy strode toward the gate, the sight of her head gardener Phillipe's tow-headed children distracted him. Phillipe had recently made arrangements for his son and daughter to be looked after by an aunt who lived in the country. Jacques and Elise were a forlorn pair, their small legs dangling off the stone bench, their eyes downcast. Another man would not have given them a second glance. But Remy hunkered down in front of the children, engaging them in some earnest conversation.

Elise shyly burrowed her face against her older brother's shoulder. To Gabrielle's astonishment, Remy straightened, raised his hands in a menacing gesture and let out a mighty roar. Squealing, the children leaped up from the bench and Remy pursued them around the rose bushes, still growling. Gabrielle gaped, leaning so far out of the casement, she was in danger of tumbling to the ground below.

Remy cornered the children near the hawthorn tree. He dropped to his knees, his hands crooked into mock claws. Jacques shrieked and brandished a stick to hold Remy at bay. Elise crouched behind her brother, wide-eyed and shivering with excitement. Remy flung back his head and emitted a roar worthy of a dragon.

Remy chanced to glance up and spied her at the window above him. He waved and cast her a grin that was endearingly boyish. She saw that she was not the only one who had been changed by all they had shared last night. It was as though years had fallen away from Remy, leaving him much younger. The sunlight glinted off his tousled hair and the chain visible beneath his half-open doublet.

He still insisted upon wearing Cass's useless medallion, much to Gabrielle's dismay. Remy only did so because Gabrielle had given it to him. He cherished the amulet as a sign of her love and desire to protect him, which in a way it was. But if Remy really knew how she'd come by the medallion, he would feel far differently.

No more secrets, she had promised Remy. She ought to tell him the truth, but she could not find the courage to do so. The love that had blossomed between them seemed too new to risk trampling it underfoot in a quarrel. Some night while he slept, she would see to it that the medallion went missing, then fashion for Remy some love token of her own to take its place. For now she refused to let anything threaten the harmony between them. She smiled tenderly down at her dragon and waved back just as Jacques poked Remy in the ribs with his stick.

The blow clearly caught Remy by surprise because he let out a startled ooff. Gabrielle pressed her hand to her lips to stifle a laugh. Remy staggered, enacting his part with a panache that would have done a strolling player proud. He flopped onto his back, growling and kicking his boots out in the throes of a dying dragon. Flinging his arms wide, he lay still. Jacques and Elise crept closer for a peek. When the children were within range, the dragon sprang back to life with another roar, seizing and wrestling them down on top of him. And yet what a gentle dragon her Scourge was, fearsome enough to delight the rowdy Jacques, but taking great care not to play too rough with little Elise.

Remy would make a good father. The thought caught Gabrielle by surprise and her hand flew to the region of her womb. She had employed every wise woman's trick she knew to prevent getting with child by any of her other lovers. But she had taken no precautions with Remy last night. She could easily have conceived.

Rather than alarming her, the notion of giving birth to Remy's babe filled her with wonder, made her feel all soft as though she were melting inside. She might give Remy a son perhaps, a little boy with sturdy limbs, tousled gold hair, and Remy's brown eyes . . .

A knock at the bedchamber door roused her from her

dreaminess. Gabrielle dragged her gaze reluctantly away from Remy. "Come in."

Bette pushed into the room, the pert maid looking somewhat harassed. "Begging your pardon, mistress, but there is someone here demanding to see you."

Gabrielle yawned and stretched. "Tell whoever is here to go away and come back later. It is hardly a reasonable hour for receiving callers."

"But it is that Lascelles woman."

Gabrielle fixed Bette with a startled gaze. "Cass? She—she is *here*?"

"Aye and insisting upon seeing you. She is below stairs with her maid and some brute of a dog that looks ready to tear the throat out of anyone who comes too close. The footmen are afraid to get anywhere near her. But I believe I heard Captain Remy in the garden. I am sure he could get rid of—"

"No!" Gabrielle rose hastily from the window seat. "I would as soon Remy knew nothing of Mademoiselle Lascelles's visit. He would not approve of our friendship."

"No doubt he wouldn't, milady. She is a dangerous creature from what I've heard tell of her. Obviously she has come here bent upon some mischief."

"And obviously you have spent too much time gossiping with Miri's cat," Gabrielle retorted. "Escort Mademoiselle Lascelles into the small parlor at the back of the house. I will be down directly."

"Very good, milady." But Bette's sniff of disapproval showed that she did not find it good at all.

As Bette left to carry out her commands, Gabrielle made a hasty toilette, shrugging into one of her simplest gowns, bundling her hair into a fine net. Before she quit her bedchamber, she stole one more anxious glance down into the garden. Remy was still absorbed with the children. With any luck, he would soon depart on the errand to his lodgings. She could find out what Cass wanted before Remy returned.

This was not the best time for Cass to have decided to emerge from her seclusion. Not with Aristide and his witch-hunters prowling about Paris. If Cass's family history and her connection with the Maison d' Esprit were discovered, Gabrielle shuddered to think what might befall her friend.

Gabrielle hurried downstairs and headed toward the small parlor. To her annoyance, she found Finette leaning up against the door, her skinny arms akimbo as though she were guarding the entryway. Gabrielle winced as the slatternly woman's sour odor carried to her nostrils.

"Mistress is waiting for you inside," she announced as though it was Cass's house instead of Gabrielle's.

"I am aware of that," Gabrielle replied coldly.

Finette plucked at the dirty folds of her dress as she curtsied. She regarded Gabrielle with that sly smirk that always made Gabrielle want to slap her. Gabrielle edged past the maidservant, making no effort to conceal her distaste.

She entered the room, firmly closing the door in Finette's face. The small parlor was primarily used as a sewing room. It was simply but comfortably furnished with a worktable, a few stools, and a settle piled with embroidered cushions. The windows faced full west, affording excellent lighting for needlework in the late afternoon.

Cass waited near one of these windows, her dog hunkered down by her side. The mastiff attempted to leap up when Gabrielle entered, but he was held tightly to Cass's side by a stout leather leash. Gabrielle drew up short, blinking in surprise at the transformation in Cassandra Lascelles. No trace remained of the recluse with the unhealthy pallor, often bloodshot eyes, and wild tangled mane. Cass's hair flowed in soft dark waves over her shoulders, a plain gold circlet banding her forehead. Instead of one of those faded gowns that half fell off her thin shoulders, Cass was attired in a new dress. The design was simple, no full skirts, no farthingale, the wine-colored silk an excellent foil for her white skin and ebony hair. She wore no ruff around her slender throat, but a heavy silver chain disappeared beneath the embroidered bodice of her gown.

She stood erect, her head held high, a strange luster in her usually dull eyes. She reminded Gabrielle of the regal way she had looked when she had conducted the séance, unexpectedly strong and powerful. Her hearing always so acute, Cass did not seem to notice Gabrielle's entrance into the room. She cocked her head to one side, her attention claimed by sounds drifting through the open window, Remy's laughter mingling with the delighted cries of the children.

Gabrielle had been so eager to arrange her meeting with Cass in one of the more remote parts of the house, she had forgotten the sewing room windows were angled near the gardens. The realization made her as uneasy as the rapt expression on Cass's face.

"Cass?" As Gabrielle stepped closer, Cerberus barked, but his tail thudded against the floor in a friendly fashion.

Cass smiled warmly, extending her hand in the direction of Gabrielle's voice. As soon as Gabrielle came within range, Cass groped for her and wrapped her arm around Gabrielle in a strong hug. Even Cerberus licked her hand as though glad to see her.

Gabrielle returned Cass's embrace and murmured, "This is a great surprise."

"Not an unwelcome one, I hope."

"N-no." Gabrielle peered over Cass's shoulder to the gardens where Remy was giving little Elise a ride upon his strong shoulders. She was relieved to see him moving farther away from the house, back toward the garden gate. Taking Cass by the elbow, she steered her out of range of the windows. "Do come and sit down. I will summon my housekeeper to fetch us some wine."

"No!" Cass said sharply. She moistened her lips and softened her tone. "I—I mean no, thank you. I have been trying to conquer my old demon, avoid any manner of strong drink. I need to keep my wits clear, but it has not been an easy battle."

She lifted her hand to display a marked tremor. Gabrielle

clasped Cass's fingers to steady them and exclaimed, "But this is wonderful. You are obviously succeeding. I have never seen you look so well. So strong and beautiful."

"I will have to take your word for that," Cass replied dryly as Gabrielle helped her find the settle. Cass eased down onto it, Cerberus sinking onto his haunches near her feet. When Gabrielle attempted to move away, Cass retained her grasp on her hand.

"There is no need to ask how you are faring. I can feel it. You are positively glowing. You and Captain Remy must be getting along well. Very well indeed."

Disconcerted by how Cass was able to read her with but a touch, Gabrielle squirmed until her hand was free. A hot blush rose to her cheeks.

"Yes, things are going well. I have much to tell you." Settling onto one of the stools, Gabrielle positioned herself near the windows where she could keep an eye out for Remy. As succinctly as possible, she told Cass all that had happened at the tourney, the decisions that she had reached.

Cass listened without interrupting, Cerberus's massive head resting in her lap. She leaned against the back of the settle, absently scratching the dog's ears. When Gabrielle had finished, Cass shook her head, a note of fond amusement creeping into her voice.

"So you intend to fly in the face of your great destiny and count it all well lost for love? Ah, my foolish Gabrielle."

"Perhaps. But then again, perhaps I am being wise for the first time in my life."

"And you meant to quit Paris without even saying good-bye to me?"

"Of course not. If you had not come here, I intended to visit the Maison d'Esprit and warn you about the witch-hunters, make certain you were all right."

"Would you have remembered to do so? I wonder." Cass's hand stilled on top of her dog's head.

"Certainly I would have," Gabrielle said, surprised by the

brooding look that clouded Cass's features. "We are friends, are we not?"

"Yes . . . like sisters, so likely you will have guessed why I have come."

"No, I must confess I am quite at a loss. You rarely leave the Maison d'Esprit and for you to risk it now when the witch-hunters have invaded Paris—"

"Bah!" Cass lifted her hand in a dismissive gesture. "I told you. Witch-hunters don't worry me. I have had experience of them before."

That experience had been horrible enough to scar any woman for life. She had lost her entire family. Gabrielle did not know how Cass could speak so cavalierly of such a dire event, but perhaps it was her way of coping with the grief.

Cass returned to stroking her dog. "I only came here today to redeem your pledge to me. The promise you made to do me one favor in exchange for your use of my ability to conjure the dead. You do remember, don't you?"

"Certainly I do. I have long been anxious to repay you, especially if it involves helping you remove from that dreadful dungeon of a room where you keep hiding. Just tell me what you require."

"Only one small thing. Nicolas Remy."

"W-what!"

"Before you get too distressed, let me explain. I only want to borrow him for one night."

Gabrielle was too stunned to say anything for a moment. She gave an uncertain laugh. "Great heavens, Cass. Whatever would you want to borrow Remy for?"

"My dear Gabrielle," Cass drawled. "What reason would a woman have for wanting a fine specimen like your captain for the night?"

"To—to bed him?"

"Don't sound so shocked. You are not some prim creature with a rigid sense of morals. You've had lovers. You can easily spare me the use of this one."

Gabrielle shot to her feet, the sudden movement causing Cerberus to lift his head and regard her warily. But Gabrielle could not contain herself. She was not merely shocked. She was thunderstruck by Cass's casual request.

"We are not just talking about a lover, but the man I love," she said indignantly. "And you are asking me to lend him to you like—like he was a horse."

"He will turn out to be a prime stallion, I hope." Cass's lips curled in a lascivious smile. When Gabrielle gasped, she added impatiently, "Good lord. I only want him for the one night."

Gabrielle paced before the windows only to check her steps when she realized she was making Cass's dog nervous, never a wise idea with Cerberus. Her mind reeled with the extraordinary nature of Cass's request. Never in her wildest dreams could she have imagined Cass would demand anything like this.

"I don't understand," she said. "If you have a desire for a lover, I could find you plenty. Why does it have to be Remy? A man you've never met, never even seen?"

"I have never *seen* any man," Cass reminded her acidly. "But I sensed something about Remy that night you placed the hilt of his sword in my hands. I suspected even then that he was the one to serve my purpose."

"What purpose?"

"To get me with child."

Gabrielle regarded her incredulously. "You want Remy to sire your child? But you once told me you had no interest in children, that you don't even like them."

"This would be my child, my daughter. You are not the only one who has a great destiny before her. You may choose to turn your back on yours, but I do not."

"What destiny?"

"Nostradamus has predicted that I will be the mother of a woman who will change history. A queen among queens. You thought you would gain power by becoming a king's mistress.

That would be as nothing compared to the power my child will have."

Cass sat up straighter, an impassioned look chasing across her features. "It will not be a power given to her by any man but rather taken, through revolution."

"Revolution?"

"A revolution of wise women. You know the legends as well as I, Gabrielle. There was once a time when the daughters of the earth were not the slaves or playthings of men, when they could practice their magic and be revered, not burned for sorcery. Nostradamus has seen a time in the future when women will begin to resume their rightful place as the equals of men. I have no intention of waiting for eons to pass when I will have long been moldering in my grave. These changes will be effected in my lifetime and even more. The daughters of the earth will topple thrones, strip all men of their rights. They will become *our* slaves. We have all been wandering in darkness, but my child will lead us back into the light. She will be our messiah. Just think of it."

Gabrielle's only thought was that Cassandra had been alone down in her cellars far too long. The woman had run quite mad. Gabrielle bit back the urge to tell her so, finding the fierce intensity of Cass's expression more than a little unnerving.

"Even if what you are telling me should come to pass," she said. "Why do you want Remy to sire this child of yours? Why does it have to be him?"

"Because when I touched his sword, I sensed valuable qualities in him, rage, ruthlessness, the ability to destroy without mercy."

"That is the part of himself that Remy deplores."

"Then he can pass his darkness on to our daughter and be at peace."

"No!"

"No?" Cass echoed, the hint of a frown gathering between her eyes.

Gabrielle moistened her lips, then said in as gentle but firm a tone as possible. "I am sorry, Cass. You have demanded the one thing I cannot grant. Ask me for anything else and I will be happy to keep my promise, but as it is . . ."

Gabrielle trailed off, bracing herself for an explosion of anger. Cass heard her refusal with an astonishing calm, merely issuing a faint sigh. Bracing one hand on the arm of the settle, she levered herself to her feet, her dog rising with her.

"You are so foolishly in love with the man, I was afraid you might not be inclined to be reasonable. But unlike you, I have learned not to leave my destiny to chance. Tell me. Where is the good captain right now?"

"Remy is gone," Gabrielle said, fervently hoping that it was true, that Remy had departed on his errand. "He—he just left and won't be back for some time."

Cass fingered the silver chain beneath her bodice, cocking her head to one side with an air of marked concentration. "Actually I think the captain is still here. Look out the window. I am sure you will spy him at the far end of the garden."

Heart thudding uneasily, Gabrielle glanced out to discover Cass was right. Remy was still in the gardens, but no longer within earshot. Beneath the shade of the oak tree, he bent down, carefully letting an awed young Jacques examine his sword.

"Am I right?" Cass prodded. "Is he there?"

"Yes," Gabrielle replied, whipping her head around to stare at Cass with a mingling of confusion and suspicion. "But how could you possibly know that?"

"Because he is wearing the amulet I made. The one that is just like mine." Cass tugged at the chain around her neck, pulling it from her bosom to display a medallion that appeared similar to Remy's down to the last detail. Gabrielle felt a chill of apprehension sweep through her.

Cass said, "The two amulets were fashioned from the same mold, the same metal, the same charm. They are linked just as I am linked with your captain when he wears his amulet. Do you remember what I told you the charm could do?"

"You told me it would help Remy sense danger, but obviously it does not work."

Cass gave a throaty laugh. "Those were not precisely my words. I said it would enable the captain to feel malice. Observe what I am about to do and keep an eye on your Scourge as well."

Cass cupped the medallion and pressed the amulet to her shoulder, her eyes glazing as she muttered some guttural-sounding words beneath her breath. Gabrielle turned uneasily back to the window. Despite the distance that separated them, she could see Remy pale and drop his sword. Staggering back against the trunk of his tree, he clutched at his shoulder, doubling over with pain. The frightened gardener's children backed away from him.

Gabrielle froze for a moment, unable to believe that Cass actually could—She rounded on the other woman, crying shrilly. "What are you doing to him? Stop it!"

She surged toward Cass to rip the amulet from her grasp. Cerberus growled and snapped, keeping her at bay. As Gabrielle glanced frantically around her for some sort of weapon, Cass released the pendant. Gabrielle pressed her face back to the glass, looking anxiously at Remy. To her relief, he straightened up, his features clearing. Looking puzzled, he gave his shoulder one final rub before bending down to retrieve his sword.

"Give me that thing. Right now!" Gabrielle advanced on Cass, holding out her hand in demanding fashion, ignoring the savage barks her tone elicited from Cerberus.

"Calm down, Gabrielle. And you too, sir." Cass lowered her hand to Cerberus's head, quieting the dog with a low command. The mastiff settled back at Cass's side, but fixed Gabrielle with his menacing stare.

"That was but a small demonstration of my power, Gabrielle. I only touched the medallion to my shoulder. What do you think would happen to Remy if I placed the amulet against my heart? I'll tell you what would happen. I could stop Remy's heart before you can even draw breath to warn him."

"No, please. For the love of God, Cass. Don't!"

"I have no intention of harming your Scourge. Not as long as you are reasonable and cooperate with my plans. But entertain no notions that you can overpower me because you think me blind and helpless. I can move far quicker than you. It will only take a touch, a word. Try to take this medallion from me and he is dead. And from this moment on, if he tries to remove his, he is dead. Now keep back."

Cerberus reinforced Cass's command with another growl. Reluctantly, Gabrielle obeyed. The dog that had licked her hand only minutes ago looked ready to rip out her heart and the woman she had foolishly counted as friend appeared just as capable of it.

Torn between feelings of hurt and anger, she cried, "Why are you doing this? You said I had become like a sister to you."

"A selfish sister," Cass replied bitterly. "You have everything. Beauty, intelligence, a loving family, and you have your sight. You also possess a magnificent man who loves you, who will continue to love you after I've done with him. You can surely be generous enough to let me have him for one night."

"Even if I did agree to your insane scheme, Remy is not my slave to do with as I will. He will never lie with you, even if you threaten his life. He is not the sort of man to carelessly bed a woman and sire a child."

"I am aware of the captain's troublesome sense of honor. All you have to do is find a way to get him to visit me. You are a clever girl. You can think of something. Once he is with me, I will see to the rest." Cass's lip curled with scorn. "I can brew perfumes and aphrodisiacs powerful enough to overcome even his noble scruples. You get a man hard enough and very few of them have any. I could seduce the Pope himself if I wanted to."

"Then why didn't you just go and seduce Remy?" Gabrielle demanded. "Why bother to involve me?"

"Because I need to make sure he will be available the exact night I require him, not otherwise engaged. Besides it will mean more if he comes to me as a gift from you. It will strengthen the bonds of our friendship."

"If this is your idea of friendship, I would hate to be your enemy."

"Yes, you would," Cass replied with a chilling smile.

"You—you are worse than Catherine."

Cass shrugged. "I'll take that as a compliment. I am sorry our transaction has had to degenerate to such unpleasantness. After my night with your captain, I promise I will let you have my medallion. Trust me. No woman could have a more effective method of keeping her lover under control."

"Miri's cat was right about you. You—you are evil."

"No, I am a practical woman seeking to fulfill my destiny the best way I can. The same as you once were until you succumbed to love. You have had a great shock. I will give you a while to think about my proposition. The moon will have ripened to its fullness two nights from now. According to my chartings, my womb will have as well. Send me word before the sun sets today. Of course, we already both know what your answer must be."

＊＊＊

LONG AFTER CASS HAD GONE, GABRIELLE REMAINED IN THE PARLOR. The sun still poured through the windows, the birds in the garden chirping just as brightly, the leaves making a soothing shushing sound as a breeze rifled through the trees. But Gabrielle was numb to it all. She sagged down upon the settle and buried her face in her hands, the recent visit of Cassandra Lascelles assuming the proportions of a nightmare. A nightmare of Gabrielle's own making. If only she hadn't lied to Remy about the medallion. If she had told him the truth, he would have discarded it at once and be in no danger now.

She would have time enough later to castigate herself for her folly. All the self-blame in the world could not help Remy. She needed to clear her head, to find some way to thwart Cass. If only she could have prevented Cass from leaving the house with that cursed medallion still in her possession. Standing helplessly aside, letting Cass walk away with the power of life and death over Remy, had been one of the hardest things Gabrielle had ever done.

But what choice had she had? Cass had gripped the medallion tightly, ready to carry out her threat should Gabrielle make one wrong move. Cass's extraordinary senses had been reinforced by Finette's sharp eyes and the vigilance of her dog. Any attempt at outright force to retrieve the amulet posed far too great a risk to Remy.

Gabrielle needed to find some way to trick Cass into surrendering the medallion. But how? The deadline Cass had given her, terrible images of Remy clutching at his heart, flooded Gabrielle with panic, rendering her unable to think clearly. The beginnings of a headache throbbed behind her eyes. She massaged her temples just as the door to the parlor was thrown open. Wolf bounded into the room, only to draw up short, appearing mightily disconcerted by the sight of her.

"Your pardon, milady. I did not realize you were in here. I was just searching for Mademoiselle Miri's cat. The wretched beast has gone into hiding. Mademoiselle Miri thinks Necromancer is angry with her because she—she—. Well, never mind about that. It is of no importance. I am sorry to disturb you."

Wolf bowed and stumbled back, preparing to beat a swift retreat. Gabrielle acknowledged his intrusion with no more than a bleak nod. She had no idea what sort of picture she presented to the younger man. But his sharp green eyes honed in on her face and something that he saw there arrested his movement just shy of the door.

"Mon Dieu!" he exclaimed softly. "Are you all right, milady? You look as though you have seen the devil himself."

"Herself," Gabrielle whispered.

"Pardon?" Wolf looked bewildered.

"Actually it turns out the devil is a woman." Gabrielle made a weak effort to smile and was horrified to feel a lump rise in her throat. There were few people she had trusted in Paris, only one she had considered a friend, and that had been Cass. She was as distressed by her own lapse of judgment as she was by Cass's betrayal.

Wolf took a timid step closer. "You do not seem yourself, milady. Is there something I might do to help?"

"No, I—I thank you, Martin. But there is nothing that anyone can do. Please. Just—" She made a helpless gesture, indicating he should leave. Wolf hunkered down in front of her, capturing her hand and giving it an awkward pat.

"Nothing is ever that hopeless. Trust me, milady. I have been in many terrible scrapes myself over the years and you would be astonished by my ability to wriggle out of the worst situations. I have been living by my own wits ever since I was three. I am amazingly clever. You tell me what is wrong and I will fix it, non?"

The look on his face was beguiling, but Gabrielle shook her head.

"Is it this threat of the witch-hunters that worries you?" Wolf insisted. "Some danger to Mademoiselle Miri?"

"No," Gabrielle said. "What makes you ask that?"

A guilty look chased across Wolf's features. "No particular reason. If your distress is not on account of your sister, then who does it involve? The captain?"

The way Gabrielle started answered him far better than any words.

"Anything that threatens the captain concerns Martin Le Loup," Wolf said fiercely. "Tell me."

Gabrielle tried to draw her hand away, but Wolf tightened his grip. Gabrielle desperately felt a need to share her burden with someone, but she would have never thought of making Martin her confidant. He was little more than a boy in her eyes, and was terrified of anything to do with the supernatural or witchcraft. She could not see in the least what help he could offer. Yet there was something about Martin, a worldly wisdom that seemed to go far beyond his years, and he was the one person in the world who loved Remy as much as she did.

"Tell me," Wolf demanded again in a softer tone.

Gabrielle swallowed hard and reluctantly did so. As he listened, Wolf backed away from her, his face blanching with horror. He crossed himself once, twice, three times, muttering, "By all the saints and the holy mother of God, protect us. I believed that I knew all there was to know of the evils of witchcraft, but even I never—never dreamed it possible . . ." He faltered.

"Nor did I," Gabrielle said. "Perhaps now you regret that I told you."

"N-no, mademoiselle. You were right to confide in me." He prowled about the room, lapsing into an uncharacteristic silence. She had expected more exclamations of horror from him and furious invectives against her for her stupidity. She wished Wolf would turn on her and roundly curse her. She certainly deserved it.

Gabrielle endured his silent pacing for as long as she could before bursting out, "Well, have you nothing more to say? No angry reproaches? No telling me what a damned fool I've been to place Remy in such danger?"

Her sharp words roused Wolf from his grave reverie. "I am never so free with reproaches, mademoiselle. I make far too many mistakes of my own."

The lad's generous response to her folly nearly reduced Gabrielle to tears. She managed a wan smile. "I only hope Remy can be that forgiving. Of course, I have no choice now but to tell him."

"No!" Wolf came to an abrupt halt, waving his hands in a warning gesture. "That is exactly what you must not do. The captain is not a subtle man. He would want to go straight to this witch and confront her. He will either end up dead or—"

"Or in Cass's bed," Gabrielle said bleakly. "Another man would not mind so much being seduced and used in such a way, but—"

"The captain is a man of pride and honor and—"

"And he has suffered so much already. He needs no more—"

"Nightmares." They finished in unison, their eyes locking in silent understanding of the man who they both loved so well. For Gabrielle to let Cass suborn Remy's reason and have her way with him would be as bad as what Danton had done to her.

"But what am I going to do to save him?"

"Why, the solution is obvious, milady. You must use your own magic to counter-curse this terrible witch."

"Counter-curse her?"

"Oui. Conjure up some dark spell or—or brew up a poison that will send her off into horrible fits until her eyes roll back in her head and she foams at the mouth, screeching and clawing at herself in agony until she drops down dead."

"Martin!" Gabrielle cried, taken aback by his ferocity. Wolf tipped his chin to a pugnacious angle.

"Why not? This evil sorceress threatens our captain. She deserves to die."

"Perhaps she does, but I don't know how to brew poisons and—and even if I did—" Gabrielle floundered, seeking to explain to Wolf the tangle of her feelings toward Cassandra, the mingling of anger, horror, and pity. "Cass is a dangerous woman, but there is something truly pathetic about her as well. In some twisted way, I do think she regarded me as a friend, but she has known so little of love herself, she doesn't even understand why the demand she made of me is wrong."

Wolf rolled his eyes in skeptical fashion, but he conceded, "Oh, very well. Don't kill her then. Just brew up some draft that will send her off into a death-like sleep."

"I don't know how to do that either."

Wolf eyed her reproachfully. "*Ma foi!* What sort of witch are you?"

"A very inept one it would seem," Gabrielle replied forlornly.

Wolf vented a frustrated sigh, but he crossed over to her, resting his hand on her shoulder. "Ah, never mind, mademoiselle. You are one of the cleverest women in all the French court, and I have all the cunning of the wolf. Between the two of us, we will find some way to defeat this evil woman even without witchcraft."

Gabrielle covered Wolf's hand with her own, too comforted by his support to do more than nod. He gave her shoulder a light squeeze, then drew away saying briskly, "Now reflect, milady. What all do you know of this creature? Even a terrible sorceress must have some weakness. To begin with, she is blind. That gives us some advantage."

"Very little. Cass's other senses are uncannily acute, and she has that beastly dog and wretched maidservant to be eyes for her. She did have one great weakness, but—"

"Yes, what is it?" Wolf prompted eagerly when Gabrielle hesitated.

"Cass had a terrible fondness for strong drink, so much so that her wits often became dangerously befuddled." Gabrielle frowned as she recalled the story that Finette had sniggered and related to her. "According to her maid, when Cass becomes too inebriated, she can't even tell one man from another."

"That is it then. We must get her so drunk, she falls into a stupor. Then we can steal the amulet—"

"You are not listening. I said *had*. Cass has recently sworn off all strong spirits."

"Bah!" Wolf gave a contemptuous sniff. "I have known many men and women with this fondness for the bottle. It is not a demon so easily conquered. Just wave a glass of whiskey beneath this witch's nose and we will see how quickly she succumbs."

"Perhaps she would, but if I were to turn up on Cass's

doorstep now, seeking to ply her with strong drink, I think she would be a trifle suspicious," Gabrielle said wryly.

"That is why we must lure her out of her lair to—to some inn or other and I must—" Wolf paused, swallowing thickly. "I must be the one to trick the witch and steal the medallion away from her."

"No! I am grateful for your offer, Martin, but there is no way I will allow you to take such a risk."

"You have no choice. You said it yourself. She will be wary of you. Me, she does not even know."

Gabrielle vigorously shook her head, but he continued doggedly, "You will send the sorceress word that the captain agrees to the tryst, but does not wish to come to the cursed Maison d'Esprit. Tell her he has engaged a room at the Cheval Noir on the rue de Morte. I know people at that inn and it will be easy for me to—"

"Absolutely not," Gabrielle snapped. "You have no idea how dangerous it might be, for you as well as Remy. I cannot predict what Cass might do to the person who seeks to thwart her mad ambitions, but I promise you, it won't be pleasant."

"I don't care. Let her conjure up her darkest curse. I am no coward."

"Nor am I. I am the one responsible for this disaster. I will not permit a mere boy—"

"I am not a boy," Wolf growled.

"You are not a wise woman either."

"Apparently, neither are you," he snorted, giving his wild dark mane a toss. "Who is the one who was clever enough to smuggle the captain into the Louvre? Who is the one who saved his life on St. Bartholomew's Eve? And of the two of us, which one is the most skilled thief? Hah! Tell me that."

They squared off, close to shouting at each other. Gabrielle was the first to seek to recover her temper, locking her arms across her chest and flouncing to the opposite end of the room. Martin's jab about her lack of abilities as a wise woman had cut deep, the more so because Gabrielle realized he was right. But she was already ashamed enough of what her own deceit and folly had wrought. She was not about to step meekly aside and let Martin deal with Cass for her. After long moments of terse silence, Wolf slunk back to her side. His usual bluster was markedly absent as he tentatively touched her sleeve.

"I am sorry if I offended you, mademoiselle. How can I make you understand? Before I met the captain, I was no one. Nothing. A rogue, a cutpurse, the lowest scum of the streets. But for him, I would likely have had my neck stretched long before now."

"Martin, I fully understand your devotion to Remy—"

"Not just to Remy, but to you and—and Miri." A tide of color surged into the lad's cheeks and he hung his head. "No doubt you will think me a cheeky upstart, a bastard who has no name but what I have given myself." Wolf shuffled his feet. "But—but you all have become like my family, the family I never had."

"Oh, Martin." Gabrielle enveloped him in hug, which Wolf returned fiercely before easing her away from him.

"That is why you must let me be the one to deal with this witch. I beg you, mademoiselle." His dark eyes were so wistful, Gabrielle felt herself yielding despite her better judgment.

"But, er, are you not a trifle afraid of witches?" she asked.

He puffed out his chest, declaring, "You forget who I am, milady. Martin the Wolf fears no one. I would fight a dozen such, nay a hundred, nay a thousand—"

"All right. All right. I believe you," Gabrielle interrupted with a wry laugh before Wolf could work his way up to a million.

She still attempted to dissuade him, but Wolf countered every argument until he wore her down, simply because she could think of no other plan besides his that had any chance of success. It was with great reluctance that she left him to compose the message that would lure Cass into the trap. Gabrielle only prayed fervently that it was a witch who would be caught in it, not a Wolf.

Chapter Twenty-two

R AIN LASHED THE SIGN OF THE CHEVAL NOIR, THE SIGN CREAK-
ing in the wind. Lightning flared over the painted symbol of the
black horse rearing up, like a demon beast prepared to carry its
rider off to hell. Most of the patrons who frequented the Cheval
Noir looked as though they had already been there. The inn was
the haunt of a rough crowd, naval deserters, smugglers, thieves,
cutpurses, prostitutes.

And tonight one witch, Wolf thought grimly as he wended
his way through the taproom. The inn was more packed than
usual owing to the storm, the air reeking with the stench of unwashed bodies, damp clothing, and stale spirits. The din of
coarse voices and drunken laughter rivaled the lash of wind and
rain beating against the dirty windows.

Stripped to his shirtsleeves and an apron knotted round his
waist, Wolf blended with the other inn servants. But he stead-
fastly ignored the meaty fists beating on tables demanding more
wine. Balancing a tray, Wolf marched determinedly toward the

stairs leading to the chambers above, trying to ignore the unsteady beat of his heart. As his foot touched the first riser, a loud clap of thunder seemed to shake the inn to its foundations. Wolf started so badly, he nearly dropped the tray. One of the bottles of the inn's most potent brandy teetered, threatening to tip and shatter upon the stairs. Wolf caught it just in time.

Steadying the tray, he swore softly, knowing it was more than the fury of the storm that had his nerves stretched taut. It was the prospect of facing the woman waiting above stairs. Despite the bravado he'd maintained for Gabrielle, Wolf could no longer deny it, at least to himself. He was terrified of Cassandra Lascelles. Gabrielle hadn't needed to warn him of the dangers of crossing a witch, the vengeance Cass might take.

Wolf's own vivid imagination supplied the details, supplemented by every horrific story he'd ever heard in his childhood. Of curses capable of shriveling up one's man parts, rotting away one's flesh, or reducing one to complete madness. The only thing that kept Wolf steady to his course was the images of the people he had come to care about so deeply. His brave captain, Gabrielle, who had brought peace to Remy's troubled heart, but most of all Miri, with her shimmering moon-gold hair and unforgettable eyes.

By preying upon the captain, this cursed witch threatened the happiness of all of them and Miri already seemed sad enough. Wolf had no idea what had passed between her and that damned Aristide, but Miri had returned looking heartbroken, her golden aura dimmed. Martin hoped that once he got her far away from Paris, the devotion of her humble Wolf might be enough to make her forget that bastard of a witch-hunter.

But before that could happen, there was a witch to be dealt with. Wolf flung back his shoulders and tightened his grip on the tray as he marched upward. He would willingly lay down his life for Captain Remy and his lady. Ah, but for Miri, his beautiful lady of the moon, Wolf was prepared to hazard his very soul.

As Wolf reached the upper landing, his attention was caught

by two figures, a man and woman linked in an embrace so heated, they were in danger of toppling over the balustrade. Despite his own tension, Wolf's lips twitched as he realized that Pierre Tournelles was already hard at work. A comrade from the days when they had been two raggedy street urchins stealing bread from furious bakers, Pierre had grown into a tall, strapping young man.

Pierre eased Finette's dirty gown off her shoulder and elicited squeaks of pleasure as he rubbed her meager tit. The wench was all over Pierre, nearly scrambling up him like a scrawny cat in her excitement. Lost in her own bliss, the girl didn't see Pierre cringe in disgust or the disgruntled look he cast Wolf over her shoulder. No doubt Pierre would be demanding double for his services, but it would be worth every penny.

Slipping past unnoticed by Finette, Wolf made his way to the end of the corridor, another flare of lightning illuminating the last door. Fortifying himself with a deep breath, he rapped lightly on the wooden panel. His summons was greeted by a menacing bark, then a sultry voice demanded, "Who is it?"

Wolf darted a quick look back down the corridor, fearing the sounds would alert the maid, but Pierre had tossed the girl playfully over his shoulder and carted the giggling wench downstairs for a drink. Wolf turned the knob. Carefully balancing the tray with one hand, he eased into the room, softly closing the door behind him.

His action produced a fearsome growl from the dog. At least, he hoped it was the dog. Wolf froze with his back to the door, the bottle and glass on the tray rattling in his trembling hands. The room was all fire and shadow, the chamber illuminated by no more than the logs blazing on the hearth. He caught the silhouette of the hell-beast crouched but yards away, looking ready to go for his throat. He saw no sign of the witch, but her voice came from the deepest shadows pooling near the four-poster bed.

"Who is there?" she cried. "What do you want?"

"I—I—am no one, milady. Only er—ah Guillaume, your humble servant, bringing you the finest refreshments the Cheval Noir has to offer."

"I ordered nothing."

"Ah, no, but your maid thought—"

"Damned idiot girl," the witch muttered, then called out sharply, "Finette!"

"She has gone downstairs to look out for the arrival of your gentleman."

This information elicited a furious hiss. "Stupid wench. I told her to wait outside and keep her eyes open. Tell her that I command she return at once and take whatever you've brought away."

This fierce command was seconded by another savage bark from the great black dog. Wolf felt as though the entire success of his mission hung by a thread. He summoned up his most wheedling tone, "But I have cheese and bread, mistress, and a brandy so exquisite, you will think you are drinking the nectar of the gods. On such a foul night, surely you—"

"*Be gone.*" The woman's bark was worse than her dog's. The mastiff crept a step closer. Wolf could see the baleful gleam of its eyes, the glint of canine incisors, but he stubbornly stood his ground.

"Think of your gentleman, mistress. It truly is a foul night out there. He will surely welcome a drop of something. It is a shabby thing not to offer a lover one drink."

The silence that answered Wolf was so cold, he feared he'd gone too far. She finally said impatiently, "Very well. Set the blasted tray down, then be off with you."

Wolf took a tentative step forward only to find his way barred by the growling mastiff. "Um—your dog, milady? He is a magnificent beast to be sure, but I am so tough and sinewy, if he chomps into me, I would not want him to hurt his teeth."

A snort of something close to a laugh escaped the witch. "Cerberus. Come here!"

After one final warning woof, the dog backed off, trotting toward his mistress. Wolf blew out a deep breath, then carried the tray over to a small table positioned near the windows. The storm continued unabated, the wind howling and the rain pelting at the glass like the fingernails of a banshee seeking to claw her way inside. Despite the raging tempest, Wolf longed to crack open a window. A whiff of some strange cloying perfume tickled his nostrils, making him feel a trifle light-headed. He felt beads of sweat gather on his brow and mopped his forehead with the back of his hand.

The sooner he completed his mission and got the devil out of here, the better off he would be. As he unloaded the tray, the witch emerged from the shadows, her hand on her dog's collar. The beast guided her over to the fire. Her movements were graceful, only a certain caution in her steps betraying the fact that she was blind.

Out of the corner of his eye, Wolf took his first good measure of Cassandra Lascelles. She was younger and lovelier than he had expected. Was there no such thing as a witch that looked like an old hag anymore? Her carnelian silk dress displayed her willowy figure to advantage, the low-cut décolletage exposing a collarbone so delicate very little effort would have been required to snap it. But any illusions of her fragility vanished when she shook back her heavy mane of ebony hair, revealing a face that was strong and terrible in its seductive beauty. Her slender fingers fretted the chain fastened about her neck, twisting the medallion to and fro so that it gleamed in the firelight.

The sight of her playing with the deadly amulet caused Wolf's gut to tighten with apprehension. He longed to leap at her, wrench the cursed charm from her neck, but the risk to the captain would be far too great.

"Steady, Wolf. Patience," he admonished himself. He moved slowly, taking his time about arranging the plates and bottles upon the table.

The witch clicked her nails against the medallion, her foot

beating out a tattoo against the floor. "What the devil is taking you so long?"

"Nothing. I am nearly finished, milady." The rasp of her fingernails against the metal amulet set his teeth on edge until it dawned on him. The witch was as nervous as he was and why wouldn't she be? All her own mad ambitions were riding on the wind this night. Her tension might make her more ready to succumb to temptation.

And it also might make her more dangerous. Tigresses were far more likely to unsheathe their claws when they were nervous. He needed to handle Cassandra with great care, but first he had to get that damned dog out of the way. The mastiff had sunk onto his haunches, close by her skirts, but those wary canine eyes never shifted from Wolf. Wiping his sweat-slick palms on his apron, Wolf lifted the napkin from the one plate whose contents he had failed to mention to the witch.

A glistening cluster of purple grapes. Wolf eyed them dubiously. It looked like a rather pathetic offering to tempt such a great black brute. Wolf would have thought the hell-beast would far prefer an oozing slab of raw meat. Wolf only prayed that Gabrielle was right when she had advised him to come armed with fruit.

Wolf stripped off a handful of the grapes, and dropped them surreptitiously in a trail leading back toward the bed. To his astonishment, the mastiff perked up immediately. Tongue lolling, he snuffled his way to the nearest grape and pounced on it and then another, moving farther away from the witch.

Wolf feared the dog's greedy gulping noises would alert his mistress, but Cassandra didn't seem to notice. It was the sound of Wolf uncorking the brandy and sloshing some into the glass that caused her to stiffen.

"What is that? What's going on?" she demanded. "What are you doing?"

"Nothing, milady. 'Tis only that it is a foul night—"

"Stop saying that," she shrilled.

"And I couldn't help noticing how ill at ease you are," Wolf rushed on. "Such a shame for a beautiful woman like you to be kept waiting. No man in his right senses could bear to stay away from you for long. Your lover has likely been delayed by this terrible storm. In the meantime, can I not persuade you to try our fine brandy? Just a small sip to help you relax."

"No! I already told you I don't want any." She wrapped her fingers around the amulet in a white-knuckled grip.

The dog had chased one of the grapes around the side of the bed. Wolf trembled as he lifted the glass of brandy, but he steadied himself as he approached Cassandra. The scent of her strange perfume was much stronger up close, almost overpowering. Heady, sickly sweet, curling up his nostrils, weaving cobwebs over his mind. He found himself staring stupidly at her breasts, her nipples outlined beneath the taut ruby-red silk.

Wolf shook his head to dispel the image. Clearing his throat, he said, "If you please, milady, one swallow would do you no harm and this is too good a brandy to refuse. So mellow on the tongue, so smooth, it slides down your throat like fiery gold."

Wolf thrust the glass under her nose where she would be forced to smell it. Cass inhaled sharply, a look of naked longing chasing across her features.

"No! Take it away." She lashed out with her hand and smacked against the glass, splashing brandy over her sleeve.

"You damned clumsy fool!" She held up her hand, brandy dripping from her lace and her fingertips. "Fetch me a napkin. Hurry!"

"Yes, milady," Wolf mumbled. Retreating to the table, he felt like cursing himself. Now he'd done it, made her furious and the angry tone of her voice had brought her dog loping protectively back to her side.

Wolf rested his palms on the table, overcome by a wave of despair. All that boasting and bragging he'd done to Gabrielle about how cunning he was, convincing her she could trust him, place the captain's life in his hands. His clever plan to render the witch drunk was never going to work. He'd have done far better to have brought a pistol and shot her dead, the risk of being caught and hung for it be damned. Except that no matter what he said to Gabrielle about Cassandra deserving to die, Wolf knew he could never have murdered any woman in cold blood, not even a witch. Besides, he would likely have had to kill the dog, too, and he doubted Miri would ever forgive him for that.

So what the devil was he going to do? He'd better fetch her the napkin before she had her dog rip him apart for ruining her gown. Snatching up the cloth, Wolf spun around only to halt in his tracks. Cass trembled from head to toe, but not, he realized from fury. Sucking in her breath sharply, she held her brandy-stained fingers up to her face and sniffed.

The witch brought her fingers closer to her mouth. She hesitated for a moment, then her tongue flickered against the back of her hand, tasting, sucking, and savoring the droplets of brandy. A deep sigh shuddered through her. Wolf held his breath, waiting, sensing the battle the sorceress waged within herself, as titanic as the clash of elements raging outside.

Mumbling his apologies for spilling the drink, Wolf crept close enough to press the napkin into her hand. Cass moistened her lips.

"It—it is all right," she rasped. "As you said, it is a foul night. Perhaps you should pour me another drink. Just one . . ."

❦❦❦

GABRIELLE PACED BEFORE HER BEDCHAMBER WINDOWS, HER DRESS-ing gown rustling around her ankles. For most of the evening, she had flitted about the room like a moth trapped in a glass jar, frantically seeking some way out. She squinted in the direction of the stables behind the house, hoping to see the flicker of a lantern, marking Wolf's triumphant return. Despite the intermittent flashes of lightning that lit up the ground below, it was near impossible to see anything, the panes of glass darkened by night and the relentless deluge of rain.

The tempest seemed like an ill omen, a portent of disaster. Gabrielle tried to shake off such superstitious notions, but the storm outside was as nothing to the turmoil raging in her soul. How could she have ever let Wolf go alone to deal with Cassandra? Why had she ever agreed to his plan? She must have been mad.

But as Wolf had pointed out, she had had no other choice. Any attempt on Gabrielle's part to interfere would be enough to visit dire consequences upon Remy. Besides, if Wolf should fail, perhaps Gabrielle could still manage to wrench the medallion off of Remy in time. But she did not even want to think about that.

Wolf would not fail. He was cunning and resourceful. He had saved Remy's life under far worse circumstances on St. Bartholomew's Eve. Compared to that, Wolf's task tonight was a far simpler one. Distract the maid, bribe the dog, get Cass drunk, steal the amulet. What could possibly go wrong? Far too many things.

Gabrielle jumped at a loud clap of thunder. Pressing a hand to her racing heart, she stole a glance toward Remy to see if he had noticed. He sprawled on the bed, lying on his side, propped up by one elbow as he studied a map. Caught earlier by the first onslaught of rain, his soaked clothes were drying by the fire. Clad only in his drawers, Remy was absorbed in plotting the escape route for his king, as oblivious to the storm as he was to the danger that threatened him tonight. Danger in the form of the innocuous-looking amulet suspended around his neck.

He toyed absently with the chain as he pored over the map. Firelight played over the rippling muscle that sculpted his shoulders and arms, the powerful expanse of his scarred chest. Strands of damp hair straggled across his brow and he swept them back in an impatient gesture. Whenever Remy fully concentrated on anything, the dark brown of his eyes seemed to grow richer in intensity, his long lashes casting shadows on his rugged cheeks.

Staring at him, Gabrielle longed to hold him fast in her arms, to recapture the glorious abandoned lovemaking she had experienced when Remy had first roused her daunted sensuality. But of late when she gave herself to Remy, she was unable to relax, lose herself completely to his loving, that hateful medallion coming between them along with the shadow of her lies. How many times had she ached to make full confession of what she'd done, tell him the truth? No more intrigues, she had promised Remy and she had already broken her vow. It seemed only right to warn him of the danger. She and Wolf had debated the question over and over again.

"I know Remy will be furious when he finds out about Cass," she had said. *"But this is a question of his life. He must be consulted before we proceed with the plan and when everything is explained, surely he will see the prudence of—"*

"The captain? Prudent?" Wolf had interrupted her with a snort. *"Milady, are we talking about the same man who insisted upon jousting with Danton even when he well knew it was a plot to destroy him?"*

"Remy did that for me. He was avenging my honor."

"Oui and that is what always rules our captain, even to his own detriment. He would think it ignoble to ply a blind woman with drink, trap her with her own weakness, even if she is a witch. He will want to find some way to deal with her honorably and fairly, and you and I both know that is impossible. The captain is a hero, and that is how heroes behave. That is why we must tell him nothing. This is no task for a hero, but for someone who is a thief and a bit of a scoundrel." The lad's teeth had flashed in one of his wicked grins. *"A mission only suited to a wolf."*

Gabrielle had been forced to agree with him, but she was honest enough to admit that it was not just fear of Remy's heroics that kept her silent. It was a far more shameful sort of cowardice. She could well imagine Remy's rage, his sense of betrayal if he ever found out, not only the truth about the medallion, but that she had allowed Wolf to venture into danger in Remy's place. If anything happened to Wolf, no one would blame Gabrielle more harshly than she would blame herself. She had always been far too good at keeping secrets, but never had one pressed so heavily upon her heart.

She gave a guilty start when she realized Remy's steadfast gaze was fixed on her, a quizzical look on his face, despite that slow, sweet smile that he offered her. She was unable to return his smile. Averting her face, she fluttered toward the fire to check his wet clothing draped over the chair, lifting his damp shirt and putting it back again.

The bed creaked as Remy levered himself into a sitting position. "My love, you have checked my clothes at least a dozen times. I don't think rearranging them again will help them dry any faster."

"It—it might," she replied, smoothing out the shirtsleeve.

"Gabrielle." Remy's voice was low, but insistent enough that she could no longer avoid looking at him. The concern on his face combined with the simmering heat in his eyes was nearly her undoing. She actually felt her knees grow weak as he commanded huskily, "Come here."

She had never realized before that it was possible to be ruled by the mere sound of a man's voice. Remy's curled through her, whiskey warm, enough to melt her very bones. She wanted to fly across the room to him, cast herself into his arms. Only her guilt caused her to approach him with reluctant steps. As soon as she was within range, his sinewy arm stretched out, his warm strong hand enveloping hers.

He drew her down beside him on the bed, easing her onto her back before she could protest. Not that she really wanted to. As he braced himself above her, heat seemed to radiate from the hard planes of his bared chest. He whispered his lips across hers in a kiss that was so tender, coaxing her lips apart. His tongue brushed against hers, tentative, teasing at first, then deepening to a kiss that threatened to steal her senses, drive every thought out of her head except for him.

But the medallion pressed between them, like the cold tip of a dagger suspended over Remy's heart. She had to fight hard not to make a grab for the malignant charm. What if Cass had only been bluffing? What if she really couldn't sense if Remy was wearing the amulet or not? What if the link between the two medallions was not as strong at such a distance? Gabrielle was afraid to take the risk, the memory of the painful way Cass had demonstrated the amulet's power etched terribly in her mind.

Remy's mouth moved hungrily over hers, but as much as she ached to be swept away by his embrace, she couldn't. She felt too much like a Judas. Panting, she wrenched her lips from his, turning her head to one side. Remy remained braced above her. She could feel the weight of his gaze.

"What's the matter, dear heart?" he asked softly.

Oh, God. Gabrielle had to bite down upon her lip to suppress a groan. It was a fortunate thing Nicolas Remy had never pursued a career as a witch-hunter. The man would have never had to resort to torture. His kiss, that tender tone, those steadfast brown eyes would be enough to make any woman confess to anything.

Continuing to lie to him was the hardest thing Gabrielle had ever done.

"N-nothing," she faltered.

"Nothing?" He gave a wry chuckle. "You have never been what I would call a placid sort of woman, but this is a new degree of restlessness even for you. I've seen fillies about to be ridden into battle who were far less tense."

"It—it is the storm. Storms always make me edgy."

"Do they?" He drifted the back of his knuckles across her cheek. "I feared it might be my fault."

"Yours?"

"I realize I have not been the most attentive lover these past few days. I have been so absorbed with my plan for the escape, no doubt I have been boring you to distraction."

Gabrielle cast him an agonized glance. Remy was blaming himself for her tension, her restlessness? She cupped her hand against his cheek, felt the scrape of beard just beneath the surface of his skin. "Oh, Remy," she choked. "How can you even think such a thing? Of course I am deeply interested in your plan to rescue Navarre."

"Are you? Do you realize that earlier I told you I had engaged a party of elves to help me and you never batted an eyelash?"

Gabrielle felt a telltale flush mount into her cheeks. "Well, elves can—can be useful creatures when—when one can find them."

Remy laughed, but he continued to study her, his dark eyes full of unasked questions and a shadow of hurt. Gabrielle could not bear it. She squirmed out from beneath him, springing from the bed. She returned to continue her vigil at the window. Oh, where was Wolf? Would this terrible night never end?

Remy slowly sat up, watching Gabrielle's flight from him with a troubled heart. A flare of lightning illuminated her restive features, her slender fingers pressed to the windowpane. What was it she kept looking for out there in the storm? Obviously something she wasn't finding with him.

Men were supposed to be notorious for making their conquests and being ready to move on. Was it possible for a woman to tire of a man after only one night? Gabrielle had had other lovers, at least two of them far wealthier, more noble than he. Was she already having regrets, second thoughts about abandoning the ambitions she'd once had? Was that why she had displayed so little interest in his plans to spirit Navarre out of Paris, something she had never wanted?

Stop it, Remy told himself in disgust. These doubts of his were pathetic. She had said she had never loved any man but him. She had proved it the night they had made love. Daunted as she had been by Danton's brutal treatment, Gabrielle had opened herself to him, trusted him. Nor could Remy complain about the number of times she had made love to him since then. No woman could be more generous, more free with the delights of her body than Gabrielle. Then why was he plagued with the feeling that she was holding something back from him?

Was he being unreasonable to want not to just be in possession of her flesh, but every corner of her heart, her mind, and her soul as well? Would he always be tormented by the thought that there was some part of Gabrielle he'd never be able to touch? Rising from the bed, he strode toward her. When he wrapped his arms around her, she resisted but only for the fraction of a second.

She melted back against him and he nuzzled his lips at her temple, the silk-spun threads of her golden hair whispering along his jaw. The lush warmth of her body was soft and inviting beneath the silk of her dressing gown. And yet she still felt so far away from him, it nearly drove him mad.

He shouldn't keep harping at her like a prosecutor badgering a reluctant witness, but he couldn't seem to stop himself. He breathed a kiss against her ear.

"Gabrielle, are you positive nothing is troubling you?"

"No, it's just that—that—"

"Just what?" he prompted.

"I—I am worried about Martin. He hasn't come back yet, and for him to be out there alone with—with such a terrible storm."

"Wolf?" Remy's eyes widened in surprise. Of all the things that might be troubling Gabrielle, he wouldn't have expected that. "He's a canny lad and he knows this city better than either one of us. I am sure he is holed up at some inn, drinking wine with some of his old comrades and flirting with some pretty girl. I was rather relieved when he asked if he could go out this evening. The boy's been closer on my heels than a shadow of late. I can hardly go to the privy without him trailing after me."

Gabrielle ducked her head, her face disappearing behind her

curtain of hair. "We have both been afraid for you, Remy. You have more enemies than you even know."

"Doubtless I do. But I assure you I have been watching my back."

He turned her to face him, brushing back her hair. "Is that truly what has been troubling you? You have been fretting about my safety?"

She gave an unhappy nod.

He pinched her chin playfully, commanding in a mock stern voice. "Well, stop it. I can look out for myself. Besides, I have your amulet to protect me. As you so ferociously made me promise the other day, I haven't removed it again. Not even to bathe."

He lifted the medallion, dangling it teasingly before her eyes, hoping to coax a smile from her. She paled instead. "Yes, you always keep *your* promises."

Implying what? That she didn't?

He cradled her face between his hands. "Gabrielle, I realize we are still surrounded by intrigue and danger. From the Dark Queen, from witch-hunters, from every Catholic noble who has ever hated me. And yet, call me a fool, but I can't help feeling that as long as you and I remain true to each other, we will be all right.

"Are you *sure* there is nothing that you want to tell me?" He searched her face anxiously. Did he only imagine the stricken look in her eyes, the way her lips parted as though weighted down by some secret, hovering just on the tip of her tongue?

Remy held his breath, waiting.

"No. Nothing." She buried her face in his shoulder. Even as he strained her close, Remy was heartsick with the idea that she was lying. But he thrust the fear aside.

She had given him her word. That ought to be good enough. If he loved the woman, he had to trust her as she did him. Cradling the nape of her neck, he tipped her face up to his and their lips met in a fierce kiss. He untied her dressing gown, seeking all her warm curves while her hands roved feverishly over him, the heat building between them, his body hardening with need. If there was a quality of desperation to Gabrielle's kisses, to her touch, Remy chose to ignore it.

She clung to him, her breath a ragged plea as she whispered in his ear, "Oh, Remy, please. Make love to me. Make love to me as though there is no tomorrow."

❈❈❈

CASSANDRA LASCELLES HAD DISCARDED HER SHOES AND SPRAWLED on the bed, her gown riding up to expose shapely white ankles and calves. Wolf struggled to keep his eyes averted as he refilled Cass's glass. If he'd ever entertained any doubts about her being a sorceress, he'd be a firm believer by now. No normal woman could consume the amount of brandy that she had and remain conscious. She was nearly through her second bottle and although her speech was getting slurred, she showed no signs of passing out.

Of the two of them, he was the one the worse for wear. Deep patches of sweat stained his armpits from sheer tension and the stifling heat of the bedchamber. His hair straggled across his perspiring face, his mouth set in a harassed expression.

The fury of the storm had abated, settling into a dreary patter of rain. Tipping the bottle, Wolf shook out the last drops of brandy into the glass. The witch's dog curled up in front of the fire, watching him, the mastiff's eyes filled with a mournful reproach almost as if it knew what Wolf was doing to his mistress.

"Not my fault, friend," Wolf muttered. "Your lady left me no choice."

"Who're you talkin' to?" Cass called out. "Izzat the Scourge? Izzy here at last?"

"No, milady. I was only conversing with—with Cerberus."

A fit of mad giggling erupted from the region of the bed. "S-silly ass. M'dog can't talk."

Wolf carried the brandy over to the bed. Cass struggled into a sitting position, leaning on her elbows and dangling her toes over the side of the mattress. It was clear that the maneuver had cost her some effort. Wolf studied her through narrowed eyes, wondering if he dared fling her back on the mattress and hold a pillow over her face. Just long enough for her to pass out and—

No, at the first sign of her distress, that damn dog of hers would tear his head off. Wolf gritted his teeth in frustration, then said brightly, "Your brandy, milady."

Instead of scrambling eagerly to get it as she had done the first eight or nine glasses full, she just sat there, her long black hair spilling over her sullen features.

"Where's m'Scourge? Why izz'in he here yet? Don't think 'es comin'."

"Oh, no, milady, I am sure he has only been delayed."

"No." Cass managed to sit up straighter, shaking her head slowly from side to side as though it had become too heavy for her. "Man's not comin'. Be—betrayed me. Gabbyelle did too. Shouldna done that. I'm a wish—a witch, y'know. Warned her what would happen if she didn't be good frien' and share. Now her captain . . . goin' to pay."

Wolf's heart constricted with alarm as Cass groped for the medallion dangling around her neck. He caught hold of her wrist and thrust the glass of brandy into her hand instead.

"Here. Have another drink and forget about Captain Remy. If the man fails to show, he's completely unworthy. Neglecting a lovely lady like you. The cad."

Cass's mouth twisted as though vacillating between revenge and the drink in her hand. The brandy won out. She took a sip and said, "You—you think me lovey?"

"Undoubtedly. You are as beautiful as—as a summer night lit bright with stars."

"It's rainin'," Cass said morosely.

"Never where you are." Wolf settled himself beside her on the bed. He was grateful for the fact that her strange perfume was no longer as strong as it had been earlier. He was able to keep his head clear, his gaze focused on the medallion, dangling so tantalizingly near. He forced himself to bide his time.

Boldly stealing one arm around her waist, he urged her to drink up, saying, "Other men would line up in the streets just for the privilege of kissing the hem of your gown. You shouldn't give this captain another thought."

Cass downed the rest of the brandy in a great gulp. "Thash right. F—the bastard. Oh, I forgot. Thash what I wanted to do."

She erupted into another peal of laughter in which Wolf forced himself to join her. His gaze locked on the amulet. His fingers twitched. With one of those abrupt shifts of mood Wolf had found not uncommon in drunks, Cass stopped laughing, her eyes filling with tears. "Didn't want to f—him. Needed to. To have m'babe. M'little girl."

Wolf started to pat her hand, only to stay the gesture. Gabrielle had warned him.

"Take great care. Don't let her touch your palm. Cass can read hands like other wise women read eyes. She'll draw out all your secrets, all your thoughts."

Wolf caressed her sleeve instead. "The captain is not the only man in the world. You are a young woman. You have plenty of time to find someone to father your child."

"No." Cass sniffed. "Runnin' out of time. Has to be tonight."

Wolf scarcely heard her. Heart beating with trepidation, he carefully crooked his fingers around the chain suspending the medallion. One good yank, that's all it would take. Cass was drunk, but not that drunk. She must have felt the tug on the chain, for her hand lashed upward, colliding with his. She curled her thin fingers around his wrist like a manacle snapping closed. Moments before her features had appeared slack with drink, but now an odd sharp look crossed her face.

"What 'bout you?"

"What about me?" Wolf said, carefully trying to disengage himself.

"What're you like? Young? Vir-virile?"

The witch groped until her hand struck up against his chest, patting him down, pawing at him. When Wolf realized the direction her thoughts were taking, the hairs prickled along the back of his neck.

"Are you fer-ferocious? Ruthlesh? Handshome? You said somethin' before about being tough, sinewy?"

Wolf gulped, edging away from her. "I have a tendency to boast far too much."

Cass scooted after him, her fingers fumbling over the region of his stomach. "You feel hard 'nough to me to—to father a fierce babe."

"I'm more of a lone wolf. I'm not really the fatherly sort."

"Who cares 'bout that? As long as you're the f—ing sort."

Before he could stop her, her hand caught him between his legs. Wolf emitted a gasp, wondering if this witch was as good at reading bollocks as she was with palms. Not that there was any great mystery there. His shaft stirred in inevitable response.

Wolf shoved her hand away and leaped up from the bed. "Milady, the—the bottle is empty. I should go fetch you more brandy."

"Don't need more. Had 'nough." With a low groan, she flopped back on the bed. Rolling over, she crept up toward her pillow.

Please let her pass out now, Wolf prayed fervently, so I can take the damned amulet and get the devil out of here. Cass lolled on her back, her knees bent, her legs flopping apart in wanton fashion. "C'mere," she said, patting the mattress beside her.

Wolf would have sooner dived out the window, but he was afraid if he did not comply, her muddled thoughts would revert to Remy and to seeking revenge. Courage, Wolf, he admonished himself. It wasn't as though the woman could pounce and ravish him. Witch or no witch, she was drunk on her tail and a thin slip of a creature to boot. Grimacing, he settled himself beside her on the bed, keeping his own knees locked together lest her fingers come a-roving again.

Cass had something clutched in her hand, but it wasn't the amulet. It was a small vial of some sort she had retrieved from beneath the pillow. When she uncorked it, the heady essence of that perfume of hers leaked out like a genie escaping from a bottle.

The potent scent assaulted his nostrils. He got a good whiff before he could help himself, the perfume fogging his brain. Cass spattered droplets over her neck, practically bathing in the stuff. She even rubbed some over her lips. With a sensuous sigh, she splashed the rest into the valley between her breasts, working her fingers beneath the bodice of her gown. Wolf watched the rhythmic stroking as if mesmerized.

Beautiful breasts they must be, creamy with pert, thrusting nipples. A savage hunger coursed through Wolf. To tear her gown away, have himself a really good look and—and what the blazes was he thinking? He had started to raise himself up over her, only to recoil. It was that cursed perfume of hers. There was something damn strange about it, a siren's brew, wreaking havoc with his head. No, worse still. With other parts of his anatomy.

He tried to hold his breath, to focus on the medallion. Not on those round ripe breasts, not on Cass's parted moist red lips. She tossed the empty perfume vial to the floor, saying huskily, "Are you there, m' lone wolf? Are you ready?"

She felt for him, her hand coming to rest on his thigh. She was so pale, this witch, her touch should be like ice. But he could feel her fingers through the fabric of his breeches and they were hot, throbbing. Or was that the blood that rushed through his veins, causing his shaft to lengthen, harden to a degree that was painful?

Wolf's breathing quickened. Lured on by those teasing fingers, by her perfume, he braced himself above her again. Sweet Jesu. She was seducing him, this witch, his body aroused to an unbearable degree. Some dim corner of his mind struggled to resist.

No, remember what you are here for. The medallion. Think

of ice-cold showers of rain, think of nuns. Think . . . think of the
captain. Think of Miri.

But the last admonishment proved a grave mistake. Cass's
features blurred before his eyes and suddenly it was Miri he saw
sprawled beneath him, her moon-gold hair fanned across the pillow, her silvery eyes beckoning him like fairy lights. Wolf dipped
down, feverishly pressing his mouth to hers. As soon as their lips
touched, Miri's image vanished and he realized it was the witch
he was kissing, her tongue snaking into his mouth. But he didn't
give a damn. The honeyed poison of her lips destroyed what remained of his reason, leaving nothing but a raw, animal need.

With a fierce growl, he fell upon her, ripping away the bodice of her gown . . .

꙳꙳꙳

GABRIELLE LAY PERFECTLY STILL SO AS NOT TO DISTURB THE MAN
slumbering at her side. His skin still damp from the heated passion of their lovemaking, Remy slept with one arm draped possessively across her waist, a deep, untroubled sleep that Gabrielle
envied him.

Exhausted as she was, she dared not give way to it. Her eyes
felt strained from struggling to remain awake, keeping vigil over
Remy, doing the only thing she could to protect him. She cupped
her fingers around the medallion like a shield, praying that if
Cass did do her worst, the charm's evil power would somehow
be absorbed by her, not Remy.

The storm had ceased, even the rain, but Gabrielle found the
silence even more oppressive. What time was it? She could not
make out the hands of the clock perched atop the mantel without drawing away from Remy. But it surely had to be past midnight. If anything was going to happen, it must have done so by
now. Wolf must have succeeded.

Gabrielle's grasp tightened on the amulet. Surely she could
remove the hateful thing from around Remy's neck, but she hes-

itated, still not daring to take the risk. She had agreed to wait for Wolf's return. But why wasn't he back? He certainly should have been if all had gone well, if nothing had happened to him. Fear caused her to jump at the sound of a soft rap at her bedchamber door.

It was more of a light scratching, followed by a fierce whisper. "Mademoiselle?"

Gabrielle's heart gave such a mighty leap, it was almost painful. Remy stirred in his sleep as she drew away from him. She eased herself out of his embrace and off the bed. Remy frowned, muttered something, then sank back deep into his pillow. Gabrielle scrambled into her dressing gown and padded to the door, cracking it cautiously open. Wolf waited, his features shadowed by the wild mane of his dark hair.

He said nothing, merely held up Cass's medallion, dangling from the chain between his fingers. Gabrielle pressed her hand to her mouth to smother a sob of relief. Her first impulse was to snatch the cursed charm from Wolf, but the full nature of the thing's evil power was unknown to her. She took hold of it gingerly.

She whispered, "Oh, Martin, you—you did it. You are wonderful."

"Oui, mademoiselle," he replied.

She expected a flash of his insouciant grin, his usual swagger, but he appeared strangely subdued. Fearful of waking Remy, Gabrielle slipped out into the hall.

"Then all went smoothly? Cass? Is she—"

"Passed out cold, milady. It will likely be some time before she rouses herself tomorrow and realizes that the amulet is gone."

"And she never suspected? She had no idea who you were?"

"No," he rasped.

Gabrielle leaned back against the door, weak with relief. No doubt there would be the devil to pay when Cass awoke from her drunken stupor and discovered how she had been tricked. But if she had no idea who Martin was, she could hardly seek to wreak vengeance upon him. She no longer had any weapon to use against Remy or Gabrielle. By the time she recovered herself to plot new malice, all of them would be long gone.

The danger was over. Gabrielle's eyes blurred with grateful tears.

"Oh, Martin, how can I ever thank you? I owe everything to you." She took an impulsive step toward him, wanting to envelop him in a fierce hug.

"No, mademoiselle." Wolf warded her off, retreating deeper into the shadows. "No—no thanks are necessary. You should return to the captain, get rid of both those cursed charms. I must go to bed. I—I am very tired."

"Of course. It has been a long night for both of us." Gabrielle summoned up a tremulous smile. As eager as she was to pour out her gratitude, she longed to return to Remy. She would not feel truly safe until she had divested him of that evil charm. As she slipped back through her bedchamber door, she said, "We will talk more tomorrow and then you must tell me everything that happened."

Wolf merely gave a weary nod. Before Gabrielle disappeared back into her bedchamber, he thought he heard her whisper, "Bless you."

Was it possible? he wondered dully. To bless a man who was damned. Gabrielle and he would likely have their talk tomorrow, but he would never tell her all that had happened. There were some secrets about this night Wolf intended to carry to his grave.

He stumbled back down the stairs, making his way out of the vast silent house through a side door that led into the gardens. Since the captain had taken to sharing his lady's bed, Wolf had quartered himself with the groom above the stables.

He trudged without seeing along a path thick with mud, brushing up against leaves still damp with rain. The sky above had cleared, clouds lifting like a veil from the beautiful face of the night, the moon full and bright. But Wolf shivered, shrinking from its light. He rubbed his shoulder, his skin throbbing where the witch had bitten him in the heat of her passion, his back raw with the lacerations from her nails.

Far worse was the smell of her, the fleshy aroma of her skin, the stale sickly odor of her perfume. No matter how many times he bathed, he feared he'd never be rid of the stench of her. That perfume that had enticed him to madness now only filled him with an urge to be sick. His stomach heaved and he sank to his knees, retching into the bushes. The spasms went on and on until he was so spent, all he wanted to do was curl up and die, right there on the muddy path.

He scrubbed his hand across his lips. He could still taste the witch as well. It was enough to sicken him all over again. He took a deep gulp, managing to control himself this time. Wolf tried to rise to his feet, but didn't have the strength to do so.

Oh, God, what had he done? Was it but mere days ago he had declared his love for Miri, and he had already betrayed it? And not just with any other woman, but with a witch. Never mind any excuses that Cass had somehow seduced him. He should have resisted. He should have been stronger. Even if he ever should be so fortunate as to win Miri's heart, he was no longer worthy of her.

He had made love to a witch. He might even have fathered her devil child. He was glad and proud he had saved his captain, but Wolf knew he'd never be free of the consequences of this night. The mark of the witch was upon him, tainting him for all time. How could he ever presume to even touch the hand of someone as pure and innocent as Miri?

He lifted his head, scarcely daring to look up at the brilliant orb suspended in the sky, so far out of his reach, so unattainable. Tears streamed down Wolf's cheeks and he let out an anguished howl.

She was lost to him, his lovely lady of the moon. Lost forever.

LIKE AN ANIMAL GONE TO GROUND IN HER LAIR, CASSANDRA LAS-
celles huddled in her underground chamber. She had no idea if it
was day or night or even how much time had passed since that
fateful evening at the Cheval Noir. Her temples still throbbed as
she nursed the lingering effects of the worst hangover of her life.
But not nearly to the degree that she nursed the hatred in her
heart.

Cerberus pressed close to her, attempting to thrust his head
in her lap for perhaps about the hundredth time. Cass had lost
count. He pawed at her skirts and whined, clearly unable to understand his mistress's coldness to him.

Cass kneed him hard in the chest, driving him away from
her. "Go lay down."

The dog slunk away, whimpering. It was the height of folly
to vent her displeasure upon a dumb brute who had no idea what
he had done to offend her. But she had already exhausted herself
exorcising her wrath upon the only other object available. She
could hear where Finette crouched in the far corner of the room,
snuffling quietly as though terrified to remind Cass of her existence. And well she should be. Cass had nearly pulled the girl's
hair out by the roots, hanging onto Finette while she laid into her
with the fireplace poker.

The miracle was that Cass hadn't killed the stupid wench,
beaten her to death. She didn't know why she hadn't done so,
perhaps some small whisper of reason reminding her she still
needed Finette. Though little use the unreliable chit had proved
so far. She had failed Cass when she had needed her the most.
Just as Cerberus had failed her. But that didn't rankle so much as
Cass's realization that she had failed herself.

It was that thought that made her want to claw out her own
useless eyes. Bad enough she could not see, but what must she
do but dull her wits by diving back into the bottle, succumbing

to the old demon. And on the most important night of her life, when she was at last taking the first step toward her great destiny, the conception of the child she had dreamed of for so long.

How could she have been such a bloody weak fool? How could she have surrendered to temptation? Of course it wasn't as though she hadn't had help, she reflected bitterly. That waiter with his persuasive voice, so assiduous in his attentions, so honeyed with his compliments, wafting the brandy under her nose, all but pressing the glass to her lips. Cass had no idea who he was, but she was certain he was no servant of the Cheval Noir.

She had no trouble guessing who he served. Gabrielle Cheney. That selfish, conniving, double-dealing bitch. No doubt she and that wretched man were having a good laugh, congratulating themselves on how they'd gotten the better of the poor, weak-willed blind woman. Cass bit down on her lip so hard, she tasted blood. Well, she would show them how weak and helpless she was. But the edge of Cass's fury was dulled by despair that made her want to whimper like Finette and whine like her dog.

Gabrielle, how could you do this to me? Cass had had no desire to harm Nicolas Remy. She would have kept her word. She would have given Gabrielle the medallion. She had only needed Remy for one night. One miserable night.

Now instead of her child being sired by a man as magnificent as the Scourge, some nameless nobody had fathered her babe. Cass pressed her hand over the region of her womb, her uncanny sixth sense leaving her in no doubt that conception had occurred. That her child was growing there and she wanted to take steps to rid herself of it. But she couldn't. Nostradamus's prophecy had been quite clear. Last night had been her only chance. She would simply have to pour enough of her own steel and dark will into her daughter that it would never matter who her father was.

Oh, but he was going to pay for what he'd done. This cunning rogue, this lone wolf. Cass would figure out who he was, track him down if it took her the rest of her life. And when she did, he would beg her to die. Death would be a blessing compared to what awaited him. In the meantime, there was an object more worthy of her vengeance, one she didn't have to go searching for, her erstwhile friend, the woman she had offered everything, the use of her dark magic, her sisterly devotion.

Gabrielle deserved a fitting punishment for her treachery and fortunately Cass didn't have to wrack her brains very hard to think of one.

Chapter Twenty-three

THE WINDOWS OF THE TOWN HOUSE WERE LOCKED UP TIGHT, most of the servants gone, the costly furniture shrouded in ghostly covers. It was as though the house had been put to sleep, cast under a spell like a castle in a fairy tale, awaiting the arrival of the next princess to come seeking her dreams. Gabrielle's footsteps made a lonely echo as she took one final look around the place that had been her home for the past few years. No, never a home, she corrected herself. Only a glittering shell that had housed her equally empty ambitions.

She knew Remy still feared a part of her would miss all this, the gowns, the jewels, the elegant house, the excitement of the French court. But Gabrielle regretted nothing she was leaving behind. None of it seemed as real as the strong, silent man who had claimed her heart.

It was difficult to remember now how hard she had fought to possess this property, even to the point of severing all ties from Ariane. This house that had come at such a painful cost no longer meant a thing to Gabrielle. She supposed the crown would confiscate it. That was what usually happened to the possessions of those who displeased members of the royal household and there was no doubt that the Dark Queen was going to be mightily displeased.

Remy's plans for the rescue had finally fallen into place. The French king, after the excitement of the tourney, appeared to have grown restless and bored. He intended to remove the entire court to Blois. The royal train of courtiers, servants, horses, baggage, and wagons would be immense, the expedition's progress slow and cumbersome. There were many places en route where a diversion might be created, enabling Navarre to wheel his horse away from the guard and gallop off to lose himself in the French countryside.

The Dark Queen had not been herself of late, her usual watchful gaze vague and distracted. Perhaps because of the presence of the witch-hunters in Paris, although Simon Aristide had not made a single arrest as yet. By all reports, the man was doing nothing more than gathering evidence and taking statements.

Citizens of Paris who had been all agog for the sensation of witch trials and burnings were keenly disappointed. The dread Le Balafre was behaving more like some attorney's clerk than a real witch-hunter, they grumbled. Gabrielle, however, was left with the disagreeable impression of a cat, crouching for hours at a mouse hole, patiently waiting until it was secure of its prey. Simon's inactivity made her nervous and no doubt Le Balafre was having the same effect on Catherine, rendering the Dark Queen far less vigilant in the matter of Navarre.

Never would Remy find a more propitious moment for the rescue of his king. He had gone to complete the purchase of another pair of geldings, which would provide Remy and the king a swift change of horses. Gabrielle and Miri were to leave Paris by a separate route, meeting up with Remy, Wolf, and Navarre at a prearranged rendezvous. Gabrielle hated this part of the plan, the idea of being separated from Remy while he placed himself in such danger. But Remy had been adamant. He would bring off the rescue more easily if he knew Gabrielle and Miri were safely out of the way. For once Gabrielle had meekly acquiesced.

Perhaps because she was still feeling guilty over the deception she had practiced in the matter of the medallion. Remy had been puzzled when after making him promise to wear the amulet always, Gabrielle had been just as eager for him to be rid of it. But he'd handed it back to her with a laugh and kiss, muttering, *"Women."*

Gabrielle still had not found the courage to tell him the truth. She was ashamed to admit that a cowardly part of her hoped it would never be necessary. She had not heard a word from Cass since that terrible night. Perhaps Cass had come to her senses and abandoned her mad ambitions or she had accepted her defeat. But Gabrielle didn't believe that for a moment. It was just as well that they were leaving Paris today.

Taking one last look around her bedchamber, Gabrielle gathered up the final item she intended to take away with her, the small locked chest that harbored her most guilty secrets. The signet ring that the Dark Queen had given her and both of the medallions were nestled in the box's silk lining. Tucking the casket beneath her arm, Gabrielle wended her way downstairs. Her fellow conspirator awaited her in the lower hall. Gabrielle could not help perceiving the change that had come over Wolf since the night he had stolen the medallion from Cassandra.

He seemed older and far more subdued, as though the events of that night had left some indelible mark upon him. The thought troubled Gabrielle and she tried to tell herself she was only imagining things. They would all be on edge until the rescue of the king was complete. When all danger was past, when they were long gone from Paris, Wolf would be his jaunty self again.

"The carriage is ready, mademoiselle," he informed her as she descended the stairs. He frowned at the wooden chest she carried. "You are going to bring *that*?"

"It would hardly be safe to leave it behind," she said, and

Martin was forced to agree with her, although he looked deeply troubled. Disposal of the medallions had posed an unexpected problem. Gabrielle's first impulse had been to throw them out, but they were far too dangerous to be lightly discarded. Their mysterious power even made her nervous of attempting to melt them down.

"Perhaps we could weight the box with chains and sink it to the bottom of the Seine," Wolf suggested.

"I have thought of that, but I think it will be better done in the sea off the coast of Faire Isle."

Wolf scowled but nodded. "Mademoiselle, do you not find it odd that we have heard nothing more from her? That she returned to her cursed house and left us alone?"

There was no need for Gabrielle to ask whom he meant by *she*. Since that night, Gabrielle and Martin had never spoken Cass's name aloud, not even to each other.

Gabrielle sighed. "Yes, I am afraid I do find it odd. Although I suppose it is no stranger than witch-hunters who bide their time or the Dark Queen going into retirement." She smiled ruefully. "I fear you and I are unquiet sort of people, Martin. When we are granted a spate of calm, we don't seem able to appreciate our good fortune."

Martin smiled, a pale semblance of his old wolfish grin. "I mistrust calm, milady. I prefer storms. At least when the thunder roars and the lightning flashes, one has enough warning to seek shelter. We had best be out of here, the sooner the better."

He strode ahead to fling open the door for her and Gabrielle left the house without another look back. She followed him to the stableyard, where the coach was waiting, the team hitched in the traces. Bette and Miri were already settled inside.

Besides her maid, the only other servants that Gabrielle had retained were her coachman and two footmen to act as outriders. The stalwart young men sprang to attention, one of them hastening forward to relieve Gabrielle of her burden.

Wolf waved the man aside, taking charge of the wooden

chest as carefully as he would have handled a pistol with a hair trigger. He stowed the casket inside the coach, then turned to hand Gabrielle up the steps.

One of the footmen had just hastened forward to fling open the gate that led to the street when it was wrenched out of his grasp. Gabrielle stared in dismay at the riders who barred their coach's path, hard-faced men in helmets and tunics with stark white crosses. As in the old Greek tale of the deadly army sown from dragon's teeth, they seemed to have sprung up out of nowhere.

"*Nom de Dieu,* mademoiselle," Wolf muttered in her ear. "It appears our weather has taken a turn for the worse."

He started to draw his poniard. Gabrielle seized his wrist to stop him, staying the gesture with a warning shake of her head. There were six of Aristide's brutish witch-hunters blocking the way, far too many to fight, especially since neither Wolf nor her footmen possessed Remy's warlike skills.

Miri's pale face appeared at the coach window as the leader of the troop nudged his way forward. For her sister's sake, Gabrielle was relieved to see it was not that damned Aristide himself. With a show of calm that belied her pounding heart, Gabrielle stepped forward. She angled her face up to the leader of the group and said in accents of icy politeness. "Your pardon, monsieur. But we were on the verge of departing and you appear to be in our way."

The witch-hunter subjected her to a stone-like stare. He was an older man with deeply creased features, his gray shock of hair doing little to disguise the fact he was missing an ear. "Mistress Gabrielle Cheney?"

"And if I am?" Gabrielle replied with a haughty lift of her brows.

"Monsieur Le Balafre would like a word with you, mademoiselle."

"At any other time, I should be only too delighted, but today is most inconvenient. Tell monsieur I will be happy to wait upon him as soon as I return to Paris."

The witch-hunter grinned and spat, his men drawing their swords. "Monsieur Le Balafre would like to see you. *Now.*"

Wolf swore, making another attempt to surge forward. Gabrielle barely caught him in time. "No, don't."

"But mademoiselle, there is no way I will allow you to be taken anywhere by these—these devils."

"I will be all right." Gabrielle insisted, praying it was true. "Please, Martin. There is only one thing you can do for me. Go and find Remy."

⭐⭐⭐

THE SHADOWS LENGTHENED ACROSS THE TAPROOM. NO DOUBT THE Charters Inn had once been a cheerful, bustling place before witch-hunters had commandeered it. Now the fading light cast a gloom-ridden atmosphere over tables empty save for the one where Gabrielle sat waiting. Two of the witch-hunters mounted guard at the door while the rest milled about the yard. There seemed to be so many of them, Gabrielle regretted her decision to send Wolf to fetch Remy. But he had to be informed of the delay to their departure. She just prayed her Scourge would not be impelled to do anything rash.

She was in no immediate danger unless it was perishing from a mix of tension and boredom. She slumped back in her chair, resisting the urge to drum her nails upon the table. For someone who had been in such a blasted hurry to have her detained, Le Balafre was taking a long time to put in an appearance.

Gabrielle had no idea how long she had been left to cool her heels in this wretched taproom. Of course, she understood his tactics. This delay was nothing more than a pathetic attempt to demonstrate his importance and power. To increase her fear by suspense. It had worked for a while. Now Aristide was simply making her angry. Who the devil did he think he was? Just some upstart who had once been no more than one of Vachel Le Vis's flunkies, the perfidious wretch who had wounded Miri's heart.

Gabrielle could have endured this ordeal much better if she had been able to persuade Miri to remain behind with Bette and her cat. But she doubted that the entire squad of witch-hunters could have dragged Miri away from her. The leader of the troop had not even really tried, merely shrugging his beefy shoulders and remarking it was no skin off his hide if the girl wanted to tag along.

Miri sat across from Gabrielle looking composed, but very quiet and withdrawn. Gabrielle could only imagine the painful memories that must be racing through her sister's mind, of the time Miri herself had faced accusations of witchcraft, of the way Simon Aristide had betrayed her trust in him. Gabrielle reached out to her little sister, wanting to offer comfort. But it was Miri who squeezed her hand, saying bracingly, "Don't worry, Gabby. Everything is going to be fine. Truly. Simon is not like his old master, Le Vis. He does not resort to torture. He—he tries to be fair and reasonable."

Gabrielle was heartsick to see how hard Miri still struggled to believe in that wretched man, to find some trace of good in him. "Miri . . ."

But as though sensing what Gabrielle meant to say, she drew her hand away. "Simon will not hurt you. I won't let him," Miri added fiercely.

Gabrielle had no idea why Aristide had brought her here, what information he sought, what charges he might be prepared to level. But he was a witch-hunter and she knew reason would have nothing to do with it. The last thing she wanted was Miri trying to be her champion.

Before she could say anything more she was distracted by one of the inn's servants shuffling down the stairs. She would never have noticed him had he not stumbled on the last riser. His hand clutched the rail to halt his fall, his thin fingers far too white and well manicured for someone who had spent a life in menial servitude.

As he edged past their table, he ducked his head, his face lost behind a straggling fall of white hair. She studied him narrowly before experiencing a start of recognition.

Bartolomy Verducci.

At great pains to avoid Gabrielle's gaze, the man scurried off toward the kitchen. Despite the wig and his hunched gait, there was no mistaking Catherine's favorite hound. But what the devil was Verducci doing here? The answer was obvious. Spying for Catherine. It made perfect sense that the Dark Queen would keep apprised of the doings of her enemy. She had been far wiser than Gabrielle, who had let herself be caught off guard. Maybe Catherine was even plotting to have something slipped into Simon's wine.

Much as she deplored the Dark Queen's methods, that would not exactly break Gabrielle's heart, but she knew someone whose heart it would. Wrapped in her unhappy thoughts, Miri had not even noticed the old man, nor would she have recognized the possible danger to Simon if she had.

Gabrielle squirmed, wondering if she should say something. Before she could decide, the guards at the door snapped to attention, their gazes shifting to the gallery above them. How long Aristide had lurked there in the shadows, quietly watching her, Gabrielle could not have said. He descended the stairs with a slow, measured tread. Gabrielle rose to her feet, although she scarce knew why. Perhaps because to remain meekly seated gave far too much an advantage to such a man. Aristide certainly knew how to create a presence. She had to give the devil that much.

He was clad in unrelenting black from boots to doublet, his close-shaved head adding to the aura of menace. His eye patch mercifully concealed the worst of the damage to his scarred face. As he reached the foot of the stairs, his steely gaze flickered over Miri.

"What is she doing here? I only asked to see Mistress Gabrielle. Why did you fetch the other one?"

Gabrielle almost choked on her outrage. Her sister had broken her heart over this miserable wretch and he dared callously term her "the other one." Simon's men stammered over their excuses as Miri rose from her chair.

Gabrielle stole an arm about her waist, trying to hold her back. But Miri tugged free, moving to stand in front of Aristide where he would be obliged to look at her.

"Don't be angry with your men, Simon. I insisted on coming. You should have known I would."

"This has nothing to do with you."

"It has everything to do with me. Gabrielle is my sister."

"I have no quarrel with you, Miri. I warned you to stay out of my way."

"If your way threatens my family, you can hardly expect me to do so."

Miri tipped up her chin and they glared at each other. Even though they were separated by more than a yard, there was a strange suggestion of intimacy between them as well. A familiarity at odds with two people who hadn't seen each other in three years.

Gabrielle didn't know when or how, but her little sister had managed to steal away. Despite all of Gabrielle's warnings, she had risked going to see this dangerous bastard. But there would be time enough later to scold her little sister for her folly. At least Gabrielle hoped there would be.

Miri and Simon squared off, each with arms crossed. Gabrielle feared the man was on the verge of ordering his guards to evict Miri when he surprisingly relented.

"You may remain as long as you promise to sit over there and be quiet."

Miri made no such promise, but she stalked to the bench he indicated with such grace and dignity, Gabrielle swelled with a fierce pride in her little sister. Shaking back her pale shimmer of hair, Miri lowered herself gracefully, folding her hands calmly in her lap. As Simon stared at her, something almost warm flickered in his gaze. It was gone when he turned to face Gabrielle.

But for the past two years Gabrielle had held her own among the vipers at court and against all the wiles and malice of a Dark Queen. She was not about to be intimidated by one witch-hunter, even if he was possessed of the devil's own eye.

Before Aristide could say a word, Gabrielle drew herself up haughtily. "First, let me make one thing clear, monsieur. This doesn't look like any church or law court that I've ever seen." She swept her hand toward the room with a contemptuous gesture. "This is only the taproom of an inn."

"I am aware of that. I have eyes." He added dryly, "At least one."

"Nor do I see any justices or church prelates. Where is your authority to arrest me?"

"My authority comes from special appointment by the king, as you well know. And you are not under arrest. *Yet.*" he added.

"Then why am I here?"

"Merely to answer a few questions."

"Really?" Gabrielle replied with a skeptical lift of her brows. "That sounds a bit like the devil saying he only wants to borrow your soul for a while."

Simon's lips twitched with a hint of unexpected humor. "You relieve my mind, mademoiselle. I was afraid you might have already entirely deeded yours over."

When Gabrielle opened her mouth to retort, he held up one hand to stay her. "All I want to do is make a few inquiries. There is a distressing matter that has been brought to my attention. I am hoping you will be able to clear it up for me."

He held out a chair for her. "Please. Sit."

Gabrielle trusted neither his courtesy nor his reassurances, but it was not as though she had much choice. She lowered herself into the chair. Before Aristide could assume the seat opposite her, one of his men rushed into the room. He drew Aristide aside and whispered urgently in his ear. The guard seemed quite agitated, but whatever he imparted, Aristide remained unperturbed.

"Certainly," he replied. "Show him in."

The guard never had a chance to obey the order. There was a scuffling in the doorway and Gabrielle heard a familiar battle-roughened voice growl, "Get out of my way unless you want to part with your other ear."

Remy.

Gabrielle's heart leapt. She twisted in her chair just as he stormed into the room, closely followed by Wolf. Several witch-hunters rushed after them, drawing their weapons, but at a quick command from Simon, they all stood down. Remy paid no more heed to any of them than if they had been an annoying swarm of flies. He'd obviously ridden hard to get here, his face streaked with sweat, damp strands of dark gold hair spilling over his brow. His gaze darted about the room until he found Gabrielle, the barest hint of relief softening the hard set of his jaw.

"What the devil is going on here?" he demanded as he strode toward her. "Gabrielle, are you all right?"

It was all she could do not to leap up from her chair and cast herself into the strong comfort of Remy's arms. But she was far too proud to put on such a display of weakness in front of the witch-hunters. She stretched out one hand instead. "Yes, I—I am fine."

He took hold of her fingers in a hard clasp, his gaze raking over her as though he needed to ascertain that fact for himself. Wolf had dashed over to Miri, looking very much like he wanted to do the same. But he stopped just short of touching her, whirling to snarl at Simon. "You evil bastard. You keep your foul hands off her, do you hear?"

"I wasn't aware that I'd ever had my hands on her," Simon

replied with a look of contempt. He and Wolf locked eyes, an inexplicable amount of hostility seeming to radiate between the two young men.

Simon was the first to look away, turning toward Remy. "I assure you there is no need for all of this heroic exertion, Captain."

"Isn't there?" Remy took a belligerent step closer. "You know who I am?"

"From what you told my guard when you were demanding admittance, you are Mademoiselle Cheney's betrothed. My congratulations. You also happen to be Nicolas Remy, otherwise known as the Scourge. Our paths crossed once before on Faire Isle, although we never officially met."

"Perhaps because I was in the cellar of the house you tried to help burn down while you were safely on the outside."

A hint of color surged into Simon's face, a look in his eye that might have been shame, but he rallied, saying smoothly, "A regrettable incident and one best left in the past. I am more concerned with the present."

"So am I. I would like to know why you've arrested my betrothed."

Simon fetched a wearied sigh. "Not arrested. As I was explaining to Mademoiselle Cheney, I merely need to ask her a few questions."

"So ask her already," Remy snapped. "Then we are leaving."

"Of course. As long as Mistress Cheney's answers are satisfactory."

Answers regarding what? Gabrielle fretted. What the devil was he up to? If Aristide was not laying charges against her, what did he want from her? Testimony against some other daughter of the earth. He'd never get anything from her, especially if he was trying to gather evidence against Catherine. If the man was fool enough to take on the Dark Queen, he was entirely on his own.

Aristide commanded one of his mercenaries to fetch him a

leather portfolio while he invited Remy and Wolf to take a seat. Wolf arranged himself protectively beside Miri on the settle, but Remy brusquely declined the invitation. He positioned himself behind Gabrielle instead, resting his hand on her shoulder. She reached up to curl her fingers over his, grateful for the strong feel of him at her back. Aristide sat across from both of them, undoing the ribbon that bound the portfolio. He opened it, sifting through the documents. He perused one at great length, although Gabrielle was sure the witch-hunter knew by rote every line that was written there.

This was simply more delaying tactics, another attempt to increase her tension. Simon might not resort to hot irons, but he was a master at more subtle forms of torture. She felt on the verge of shrieking at him to get on with it when he finally looked up. When his question came at last, it was far worse than anything she had expected.

"Mademoiselle Cheney, you are perhaps acquainted with a woman named Cassandra Lascelles?"

Gabrielle's hand tightened convulsively on Remy's fingers. Wolf started, but Gabrielle did not even dare meet the young man's eyes. She stared at Aristide, trying to gauge just how much the witch-hunter might know. His mocking gaze told her nothing. She decided that outright denial might be less than wise. "Cassandra Lascelles, you say? The name sounds familiar. I—I— perhaps I have heard of her."

"She has definitely heard of you. By all reports, the young woman is blind and something of a recluse, but she sent her maidservant—" Aristide paused to consult his notes again. "One Finette Dupres, to lay some rather disturbing charges against you."

So this was to be Cass's revenge? Gabrielle could scarce believe it, not even of Cass, not after the way the woman had lost her mother and sisters. Cass might be furious with Gabrielle, but she had far more cause to hate witch-hunters.

Remy gave Gabrielle's shoulder a comforting squeeze as he

demanded, "Who the devil is this woman? What does she say Gabrielle has done?"

"Mistress Lascelles claims that mademoiselle has been employing evil magic, to ensnare men and keep them in her power." Simon directed an insolent smile at Remy. "You in particular, Captain."

"I admit I have long been charmed by Mademoiselle Cheney, but she has never had to resort to black magic. I assure you my love has been most freely given." The tenderness in Remy's voice, his complete faith in her made Gabrielle want to shrink down in her chair from guilt.

"How very romantic," Aristide sneered. "Then no doubt mademoiselle has an innocent explanation for certain objects that have been found in her possession."

"What objects?" Gabrielle asked hoarsely, although she already knew, even before Simon snapped his fingers, summoning one of his guards. The man strode forward and set her wooden chest down before Simon, the lock smashed open.

Her stomach took a sickened dive. She now understood the reason she had been kept waiting for so long. The bastard had been having her abandoned house and her carriage searched for evidence. Not that it would have taken that long to find. Not when she had been obliging enough to leave the casket in plain view on the carriage seat.

Wolf hitched in his breath, poised on the very edge of his seat. Gabrielle exchanged an apprehensive glance with him. She had been so grateful to have Remy with her, strong and supportive by her side. Now she wished him miles away, anywhere but here. She slid her fingers from his grasp, clutching her hands tightly together in her lap as Aristide cracked open the lid of the wooden chest.

He drew out the medallions and laid them on the table side by side.

"Mademoiselle Cheney, do these belong to you?" Aristide asked quietly.

"Well, I—I—" she stammered.

"They were found in this box, in your carriage," he added, making futile any attempts at denial.

Remy stepped from behind Gabrielle's chair. He picked up one of the amulets to inspect it, comparing one to the other. He appeared bewildered to find the two identical, but he shrugged, tossing them back on the table. "And so what if Mademoiselle Cheney does possess such medallions? They are harmless trinkets, nothing more."

"Not according to Mademoiselle Lascelles," Aristide said. "She claims these amulets are imbued with the most evil kind of sorcery. The witch who wears one of these can control the person who wears the other."

"That's ridiculous—" Remy began.

"By inflicting severe pain that can strike without warning, anywhere on the body, an arm, a leg, a shoulder. Apparently they even have the power to kill."

Remy fell silent. His hand crept involuntarily toward his shoulder, the first look of doubt clouding his eyes.

Unable to contain himself any longer, Wolf shot to his feet. "Mademoiselle Lascelles seems to be an expert on those evil medallions," he cried hotly. "And why shouldn't she be? She is the one who is the evil witch. She is the one who made those damned charms and gave one to Mistress Gabrielle for Capt—"

Wolf stopped abruptly. Whether it was Simon Aristide's smile of triumph, Miri's look of horror, or the way that Remy paled, it dawned on Martin he was making everything worse. He closed his mouth and slumped miserably back down in his seat.

A terrible silence ensued. Gabrielle could not bring herself to look at Remy. She was aware of how rigid he had gone. When he spoke, his voice was low, almost fierce.

"None of this is true. The medallion that I wore was fashioned by Gabrielle's sister, Ariane. The Lady of Faire Isle, a wise woman of great virtue. A healer who would never have anything to do with the dark arts. Tell him, Gabrielle."

Her throat had squeezed so tight she could not speak.

"Gabrielle? *Tell him.*"

She flinched when he seized hold of her chin, forcing her to meet his gaze. The look in his eyes was more than she could bear, hope warring with desperation, his need to believe in her battling with a stark sense of betrayal.

"Remy, I—I—" she faltered. It would have been so much easier to make Remy understand, to confess what she done if they had been alone. If Simon Aristide had not been dispassionately observing them as though they were mummers in some pageant, their most private emotions on display for his entertainment.

Remy searched her face. Whatever he saw caused him to release her. He recoiled a step as though he had taken a severe blow and still that bastard Aristide was not finished. He delved inside the box, pulling out the remaining object and set it carefully alongside the medallions.

"And what of this, Mademoiselle Cheney? It appears to be a signet ring of some sort emblazoned with the letter C. Did Cassandra Lascelles manufacture this, too?"

Gabrielle swallowed. "No, that—that was a gift from someone else."

"Both costly and exquisite, a very *regal* gift, one would almost say." Simon's mouth curved into a taunting smile. The witch-hunter likely knew full well who had given her that ring and she feared that Remy did too. If he looked as though he had been kicked in the gut earlier, he now appeared as though he had been dealt a mortal blow.

Aristide gathered up his notes, arranging the parchment into the leather portfolio. "Regrettably, I am going to have to detain you further, Mademoiselle Cheney. I fear there is enough evidence here to warrant a trial for witchcraft."

"Simon, no!" Miri cried.

He ignored her, directing his words only to Gabrielle. "Your trial will be held in, say . . . a fortnight's time. That should give you ample time to prepare a defense."

Gabrielle scarcely heeded him, her gaze fixed imploringly on Remy. But now it was he who could not bear to look at her. He was pale and silent, his gaze fixed numbly on the Dark Queen's ring and those damning medallions.

But Cass's evil charms no longer had the power to wound Remy, Gabrielle reflected. She was the one who had done that, with her own foolish lies.

⚔⚔⚔

ARISTIDE WAS MORE MERCIFUL THAN GABRIELLE WOULD HAVE EXpected. He had made no immediate move to have her clapped in arms or carted off to the prison where she would be held until her trial. The witch-hunter was even gracious enough to permit her a few moments alone with Remy in the inn's small private parlor, although making it clear that any attempt at escape was not to be considered.

Guards were posted outside both the parlor's doors and windows. Gabrielle had feared that Remy might make a rash attempt to free her then and there, despite the impossible odds. But the fight appeared to have been bled out of her Scourge to an alarming degree. He was like a man who had taken a hard fall and was unable to regain his wind. He had not even protested when Simon had demanded that he surrender his sword as a condition for this moment alone with Gabrielle.

Gabrielle paced before the parlor windows, rubbing her arms as she sought to contain her desperation, knowing that she had only a brief time to explain to Remy, to try to repair the damage her lies had done. But as she unraveled for him the whole tale of her dealings with Cass, her excuses sounded halting and lame even to her own ears.

Remy heard her out in grim silence, his arms locked across his chest. Whatever hurt she had inflicted upon him was now shelved behind an expression so stony, a stance so forbidding, Gabrielle's heart quailed. It was all she could do to finish.

". . . and—and this laying of charges against me must be Cass's idea of revenge. I should have anticipated her doing something to get back at me. But when Martin and I didn't hear anything more from her, I suppose we hoped that—that—"

"That you'd gotten away with everything?" Remy asked icily.

"Yes. I—I mean no."

Knowing Remy's temper, she braced herself for the blast. But instead of raging at her, he shook his head in disgust. "If you were going to meddle with the dark arts, at least you might have had the wit to get rid of the evidence or keep it better hidden."

"I didn't have enough time to decide what to do with the medallions. I thought after we were away from Paris, I could consult Renard—" She broke off as the full import of Remy's words struck her. "I wasn't *meddling* with the dark arts. I explained to you that I didn't know what the medallion really was. Surely you don't believe that—"

"I don't know what the devil to believe." Remy took an agitated turn about the room, raking his hand back through his hair. "I hear that my betrothed has been taken up by witch-hunters and nearly break my neck getting here to defend her innocence. Only I end up making a fool of myself because it is obvious I don't have a clue about what has really been going on. Then you feed me some incredible tale about owing a favor to this sorceress and that what she wanted was me for one night. To father her child, a little she-devil that will rise up one day and take over the world. And if I didn't comply, she was going to kill me, use the medallion to strike me dead."

"I know it sounds completely mad," Gabrielle faltered. "But is it easier for you to believe that I was the one who wanted to hurt you?"

Remy's hard gaze drilled into her. "You were the one who fastened that medallion around my neck and never gave me one word of warning about its origin. Instead you lied to me, told me that Ariane had fashioned it."

"Because I knew you'd never wear it otherwise. I thought I was protecting you."

"I don't need that kind of protection," Remy snapped. "How many times has Ariane warned you to stay clear of black magic? How many times have I told you the same thing? But you always go your own headstrong way. Never listen to anyone."

He stormed toward her and for one moment Gabrielle thought he was going to seize hold of her, shake her. She would almost have welcomed his fury. Anything but that disillusionment in his eyes, the way he drew back as though he could not endure the thought of touching her. He stalked over to the windows and stared out, sunlight pouring mercilessly over his hard-chiseled features that suddenly looked incredibly defeated.

"I thought that we had finally established some level of trust between us, no more lies, no more secrets. But clearly I expected too much. Deception comes as naturally to you as breathing."

Gabrielle knew that she deserved his reproof, but his words wounded her all the same. "Remy, that—that is not entirely fair."

"Isn't it? You appear to be once more neck deep in intrigue to me. And what is worse, you involved Wolf in all of this, laid him open to this Lascelles woman's vindictiveness. It is a wonder she didn't include him in the charges she laid at your door, have him arrested as well."

"Cass doesn't even know who Wolf is and I tried to dissuade him from getting involved, but he can be as stubborn as you are. He insisted upon taking the risk to help because he cares about you. As deeply as I do."

"All right. That clears up the little mystery of the medallions, I suppose. But what have you got to say about the other little trinket in that box? That ring. I know whose it is. I remember seeing it on the Dark Queen's finger the night of the masquerade. So don't even bother trying to deny it."

"I wasn't going to," Gabrielle replied sadly.

"So why do you have it? Why did she give it to you?"

"It was a token to seal a bargain between us. A pact she

forced upon me. I—I always meant to tell you about it, but I—I—"

"You forgot? It slipped your mind?" Remy asked so acidly that she flinched.

The unbelievable truth was that so much had happened during these past days, Gabrielle had nearly forgotten about Catherine's ring. Between the witch-hunters, dealing with Cass, and most of all, the miracle of rediscovering herself in Remy's arms, Gabrielle had had little thought to spare for the Dark Queen. But she realized she was going to be hard-pressed to convince Remy of that.

"What kind of pact?" he demanded.

Gabrielle rose and stole up behind him. He appeared rigid and unyielding, scarce inviting her touch. But she ached with the need to do so, to reestablish some intimacy, some connection between them before it was broken forever.

She rested her hand tentatively on his shoulder. He didn't brush her away, but she felt not the faintest tremor of response either. She said softly, "I was afraid Catherine would seek to harm you. She promised she would not if—if I seduced you and prevented you from rescuing Navarre."

"Congratulations. I would say that you succeeded admirably."

"Remy, I never intended to keep my bargain with her."

"Lied to her, too, did you? I daresay the Dark Queen understands the rules of all these games far better than I do."

Gabrielle pressed herself in front of him. "Remy, I realize I have made mistakes, dreadful ones, and I will do everything I can to make things right between us. But you can't for one minute imagine that I only made love to you on Catherine's command, that I was only trying to come between you and Navarre."

Remy seized hold of her wrists and thrust her away from him. "It doesn't really matter what I imagine, does it? The result is the same. You *have* come between me and my king."

"I—I don't know what you mean."

Remy shot her a look rife with frustration and anger. "Don't you? I made a pledge to my queen when she lay dying. That I would look out for her son. I failed him on St. Bartholomew's Eve. For three years, I have waited for the day I could redeem my honor by helping my king escape from his enemies. At long last, I find the opportunity and now I have to let it go because I am obliged to rescue you instead."

Gabrielle stumbled back from him, the realization striking her with as much force as though Remy had drawn back his fist and leveled her to the ground.

"My God. That is what you are really angry about, isn't it? Not that I lied to you, but that I am preventing you from fulfilling your—your precious duty."

"You don't understand. You never have. I lost nearly everything on St. Bartholomew's Eve. My sense of honor, my duty are all that is left to me."

It was all she could do to keep the tremor from her voice as she said, "I thought you had me."

"So did I. But apparently I was wrong. I may have possessed your body, Gabrielle, but I don't think I ever came close to touching your heart. I suspected something was amiss that night of the storm, that you were holding something back from me. I gave you every chance to tell me the truth, to the point where I felt guilty for pressing you." His mouth twisted in a bitter smile. "No, I told myself. If you love a woman, by God, you should trust her. What is love without trust? And the whole time, you looked me straight in the eyes and continued to lie to me. You even let me make love to you, pretended nothing was wrong."

Gabrielle supposed she could try to explain to him her hope that if she held him in her arms, that if Cass did her worst, the power might strike her down, not him. But what would be the use? Remy was clearly beyond listening to anything she had to say. Besides, it wasn't the medallion or even Catherine's ring that was driving them apart. It was because she had come between

Remy and his honor and nothing mattered to him as much, not even her.

Gathering up the pride that had long served her as a protective mantle, she said, "If you are troubled about Navarre, you needn't be. You may go rescue him with my blessing. You are under no obligation to me. I can look out for myself. I have managed to do so for a long time."

"We are betrothed, Gabrielle. Or is that something else that also slipped your mind? I trust I know where my first duty lies."

"I won't be any man's duty, Nicolas Remy. As for our betrothal, I entirely release you. We were always a rather hopeless match. The courtesan with no honor and the soldier with entirely too much."

She stalked away from him, head held high, putting the length of the room between them, her haughty demeanor belying the ache inside her, the hope that he'd come after her, seize her in his arms and roughly order her to stop talking like such a fool.

But he didn't. He said nothing until one of the guards flung open the door to announce that their time was up. Remy strode after the man, only pausing by Gabrielle long enough to mutter, "I'll be back for you. For once in your life, show some prudence and don't do anything to provoke that witch-hunter. You will be all right until I can get you out of here."

"Did you not hear anything I have said?" Gabrielle shot back. "I don't need your help. I don't *want* your help."

"I heard you perfectly, but one way or another, I will have you out of here, get you and Miri safely back to Faire Isle as I promised."

"And then?"

He didn't answer, but the hard set of his jaw as he followed the guard from the room said it all. Remy would once more ride out of Faire Isle to do his duty to his king. And this time he would not be coming back to her.

Chapter Twenty-four

SIMON GATHERED UP HIS PORTFOLIO AND THE BOX OF EVIDENCE, retreating upstairs to his inner sanctum with Miri hard at his heels. He didn't know why he didn't order his guards to stop her, why he had permitted her to be present at the inquiry at all. His old master Le Vis had been fond of flagellating himself with a stout whip to purify his flesh, an action Simon had always found quite mad. But he wondered if he didn't subject himself to torture in a far more subtle way. There was no reason why he had to face Miri, endure the sight of her reproachful eyes. But he made no protest as she followed him into his chamber, slamming the door behind him.

Ignoring the girl, he strode over to the huge wooden trunk at the foot of the bed and hunkered down. He took his time about locking away his notes and the evidence, all the while marshaling his forces for this scene with Miri. He knew it wasn't going to be pleasant. He only hoped she wouldn't cry. But when he chanced to look up at her, he was startled to find not a pleading maiden but a wrathful goddess. Miri towered over him, hands splayed on the gentle swell of her hips, her fey eyes darkened to the hue of a summer storm, her delicate chin tipped to a pugnacious angle.

"Simon, how—how could you? You told Gabrielle you only wanted to ask her a few questions. Then you would let her go."

Simon finished locking the trunk. He rose to his feet, dusting his hands. "I said if her answers were satisfactory. Which even you have to admit they weren't."

A ripple of uncertainty played across Miri's features. It was clear to Simon she had been stunned by the contents of that box and had known nothing of what her sister had been up to. But Miri was unwilling to concede that Gabrielle had done anything wrong.

"You never even gave Gabrielle a chance to properly explain," she said.

"She will have plenty of opportunity to defend herself at her trial. All things considered, I have been more than fair. I could have arrested that friend of yours, too."

"Martin?"

"Yes, *him*." Simon was annoyed to hear an edge creep into his voice. He didn't know what it was about Miri's companion that raised his hackles. Maybe it was the proprietary way the lad hovered over Miri. Maybe it was simply the boy's handsome, unblemished face. But jealousy was an unproductive emotion and one that Simon could ill afford.

"Monsieur Le Loup appears to have been heavily involved in your sister's activities," he went on. "The lad looks to me like gallows meat if I ever saw it."

"How strange," Miri retorted. "Martin says the same thing about you."

Simon accorded her riposte a taut smile. Stalking over to the hearth, he locked his hands behind his back, adopting a rigid stance to indicate plainly that all further debate on this matter would be useless. "I am sorry if your sister's arrest has distressed you. I promise you she will be treated decently while she awaits her trial. I will even arrange for you to visit her if you like. But that is all I have to say. So if you will excuse me, I have other affairs that require my attention."

Miri ignored his hint to be gone. She nibbled her nails, a habit of hers when she was thinking. "What if I were to say that the medallions and the ring belonged to me, not Gabrielle?"

"I would say you were a liar. A beautiful one, but a liar nonetheless."

She scowled at him. "You are a very strange witch-hunter, Simon Aristide. It is the usual practice of your sort to drag in as many women as possible, especially those of the same family. All tainted by blood, by mere association." Miri strode toward him, coming so close he could not help but catch her scent, something as sweet and wild as the kind of flowers that only thrived on windswept meadows.

"So why will you not arrest me?"

Because no matter what sort of witchcraft Miri might practice, Simon didn't think he could ever bring himself to raise a hand against her. He averted his gaze from her lovely upturned face, muttering, "I have made all the arrests that I intend to for today."

"And what about Cassandra Lascelles?" she demanded. "I would never wish to speak ill of another daughter of the earth. But she is your true witch. Why aren't you going after her?"

"Never fear. I will deal with Mademoiselle Lascelles eventually. Your sister is my first arrest. She certainly will not be my last."

"And exactly why is that? You have been gathering your evidence for days. I find it very strange that the first woman you decide to take action against is my sister."

Miri was far more perceptive than she had once been.

"Why, what is this? Suspicion from Miri Cheney?" he mocked. "You were always wont to be so trusting."

"I'm learning," she replied tersely. "Why were you so quick

to seize an excuse to arrest Gabrielle? What are you really after?"

Simon stalked over to the table and shuffled through some papers to buy himself time to consider. There was no reason to confide his true design to Miri, except for one. He might possibly be able to make use of her. But he didn't want to. A part of him quailed at the thought of wounding her trusting heart a second time. But he knew what was at stake, the suppression of an evil greater than he'd ever known. He struggled with his weakness for this strange girl with the fairy eyes before responding.

"All right. I concede that arresting Gabrielle was not my primary goal, that I hope she may be no more than a means to an end of a far greater menace."

"Menace? What menace?" Miri gaped at him. "Great heavens, Simon. If you are thinking of using Gabrielle in an attempt to trap the Dark Queen, you are quite mad."

"Not the Dark Queen. Though I admit that I am ambitious enough to hope that I may one day put an end to the Italian woman's reign of evil. But there is one who I have long regarded as her equal in darkness. Your brother-in-law, the Comte de Renard."

"Renard. But—but Simon—"

"If you are going to try to convince me I am mistaken in him, don't. The comte is a devil who should have been brought to justice a long time ago."

"Justice or vengeance?" Miri asked. Her clear gray eyes seemed to pierce Simon clean through. His hand crept instinctively toward his scar, but he caught himself in time, staying the gesture.

"I try to keep my own enmities and grudges out of my work. The comte is guilty of far greater offenses than splitting open my face. I have seen the extent of his evil influence over your family, watched him slaughter the brethren of my old order."

"He was protecting me and my sisters from your lunatic

Master Le Vis," Miri protested. "Or have you entirely forgotten that? Renard is a good and honest man—"

"Good and honest men don't pay out king's ransoms to acquire something as evil as the *Book of Shadows*."

Miri let out a wearied groan. "Simon, we've been through this before—"

"The *Book* exists, Miri. And your brother-in-law has it. I am so convinced of that, I am prepared to send an emissary to him. Offer him Gabrielle's freedom in exchange for him coming in alone and surrendering the book. You could help to facilitate this exchange."

"Me?" Miri stared at him as though he'd lost his mind.

"The comte might well strike down any of my men on sight before he had a chance to deliver my offer. But I know you have extraordinary means of keeping in touch. I once shot down one of those birds your kind bewitches to carry messages."

"Not bewitches, *trains*," Miri said indignantly. "Birds possess a remarkable degree of intelligence, much more than some men I have met."

Her pointed barb was not lost on Simon, but he chose to disregard it. "Send word to the comte. Tell him of my proposal."

But Miri was already shaking her head.

"You wished to do something to help your sister, did you not?"

Miri cast him a look of blistering reproach. "You expect me to save one sister by breaking the heart of another? Renard is Ariane's husband. She adores him."

Simon thought that Lady Ariane would be far better off without such an evil man. Break her heart to save her soul, but he knew he would never convince Miri of that. He toyed with his papers, stacking them in a neat pile. He abhorred falsehood and deception, but Simon had learned long ago that in order to defeat the devil, one was sometimes obliged to resort to his methods. He took great care not to meet Miri's eyes as he said, "My main concern is not destroying either Gabrielle or the comte, but getting my hands on that book, making sure it is burned."

"You expect me to believe that?"

"You have little choice. Not if you want to save your sister. I doubt Gabrielle will be able to mount an adequate defense at her trial."

"Because you have no intention that she should."

Simon avoided her accusing frown by striding over to the window. He had a clear view of the inn yard below, where Miri's friend Martin Le Loup prowled back and forth. A tame wolf, Simon thought scornfully. Waiting just as Miri had commanded him to do. Simon could never allow the girl to gain that kind of power over him. She followed him over to the window. All anger had drained from her eyes, leaving her face pinched with a deep sorrow.

"I have been warned against you, Simon. Time and again, by my family, by Martin, even my cat. My head tells me I would be wise to place no faith in you. And yet my heart keeps looking for something I glimpsed in you long ago. Someone more kind, gentle, and compassionate than the man I see before me today."

She breathed a deep sigh. "I don't believe for a moment my brother-in-law has this evil book you are seeking, but I will get word to him, tell him of your proposal. But know this, Simon Aristide. If you harm either Gabrielle or Renard, I will never be able to forgive you for it. You once told me I had never learned to hate. Please don't let my first lesson come from you."

Simon stared rigidly out the window. By the time he turned to acknowledge her words, she was gone, the sweetness of her scent lingering in the room. Even after all this time, Miri Cheney never failed to astonish him. She was by no means a fool and yet surrounded by a world steeped in evil and perfidy, she still looked only for the good, struggling to believe the best of everyone, even him.

"I have never learned to hate. Don't let my first lesson come from you."

Simon bowed his head in despair, knowing her plea was impossible for him to heed. He was a witch-hunter. She came from a family of witches.

He was doomed to become her teacher.

※※※

REMY THUNDERED THROUGH THE GATES OF THE CITY, GALLOPING into the countryside, unable to endure the noise, dirt, and bustle of Paris. Both his heart and his head in turmoil, he needed to get away to catch his breath, to think, to plan what to do next. The logic and legendary calm that had stood him in such good stead on the eve of so many battles had deserted him. He galloped down the dusty track, scarcely heeding where he was going. The sun blazed down upon him until he was drenched and his mount lathered in sweat. He felt obliged to draw rein for the sake of his horse, if not himself.

A small hamlet lay ahead comprising little more than a scattering of cottages, tidy gardens, a pond, and a copse of trees. Remy dismounted and walked the gelding until it had cooled down enough for him to tether the horse near the pond. He splashed the water over his own face before collapsing beneath a large elm, fighting to cling to his anger.

His fury was nearly spent and he regretted that, because he knew when his anger was gone all that would be left would be despair and bitterness. He could not remember feeling such an overwhelming sense of defeat since St. Bartholomew's Eve. It was hard to believe that only a few hours ago, he had been bristling with excitement and confidence, feeling so strong and sure of everything, on the verge of achieving all he had ever desired. Rescuing his king, redeeming his honor, embarking on a new life with the woman he loved far from all the peril and intrigue of Paris. Now the future that he'd dreamed of was in ashes. He had lost his opportunity to help Navarre escape and Gabrielle was in the hands of witch-hunters.

As furious as he'd been with her, it had damn near killed him to leave her a prisoner. Not that Gabrielle had been reduced to tears or shown any sign of fear as a normal woman would have. Oh, no, not Gabrielle Cheney. Even facing trial for witchcraft, the woman was still proud, stubborn, and defiant. Remy scarcely knew what he had wanted to do most, curse her or kiss her until she whimpered for mercy.

He had to remind himself that she was no longer his to do either with. She had ended their betrothal. He was tormented with doubts, the thought that maybe Gabrielle had never intended to marry him. Maybe she really had been intriguing with the Dark Queen all along to—

No, Remy could not believe that of her. Those moments Gabrielle had spent in his arms, the intimacies they had shared, she could not have faked that. Why not? an ugly voice whispered in his ear. She was a courtesan, after all. Remy dragged his hand over his jaw. He didn't know what to think. He wasn't sure of anything anymore.

"Damn it, Gabrielle," he railed inwardly. "Why couldn't you have just been honest with me? Why did you have to continue playing these games?"

Maybe she had been right to end it between them. Maybe they would both be better off. Then why did he feel like plunging headfirst into that pond and drowning himself? As he shook his head to dispel such thoughts, he became aware of the approach of a rider. Squinting into the sun, he discerned Wolf's familiar features.

The last thing he needed right now was to deal with any more of Martin's high drama. The lad had been pure spoiling for a fight, eager to take on the entire cadre of witch-hunters right then and there. He seemed to have taken a particular dislike to Aristide. It had been all Remy could do to drag the lad away from the Charters Inn before he got them all killed. When Remy had ridden away from the city, he had ordered Wolf to remain behind, entrusting him with one simple task. To look after Miri, make certain she got into that coach and departed for Faire Isle.

Wolf drew rein and slid down from the saddle. The lad had never learned to be adept at handling horses, but his mount was a sweet-tempered mare. She ambled docilely at Wolf's side as he led her toward Remy. Grimacing, Remy levered himself to his feet. Wolf's thick mane of hair tumbled more wildly about his sharp features than usual. He regarded Remy with a mingling of reproach and confusion.

"Captain—"

"What the devil are you doing here? I told you to look after Miri, not come trailing after me. Is she on her way back to Faire Isle?"

"She won't go, as I could have told you if you'd have given me half a chance. She won't leave Paris without her sister."

"Damn those Cheney women. Do none of them ever do as they are told?" He glowered at Wolf. "Or you either for that matter. You could have at least stayed with her. Her safety would be one less thing for me to worry about."

Wolf bristled with indignation. "Miri is back at her sister's town house. She is safe enough for the moment or I would never have left her. Not like you did your lady."

"What did you expect me to do? Cleave my way single-handed through a score of armed men? Risk Gabrielle and Miri being killed in the process?" Remy added bitterly, "Besides, Gabrielle is no longer my lady."

"What!" Heedless of his mount, Wolf dropped the mare's reins to seize Remy by the sleeve. While the horse meandered down to the pond, Wolf stared at Remy in dismay. "Mon Dieu, Captain. I know you are upset with mademoiselle and—and you have some reason to be. But will you cast off the woman you love simply because she made one small mistake?"

"I didn't cast her off. She is the one who ended our betrothal."

"And you just allowed her to do it?"

"You don't understand anything, boy. She—" Remy shook Martin off impatiently. "Never mind. This is none of your concern."

"I must make it my concern if you intend to abandon Mademoiselle Gabrielle."

"Damn it, Martin. I am not abandoning her. You should know me better than that." Remy felt his temper rise and he checked it even though he had cause enough to be angry with Wolf. He knew this disaster was more Gabrielle's doing, but Wolf's share in the deception cut him almost as deep.

"Look. Will you just get back on your horse and return to Miri? I will join you presently. I don't want to quarrel with you as well. I don't really blame you for anything that has happened."

Wolf stared at him, clearly thunderstruck. "You don't blame me for saving you from a witch's curse. How damned noble of you."

"It is not that I don't appreciate what you did," Remy replied tersely. "But you should never have taken such a risk. You should have come to me and warned me of what was going on and so should Gabrielle instead of involving you. She promised me no more secrets, no more intrigue."

A furious shade of red surged up Martin's neck, spreading against his cheeks. "Mademoiselle Gabrielle did nothing wrong. Neither did I. All right, so we felt obliged to tell you a few small lies. That is no great crime. It was for your own good."

"I have never known anything good to come out of lying. I wouldn't have been pleased to learn the truth about the medallion, but if I had been warned, I could have—"

"You think you could have handled that witch any better? It was not a task for a soldier, the great Scourge, but for a rogue and a thief, for someone who understands the need to bend the truth now and again. Someone like Martin Le Loup." Wolf struck his chest for dramatic emphasis. "You think you are the only one who can be the hero? I may not have your sense of honor, but I have as much courage and heart as you. Maybe more. *I* certainly would never give up on a woman like Mademoiselle Gabrielle so easily. She loves you—"

"But apparently not enough."

"Not enough?" Wolf advanced upon him with clenched fists. "Mon Dieu! If you say such a thing again, I—I will mill you down. Oh, I don't doubt you'll make complete hay out of me, but at least I'll have the satisfaction of trying to knock sense into you."

Remy retreated a step, but he growled warningly, "Martin—"

"No! You—you just shut up and listen." Wolf wagged his finger furiously in Remy's face. "You want to know why Mademoiselle Gabrielle was afraid to come to you and confess about the medallion? I will tell you why. It is because to you everything is so clear, right and wrong, black and white. Well, the rest of us poor mortals tend to stumble along through shades of gray. We can't always live up to your high standards."

Remy opened his mouth to hotly refute Wolf's words, only to be brought up short by a memory of something Gabrielle had once said to him, something disturbingly similar. *"You demand far too much from everyone, Remy."* Her blue eyes had gazed sorrowfully up at him. *"Including yourself."*

The memory was a disquieting one. Remy sought to thrust it stubbornly from his mind as Wolf raged at him. "You tell me how much you love Gabrielle Cheney, how she is this beautiful enchantress, so flawless, so far out of your reach. Then we come to Paris and you discover that she is not so perfect, that she has become the courtesan. It breaks your heart."

"I got past that—" Remy tried to interrupt.

"No, you haven't. You still want her to be perfect for you."

"All I want is for her to keep faith with me. To love me."

"And you think she does not?" Wolf rolled his eyes with exasperation. "Ever since you returned to Paris, she has done nothing but love you. You remember the night of the masquerade, when Mademoiselle Gabrielle risked everything, her own interests, her ambitions, even her very life to smuggle you in to see your king? That moment in the corridor when she whispered something in my ear?"

"Yes, I remember," Remy conceded.

"You know what she said to me, m'sieur? She said, '*You look out for him, faithful Wolf. You take care of our Captain.*' And that is all she has ever tried to do. Why did she acquire such an evil medallion and trick you into wearing it? Because she didn't know it was evil. Because she thought she was protecting you.

"Why did she take that ring from the Dark Queen, enter into a pact with a woman whose power she fears? Once again, she was trying to protect you! Mademoiselle Gabrielle would do anything, risk anything to keep you safe, even her own life."

"And I would be more than willing to risk my life for her, but—"

"Ah, but would you be willing to sacrifice your honor for her?" Wolf's sharp green eyes bore into him to an uncomfortable degree. "Because she would do that for you. Unless you believe she has no honor?"

"No, of course I don't think that."

"I am glad because then I really would have to hit you." Some of the fierceness faded from Wolf's voice. He went on more quietly. "I know you will save Mademoiselle Gabrielle because you are a hero and that is what heroes do. But then what? You will ride out of her life because she disappointed you, because she thwarted your effort to rescue your king. You will continue your quest to do your duty.

"But me, I think that kings, noble causes, even kingdoms all eventually fade to nothing. Only love endures and you were offered a chance at a love like few men ever know. The kind that I will never—" He broke off, a shadow clouding his eyes.

His throat worked as he continued, "If you let this love slip between your fingers, then it is clear to me that I have wasted my time these past three years. Because I have been following a great thundering idiot."

Wolf spun on his heel and stalked away. Remy half-expected him to fling himself on his horse and simply ride off. But the lad ground to a halt at the edge of the pond and stared moodily down into the water. The silence that descended seemed so heavy to Remy that it stilled even the whisper of the breeze through the grass, the whickering of the horses. He felt his face sting with heat, not of anger this time, but shame.

A shame so strong, it threatened to overpower him. It was as though Wolf had thrust a mirror up in front of his face and Remy didn't like the man he saw reflected there. A man who had become so consumed by his notions of honor and duty that they had blinded him to all else, turned him hard and uncompromising.

He had been outraged when Gabrielle had accused him of being angrier that she had frustrated his plan to rescue Navarre than he had been concerned with her deception. Remy was mortified to realize that she was right.

Ever since St. Bartholomew's Eve, he had carried with him this sense of failure, this burning need to redeem himself. As though he had come to believe in his own legend, the great Scourge. As though somehow he alone should have been able to turn the tide of history that night. Gabrielle said he had too much honor, but that wasn't his true sin. What he suffered from was too much pride.

Remy tortured himself, recalling those few precious moments Aristide had accorded him alone with Gabrielle, how he'd wasted them on anger and recriminations when he should have held her in his arms, reassured her. She'd acted so defiant, it had further infuriated him, but he should have seen her behavior for what it was, an act. He ought to know Gabrielle at least well enough for that. How often had he watched her employ that stubborn bravado to cover up her hurt and fear?

He had been far too busy brooding over his own wrongs to realize how much she had needed him to tell her he forgave her, that everything was going to be all right. If those ended up being the last moments they ever shared—

No, he would not let himself think that, not even for a moment. He would save her or die trying and perhaps somehow he would find a way to mend matters between them. But there was someone else with whom he needed to make amends. Martin waited by the edge of the pond, scowling as he attempted to skip rocks along the surface. All he was doing was creating great splashes that threatened to spook the horses.

The lad tensed at Remy's approach. He threw Remy a furtive look and Remy could tell the lad was a little daunted himself by his recent outburst. But he threw his shoulders back and announced gruffly, "I realize I have addressed you with great impudence, Captain. Moreover, I did lie and practice a great deception upon you regarding the affair of the medallion. So if you wish to dismiss me from your service or—or even if you want to call me out, demand satisfaction, I—I quite understand."

After such a grim morning, Remy was surprised to discover he had the least inclination to smile. For the sake of Wolf's dignity, he managed to maintain a grave demeanor. "Actually I don't want either of those things." Remy extended his hand. "All I want is to ask your pardon for being—er, how did you put it—a great thundering idiot."

Wolf scratched his nose, looking somewhat abashed. But he clasped Remy's hand in a hearty shake. "Thank you, Captain, but I don't think it is only my pardon you should be asking."

"I know that. I fear I have always behaved like a fool where Gabrielle is concerned. She is the most damned exasperating woman I have ever known. Also the most extraordinary. That is part of my problem. I am haunted by the fear of losing her, that I will never be able to hold her forever. Perhaps that is why when she ended our betrothal, it just seemed easier to let her go."

"Ah, but you have never been a man to take the easy road,

Captain. I am confident you will find a way to get your lady back into your arms."

"I have to get her away from those witch-hunters first," Remy said. He fetched a grim sigh. "I also must send word to Navarre, let him know what has happened. Pity that he is no more than a shadow king. I might have been able to call upon his influence to gain Gabrielle's release."

Martin shifted with some impatience at the mention of Navarre, but the lad's gaze was not entirely unsympathetic as he said, "Captain, I know how your king's captivity chafes you, that you are bitterly disappointed that you have not been able to redeem your pledge and secure his freedom. But from what I have observed of this Henry of Navarre, I think that when he truly wishes to escape from the French court, he will do it, with or without your help. He pretends to be so indolent, so careless, but this is a man who knows how to survive. A truly clever and cunning fellow."

"A fellow much like you, my faithful Wolf."

Wolf shrugged, tried to look modest, but failed utterly.

Remy gave him a fond cuff on the shoulder. "Incidentally, speaking of your cleverness, I have not thanked you for saving my life again. Though I have never been sure why you did so the first time."

Wolf's teeth flashed in his old familiar grin. "It was because of the boots."

"But you could have had those. All you had to do was let me die."

Wolf cocked his head, studying Remy curiously. "You don't really remember, do you, monsieur? I was hiding in the alley while you fought so bravely against your enemies until you were finally overwhelmed. It was only when the soldiers were gone, when I thought you were dead, that I crept out of the shadows like the street rat that I was to rob you.

"But as I was working off your boots, your eyes opened. Instead of cursing me as you should have done, you just stared at me. You were in pain, your life spilling out of you and yet you noticed I had no shoes and you said—you whispered—'Take the boots, lad. You have more use for them than I do.' And you told me where your money was hidden in your belt as well."

Wolf's eyes waxed overbright. "Never in my life had anyone offered me anything. It was then I said to myself, Martin Le Loup, so this is what a hero is. Not just the courage, but this greatness of heart."

He shrugged. "So that is why I sought to save you and why I have been willing to follow you ever since. Even to the depths of hell."

The lad's words moved Remy more than he could show. He gave Wolf's shoulder a hard squeeze. "Thank you, lad. Unfortunately, hell is where I have to go."

"M'sieur?" Wolf gave him a puzzled frown.

"Believe it or not, I didn't ride all the way out here just to stare at the clouds. I have been thinking. I have two weeks before Gabrielle's trial. I may well have to resort to force to free her, but I would like to at least make the attempt to establish her innocence."

"How could you possibly do that?"

"By finding the real culprit. By dragging Cassandra Lascelles and her maid out of hiding. By forcing them to confess the truth."

Wolf paled at the suggestion. "That would never work, Captain. You have no idea how dangerous that woman is and besides, do you think that Aristide bastard would recognize the truth even if he heard it, if he would even listen?"

Remy supposed the Wolf was right and yet he hardly knew how to explain it to the lad. That something about Simon Aristide had struck an unexpected chord with Remy. That man didn't seem to be acting out of malice or mindless superstition. He was motivated by a belief in his cause, by a sense of duty that Remy understood far too well.

"Aristide doesn't strike me as being entirely beyond the pale of reason," Remy said. "He seems to be a bit above the common cut of witch-hunters."

Wolf snorted. "No, he isn't. Let's just kill him. I'll do it," he added cheerfully.

"Not until I make a stab at convincing him to release Gabrielle."

When Wolf started to register a stronger protest, Remy cut him off. "I have to try, Martin. I have lived as a fugitive, an exile from my country. I know what it is like. There is little enough I can give Gabrielle, but I can at least attempt to spare her such a fate. Living out the rest of her days under the shadow of an accusation of sorcery, constantly looking for witch-hunters over her shoulder."

"Oh, very well, monsieur." Wolf sighed, but he looked deeply troubled.

Remy had an idea what was bothering the lad and he said as delicately as he could, "Er—Martin, I know how you feel about the Maison d'Esprit and about witches in general. Nor do I want to expose you to the possibility of this Lascelles creature's wrath. There is no need for you to accompany me."

Remy braced himself for vehement protestations from Wolf, fierce indignation against anything that he would perceive as an aspersion on his courage. To his surprise, Wolf merely essayed a low mirthless laugh.

"No, Captain, I will go with you. I am not afraid of that woman."

At least not anymore, Wolf reflected bitterly. He had already experienced the worst of Cassandra Lascelles. She had tainted him, stolen away forever his dreams of loving Miri. Wolf did not see what more the witch could possibly do to him.

Chapter Twenty-five

GABRIELLE SHIFTED ON HER NARROW BED, WATCHING THE MOON conjure patterns of light across the ceiling. She had long ago surrendered any attempt at sleep, although she was well nigh exhausted. How many nights had it been since she had last slumbered peacefully in her own bed, cradled in Remy's arms? Six? Seven?

She was beginning to lose track of the empty hours that left her too much time to think, to worry, and to regret. Otherwise she had to admit she had little cause for complaint about her captivity. Aristide had kept his word thus far. She was being decently treated, well fed, provided with hot water for bathing.

She had never been moved to the Bastille or any other grim, dank prison as she had feared. She was being kept confined in one of the more modest rooms at the Charters Inn. The attic chamber had been stripped down to its bare elements, little more than the bed, a table, and a candle remaining. Nothing that would furnish an adequate weapon for escape unless she was rash enough to try braining her guard with the chamber pot.

Of course, she understood why she was being held at the inn. She was more Aristide's hostage than she was his prisoner. During the one brief visit Aristide had allowed her younger sister, Miri had explained to her what the witch-hunter was after.

Gabrielle was not as quick as Miri to dismiss the possible existence of a *Book of Shadows.* What she doubted was that Renard had it, but she feared he would still come, make some rash attempt to save her life. Despite their constant bickering, she loved her great ogre of a brother-in-law and hated the thought of being used to lure him into a trap. Miri might desperately want to believe that Aristide only wanted to destroy the book, that he would not harm Renard. But Gabrielle didn't trust the bastard in the least.

If it was Aristide's plan to kill Renard, he needed to be stopped. The question that plagued Gabrielle's every waking moment returned to torment her again. Oh, where was Remy? What was he doing? Miri had not been able to give her any satisfactory answers, only that Remy and Wolf were working on some plan to free Gabrielle. But Remy had not been anywhere near the Charters Inn since their terrible quarrel.

Was he still angry with her, still unable to forgive her? What if he had taken Gabrielle at her word when she'd proudly insisted she didn't need his help? What if he had left Paris, simply carried on with his quest to rescue Navarre? No. Remy would never do that. The infuriatingly stubborn man considered it his duty to save her. But after that, once he had transported her safely back to Faire Isle . . .

Gabrielle could not even bear to think about that, what it would be like to spend the rest of her life without him. She had to take things one moment at a time, concentrate on the difficulties of her present situation, or she would run mad. She wrestled with the covers, seeking a more comfortable position, only to flop on her back with a gusty sigh. What she truly loathed most of all was her own helplessness. She was the one who had gotten herself into this situation. She ought to find a way to get herself out of it without putting either Renard or Remy at risk.

Witch-hunters were always arresting and persecuting women for witchcraft, exhorting them to repent. Gabrielle wondered wryly how many of these hapless prisoners were just like her and spent their captivity wishing they had actually learned some dark magic in order to save themselves.

She fretted the ends of the sheet between her fingers, noticing how thin the fabric was, how easy it would be to tear into strips. She'd considered the possibility of forming a rope ladder, forcing open one of the chamber's narrow windows. But her room was on the inn's uppermost floor. It was a long way to the ground. If she didn't end up breaking her neck, there were still Simon's men to contend with.

She contemplated getting Bartolomy Verducci to help her either by bribing or threatening to expose the man. When she had been served one of her meals, Gabrielle had noticed Catherine's spy lurking down the corridor of the inn. So why was the Dark Queen's hound still hanging about? If Catherine had sent Verducci to dispose of Simon Aristide, the man had already had plenty of opportunity to do it by now. Obviously Catherine had some other end in view.

It was maddening to sense all the plots swirling about her and to know nothing, be able to do nothing. Gabrielle feared that Remy was right when he'd accused her of having a penchant for intrigue. Long accustomed to being a player in the game, it was wretched to be reduced to the role of insignificant pawn. Was that how she'd made Remy feel when she concealed the truth from him about the medallion and the Dark Queen's ring? When she got out of here, somehow she would make Remy understand how sorry she was, how much she loved him. She would find a way to win him back. *If* she ever got out of here—

A sharp rap on her bedchamber door startled Gabrielle into sitting bolt upright.

"Mademoiselle?"

Gabrielle recognized the gruff voice of her chief jailer, Braxton, the older man with the unprepossessing countenance and missing ear. Per Simon's instructions, the man paid Gabrielle the grudging courtesy of alerting her before he opened her door. Not that he always waited for her response. Gabrielle heard the grate of the key in the lock. Although she was fully clothed, she dragged the coverlet up to her chin.

Shoving the door open, Braxton held up a candle, the taper casting a flickering light over the dismal room and his surly features. "You need to get up, mistress. Monsieur Le Balafre wants a word with you below stairs and—"

"He wants it *now*," Gabrielle finished for him in a mimicking tone that caused the man to scowl at her. But her taunt was only a bluff, a way to conceal how her heart had begun to race. She couldn't imagine any good reason for a prisoner being rousted out of bed in the middle of the night by a witch-hunter. Perhaps Simon Aristide was finally about to drop his polite mask.

So what was it to be? An effort to torture a confession from her or intentions of a more alarming nature? No, if Aristide was capable of feeling anything as human as desire, Gabrielle would not be the one to inspire it. She'd seen the way the bastard looked at her younger sister and it made her want to scratch out his remaining good eye.

Gabrielle bartered for time as she struggled into her shoes and made a desperate attempt to finger comb the snarls from her hair. Her elegant manner had long been her armor and she felt that hers had grown sadly tarnished. She grimaced to think what she must look like in her crumpled gown, her eyes raw from lack of sleep.

But she forced herself to stand tall, her head held high as Braxton prodded her from the room. He lit her way down two flights of stairs to the taproom. The inn looked eerie and empty, only a few branches of candles holding the night at bay. Aristide waited in the darkness near the windows. The man had an annoying habit of doing that, keeping himself well out of the light while his victim felt mercilessly exposed. His black garb blended with the shadows, his towering height, shaved head, and eye patch giving him a sinister edge, a figure of nightmare.

What Miri could possibly see of good in this man was completely beyond Gabrielle's comprehension. But then Miri was the one who had held longest to her belief in fairies and unicorns. Braxton gave Gabrielle a shove into the center of the room. With a bow to Aristide, the guard left Gabrielle alone with his master.

"Good evening, Mistress Cheney." The witch-hunter's voice was still all silken politeness. It was starting to grate on her nerves. "May I get you something?"

"Like what?" she snapped. "Hot brands, thumb screws, boiling oil?"

"I was thinking more on the lines of a flagon of wine." As Aristide stepped into the light, his lips twitched with the hint of a smile. The glimmer of humor softened his grim visage and rendered him surprisingly more attractive. It only irritated Gabrielle. If the man was a witch-hunter, he ought to behave like one and be completely detestable.

"No, thank you. I prefer that you just tell me what you want."

She ignored the chair Aristide offered her, smothering a feigned yawn beneath her hand. "It is the middle of the night, in case you hadn't noticed. Or is disrupting my sleep your preferred method of torture?"

"Oh, were you sleeping?" His dark eye pierced her as though he knew all too well the kind of nights she had been spending, tormented by her fears, her uncertainties, her desperate ache for Remy.

Gabrielle averted her face. Damn Aristide. She was the wise woman. If anyone was supposed to be able to read eyes, it was she. But the witch-hunter's ravaged face was inscrutable as he stalked closer, hands locked behind his back.

"I regret the inconveniences of your captivity, mademoiselle. But your ordeal will soon be at an end."

Gabrielle tried hard not to give him the satisfaction of showing her alarm. "But you said I had a fortnight until my trial. I have at least another week remaining to prepare my defense."

"Your trial may not be necessary. If I do pardon you, I hope you will go on your way a sadder, wiser woman and avoid the company of witches like Cassandra Lascelles."

Gabrielle glowered at him. "So you have known all along Cass was the one responsible for the medallions."

"Not all along, no," was his cool reply. "But I admit when she sprang forward so handily to offer information against you, her name struck a chord with me. I still have the journals of my former master, Vachel Le Vis. I went back through them and discovered I was right. I had heard of Mademoiselle Lascelles before.

"I was not much more than a boy at the time, new to my master's service, when he took up the case of a girl suspected of practicing the worst kinds of sorcery, necromancy, and curses. Because she was young and blind as well, my master was moved to spare her. Especially when Cassandra bargained for her life by offering up her mother and sisters instead, exposing their hiding place within the Maison d'Esprit."

"Dear God!" Gabrielle had resolved to display no emotion before the witch-hunter, but she felt herself blanch with horror. This was a far different version from what Cass had told of the destruction of her family. Her grief and torment over the death of her mother and sisters had always seemed quite genuine and perhaps it was, the torment of guilt. Gabrielle would like to believe Cass possessed at least that much conscience.

"So you see," Aristide concluded. "You are not the first of her confederates Mademoiselle Lascelles has ever betrayed."

"I was not her confederate. But for a time, I did believe I was her friend."

"You should choose your friends more carefully."

"So should my sister," she shot back.

A muscle twitched in Aristide's cheek and his eye clouded with something that might have been regret. The emotion was quickly shuttered away as he continued, "Mademoiselle Lascèlles and that serving wench of hers appear to have vanished. But I will track them down eventually and the Lascelles witch will answer for her crimes."

So Cass had fled the Maison d'Esprit. Gabrielle heard the tidings with mixed emotions. It was alarming to think of Cass on the loose with no idea of where she might turn up next. On the other hand, her disappearance did give Gabrielle one advantage.

She cast Aristide a triumphant smile. "If Cass and her maid have vanished, you no longer have a witness against me."

"I don't need one. I still have the evidence of the medallions." He gestured toward where the chest rested upon one of the tables.

Gabrielle's smile dimmed.

"But as I said before," he went on. "I am hoping no trial will be necessary."

"I know what you are hoping," Gabrielle said scornfully. "Miri told me all about the trade you have offered Renard. Did you know that every Midsummer's Eve, my little sister attended a ceremony at the stone circle on the far side of Faire Isle?"

"Yes." A brooding look stole over Aristide's face. "That is where I first met her."

"Miri actually believed that the dolmens were frozen giants who might return to life on that one magical night. Well, there is about as much a chance of that happening as the Comte de Renard ever—"

Gabrielle stumbled to a halt as she realized that the inn door had swung open, letting in a breath of crisp night air and the massive figure of a man.

"Yes? Renard will ever what?" her brother-in-law demanded affably.

Gabrielle's jaw dropped. She knew she must look like a witless idiot with her mouth hanging open, but she couldn't seem to close it any more than she could stop staring at the huge man who filled the doorframe. It was as though she had conjured up Renard with the mere mention of his name. But the comte had always had a disconcerting way of doing that, springing up out of nowhere.

Small wonder that Simon Aristide suspected the man of being a demon. Although the witch-hunter had clearly been expecting Renard tonight, Simon paled at the sight of him. Aristide's fingers twitched as though he wanted to reach for a cross to fend Renard off. Appearing as unperturbed by the sensation he had aroused as he was by the two stout witch-hunters who flanked him, Renard ambled into the room, the floorboards creaking beneath his heavy boots. He leisurely stripped off his riding gloves, his hooded green eyes sweeping the taproom with that laconic expression that masked a sharp and cunning intelligence.

"Monsieur Le Balafre, the comte has arrived," one of Renard's escorts announced.

"I can see that," Simon snapped. He dismissed the men, only Braxton remaining to post guard at the door. The comte ignored Aristide, turning to Gabrielle instead.

Gabrielle tipped up her chin, bracing herself for her brother-in-law's anger and contempt. The comte had little tolerance for anyone who caused his beloved wife grief and she had never been anything but trouble to Ariane. She was completely disarmed when he took her hand and carried it to his lips.

"My dear sister-in-law. I am as ever charmed to see you." Despite his teasing tone, Gabrielle found something astonishing beneath his hooded lids. Warmth, gentleness, and concern as his eyes searched her face. "I find you well, I trust?"

A lump rose to her throat. Ariane's ogre appeared so comfortingly large and solid, Gabrielle had to master a strong urge to sag against his chest and burst into tears.

"T-tolerably well," she managed to reply with a tremulous smile.

Renard gave her cheek a reassuring pat before turning to Aristide. The comte possessed an overwhelming presence. Even someone as formidable as the witch-hunter Le Balafre seemed to dwindle before him. Simon suddenly looked much younger and more vulnerable as Renard's scornful gaze swept over him.

"Ah, and this would be our young Master Aristide. You've grown so much I would have scarce recognized you."

Simon flushed, his hand flying to his scar. "Yes, I suppose I have changed."

"I am sorry about the damage to your pretty face, lad," Renard said in a softer tone. "It was never my wish to fight you that day. I had no desire to be your enemy."

"You were born to be my enemy." The hate radiating from Aristide was so strong, it sent a chill through Gabrielle. He inhaled sharply as though fighting to contain the virulent emotion. "I believe you came here to barter for mademoiselle's freedom, not thrash over old times. Did you bring the article I require?"

After a hesitation, Renard nodded, reaching for a pouch slung round his shoulder. Gabrielle watched, almost breathless with suspense as Renard undid the straps that held the pouch closed. He slowly extracted a plain volume bound in black leather. Of no great size or thickness, the book appeared no more threatening than a folio of poems.

Gabrielle's heart sank. Aristide was no fool. Did Renard really think he could trick the witch-hunter with a text as harmless looking as that? As the comte handed over the volume, Simon's sneer showed his skepticism.

"This is the infamous *Book of Shadows*?"

"I hope so. I paid dearly to acquire it."

"Not yet you haven't," Simon muttered. Snatching the book from Renard, he carried it close to the lit branch of candles and cracked the cover open.

Gabrielle strained on tiptoes, craning her neck. From what she could make out from her vantage, the pages looked aged and brittle enough to crumple to dust. Yet as Simon thumbed through them, the leaves crackled with a surprising resilience.

They were covered with strange bold markings, the ancient writing of a language all but forgotten, the symbols somehow dark and threatening. Gabrielle would never have thought it possible that a mere book could convey such an aura of mystery, power . . . evil.

There was little doubt in her mind that it was indeed the *Book of Shadows*. But whatever had possessed Renard to acquire the cursed thing, worse still to keep it? If the comte had ever intended to destroy it, he surely would have done so by now.

Gabrielle cast an uneasy glance at her brother-in-law. Much as Ariane loved her husband, she had ever feared that part of Renard that took too keen an interest in the dark arts, a fascination he had inherited from his wicked old grandmother, Melusine. With Aristide absorbed in the book, Gabrielle sidled closer to Renard and muttered, "You're an idiot. You know that, don't you?"

Renard bent down to reply in her ear. "Thank you. I have always been excessively fond of you, too, dear sister."

"Ariane is going to kill you," Gabrielle whispered fiercely. "You know how she feels about black magic. What possessed you to be messing about with that book?"

"*Love*" was his unexpected sad reply. "Your sister is so desperate to have a child, she's willing to die for it. But I can't lose her. It would be easier to part with my soul. I thought I might find an answer in that book, a way to let her have her babe, but keep her safe forever. I would risk employing even the darkest magic for that."

Gabrielle understood his desperation all too well. Hadn't it been the same feelings of love, fear, the need to protect that had driven her to place that dangerous medallion around Remy's neck? If Renard was an idiot, then so was she. She slipped her hand into his huge callused fingers and gave him a comforting squeeze. Renard returned the pressure with a rueful smile.

The minutes crawled by as Aristide inspected the book. Would the man have the wit to see that it was genuine? He appeared to be trying to take it apart, running his fingers over the cover, poking his thumbnail along the ridge of the spine. To Gabrielle's amazement, part of the leather peeled back, revealing a hidden pocket. Aristide turned the book over and shook it vigorously, as though expecting something to fall out.

When nothing did, he glared at Renard. "Where is it?"

"Where is what?" the comte asked blandly.

"You know damned well what. The list that should be hidden beneath the cover. The names of every known witch and sorcerer on both sides of the English Channel."

Gabrielle emitted an outraged gasp. "That is what you are after? You bastard. You told Miri you only wanted the *Book of Shadows,* to destroy it when what you really want is—is—"

"The destruction of evil itself and every man or woman who practices it." Simon stalked toward Renard. "Where is that list, monsieur?"

"Dear me. I suppose I must have lost it. Careless of me."

Simon's face darkened with such fury and frustration, Gabrielle stepped protectively in front of her brother-in-law. But Simon pivoted on his heel. He strode over to the chest that contained the medallions and the Dark Queen's ring. Wrenching open the lid, he flung the *Book of Shadows* inside.

He stared down at it for a long moment. When he turned back to face them, Aristide's eye was steely and cold. "I regret to inform you our agreement is terminated, Monsieur le Comte. Mademoiselle Gabrielle will remain to stand her trial and you also are under arrest."

Renard folded his arms across his chest, looking completely unfazed. "I was afraid you might say something like that. If I were you, I'd think better of it, boy."

"Why? Because you are expecting the armed men you had

concealed out there in the darkness to come storming to the rescue?"

Renard started, although he did his best to conceal it.

Simon's mouth twisted in an unpleasant smile. "I remember your tricks, monsieur, how you were always wont to come charging in, followed by a small army of retainers, how you pitilessly slaughtered all of Master Le Vis's order. My witch-hunters aren't monks, they are mercenaries, and I prepare better to meet my enemies than my old master did. Most of your servants are either dead or captured. The only men who will be coming through that door are mine. Braxton!"

As though he'd been waiting for this signal, Braxton flung the door open and three other witch-hunters swarmed into the room, surrounding them, swords drawn. Renard wrapped one arm about Gabrielle, drawing her protectively close to him. He remained remarkably calm, although she doubted that he'd anticipated this turn of events. She noticed him fingering the ring on his left hand, the curious metal band that linked his thoughts to Ariane. Was he reaching out to her in his mind, warning her what was happening, perhaps telling her how much he loved her, asking for her forgiveness?

Gabrielle only wished she could have the same chance with Remy. Her stomach dipped when she realized that Renard was not even armed. He had likely been obliged to surrender his sword before entering the inn.

"Take Mademoiselle Cheney back to her room," Aristide commanded. "As for the comte, there is no point wasting the time for a trial. His guilt has always been more than evident. Take him outside. He is to be executed at once."

"No!" Gabrielle shrieked. She clung desperately to Renard, but Braxton's rough hands pinned her arms behind her back. She struggled to break free, find some way to help Renard, but to no avail. A sob of despair escaped her as Renard was forced toward the door, the tip of a blade pressed to his throat.

"Stop!" a voice suddenly rang out. A voice as silvery and

clear as a pure forest stream. Everyone froze, all eyes turning toward the cloaked figure that emerged from the shadowy passage leading from the kitchens. Throwing back her hood, Miri Cheney stepped into the light.

How her sister had managed to gain access to the inn, surrounded by Simon's guards, Gabrielle had no idea. The answer perhaps lay in the familiar black shape crouched by Miri's skirts. Necromancer. Miri's cat had always had an uncanny ability to slink his way into forbidden places. No doubt he had found an entrance for Miri. Gabrielle wished the cat hadn't been so damned helpful.

This was the last place on earth Gabrielle wanted her little sister to be right now. From the expression on Aristide's face, the witch-hunter concurred. He advanced on Miri, growling, "What the blazes are you doing—"

"You lied to me, Simon. You did not keep your word."

Miri looked up at him, her gaze so clear and direct Gabrielle did not know how Aristide had the courage to meet it without flinching. But he offered no excuses, made no effort at apology. "I am a witch-hunter, Miri. You should have understood that. I do what I have to do."

"Then regrettably so must I." Miri's cloak fell back as she raised a pistol and leveled it at Aristide. "Tell your men to back off, Simon. Release my sister and Renard."

"Or what? You'll shoot me?"

"If I have to." Miri's face hardened, her eyes growing as cold as the distant stars. "Let them go. *Now.*" Miri adjusted the pistol, aiming directly at Simon's heart.

He simply stared at her, a storm of emotion rippling across his scarred face. Disbelief, regret, despair. Gabrielle's captor tightened his grip on her arms, but she sensed Braxton's uneasiness. The men restraining Renard had come to an uncertain halt near the door. The comte might have used the moment to make a bid for freedom, but like everyone else he was staring at Miri.

"No. Put the pistol down, child. *This isn't necessary.*" Renard laid unusual stress on his words, as though trying to convey some hidden message.

Braxton shuffled his feet and called nervously, "Monsieur Le Balafre?"

Neither Simon nor Miri responded, the pair locked in their confrontation, as though everyone and everything else had ceased to exist.

"Very well," Simon told her with a strange, resigned smile. "Go ahead. Do it then. Kill me."

As Simon stalked closer, the pistol trembled in Miri's hand. She steadied it, gritting her teeth. Gabrielle held her breath, wondering if Miri really could—

A deafening roar split the room as though a mighty dragon had assaulted the inn. Windows shattered, the rafters shook, the floor heaved beneath Gabrielle's feet. Light exploded, blinding her. She was flung roughly to the floor, the breath driven from her lungs. Webs of darkness danced before her and her eyes fluttered closed.

She must have lost consciousness, for how long she had no idea. When she next opened her eyes, she felt dazed and disoriented, as though her head was muffled in cotton. Something warm trickled down her cheek. She touched it and squinted uncomprehending at the red, sticky substance on her fingers. Blood.

Gabrielle shook her head in an effort to clear it, only to stop as a sharp pain lanced her temple. Her confusion receded, memory returning. The Charters Inn, the witch-hunters, Aristide ordering Renard's execution, Miri aiming her pistol . . .

But this level of destruction had never come from Miri's pistol. As Gabrielle struggled to sit up, she found herself enveloped in a world of chaos, blazing light, unbearable heat, and a heavy mist. No, not mist, but smoke that was already beginning to sting her eyes, making her cough. The inn was afire, flames licking up the walls. She had to find Miri and Renard . . . get out of here.

Gabrielle braced herself with her hand, only to recoil as she came in contact with a man's arm. The witch-hunter, Braxton, sprawled near her. Whether he was dead or merely unconscious, she could not tell. Her attention was drawn to the doorway, where she heard something above the crackle of flame. The clash of steel. Through the thickening haze, she saw that Renard had wrestled a sword from one of his captors. One man lay dead at his feet, while he battled furiously with another.

And shoulder to shoulder with Renard, his sword flashing as he held another witch-hunter at bay, was . . . *Remy*. Gabrielle's heart leapt with a painful mixture of disbelief, joy, and fear for him. She tried to call out to him, only to choke on the smoke. But Remy had already spotted her. He brought his opponent down with one swift, savage stroke. Before the witch-hunter had dropped to the floor, Remy bounded toward her.

He hunkered down beside her, his face streaming with sweat, his cheek smudged with soot. Damp strands of dark gold hair tumbled wildly across his brow, but never had any man looked so good. She flung her arms around his neck with a deep sob. "Oh, you—you came for me."

"Of course I did, you little fool," Remy rasped in her ear. He strained her so hard against him, she thought her ribs would crack. "We've got to get out of here. Are you badly hurt? Can you stand?"

Gabrielle nodded, but when Remy hauled her to her feet, she winced as her ankle throbbed. But she forgot her pain as the thought struck her—Miri. Where was she? Eyes streaming from the thickening smoke, Gabrielle glanced frantically about her, praying Miri had already made her way outside.

She was horrified to see her little sister crouched over Simon's recumbent form. One side of his face dark with blood, Aristide lay unmoving. Miri sought to rouse him, heedless of Necromancer pawing at her skirts as though the cat urged her to flee while there was still time.

"M-miri," Gabrielle choked. She yanked at Remy's arm, drawing his attention to her sister. Before he could respond, Renard was already shoving past them. One arm flung up to shield his face from the smoke, Renard shouted to Remy. "I'll get her. Take Gabrielle. Go now."

Gabrielle tried to protest, struggling to rush to her sister. But Remy's arm closed inexorably around her waist. His sword clutched in his other hand, he hauled her to the door, forcing her into a crouching position to avoid the worst of the smoke. Her lungs felt as though they were on fire. She was half-blinded by her tears. All she could do was cling to Remy, hobbling at his side as they emerged into the night.

He half-dragged, half-carried her a safe distance from the blazing inn. Gabrielle coughed and gulped in great lungfuls of the clear night air. Remy choked, his own chest heaving. His grip loosened on Gabrielle enough that she twisted free. Rubbing her raw eyes, she gazed back at the inn. A sob of relief escaped her when she saw Renard emerge, bearing Miri in his arms, Necromancer streaking before them. He strode over to where she and Remy waited, gently easing Miri down onto a stone bench beneath the gnarled branches of an oak tree.

Still struggling to regain her breath, Gabrielle leaned against Remy, taking in the madness that had erupted around them. Half the inn was engulfed in flame, the fire lighting up the night with a hellish glow as it spread to the roof of the stable. The terrified whinny of the horses mingled with the shouts of Simon's men. Their dark shapes were silhouetted against the red haze of the fire. Witch-hunters, grooms, servants from the inn darted frantically to and fro, some seeking to save the horses, others merely to get clear of the fire, contain the deadly sparks flying from the inn.

The confusion was increased by citizens from neighboring houses surging into the inn yard, many clad in their nightclothes. Some came to help, others merely to gawk, the light of the flames reflected in their faces. In the midst of all the chaos, Gabrielle thought she spied Bartolomy Verducci, the man's scrawny legs pumping as he fled the scene.

But she had little time to spare a thought for Catherine's spy. A bellow of rage went up and to her horror, Gabrielle realized their escape from the inn had finally been noted. Several of Simon's burly witch-hunters bore down upon them, weapons drawn.

She felt Remy's body coil with tension. He muttered terse instructions in her ear. "Look after your sister. Get her out of the yard. Ariane will be waiting just down the street with horses. I'll find you there."

Gabrielle was certain the explosion must have damaged her hearing. Had Remy just said *Ariane?* There was no chance to question him. He planted a hard kiss against her lips and then was gone. He charged forward to meet the onslaught of the witch-hunters, Renard thundering after him. They were reinforced by a third man, a rangy youth with wild, flowing black hair. Wolf. Where had he come from? Gabrielle stood frozen for a moment, watching the melee that ensued, a mad tangle of shifting male figures and flashing swords.

Helpless to aid her men, Gabrielle did the only thing she could and turned to her sister. Miri was still sitting on the bench, looking dazed but mostly unharmed. Her face and hands bore cuts from the flying glass when the windows had shattered. Necromancer licked one of her palms as though seeking to heal her, but Miri took no heed of him.

Her gaze was fixed on the blazing inn, an expression of horror in her eyes.

"S-simon," she whispered.

After all that had happened, Gabrielle could not believe her sister was still fretting over that witch-hunter, fearing for his life. She took hold of Miri's shoulders, gently forcing her to her feet.

"Come on, love. We have to go," Gabrielle urged.

Miri tried to wrench free of her.

"Simon," she repeated. Gabrielle tightened her grip, fearing Miri meant to dash back to the inn in search of him. Then she understood the look in her sister's eyes. It was not fear for Simon

Aristide, but of him. Both Aristide and Braxton had somehow got clear of the burning inn, their menacing forms etched against the backdrop of the flames.

Simon looked more than ever the devil's apprentice. He'd lost his eye patch, his scarred visage fully exposed, his face blackened with ash, blood, and rage. Staggering, Aristide barked some command to Braxton, gesturing toward Renard.

The comte was engaged in desperate swordplay, oblivious to the danger behind him. Gabrielle's breath clogged in her throat as she saw the weapon in Braxton's hand. The witch-hunter fitted a quarrel into the taut string of a crossbow. Gabrielle shrieked out a warning, but her cry was lost in the din of fire and battle. Before she realized what was happening, Miri tore free from her grasp. The girl went racing forward.

Heart thudding, Gabrielle surged after her, hampered by her throbbing ankle. It was like being trapped in a horrible nightmare, running, never getting closer, knowing she would never get there in time. Miri flung herself in between Braxton and Renard just as the witch-hunter took aim. Gabrielle choked on her cry, bracing herself for the worst.

But at the last possible moment, Aristide swore, knocking Braxton aside. The quarrel whistled, veering wildly off course, leaving both Miri and Renard unharmed. A second explosion rocked the night, the roof of the inn caving in with a mighty roar, sending the crowd in the yard scrambling away in panic. Sparks and burning embers flew everywhere. The world descended into a complete madness of heat, smoke, and fire. The only thing sane was Remy suddenly appearing at Gabrielle's side.

The rest of their escape was a blur to her, Remy's strong arm wrapped about her waist, supporting her, his stalwart form protecting her from the panicked rush, keeping her from tripping over the bodies of slain witch-hunters. She followed him blindly through the yard until they reached the street. Miraculously, they all arrived unharmed, Remy, Gabrielle, Renard, Miri, Wolf, even

Necromancer. The cat led the way toward the shadows pooling near an alley where Ariane and Bette waited with the horses.

Her ankle throbbing, Gabrielle stumbled, catching at Remy's arm. Her hand came away sticky with blood. "Remy. You—you are hurt."

Horrified, she pointed at the shaft protruding from his upper arm. Remy stared at it, dumbfounded. The infuriating man actually grinned at her and laughed.

"Oh, hell and damnation," he exclaimed. "Not again."

*   *

SIMON SAGGED DOWN ON THE BENCH, CLUTCHING THE WOODEN chest to him, as he watched the flames engulf the inn and stables. It was as though the earth had split open, spewing forth hell itself. Even from this distance Simon could feel the heat, his face streaked with soot and sweat. He coughed, his lips parched, his lungs straining for a breath of pure air such as he feared he would never know again. All around him, men shouted, forming a brigade, hauling buckets of water from the well. A pathetic and futile effort. How did one extinguish the fires of hell?

The inn yard was strewn with the fallen bodies of his witch-hunters, some of them no more than dark, unmoving shapes, other stirring, emitting low groans. Simon knew he ought to go to their aid, but he could not seem to rouse himself. Nearby Braxton nursed a burned hand, the older man casting a dazed look at Simon as though awaiting instructions.

Commands that Simon could not give. He couldn't seem to move or think, do anything beyond brood over that moment when Miri had leveled the pistol at his chest, the look in her eyes so cold. Had she learned to hate Simon so much? Had he taught her that well? Would she really have pulled the trigger?

That was something he'd never know. He could hardly ask her because he'd let her go. Miri, Captain Remy, Gabrielle, the comte. He'd simply let them all go, making no effort to stop them, to mount a pursuit. Simon felt as though something more than the wind had been taken out of him in tonight's explosion. He'd lost his strength of purpose, his confidence in his ability to battle evil, defeat it. And he knew whom he had to thank for that.

That devil Renard. Just like his old master, Simon had completely underestimated the demon comte. Only Renard with his dark magic could have produced a cataclysm of this fearful nature. Simon could still have brought the comte down, but once more Miri had gotten in his way. For the sake of a girl who now despised him, Simon had let evil slip through his grasp.

He dragged his hand wearily over his naked scalp. At least he had accomplished one thing. He had deprived that sorcerer of his devil's handbook. The lid of the chest was scorched black from the fire, but otherwise the wooden box remained intact.

Simon flung back the lid and blinked hard in disbelief. He had to rub his burning eyes, frantically grope the silk lining of the coffer to convince himself he was not mistaken. He wasn't. The chest was completely empty. No medallions. No ring.

Worst of all, the *Book of Shadows* was gone.

❋❋❋

THE PALACE WAS IN CHAOS, PREPARATIONS FOR THE REMOVAL OF THE court to Blois brought to a halt. Trunks remained packed, wagons half-loaded, grooms, maids, and courtiers alike left in a state of suspension, awaiting the king's command. Henry Valois had flown into a rage when he'd learned of the attack on his witch-hunters. With only a few of his chosen mignons to bear him company, he had retired to his apartments, where he had remained for the past two days.

Like a petulant boy sulking because some of his toy soldiers had been broken, Catherine thought contemptuously. Any excess of emotion seemed to exhaust her son to the point of rendering him bedridden. But Henry's ill humor was the least of her concerns at the moment, although he had all but accused her of being responsible for the assault.

She had been tempted to dryly inform him that he suspected the wrong witch. Catherine had gleaned enough information regarding the strange explosion and fire to guess who was to blame. That devilishly clever husband of Ariane's, Renard. Pity that instead of burning the Charters Inn to the ground, the comte had not succeeded in destroying all the witch-hunters, especially Monsieur Le Balafre. But that wretched young man had somehow survived. By all reports, so had Gabrielle and Nicolas Remy. They had fled Paris, along with the younger Cheney sister, the Comte de Renard, and Ariane.

The witch-hunter still alive, the Scourge on the loose in the countryside. Catherine could not seem to spare more than a passing thought for either of these disturbing tidings. As she paced her own apartments, all her energies, her entire mind was focused on one thing.

Where the devil was Bartolomy Verducci? She'd had no word from the cursed man since the night of the fire. No word for two whole days. She only prayed the old fool had not gotten himself blown to bits on the most important mission she'd ever given him—the acquisition of the *Book of Shadows*.

Her spy had been making regular reports to her and she'd been aware of the proposed trade of the book for Gabrielle's life. Verducci had had his instructions. If the manuscript did indeed surface, he was to obtain it at all costs. But she should have known better than to trust Verducci or any servant with a task so vital. Despite all risk of discovery, she should have somehow contrived a disguise and gone herself.

Verducci's disappearance left Catherine in a quandary. She could hardly search openly for the man without raising questions about what her servant had been doing secreted in the witch-hunters' quarters. She was considering how best to pursue a discreet inquiry when one of her ladies in waiting brought her the welcome intelligence of the signore's return.

Heart thudding with anticipation, Catherine quickly dismissed all her attendants. When Verducci staggered into her antechamber, even she was shocked by his appearance. He looked like a man who had just escaped from the depths of hell. He was still clad in the clothing he'd worn the night of the fire, his breeches and jerkin ashen with soot. His eyebrows had been completely singed off, likewise the ends of his beard, his gaunt cheek displaying an ugly blister. His head was wrapped in a thick blood-stained bandage that prevented him from donning his cap.

Verducci limped toward Catherine, barely able to execute a bow without tumbling off balance. "Y-your grace," he rasped.

At any other time, she would have roundly rebuked him for taking so long to return with his report, but she wasted no time on pointless preliminaries, not even asking where he had been all this while. There was only one thing she wanted to know.

"Well, sirrah? Did the Comte have the *Book of Shadows*?" she demanded. "Have you succeeded in your mission? Did you acquire it?"

Verducci held up a pouch that he attempted to present to her, but the scrawny little man swayed, collapsing at her feet. Ignoring the unconscious man, Catherine all but stepped on him in her haste to reach the pouch.

Catherine's heart thudded, and her hands trembled with eagerness as she worked the drawstrings. She was barely able to suppress her cry of triumph as she groped inside and drew out the worn leather book . . .

⁂

MOST OF THE COURTIERS WERE QUIET AND SUBDUED, THE MYSTERIous affair of the Charters Inn discussed in hushed whispers for fear that any mention of the subject might be reported and further infuriate the king. Legs stretched idly before him, Navarre sat on a bench in the Tuileries garden, affecting to read a book and act as though recent events were of no moment to him.

But it was hard to retain his pose of customary indifference. Gabrielle was safe. Navarre's relief at that was tempered with a residue of anger and hurt against both her and Remy for the deception they had practiced upon him. He reflected that he should have been accustomed to not being able to trust anyone by now, but Gabrielle, the woman he had so adored . . . Her defection had been painful enough, but if there had been one man Navarre had believed he could entirely rely upon, it had been his Scourge.

Navarre was as mystified as the rest of the court regarding what had happened at the inn two nights ago. He doubted he would ever entirely know what Gabrielle had been doing to get herself accused of witchcraft. Far more clear to Navarre was what had transpired between Gabrielle and Remy. They had become lovers. Navarre had suspected as much since the day of the tournament, although he had allowed Gabrielle to allay his doubts.

It had been Remy who had made the true state of affairs clear in his last message to Navarre. Written in the captain's plain hand, Remy had expressed his sorrow for not being able to carry out Navarre's rescue, but Gabrielle needed him more. Navarre entirely forgave Remy for that. He bitterly wished he could have played the hero himself and saved her, not as usual been completely useless, the shadow king.

No, it was not Remy's calling off the escape that Navarre found unpardonable. Truth be told, Navarre had never had much confidence in the success of the plan. It was the other matter that irked Navarre, the thing that Nicolas Remy did not even apologize for, making off with the woman Navarre had desired above all others. Remy had merely written after his blunt fashion,

"I love Gabrielle to the depth of my soul, in a way that you never can. After I have freed her, I intend to take her far from Paris and make her my bride. I will yet find a way to rescue you from your imprisonment. My duty, my life, my service will always be yours to command, my liege. There is only one thing that I will never be able to offer you, and that is my wife."

Remy loved Gabrielle to the depth of his soul? A rather passionate declaration to come from such a somber man. Navarre's lips quirked in spite of himself. It would have been amusing to finally see the mighty Scourge fall victim to a lady's charms. Amusing perhaps if it had been any other woman but Gabrielle.

But Remy's words rankled, perhaps because Navarre was forced to admit the truth of them. *"I love Gabrielle . . . in a way that you never can."* The solemn Scourge was indeed the sort of man who would love but one woman, remain true to her forever. As for Navarre, he feared that he had inherited his libertine grandfather's wandering eye. Would it have been different with Gabrielle? Navarre would have liked to believe so, but even he was not sure. Now he would never know.

Navarre sighed as he turned a page in his book, the print a blur. He saw only the image of Gabrielle's golden hair, bright blue eyes and lush, beckoning lips. Perhaps in time he would be able to forgive her and Remy. Navarre was not possessed of a vengeful disposition.

But at the moment he was consumed by envy for Remy and not just because of Gabrielle. He envied the Scourge something even more precious, his freedom. He had never allowed anyone to see how much his captivity chafed him, this degrading, shameful role he'd been forced to adopt, Navarre, the rustic buffoon, the cowardly turncoat, the puppet king. It was wearing him down to the depths of his soul.

More than his desire for Gabrielle, it had been Navarre's growing desperation that had made him consent to Remy's plans for his escape. His longing for the rugged mountains of his home, his need to be clear of all the treachery of the French court, his burning hunger to become the kind of king that he wanted to be, strong, wise, and courageous.

But Navarre found he was more relieved than disappointed that Remy's plan had to be abandoned. He had seen too many plots for his rescue come to nothing, too many of his followers executed. He had become convinced that the reason for all these failures was that the attempts had been too elaborate, involved too many people. He was more determined than ever to escape, but when the time was right, it would involve the simplest of plans and depend mostly upon the one person Navarre did fully trust. Himself.

As for right now, he needed to lull the dragons that guarded him back to sleep, dispel the suspicions that Remy's return had aroused. Hard as it was, he must continue to play the indolent young fool, concerned only with the gratification of his senses. Fortunately, that role was not entirely without its compensations.

Hearing a discreet cough, Navarre glanced up from his book to find himself being observed by a buxom brunette with laughing eyes and a pert smile. He recognized her as one of Catherine's ladies, the Dark Queen's latest offering to keep him seduced and tame. But oh, well. What the devil, Navarre thought with a cynical shrug. His breeches might be easily undone, but his counsel he had learned to keep to himself.

The young woman fluttered her fan and with a provocative look disappeared into the shrubbery. Navarre grinned, closed up his book, and followed.

Chapter Twenty-Six

THE MODEST FARMHOUSE WAS TUCKED AWAY IN A VALLEY SEV-eral leagues from Paris. Not as far away as Gabrielle would have wished, but Remy had been unable to go any farther. The last mile, only Renard's strong arm had prevented Remy from slipping from the saddle. Gabrielle was grateful for the temporary haven provided by the farm with its stone cottage, snug dairy barn, and chicken coops.

The place was the property of the Widow Perrot, noted for her fine apple jellies, sweet cream, and mellow cheese. She was also known to brew up the occasional potion to ease the pain of childbirth or monthly courses and concoct ointments that could cure anything from warts to rheumatism. Few outsiders would have guessed from her dimpled chin and plump matronly figure that she was one of the wise women who had recently attended the council on Faire Isle and that her name had likely been included on that list that had eluded Simon Aristide.

It was the widow who looked after Gabrielle and Miri while

Ariane tended to Remy. Clucking over them both in motherly fashion, she dabbed her ointment on the cuts they had sustained from the flying glass. She even applied a poultice to Gabrielle's ankle, wrapping it tightly.

"Something that I use on the pony when he pulls a fetlock," the widow said with a wink. "Ornery old cuss. If it works on him, it should work for you, m'girl."

Gabrielle mumbled her thanks, but she had little thought to spare for her own aches or exhaustion. All her mind, all her energies were focused on Remy. He'd finally sunk into unconsciousness when Ariane had worked upon his wound. After she'd finished he'd been tucked up in the widow's own bed. He slept most of that day, then spent an uneasy night, stirring restlessly.

Gabrielle hovered by his side, soothing his brow with a cool cloth, fearful he might fall prey to fever or his old nightmares. Even though Ariane had urged Gabrielle to get some rest, said that she would look after the captain, Gabrielle had refused.

She perched on a wooden chair near the bed, offering him sips of water whenever he briefly roused. The herbal brew that Ariane had administered to dull his pain left him groggy. Gabrielle doubted that he even realized she was there with him and the thought brought an ache to her heart. Despite her best efforts, she dozed off, only to be awakened by the cheerful twittering of sparrows in the apple tree outside the window. She sat up and stretched painfully, rubbing the lower area of her spine. Her neck muscles protested as she twisted to peer at the man on the bed.

Morning light flooded the small chamber, playing softly over Remy's face, his jaw coarsened by the stubble of beard. He appeared alarmingly still, his breath barely audible. Gabrielle pressed her hand to his brow, finding his skin cool to the touch. No fever. Surely that was a good sign and yet he looked so pale and drawn, like a mighty warrior who'd taken one blow too many and could not summon the strength to rise.

She couldn't help but contrast his present state with the way he'd been but a week ago, so strong, bursting with vitality and enthusiasm as he'd laid his final plans to rescue his king. She longed to thread her fingers through his tousled dark gold hair, tenderly caress his face, but she feared to disturb whatever healing slumber he had found.

Gabrielle drew back, careful not to brush against his bandaged arm resting atop the coverlet. His powerful shoulders and upper chest were likewise exposed, the scars that creased his flesh appearing even crueler in the gentle morning light. So many wounds, so much pain for one man, and now he'd had to endure one more.

But this time it was her fault. Such a stupid, senseless injury for Remy to have suffered. If not for her recklessness, her deceptions, none of the terrible events of last night need ever have happened. The creak of the door behind Gabrielle cut short her guilt-stricken thoughts. She turned from Remy as Ariane stole quietly into the room. Her older sister's eyes were smudged with exhaustion, her soft brown hair tumbled about her shoulders, but she was still very much the same calm Ariane.

"How is he?" she whispered as she tiptoed over to the bed.

"I don't know," Gabrielle confessed with a wan effort to smile. "My Scourge looks rather—rather weak and helpless lying there like that."

She stepped out of the way as her sister bent to examine Remy. Ariane's hands seemed so much more capable and confident than hers as she tested his brow for fever and checked his pulse. Feeling utterly useless, Gabrielle retreated to the window while Ariane carefully undid the bandage to inspect his wound. Remy barely stirred.

Gabrielle rested her head wearily against the window frame, taking in the soft breeze, the earthy smells emanating from the barnyard below. She spied Necromancer stalking some hapless field mouse. If Miri had noticed, she would have put a stop to it.

But her little sister was busy currying the mane of a stout gray pony while Wolf leaned up against the paddock gate watching her.

The early morning peace was broken by the dull thud of an axe. Shirtsleeves rolled up, the Comte de Renard was busy chopping firewood, not looking in the least fazed by the battle at the inn or their fatiguing flight from Paris. The man had always possessed a stamina that was downright exhausting. The pleasure he took in such simple tasks as chopping wood had once caused Gabrielle to dub him a peasant. But she found something solid and reassuring about the sight of her brother-in-law wielding his axe while he kept an eye on the track leading to the farm, alert to any possible danger.

It was good to have an ogre guarding the castle, especially when her Scourge was so vulnerable. As Ariane finished rebinding his wound, Gabrielle took some comfort in noting her sister's nod of satisfaction as she drew back from the bed. Ariane joined Gabrielle at the window, speaking low so as not to disturb Remy.

"Your captain will be fine. He is a very strong man who has survived much worse. He lost a great deal of blood, but there is no infection, no fever. All he needs is a little time to rest and heal. Pray God he will have that."

Ariane stole an anxious glance out the window. The sight of her stalwart husband must have offered her reassurance. Some of the tension melted out of her shoulders. It was a rare thing to see Ariane with her hair unbound. She usually dressed simply, but neatly, her glossy brown tresses done up in a chignon or confined beneath a veiled headdress. Her hair hanging loose about her shoulders made her look younger somehow and yet there was a shadow of sorrow lurking in Ariane's serene eyes that Gabrielle did not remember being there, not even after their mother had died.

They'd had little time alone since their hurried and perilous reunion, too many other concerns and dangers getting in the way. This was their first quiet moment together and the silence that descended felt strained with memories of their quarrels, the bitter differences of opinion that had caused their paths to diverge.

There was so much Gabrielle wanted to say to her sister but she scarce knew where to begin. She was surprised Ariane hadn't forced the issue between them before now. Her older sister had never been one to let matters simply rest, always wanting to fix everything, to heal what was sometimes not ready to be healed. Gabrielle had often resented Ariane's probing, those discerning eyes of hers that could peel back layers of the heart too easily, leaving wounds one sought to protect raw and exposed.

But Ariane didn't push, didn't probe. She waited, her eyes downcast, her hands folded before her. Gabrielle suddenly realized this was just as hard for her sister, finding a way to bridge the gulf between them.

Gabrielle cleared her throat. "It was my fault."

"I—I beg your pardon?" Ariane faltered.

"Our quarrel. The rift between us and what has happened to Remy." She gestured miserably toward the bed. "I am to blame for all of it."

"Oh, you are the one who shot the captain? Well, I am sure that is quite understandable. There have been many times I wanted to do the same to Renard, especially when I found out he really did have that cursed book."

Her sister's jest left Gabrielle reeling in astonishment. Ariane had always been so serious, almost painfully so. She saw what Ariane was trying to do, teasing to ease the situation. But her gentle humor had the unexpected effect of cracking Gabrielle's reserve. Her eyes filled with tears.

"Oh, Ari. I—I have made such a d-dreadful mess of everything." Her voice broke on a mighty sob.

Ariane said nothing, just gathered Gabrielle into her arms. There had been so many times Gabrielle had resisted her older sister's comfort. Now she melted willingly against the softness of

Ariane's shoulder, weeping out all the heartache, fear, and stress she had kept bottled up since her quarrel with Remy.

Ariane rocked her, stroking Gabrielle's hair, her gentle, healing hands so like their late mother's. "Hush, dearest. Nothing has happened that can't be mended."

"You—you don't know. You have n-no idea some of the things I have done." Gabrielle drew back, shuddering on a hiccup. She wiped furiously at her eyes until Ariane produced a handkerchief. Ariane *always* had a handkerchief.

She cupped Gabrielle's chin, drying her cheeks. "I am afraid I do have some idea of what you've been up to. It was no accident that Bette followed you to Paris, seeking employment. I sent her."

As Gabrielle's eyes widened, Ariane went on hastily, "I couldn't endure the thought of not knowing what happened to you. Not with all the dangers of the city, the court, the Dark Queen. I sent Bette, instructed her to dispatch regular reports. Those pigeons she raised in the pen behind your stables weren't for your dinner table."

"I should have suspected as much. I loathe pigeon pie and Bette knows it."

"Please don't be angry with her. It was my idea. I made her do it."

"I am not angry with her or you either." Gabrielle said. "Perhaps at one time I would have been foolish enough to have been furious. But I have been so afraid you no longer cared if you ever saw or heard of me again. That—that I'd so shamed and disappointed you by becoming a courtesan, by living in the house that belonged to Papa's mistress. I thought you must hate me."

"Oh, Gabrielle, how can you think such a thing? You and I have always had our differences—"

Gabrielle smiled. "That is a bit of an understatement."

Ariane also smiled but it was a tremulous one. "I have often been worried by your choices, afraid for you, hurting for you.

But you are my sister. I will always love you no matter what."
Ariane's eyes filled with tears. "And I have missed you so."

"I have missed you, too."

Gabrielle drew her sister to her fiercely. They hugged,
laughed, and cried over each other. Drawing apart, they peered
guiltily in Remy's direction, but he slumbered on undisturbed.
They shared the handkerchief between them, drying damp eyes.
Gabrielle had always hated what she thought of as the womanly
weakness of tears. She had especially loathed ever breaking
down in front of her composed older sister. But it was different
somehow, sharing a good weep with Ariane. She felt curiously
better for it.

Ariane composed herself with a final sniff. "Now, what is
this I hear about you becoming betrothed to Remy?"

Gabrielle shook her head sadly. "Unfortunately, that is all
over. I daresay you haven't heard the rest of the story because
Bette did not know."

"I didn't get the tale from Bette, my dear heart. I heard it
from Remy."

"Remy?" Gabrielle echoed in astonishment.

"When Miri sent word to the château about Simon Aristide's
demand, Renard and I headed for Paris at once. Our first
thought was to contact Remy, but we found him only by chance.
Your Scourge was tearing the city apart looking for that Lascelles woman."

"For Cass? But why?"

"Remy had some notion of forcing her to come forward and
tell the truth to clear you. He didn't want you to end up a fugitive, forever on the run from witch-hunters."

So that was what Remy had been doing when Gabrielle had
begun to fear he had abandoned her. She was moved that he
should have attempted such a desperate thing on her behalf and
dismayed as well.

"I am glad Remy never found her," she said. "Cass is the
most dangerous person I've ever met and that includes the Dark

Queen. You always warned me to steer clear of anyone who practiced dark magic, but of course I didn't listen. You would have never been so tempted."

A chagrined expression played across Ariane's gentle features. "I am not a saint, Gabrielle. Although you have often implied that I thought I was."

"I am sorry, Ari. I never meant—"

"No, you were quite right. I did try very hard to act the part of the all-wise, all-knowing Lady of Faire Isle. Mostly so no one would ever realize what a fraud I am. I must have been quite insufferable." She fetched a deep sigh. "The truth is, I am not wise. Far from it. It was particularly difficult for me just after Maman died. With our father lost at sea, you and Miri to look after, all the debts Papa left, and then everyone on the island turning to me, expecting me to be as wise as Maman."

Ariane swallowed hard before confessing. "I was so desperate. I turned to black magic myself to—to conjure Maman's spirit."

"*You* practiced necromancy? I didn't even realize you knew how."

"I am not as naturally skilled at it as Cassandra apparently is. But I did succeed in contacting our mother several times. Even though I promised her never to do it again, I have still been tempted. Especially this past year when—when—." Ariane broke off, her eyes darkening with sorrow.

"Miri told me about your—your difficulties, about you losing the babe." Gabrielle pressed her sister's hand. "I am so sorry, Ariane."

Ariane managed a wan smile. "Thank you, but I fear I have already dwelled too much upon my grief. I was furious with Justice when I realized he had acquired the *Book of Shadows* and didn't tell me, that he was actually attempting to read it. Worse still, he finally admitted he has been taking some concoction his grandmother taught him to brew. To render his seed temporarily sterile. I was so angry, so devastated. But all he wanted to do was protect me until he found some way for me to be safely delivered of a healthy babe."

Ariane wrapped her arms about herself and leaned wearily against the wall. "I was so consumed with what I wanted, I paid no heed to my husband's feelings. Justice lost his own mother in childbirth and I know that has always been his greatest fear for me, but I chose to ignore that. In my quest to become a mother, I was forgetting to be a wife. I—I hope he will forgive me for it."

"I am sure your ogre will tell you there is nothing to forgive. The man completely adores you, Ariane."

Ariane smiled, arching her brows. "As your Scourge does you and even though you were foolish enough to declare your betrothal at an end, I don't believe the man intends to let you get away from him so easily."

Gabrielle wished she were as certain of that. She cast a wistful look toward the man sleeping on the bed. "So what happens now, Ariane? What are we going to do? Do you think Aristide and his witch-hunters will pursue us all the way to Faire Isle?"

"I fear so."

"I wish Renard had succeeded in blowing the wretched man up," Gabrielle said bitterly.

"Uh . . . that wasn't Justice. That was me."

"What!" Gabrielle dragged her gaze from Remy to stare at her sister.

Ariane squirmed, looking guiltier than Gabrielle had ever seen her. "It was that cursed book," she blurted out. "Even I couldn't resist the temptation to peek inside the cover. Justice and Remy laid their plans for rescuing you, but there was so much that could go wrong. Just one little spell, I thought. Just in case.

"I found instructions for making an explosive device so small it could be launched like an arrow from a bow. So I made one, kept it in reserve, and when everything did go wrong and Justice's retainers were ambushed, I decided to use it. I have always been so good at deciphering the ancient language. I thought

I had followed the instructions carefully, that the device would explode in the air, go off like an enormous skyrocket and create a diversion. Instead it's a miracle I didn't destroy us all and set half of Paris on fire."

Ariane hung her head, looking so horrified by what she'd done, Gabrielle should have sought to reassure her. Instead she had a hard time suppressing a smile. Noting her struggle, Ariane frowned at her. "There was nothing the least amusing about it, Gabrielle. I could have killed a lot of innocent people."

"But you didn't," Gabrielle pointed out practically.

"But I could have. You see what a horrible person I really am. I daresay you will no longer have any respect at all for me."

Gabrielle only grinned and gave her sister another hug. "I am more in awe of you than ever. The Lady of Faire Isle is indeed a force to be reckoned with. And there is one good thing to come of the fire you set. That evil book was bound to have been destroyed and none of us need ever worry about it again."

When Ariane still looked far from comforted, Gabrielle added, "Your explosion did end up saving the day. It came at a very timely moment."

She sobered as she told Ariane what had happened with Miri. "You know how our little sister has always been, so tender-hearted, so bewildered by violence. I swear she would shift a venomous snake off the road to keep it being run over by a cart. But when she had that pistol leveled at Aristide, I have never seen such a hard expression on her face. I—I think she really was prepared to kill him to save me and Renard."

Gabrielle fretted her lower lip. "I'd like to shoot the bastard myself for what he has done to Miri, the most innocent and trusting soul that ever lived. He betrayed her yet again and then he turns around and saves her, even at the cost of letting Renard escape his vengeance. No wonder Miri ends up so confused. Why can't the blasted man make up his mind to act like a proper villain and be done with it?"

"Because no one ever is a complete villain. We are all a blend of light and darkness. Some hearts much darker than others," Ariane conceded ruefully. "I, too, am sorry for what has happened to Miri. But the world is full of evil and treachery. Miri couldn't cling to her innocence and dreams forever. She had to grow up sometime, much as we both hate to see it."

"I do hate it," Gabrielle said. "No one was more frustrated than I by her belief in such things as fairies and unicorns *and* in that perfidious Aristide. But it hurts to see her disillusioned, her heart forced to grow tougher. I never really wanted her to change."

"If it is any consolation to you, there is much about our little sister that is still the same." Ariane motioned Gabrielle to the window, gesturing toward Miri and Wolf in the paddock with the pony, Martin's dark head bent close to Miri's blond one as they conferred in what Gabrielle could only describe as a decidedly conspiratorial manner.

"Miri still retains her fixed view on the rights of animals and her faith in her ability to communicate with them," Ariane said. "Apparently that pony has been giving her some sad tale about how lonely he feels, how he would like to be on a farm where there were other horses and perhaps some children to play with him."

"Oh, no," Gabrielle groaned, guessing what was coming. Miri had been known to—what did her younger sister call it— *liberate* unhappy animals from their lawful owners.

"It would be very poor recompense for Madame Perrot's hospitality if Miri were to make off with her pony," Ariane said.

"And Martin Le Loup would be just the lad to help her do it," Gabrielle agreed. "We'd best keep an eye on those two."

Ariane started to nod, then she stiffened, an arrested expression coming over her face. She cocked her head as though she detected someone calling her name. Gabrielle heard nothing, but she noticed Renard staring intently up at the window. He touched his ring with the strange runic symbols and Gabrielle noticed her sister did likewise with the one encircling her finger.

Whatever silent communion passed between them, Ariane's eyes grew softer, a hint of color stealing into her cheeks. "I think I—I need a breath of air."

"Oh, yes, of course you do," Gabrielle drawled.

Ariane blushed even more deeply before Gabrielle's knowing look. She smiled sheepishly as she headed for the door. Before she slipped out of the room, she called, "Look after your Scourge. I am sure Remy will awaken soon and he'll be wanting you."

After Ariane had gone, Gabrielle lingered by the window until she saw her sister emerge into the barnyard below. As Ariane approached her husband, he set aside his axe. The two exchanged a long look, then with a single bound Ariane was in Renard's arms. He lifted her off her feet as their lips met in a passionate kiss.

Gabrielle watched them wistfully, envying her sister that love she shared with her husband that went beyond the need for words, that could heal all misunderstanding and hurt, enable them to begin again. Would she and Remy ever arrive at that point with each other? Gabrielle crept back to the bedside where Remy lay so still, his eyes sealed closed, so completely oblivious to her presence.

"Remy will awaken soon and he'll be wanting you."

Gabrielle sank to her knees by the bed, buried her face in the coverlet and prayed that Ariane was right.

※※※

GABRIELLE HAD NO IDEA HOW LONG SHE KNELT THERE. PERHAPS EX-haustion had overtaken her and she had fallen asleep. The feel of something brushing against her hair roused her. Her heart gave a mad leap when she realized what it was, the touch of Remy's fingers. She jerked upright to find him gazing at her with a wan smile. He still looked very tired, but color had returned to his face and his eyes were remarkably clear.

"Remy!" She sprang to her feet. "You—you are awake. How are you feeling? Are you in pain? What can I get you? Some water or some brandy perhaps? Or—or do you need more of Ariane's potion?"

In her eagerness, she would have darted from the room had Remy not sat up to stop her. He flinched, obviously paying the price for such a sudden movement. Gabrielle flew back to his side immediately.

"What are you doing?" she scolded, easing him back to the pillow. "Lie still."

"I will. As long . . . as you don't go," he grated. "I don't need anything just now except—"

"Yes?"

He exhaled a deep cleansing breath, then answered by patting the mattress beside him. Gabrielle settled herself gingerly next to him, longing to cover his face with kisses while she wept with joy and relief. But the woman who had once considered herself such a skilled seductress felt shy and awkward, afraid of aggravating his injury, of causing him any more harm than she'd already done.

Remy took hold of her hand, his grip surprisingly strong, as though he feared that if he let go of her she would vanish before his eyes. He studied her through half-lowered lashes until she felt miserably self-conscious of her rumpled gown and tangled hair. Perhaps it was a foolish moment to be worrying about her looks, but for so long she had believed that her beauty was her one gift to offer.

She essayed a shaky laugh. "I must look like a positive hag."

"No, only very tired," Remy murmured. "You should have left me, gotten some rest last night. But I am a selfish bastard. I am glad you remained."

"You realized it was me? I thought you might have mistaken me for Ariane."

"I know your touch, Gabrielle."

She warmed with pleasure at his assurance. "Oh. I—I wasn't

sure. You seemed so close to delirious. I was afraid you were going to drift into one of your nightmares."

"I might have, but you were here. I saw your face, haloed by the candle. You have always been able to keep my nightmares at bay."

"I rather thought that I had become the source of them," she said. "Oh, Remy, please believe me. I am so sorry for every—"

"Hush," he commanded, cutting her off with a gentle squeeze of her hand. "No more of that. I am as much to blame for the terrible way we parted as you. I have always known I possess the devil's own temper when roused. But I never realized what a hard and unyielding ass I could be until Wolf kindly pointed it out to me."

"Of all the impertinence," Gabrielle said indignantly. "Martin had no business doing so."

"Yes, he did. The lad has proved a good friend to me. Quite the greatest I have ever known, next to you."

Gabrielle had received many compliments in her life, but never any that moved her as deeply as that one. Remy gathered her hand more tightly in his own. "I still didn't fully appreciate how much of a bastard I had been to you until I burst into the inn and you wept with disbelief at the sight of me."

"It was only the smoke, Remy. Stinging my eyes."

"No, it wasn't, not entirely. I'll never forget the way you cried out *you came for me* as though you'd thought I wouldn't. That I truly would abandon you for the sake of Navarre."

"Oh, no, Remy." Gabrielle leaned forward, daring to touch him at last. She sought to smooth the troubled furrow from his brow. "I never doubted you would come. Not really. You swore that you would and you always keep your promises, although—" She confessed sheepishly. "As the days passed and I didn't know where you were, I did start to get a bit worried."

"I was trying to track down that evil woman."

"I know. Ariane told me."

Remy's eyes darkened with regret. "I wanted to do more

than just rescue you. I wanted to find a way to clear you of those charges so you didn't have to spend the rest of your days with witch-hunters hounding you."

"Considering the kind of woman I am and my family background, that almost seemed inevitable," Gabrielle said with a wearied laugh. "I don't mind so much for me, but I hate involving you in this."

She took a deep breath and plunged on bravely, "And if there is any way for you to get clear of me, I want you to take it."

When Remy frowned and began to protest, she laid her fingers over his mouth. "No, Remy. Listen to me. I do understand how frustrated you were at having to call off your rescue of Navarre. I fear I have always been stupidly jealous of your devotion to his cause. But your sense of duty and honor are part of what make you the man that you are, the reason that I love you so much. I don't ever want to change you."

Remy kissed her fingertips and shifted her hand away from his mouth. "I think Navarre would be the first to understand. He has flashes of wisdom that give me hope for my young reprobate of a king. He once said to me that a man's first duty should be to the woman he loves."

Remy gazed up at her with that deep earnest expression that had so long ago won her heart. "But you are not my duty, Gabrielle. You are my love, my life, my very soul."

Gabrielle's heart swelled with such emotion, her eyes filled with tears threatening to overflow. She tried to lean closer, to brush her lips against his, but Remy forestalled her by saying, "No, wait. There is something I have to do first."

He grimaced, shifting as though he could struggle from the bed, as though he seriously thought she would allow such a thing. When she sternly ordered him to lie still, he subsided with a disgruntled sigh. "All right, but then you are going to have to help me. Do you know what became of my things? My saddle-bag?"

"Everything is stacked there in the corner."

"Good." He sighed. "Open the saddlebag, will you? And look for a small leather pouch."

Gabrielle did as he asked, returning with the object he'd requested, a pouch so light it felt as though it contained nothing at all. It pained Remy far too much to move his injured arm and he was unable to work the drawstring with one hand. He surrendered the pouch to Gabrielle. She shook the contents out onto the palm of her hand, a gold ring.

"It's a betrothal ring," he said gruffly. "I know it isn't anything much. In the midst of all this madness, I didn't exactly have time to look properly and—and this was the best I could afford."

Gabrielle's eyes did overflow then. All she could do was choke out, "Oh, Remy."

"You accused me of only wanting to wed you at the king's command. Well, I couldn't have you thinking for the rest of our lives that that was the case, so I made up my mind to ask you properly. I really should get down on one knee."

"Don't you dare even think of it," Gabrielle cried fiercely.

"All right then," Remy said with a regretful smile as he took hold of her hand. "I suppose this will have to do. Gabrielle Cheney, will you do me the honor of—"

"Yes!"

"At least let me finish," Remy growled. "Do me the honor of becoming my wife, allowing me to love, cherish, and protect you until the end of our days?"

"Oh, yes," Gabrielle whispered. "As I will love and cherish you." Her hand trembled as Remy took the ring from her and slipped it onto her finger.

Her hair fell over him in a golden shower as she bent close, intending to whisper her mouth so very gently over his. But the Scourge was having none of that. Regardless of his wound, he cupped the nape of her neck and drew her mouth to his, sealing their betrothal with a fiery kiss.

Epilogue

THE SUN PIERCED THE LEAFY CANOPY OF THE TREES, SCATTERING diamonds of light over the stream that meandered lazily past the banks. A hush seemed to have settled over the forest behind Belle Haven, broken only by the murmur of the water, the occasional breeze rustling branches as though the ancient trees themselves breathed a sigh of contentment at the return of a long-lost daughter.

Gabrielle paused in her work to savor the crisp scent of pine mingling with the sweeter fragrance of wildflowers and the heavier aroma of the earth itself. Never before, she thought, had she so appreciated the calm beauty of her home on Faire Isle.

Perhaps her appreciation had deepened because she realized, sorrowfully, this peace was only fleeting. Simon Aristide and the witch-hunters would eventually come, no doubt backed by the king's troops. Henry Valois was likely to be furious at the attack upon the man he had commissioned to rid France of witches. Faire Isle itself might no longer prove a haven for the women who had long sought to do nothing more than to learn, to teach, to heal, to preserve what was best of the old ways and knowledge.

Gabrielle thrust that fear from her mind, refusing to dwell on any grim prospects on such a lovely day. She shook back her hair, curling her bare toes in the cool grass, reveling in the magic of Faire Isle, until it seemed to surge from the soles of her feet all the way up to tingle through her fingertips.

Her hands pulsed with her own unique magic, her fingers seeming to move of their own volition as she wielded her brush, applying deft strokes to the canvas mounted on the easel before her. The image reaching its final completion was in part the product of the vision in her head, the rest inspired by the man sprawled beneath the tree.

Remy had recovered well from his wound. Perhaps it was more the somnolence of the summer's day or Gabrielle's absorption in her work that had caused him to doze off. He leaned back against the trunk, cradled in the arms of old Sycamore, the dragon likewise benign on such a lazy summer afternoon.

Remy didn't bestir himself until Gabrielle was putting the finishing touches to the canvas. He was roused by the crashing of branches as two squirrels bickered overhead. Chattering and scolding each other for possession of a particular tree limb. Or perhaps it was merely the prelude to a mating. Miri would have known.

Remy sat up, stretching his arms overhead with a mighty yawn. He cast Gabrielle an apologetic smile. "Did I doze off? Sorry. I suppose I have not been the most scintillating company. Or did you even notice?"

"Of course I did. But after last night—" Gabrielle's body tingled at the memory of Remy's exertions in her bed. "I thought you could use the rest."

"Humph! More likely you welcomed the chance to work undisturbed."

Hearing the slightly disgruntled tone in Remy's voice, Gabrielle set down her brush. She padded over to offer him her hand as he struggled to his feet. She winced at the sight of her hand spattered with dried paint, her nails cut bluntly short.

But Remy carried her hand to his lips as though it was still as silken and elegant as in her days at court. "I fear that in time I could wax quite jealous of this magic of yours that absorbs you to the exclusion of all else."

Despite his teasing complaint, she caught the gleam of pride in his eyes and it warmed her more than the sun.

"So am I finally permitted to see this masterwork of yours?" he demanded.

"Well, I—I—" Gabrielle faltered. The return of her magic still felt so new, so tentative. This was the first painting she had done in years and she had guarded it jealously from everyone's sight, especially Remy's.

But when he ducked playfully past her, she made no effort to stop him. As he slipped around in front of the canvas, she caught her breath, waiting anxiously as he stared at her work. Her heart sank with dismay as Remy's jaw dropped with horror.

"Gabrielle!" he gasped.

"You—you don't like it," she cried. "You think it's dreadful."

"No. No," he reassured her hastily. "It—it is truly magic. I feel as though I could walk straight into the canvas, but—but—" He gestured helplessly toward the easel. "You've been painting me."

"It isn't supposed to be you. I only used your face for my model."

"You used a great deal more than my face, woman," Remy said accusingly. "Hell's fire, Gabrielle. You have me completely naked."

Gabrielle stepped to Remy's side, critically eyeing her own work. The beauty of the forest surrounding them seemed to live in the painting. A horse grazed near the stream, its saddle and its rider's armament—his sword, armor, and clothing—scattered nearby. But the foreground of the painting, the focus of the work, was of the knight sleeping beneath the trees, half-turned on his side, his head pillowed upon his outstretched arm, his tumbled hair an extraordinary blend of sun and shadow. Even in repose, the power and strength of the man were evident, delineated in his sinewy shoulders and limbs, the ripple of muscle across his chest, the taut curve of his buttocks. His vulnerability was laid bare as well in the scars that marred his smooth skin, in the weariness that lined his face as he slept so hard and deep. Every inch of Remy captured from Gabrielle's loving memory.

Although his reaction was not what she'd hoped it would be, she lifted her chin defiantly. "I think it is the best thing I've ever done."

"Yes, it—it's very well executed, but—" Remy looked highly discomfited. "Why is your knight naked? I would never—I mean he would never just strip off and go to sleep like that. It would leave him too open, too vulnerable to his enemies."

"The knight was hot and tired from his many quests and battles," Gabrielle explained patiently. "He cooled himself in the nearby stream and fell asleep beneath the tree. It is an enchanted wood and he feels safe here."

"If he is so exhausted, then why is he so—so—" Remy pointed uncomfortably to the rather impressive appendage between the knight's legs.

"Obviously, he is having pleasant dreams about the lady he loves."

"But couldn't you at least place a discreet bush or some weeds—"

"No, I couldn't! I am sorry if it offends you, but I find nothing shameful in the magnificence of the male body, especially yours."

Remy draped his arm about her shoulders and said more gently, "I am not offended, love. I am actually rather flattered to realize that is how I appear to you. Do I really look that—that—"

"That good? Oh, yes, you do," Gabrielle replied with a shiver and sigh.

Remy's mouth crooked in an adorably sheepish smile. "It is only that I don't know how I will ever look either one of your sisters in the eye again after they have seen that." Her mighty Scourge actually blushed to the roots of his hair. He added with a groan, "To say nothing of the bedeviling I will be forced to take from Wolf and Renard."

Gabrielle draped her arms about his neck. She said soothingly, "I never intended to embarrass you. I did this painting for myself as a celebration of my love for you and for the return of my magic. I thought it gone forever after what Danton did to me. But you gave it back to me."

Remy gazed down at her, his deep brown eyes tender and earnest. "Your magic was never any man's to take, Gabrielle. Nor mine to give. It has been there inside of you all along, just waiting for the day you'd find the courage to summon it again."

"A courage I might never have found but for you." She caressed his cheek lovingly. "And don't worry. No one will ever see this painting but you and me."

Remy responded by fastening his lips on hers, his mouth warm and coaxing. Even as Gabrielle strained toward him, eagerly returning his embrace, she felt a prickle of unease. She had vowed with Remy to be completely honest with him from now on, and she intended to be. So then should she tell him about Miri's latest dream?

Her sister had ceased having those troubling nightmares about Gabrielle becoming Navarre's mistress. Her dream had clarified, revealing the face of the lady stealing toward the king's bedchamber, another golden-blond beauty, another woman named Gabrielle.

Miri's latest prophetic dream conjured up Paris in the far distant future, when it had become a city of mysterious lights that never burned themselves out. A Paris no longer governed by a king or queen, the vast palace of the Louvre transformed into a repository of art collected from the far corners of the world. Displayed right there in one of the main galleries for millions of visitors to see was a collection of Gabrielle's paintings, including her most famous work.

The Weary Knight.

But this vision struck Gabrielle as being too bizarre and far-fetched, even for Miri. She saw no point in troubling Remy with it. She was no longer interested in prophecy or seeking her destiny in dreams or some distant stars. Let the future look to itself, Gabrielle thought as she melted before Remy's kiss, her lips parting to welcome his passion and tenderness. All that mattered to her was Remy, his love.

And their time was here and now.

Author's Note

Although the mercenary regiment of witch-hunters is a product of my imagination, sixteenth-century France was rife with sorcery trials and burnings. The populations of some villages were entirely decimated of their women. There actually was a Le Balafre, the charismatic and ambitious duc de Guise. I found his nickname, "Scarface," much more appropriate for my tormented witch-hunter Aristide and so I shamelessly borrowed it.

Catherine de Medici herself was suspected by many French people of being a poisoner and sorceress. She was known to have frequently consulted the French physician and astrologist Michel de Nostredame during his lifetime. Michel, better known as Nostradamus, is said to have foretold both the death of Catherine's husband and the downfall of her line. The predictions in his book *Centuries* are still studied to this day.

To what degree Catherine believed Nostradamus's predictions is not known, but she certainly kept close watch over other possible claimants to the French throne, most especially Henry of Navarre. Navarre was held prisoner at court. He survived all the intrigue and hostility only by sheer nerve, adopting an indolent manner that masked his keen intelligence.

After several elaborate escape plots that failed, he finally eluded his captors in the simplest manner. During a hunting party at Senlis, Navarre and several trusted attendants galloped off, disappearing into the woods. As soon as he had crossed the Loire and was well clear of any French pursuit, Navarre is reported to have said, "God be praised who has delivered me . . . I'll never return unless I'm dragged."

Events proved otherwise for the man who was fated to become one of France's most beloved kings, known as the Evergreen Gallant.

Read on for a sneak peak at
Miri's story, the next captivating novel
in the Cheney Sisters Trilogy!

The Silver Rose

❧

Coming in February 2006
from Ballantine Books

Prologue

THE SUN SLIPPED BELOW THE HORIZON, THE LAST OF THE LIGHT fading like smoke from a snuffed out candle. Darkness descended over the cliff side and the line of trees, turning the rugged Breton coastline into the kind of land Simon Aristide understood best. A land of night and shadow.

His hands encased in leather gloves, the witch-hunter gripped the reins of his mount. Like her master, the spirited ebony mare blended with the darkness. Aristide's shoulder-length hair was as black as the horse's mane and just as wild in the brisk wind blowing leeward. He was likewise garbed all in black from his thick boots to his leather jerkin. His beard-shadowed face cast no pale gleam to alert his enemies, his skin toughened from many days spent in the saddle, weathering the elements.

Simon had an angular countenance, the set of his mouth hard and uncompromising, rarely softened by a smile. His right eye was as dark as the rest of him, glinting with a piercing intelligence. His ravaged left eye was usually kept concealed beneath a black patch. A heavy scar, the result of a duel, bisected his forehead, disappearing beneath the patch only to emerge in a thin crease that marred his cheek. He was an intimidating figure; tall, with sinewy limbs. Anyone would have to be mad to have attacked him.

But Simon had concluded that the creatures stalking him *were* mad or else imbued with evil and malice to a chilling degree. On a night like this, alone, isolated from any sign of human habitation, he preferred to think his pursuers were merely insane. It was more comforting than the alternative.

As the shadows deepened around him, Simon resisted the urge to nudge Elle into a gallop. The barest pressure of his knees and they'd both be off like the wind. But it would be far too dangerous; the cliff path narrow and treacherous even in the full light of day. A full out gallop in the dark would be pure suicide. An easier road beckoned to him through the trees that rimmed the cliffs, but the gnarled trunks, the thicket of shrubs and undergrowth offered far too many places for concealment.

Simon kept the mare to a sedate walk. He heard nothing beyond the steady clop of Elle's hoofbeats, the wind rustling through the trees, the surf battering the rocks far below and yet the back of his neck tingled with the awareness that he was not alone out here in the darkness. *They were here.* At least one of them. Perhaps the one he had sensed dogging him in the last village he had passed through.

Or perhaps exhaustion and only a few snatched hours of troubled sleep were starting to get the better of him. But he didn't think so. Elle's behavior told him otherwise. The mare had been twitchy the past mile or so, skittering, tossing her head, her ears pricked.

Simon reached down to pat her neck when the sound carried to his ears. At first he thought he imagined the faint wail of an infant. It could be no more than the wind keening over the rocky headland. Simon's gut knotted with dread all the same.

Around the next bend, the land leveled off and the cries became louder and more plaintive. Simon drew Elle to a halt, tersely scanning the distance. Barely one hundred yards ahead, moonlight flooded an object abandoned perilously near the edge of the cliff. Anyone else might have mistaken it for a blanket roll left behind by a careless shepherd. But Simon had seen such bundles before, with one difference this time.

This one was still alive, the infant's cries borne to him clearly on the wind. Simon's heartbeat quickened, his first impulse to charge forward. But he'd narrowly avoided ambush too many times to be that rash.

He slid from Elle's back and drew the mare into a stand of trees, tethering her to the trunk of a sturdy, but pliant beech. Elle's eyes did not roll in terror, but she was blowing and stamping. She shifted her sleek powerful chest and shoulders as though to block him from leaving the grove.

Simon stroked the horse to soothe her. He lingered in the shadow of trees, his gaze tracking the path to the jutting of cliff. The plateau where the child had been abandoned offered no place of concealment, no cover for anyone attempting to hide. It would not offer Simon any either if some assassin lurked further down the path or even in the trees, preparing to lodge an arrow in his back.

But that was not his enemy's usual mode of attack and the cries of the infant overrode his caution. They were growing weaker by the moment. It was just possible that they had never counted on Simon being here this soon.

Easing past Elle, Simon drew his sword and started forward. He could barely hear the child now, only one final whimper and then a terrible silence. All stealth and wariness forgotten, he ran, dislodging a hail of pebbles beneath his boots.

He hurtled towards the small bundle on the edge of the cliff, dropping to his knees beside it. The wind stirred the edge of the coarse blanket, but there was no movement from the tiny figure.

Simon set down his sword and stripped off his gloves. He gathered the swathed infant into his arms with gentleness, which was as rare as his prayers.

Please. Please let me have arrived in time. Just this once.

He peeled back the flap of the blanket, his breath hitching sharply. The doll's glass button eyes fixed him with an empty stare, the jagged mouth stitched onto the canvas face sneering at him. *Tricked.*

He scarcely had time to register that fact before he heard the snap of a twig on his blind side. He jerked towards the sound and realized that there was a hollow in the ground below the place where he knelt. He caught the barest blur before the woman crouching there sprang at him.

Her teeth bared in a snarl, she launched into him, knocking him onto his back. Moonlight glinted off the weapon in her hand as she thrust at his neck. Simon deflected the blow with the doll and bucked upward, hurling his attacker off of him. She hit the ground with a furious screech. By the time he had regained his feet, she had also scrambled to hers. And she was between him and his sword. With a contemptuous smile, she kicked it further out of his reach.

She was much the same as all the others who had been sent to kill him. Clad in baggy breeches and a peasant's tunic, her dark hair, unkempt, her eyes manic, her mouth cruel and cunning. Simon kept a knife hidden inside his boot, but he made no move to go for it.

"Keep back, woman," he said. "I have no desire to harm you. Drop your weapon and I am willing to spare you if you answer my questions."

The creature threw back her head, emitting an eerie imitation of an infant's mewling cry. "What's your question?" she mocked. "Where's the babe? There is none, witch-hunter. Not this time. And that is the only answer you'll get from me. Aside from this." She brandished her weapon, circling in closer.

"No desire to harm me. Bah." She spat in Simon's direction, the spittle landing inches from his boot. "I know how you witch-hunters ask your questions. With the rack and the branding iron."

"That is not my way," he said, "If you attack me again, I will have to kill you."

"What does that matter? I am not afraid to die. The Silver Rose will resurrect me."

With a blood-curdling screech, she leaped and was on him again. Simon caught her wrists to hold her back. No mere woman should have been so strong. Whatever madness or evil surged through her veins, it was all Simon could do to keep her at bay. He felt the heat of her fetid breath, heard the gnash of her teeth as she came within an inch of tearing open his cheek.

He was more concerned with the strange weapon she clutched in her right hand. She stabbed at him, the tip tearing through his jerkin. The only thing that saved him was the light coat of mail he wore beneath. Simon twisted her wrist until she cried out and dropped the weapon. She went into a frenzy of fury, kicking, snapping, and trying to bite. When nothing else availed, she butted the top of her head beneath his chin. Simon reeled, his jaw exploding with pain. He lost his grip on her and staggered back, barely managing to stop himself from plunging off the edge of the cliff.

His attacker rushed at him in an effort to drive him over. He dodged her charge and it was she who teetered, the ground giving way beneath her. She fell, scrambling wildly for purchase. Simon flung himself to the ground and caught her arm. She dangled below him, her legs and free arm flailing, her face white with rage. Her weight strained the muscles in his arm until they burned with pain.

"Who sent you?" he growled. "Who is this Silver Rose that you serve?"

"Go to hell," she shrieked.

"Tell me what I want to know or—" Simon gasped as she clawed at his hand, digging her nails in so viciously, his grip slackened.

He felt her start to slip, and made another desperate grab for her arm. But it was too late. She hurtled into the darkness, his last view her face gloating with insane triumph. He heard the thud of her body as it struck the cliff side on the way down and then a splash. The sea was like a dark, hungry beast, frothing at the mouth as it devoured the witch's broken body and all the answers he so desperately sought along with her.

What demon possessed you, woman? Where does your coven hide when all of you are not out spreading terror and trying to kill me? And who is this she-devil you call the Silver Rose? This sorceress you all worship so much you are willing to die for her, believing she has the power to raise you from the dead.

And what if she could?

A chill went through Simon that had nothing to do with the wind whipping in from the sea. With a low groan, he retreated from the edge and rolled onto his back, seeking to recover his breath. He sat up slowly, brushing the tangle of hair from his face. He winced at the throb of his hand where the witch had lacerated him with her nails. The salty taste of blood filled his mouth. He had bitten his cheek when she had butted him with her head.

He worked his jaw carefully. It hurt like the devil, but she hadn't managed to dislocate it or loosen any of his teeth. His injuries could have been a great deal worse, he reflected as his gaze fell upon the strange weapon he had forced from her hand. He had caught glimpses of these hellish devices on other encounters with these witches, but he had never managed to gain possession of one before. Simon picked it up carefully.

The device looked like nothing more than a very thin stiletto. Closer inspection revealed that the tip was sharp, but the blade was hollow. Imbedded in the hilt was a vial of some dark red liquid. Once the stiletto punctured the skin, the hilt could be twisted or pushed, shattering the vial, sending the poisonous liquid through the blade. Simon had no idea exactly how it worked, but he'd seen the results too many times. The wound was small, looking far from mortal, but the death that it wrought was slow and agonizing.

Simon set the weapon down, seeking some safe way of transporting it. He found the discarded doll and stripped the blanket away. Out of its swaddling, the doll was a crude semblance of a child. No more than a cloth head and body carefully weighted with something to give it just the right feel of a small infant when wrapped in the blanket.

Simon seized the doll and hurled it off the cliff. But his anger was tempered with relief, that that was all it had been this time—a fake. He'd witnessed more cruelty, death and evil in the span of his thirty years than most men twice his age. But he was not certain he could endure the sight of one more dead child. He'd lain awake far too many nights, picturing the torment of those helpless babes he'd been too late to save. Left exposed in some remote locale where their cries would go unheard, abandoned to perish slowly of hunger and neglect.

What kind of woman could command others to commit such horrors? The same woman who could craft a weapon like that poisonous stiletto; the dark flower that was her emblem arrogantly engraved on the hilt. No matter what it would take, Simon intended to find the witch and put a stop to her ungodly crimes. Unless the Silver Rose got him first.

That was more than likely if he behaved as stupidly as he'd done tonight. Five years ago, even two, he would never have fallen for such a trap. But his lone crusade was wearing him so thin, he was surprised he still cast a shadow.

He wrapped the blanket around the stiletto. Retrieving his sword and gloves, he trudged back to where he had left Elle. She stamped, tossing her head and yanking on the lead, spooked by his battle with the witch. It took much soothing on his part before she settled down. He rested his forehead against the velvet softness of her nose.

"Lord, Elle, I'm so tired of all this. So damned tired."

She whickered, her dark eye gleaming softly in the moonlight. She nuzzled his hair and lipped at the neckline of his shirt as though to comfort him. As absurd as it seemed, Simon sometimes thought the mare understood him.

Miri Cheney would not have thought it absurd. She would have said . . . Simon's breath snagged in his throat as her image stole into his mind, so clear even after all these years. The memory of a young girl with hair pale as moonlight, a face as ethereal as an angel's, eyes that could be the soft hue of morning mist or the dark color of a storm at sea. Fey eyes that could almost make a man forget who he was, what he needed to do. Or worse still, forget who she was. A daughter of the earth, a wise woman. That was how Miri had always referred to herself. No matter what she chose to call herself, a witch was still a witch. And yet, there had been something different about Miri.

Despite her unfortunate family background of sorcery, she had been more misguided than tainted by evil. The girl had possessed an innocence, a shining faith in the ultimate goodness of the world, a hope for the best in people. Girl? No, she'd be a mature woman by now and that light of hers had probably dimmed since her family had been forced to abandon their home on Faire Isle, driven into exile. Simon was in large part responsible for that.

Rumors had reached him this past year that one of the Cheney sisters had dared to return to the island and was living there in quiet seclusion, a woman possessing an almost supernatural ability to cure any sick or wounded creature she came across. There was only one person that could be . . . Miri.

Simon tightened his grip on Elle's bridle as he sought to banish the woman from his mind. Remembrance of her loosed upon him far too painful regrets. But Miri had been invading his thoughts more of late and he could no longer keep the gates of his mind barred against her. His enemies were gathering strength to an alarming degree. He was alone. He was exhausted. He was desperate. Each day inched him closer to the conclusion he stubbornly resisted. There was only one way he was going to defeat the Sisterhood of the Silver Rose.

He needed the help of another witch.

About the Author

SUSAN CARROLL is an award-winning romance author whose books include *The Bride Finder* and its two sequels, *The Night Drifter* and *Midnight Bride,* as well as *The Painted Veil, Winterbourne,* and most recently, *The Dark Queen*. She lives in Rock Island, Illinois.

About the Type

This book was set in Life, a font designed by W. Bilz, and jointly developed by Ludwig & Mayer and Francesco Simoncini in 1965. This contemporary design is in the transitional style of the eighteenth century, and was intended for use in text settings where printing and production quality may be low. Life is a versatile text face that can encompass a large range of newspaper typography as well, from straight copy to advertising.

Don't miss these three captivating novels in the

DARK QUEEN series

by Susan Carroll

The Dark Queen
On sale April 2005
Set in Renaissance France, a time when women of ability are deemed sorceresses; when France is torn by ruthless political intrigues; and all are held in thrall to the sinister ambitions of Queen Catherine de Medici—Ariane Cheney, Lady of the Fair Isle, must risk everything to restore peace to a tormented land.

The Courtesan
On sale August 2005
Skilled in passion, artful in deception, and driven by betrayal, she is the glittering center of the royal court —but Gabrielle Cheney, the most desired woman of Renaissance France, will draw the wrath of a dangerous adversary—the formidable Dark Queen.

The Silver Rose
On sale February 2006
France is a country in turmoil, plagued by famine, disease, and on the brink of a new religious war. In the midst of so much chaos, Miri Cheney must face a far greater evil—a diabolical woman known only as The Silver Rose.

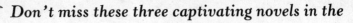 Published by Ballantine Books • Available wherever books are sold